GHOST SONG

GHOST SONG

Sarah Rayne

POCKET
BOOKS

London • New York • Toronto • Sydney

First published in Great Britain by Simon & Schuster UK Ltd, 2009
This edition published by Pocket Books UK, 2009
An imprint of Simon & Schuster UK Ltd
A CBS COMPANY

1 3 5 7 9 10 8 6 4 2

Simon & Schuster UK Ltd
1st Floor
222 Gray's Inn Road
London WC1X 8HB

www.simonandschuster.co.uk

Simon & Schuster Australia
Sydney

A CIP catalogue record for this book is available from the British Library

ISBN 978-1-41652-224-9

Typeset by Rowland Phototypesetting Ltd,
Bury St Edmunds, Suffolk
Printed and bound in Great Britain by
CPI Cox & Wyman, Reading, Berkshire RG1 8EX

For 'Frank Douglas'
1899–1963

ACKNOWLEDGEMENTS

Grateful thanks are due to Tony Duggan, for help with information on early-twentieth-century sound recordings, and also for 'Tranz', and to Paul Smith, company archivist at Thomas Cook's, for details on early-twentieth-century travel.

CHAPTER ONE

The Present

The Tarleton Music Hall was the ugliest building Robert Fallon had ever seen, and he fell instantly and overwhelmingly in love with it.

'Since you're the enthusiast when it comes to the old stuff, you'd better deal with this one,' the senior partner of his firm had said, three days earlier. 'It's a disused theatre in Bankside and it's just come under this new government directive about stricter monitoring of old buildings, so a full survey's wanted. Nobody seems to know when it was built, but apparently it closed down in 1914 and never reopened. It's regarded as a bit of a mystery locally, I think.'

'However mysterious it is, if it's been empty since 1914 it'll probably be in a disgusting condition,' said Robert. But he was pleased at the prospect of carrying out a survey in that part of London; he liked Bankside and Southwark with their echoes of Elizabethan theatre, and he liked seeing the newly renovated Globe and the Rose.

He collected the keys from the managing agents who were called the Harlequin Society and who provided him with helpful

1

directions, managed to park his car near Burbage Street where the Tarleton was and, with the sounds of the river on his left, walked along the street. Halfway along there it was: the exuberantly ugly Tarleton Music Hall.

It was surrounded by buildings whose original purposes had long since become blurred or lost altogether, but Robert hardly saw them and he barely heard the roar of the traffic which thrummed along streets built by people who had never envisaged the internal combustion engine. He stared up at the peeling facade and the chipped stonework and was vividly aware of two emotions, both wildly different. The first was dismay at the enormity of the task ahead of him. The interior of this building would probably be divided and sub-divided, and rooms would be partitioned haphazardly with no regard to proportion or logic, let alone building regulations. There would be several kinds of dry and wet rot, rampant timber infestation and miles of ancient lead pipework. The walls would be festooned with rusting gas mantles, which meant Robert would have to track down defunct gas inlets and outlets, and if there did happen to be any electrical wiring it would date back to the coronation of George V, if not Edward VII. Once he got inside, he would have to test each step he took because the floor joists would be powdery with woodworm and likely to collapse under him.

But none of this mattered because the second emotion was an instant and unreasoning passion for this tattered old music hall.

He resolutely quelled both sentiments and went along the little alleyway at the side, which was called Platt's Alley. It had begun to rain and the cobblestones were shiny and slippery. The old stage door was at the very end. Robert reached for the keys in his jacket pocket, then paused to read the inscription carved into the stone lintel over the door. It was worn, but still legible: 'Please one and please all, be they great, be they small'. He did not recognize the quote, but it was so completely appropriate for a theatre that he smiled and stopped minding about the complexity of the work ahead of him. Unlocking the stage door, he stepped inside, and the scents of dust, old timber and sheer age closed about him.

The electricity had not been switched on, but he had brought strong torches and battery-powered lamps on stands which he set up at strategic points. This took quite a while, and several times he found himself looking over his shoulder because he had a definite feeling of being watched. He didn't think it was a living person who watched; just the lingering memories of the people who had stood on this stage and told jokes, sung songs, juggled, danced or recited monologues. After the first few moments he did not mind; it was not a threatening feeling, in fact it was rather friendly.

He set the last of his lights in place, then began to work systematically through the building, making careful notes as he went. It was a remarkable old building. There was some surface dilapidation – several patches of damp suggested gutters needed attention, there was wet rot in the supper-room floor, and the electrical wiring was certainly dangerous – but other than this, the building was amazingly sound. It was almost as if the whole place had been trapped in its own little pocket of time, or as if a glaze of amber had been spread over it. Robert had checked several old maps of the area: the Tarleton was shown on one dated 1850, and he was inclined to think it had been built around 1830. His partner regarded this kind of research as unnecessary – too much attention to detail, he always said – but Robert liked detail and he thought a property's history could provide valuable clues.

Whatever the theatre's true age, by the end of that first day he had identified several building styles and materials from different eras. In most cases these could be explained: a buttress shoring up a dubious section of the ceiling of the upper circle – probably put there towards the end of the nineteenth century – and a false floor in what he thought was the old green room, most likely meant to strengthen sagging joists. But when he began his examination of the subterranean levels he came across something for which he could find no logical explanation.

Near the old doorkeeper's room on the Platt's Alley side was a small passage leading off at right angles, and at the end of this passage was a thick oak door, black with age. Robert opened it warily, wincing as the hinges shrieked in rusty protest, and pushed it back against the wall. Immediately inside was a flight of stone steps. He shone his torch cautiously, then went down them. The walls were of old London brick, crusted with grime, and Robert, who did not normally mind cellars which were an inevitable part of his work, was uncomfortably aware of the tons of brick and timber above him. The smell of dirt was almost overpowering.

At the foot of the steps was a very large room. The tape showed it to be thirty feet long and Robert thought it was directly beneath the front of the auditorium and part of the stage. He moved the torch round, picking out shadowy outlines of old canvas flats and odds and ends of furniture: broken-backed chairs and tables. Against one wall were three wicker skips containing lengths of brocade and velvet, probably once stage costumes or curtains. They were faded to an indeterminate grey and smelt dreadful. Robert thought them rather sad, because it was as if the real costumes and curtains had gone and left these ghosts in their place.

Mingling with the stench of dirt was an ominous dank aura. Sewage spillage? Robert frowned, trying to fix the Tarleton's position in relation to the Thames and the old sluice gates. He would check the maps when he got back to his office, but he thought there was a disused pumping station in Candle Square.

But whether or not there had been seepage coming in from London's old drainage system, at some time in the Tarleton's history – sometime long after its original construction – someone had built an extra brick wall, spanning the entire width of the cellars. Robert brushed the cobwebs away and shone the torch over the wall's surface, frowning because it was so obviously of a later construction than the rest of the building: the bricks were machine-made, and the wall was so crazily out of true it had the

4

effect of distorting the whole room. Whoever had built it had either been very unskilled or—

Or what?

Or had built it in a very great hurry.

Robert considered the wall. Surely this was not going to be the classic scenario of a crumbling body behind a hastily built wall? Some ancient murder discovered a century after it had been committed? It was unlikely. But why would such a wall be built down here? Clearly it was not intended to shore up what was overhead. If the foundations had needed strengthening, steel struts would have been put in or, in an extreme case, cement pumped in to fill up these rooms. No one in his right mind would have built this amateurish wall.

But perhaps it was someone who was not in his right mind, said a voice inside Robert's head. Have you thought of that?

He pushed this unpleasant idea away and shone the torch onto the upper sections. The wall bisected several ceiling joists which confirmed it had originally been one long room and this wall had partitioned it. So what was in the other part? What was on the other side? Robert spread out the ground plan he had made. As far as he could tell, there was quite a large space on the other side of this odd wall, including the under-stage void. That definitely ruled out any strengthening of the foundations. And if the under-stage area really was on the other side, there would have to be another means of access somewhere in the theatre.

He went back up the stairs, closing the oak door, and crossed the foyer into the auditorium, his footsteps echoing in the emptiness. The stage had shallow steps on one side. Robert went up these, and began to search for access to the under-stage area. But although he checked and re-checked every nook and cranny, he could not find one: there were no doors, no flaps or hatches, no extra passageways or tucked-away stairs. But there must be a way down there, because the stage had the outlines of what looked like an old trap. He had researched this as well. Most theatres had apparently had at least one of these contrivances, mostly used for melodrama and pantomime. Victims of Sweeney Todd's chair would have plunged down into the pie-making factory by this route. Demon kings and genii of the lamp would have used it as well. Robert smiled at his own childhood memories of wildly fantastical figures projected abruptly upwards, bathed in fiendish crimson or poisonous green light. Mechanical magic by the light of the limes. Taken to theatres as a child, he had exasperated his parents, who had not bargained for a son who came home from a pantomime and requested drawing paper and sharp pencils to work out how Captain Hook sailed across Never-Never Land.

The Tarleton's stage trap was rectangular: roughly six feet in length and three feet across, and Robert thought it was what was called a grave trap. According to the sources he had consulted, it owed its name to the graveyard scene in *Hamlet*. Had they been foolproof, these devices, or had it been a case of 'Hamlet, I am thy father's ghost doomed to walk the earth— Hell's teeth, the stage manager's forgotten to oil the hinges and I'm stuck . . .'

The traps had worked on the principle of a frame of four uprights, with a floor inside which could be moved up and down, rather like a lift shaft. When in place, the floor of the trap was flush with the stage, when it was winched down, with the actor standing or lying on it, it would leave a deep opening – presumably the actors had to avoid the hole until the floor was brought back up.

A section of wood had been hammered down over the trap and Robert knelt down to examine it. The wood was an irregular shape and the whole thing was clumsily done. The nails were ill-matched, several of the heads were broken off and Robert had the impression that whoever had done it either had not been used to this kind of job or had had to do it in a hurry. He remembered again the amateurish brickwork in the underground room.

In an empty theatre it was probably a sound safety measure to seal up the trap, but Robert found himself thinking that at some time, someone in this theatre had wanted to be very sure that the under-stage was completely sealed off. Why? Would the Harlequin Society be able to tell him? How comprehensive was their brief in regard to this place? He wondered who the owner was, and why he – or she – had let the theatre stand empty for so long. Bit of a mystery, Robert's partner had said about the Tarleton: closed down in 1914 and never reopened. Robert had supposed the outbreak of the first world war was the reason for the original closure, but it was still odd that it had stayed closed for so long.

He came back to the stage. The lights he had rigged up cast sharp bluish circles, giving the impression of old spotlights trained on the stage, and Robert stood for a moment, looking into the dark well of the auditorium. Most of the seats were still in place, and he could see the shadowy outline of the dress circle and of the four boxes, two on each side of the stage. Wisps of almost colourless curtains still hung over the tarnished giltwork of one of the boxes.

How would the Tarleton have looked in its heyday? On a Saturday night, with performers on this stage and a full house, how would it have looked and sounded and smelt? Hot and raucous, said Robert to himself. It'd have been crowded with people, and it would have smelt greasily of jellied eels, oysters and cigars. You'd have hated it.

He looked about him again, trying to brighten the faded colours, trying to see what might lie beneath that thick layer of amber. This auditorium would have had the florid decor of its era – crimson and gilt paintwork and thick flock wallpaper, with glossy mahogany the colour of black treacle. I wouldn't have hated it in the least, thought Robert, rolling up the tape measure. I'd have loved it.

Toby Chance always found the Tarleton's crimson flock wallpaper and dark molasses-coloured mahogany a bit overpowering in hot weather. He liked the theatre better in winter, when the stoves were lit and roaring out their heat, and the street sellers brought in bags of roasted chestnuts, and the hot-codling sellers handed round their roast apples, juicy and spiked with cinnamon.

Crossing the foyer, he made a face at the fleur-de-lys and a rude gesture to the nearest of the blow-cheeked cherubs. He was early for the evening's performance, but there were two reasons for this. The first was simply that he loved walking through the theatre when it was empty: it seemed to become his theatre more than at any other time. He liked, as well, the feeling of anticipation, as if the ghosts of audiences lingered, perhaps hoping for another show, perhaps another chance to see Marie Lloyd – getting a bit past her best now, of course, the great old girl, but still able to light up a theatre.

She had certainly lit up the Tarleton a couple of weeks previously. Toby grinned, remembering he had lit up a few things himself that night. Alicia Darke was the name of the lady who had been with him, and she and Toby had been in the stage box for Marie's act – the stage box was regarded as Toby's own particular province and it was hardly ever opened for anyone else. Alicia had worn a dark red evening gown with a demure neckline and long silk gloves covering her arms. But as Marie embarked on 'A Little of What You Fancy' Alicia's hand, still gloved, strayed to Toby's lap. It was erotic to near explosion point to sit in full view of a Tarleton audience, with Alicia's fingers exploring and caressing with such insistent intimacy. Her hand was just – but only just – out of the audience's sightline, below the box's parapet. On stage, Marie reached the line about, 'I don't mind nice boys staring hard . . .' The irony of the timing of this was not lost on Toby.

It would have afforded more privacy to draw the curtains across the front of the box, but half the audience would have noticed this, so they retreated to the back of the box. At this point Alicia removed the gloves, then she removed several other garments as well, and by the time Marie was reaching the climax of her act, Toby was reaching a climax of his own. They managed to be back in their seats by the time the lights came up, and had eaten a very decorous supper with the performers afterwards. Then they had a second, very indecorous, supper at Alicia's house in Chelsea. Remembering all this, Toby winked at the framed photograph of Marie in the foyer as he went past.

His other reason for arriving early was a practical one. He wanted to run through the new song, which was called 'All Because of Too Much Tipsy Cake'. His pianist and music partner, Frank Douglas, had said they would put Marie Lloyd to rout with it, but Frank thought every new song would put somebody to rout. He was a happy-go-lucky Irishman from Galway, and he could play the piano by ear more skilfully than anyone Toby had ever known. He shaped his tunes to Toby's lyrics, producing melodies the audiences loved – somebody had said quite recently that if you walked down any of the streets around the Tarleton you would hear at least one errand boy whistling a Chance and Douglas song.

Toby was hoping 'Tipsy Cake' would be whistled tomorrow and also that the chorus would be sung by the audience tonight. He thought it would; most of them would pick up the sly bawdiness of the lyrics – the cook tippling the cooking sherry while making tipsy cake for the mistress's grand dinner party upstairs.

> *She'd just tipped up the bottle for the smallest taster*
> *When the butler said, 'Let's have another glass.'*

They would like that – they would like the implied suggestion that the butler and the cook had become so drunk on the cooking sherry that they had ended up in bed together. Toby thought he had managed to suggest this without actually saying it, which should keep him on the right side of the Lord Chamberlain.

It was to be hoped it would keep Toby on the right side of his father as well. Toby had recently written a song, describing how the Kaiser had vainly tried to drill Prussian troops preparatory to taking over the world, and had flown into a temper over a hapless new recruit who was pigeon-toed and made the entire army look untidy. His father had found the lyrics and broken an almost unbreakable rule between them by asking Toby not to perform it.

'But he's such a silly posturing creature,' Toby said. 'You can't help making fun of him.'

'He might be a poseur, but he's a very dangerous poseur,' said Toby's father. 'Hardly anyone in Europe trusts him. For God's sake don't ridicule him publicly, Toby, you might come to grief in a way you don't expect. If you don't care about your own reputation, you might care about mine. I might come to grief as well.'

It was not often his father referred to his position within the Foreign Office in quite this way and Toby had wavered, but in the end he had gone ahead and performed his song on the Tarleton's stage. He had been horrified when quarrels broke out in the stalls where three Germans, deeply injured at the insult to their emperor, were sitting. One of them challenged Toby to a duel and in the end the police had had to be called to break things up. The next day four people were charged at Cannon Street with disturbing the peace. Toby had regretted the disturbance, but he had regretted even more the fact that his father had been proved right.

As he went into the auditorium, he realized that after all he was not on his own in the theatre. Going up the steps to the stage, he heard a sound somewhere in the shadows. In the stalls, had it been? Perhaps it was Minnie Bean – she sometimes liked to prowl around the theatre, remembering the days when she had been dresser to Toby's mother. But Minnie had been on door-opening duty at the Kensington house when Toby left, and she did not prowl – she was four-square as to build and inclined to clump. If she had taken a nip of gin in the Sailor's Rest ('Just two nips for a little bit of comfort, Mr Toby'), she clumped a wildly erratic path. For years Toby had longed to write a song about Minnie and the gin-nipping, but she was sharp enough to recognize herself and he was too fond of her to upset her.

But when he looked out into the darkness nothing moved, and when he called out to ask if anyone was there, there was only the echo of his own voice. Probably it had just been one of the inexplicable sounds old buildings sometimes made. Or it could have been rain pattering down on a section of roof somewhere – thunder had been sulking its way in from the east since lunchtime and thunder-rain was usually very heavy.

It might even be one of the theatre's ghosts he had heard. When he was fourteen he had read *A Tale of Two Cities* and been entranced by Dickens's concept of London having corners where there were resonances from the past and where footsteps echoed down the years. He thought Dickens might easily have been writing about Platt's Alley and Burbage Street and Candle Square.

But although Toby believed in the echoes and sometimes thought he heard them for himself, he was inclined to be cynical about the existence of actual ghosts. Still, most theatres were supposed to be a bit haunted – you had only to look at Drury Lane with its famous eighteenth-century gentleman who had been seen quite a few times over the years. The Tarleton was certainly old enough to have one or two spooks. There was a persistent legend of a man wearing a long cloak or coat and a wide-brimmed hat who was supposed to be occasionally glimpsed in Platt's Alley. He was said to hide his face as he slunk through the darkness and to hum snatches of song to himself occasionally, although the legend did not tell why he did either of these things. Toby had no idea when the legend had begun; he had never seen the ghost and he did not know anyone who had, but the story was part of the Tarleton's folklore.

But even if there were ghosts he did not mind. There might even be a song to be written about them – something spooky but comic. Something about the ghost walking? Would the audiences recognize that as a theatre expression? Would they know that when actors talked about the ghost walking, they meant wages were being paid? It could be written as part of the lyrics and Frank could create eerie music that sounded like tiptoeing footsteps.

Tiptoeing footsteps ... The sound came again, exactly as if someone was walking stealthily through the darkness. He looked about him, but there was nothing to be seen. Imagination or creaking timbers. Yes, but supposing it really was the ghost walking again? Don't be absurd! But the phrase and the idea had lodged firmly in his mind and he was already trying out lyrics.

> On Friday nights the ghost walks
> Rattling its chains to itself;
> Because that's the night the ghost hands out the pelf.

Not W. S. Gilbert's standards by any means, but not bad as a starting point and presumably Gilbert did not write *The Pirates of Penzance* in five minutes.

Toby, his mind full of this promising new idea, went into the green room to write it down, so absorbed that he did not hear the footsteps start up again. Nor did he see the figure that stood unseen in a corner of the auditorium, watching him through the darkness.

CHAPTER TWO

The Present

Hilary Bryant had worked for the Harlequin Society for four years, and she still found every day a delight. The society was listed in most reference books as being specialists and consultants on early-nineteenth-century theatre – people said this was a massive generalization, but Hilary thought it described their work as well as anything could. She loved everything to do with Edwardian theatre and she enjoyed tracking down freelancers who would work with television set designers, and getting involved in research for early-nineteenth-century plays or documentaries. Last year they had helped set up a series of lectures for Open University summer schools, and after that had been an exhibition of music-hall memorabilia which *The Sunday Times* had told its readers was original and well worth seeing.

Shona Seymour, Hilary's boss, was pretty good to work for. She was practical and crisply efficient, and she dealt with the administration and budgeting for the society, and inveigled money or grants out of obscure government departments and arts councils. Nobody knew much about her private life, but it was part of the office folklore that she had started out as a lowly receptionist twenty-odd years ago and worked her way up to executive manager.

'She's like those exaggerated success stories about people starting in the post room and ending as chairman of the board,' said Judy Randall, who was a freelance nineteenth-century food expert, regularly used by the Harlequin. Judy wore hand-woven cloaks like a psychedelic version of Margaret Rutherford playing Miss Marple, and rode through London on a bicycle, with long striped scarves trailing behind her like flattened rainbows. She had once invited Hilary to a meal at her flat and had served a complete five-course menu from 1880. Hilary and two of the other guests had had to walk all the way along the Embankment afterwards to work off the apple and mutton pudding and meringue glacé.

'And you know, of course,' said Judy, who on this occasion had called at the office to collect a brief for a TV programme and stayed to talk, 'that she's got a bit of a thing for young men. You've only got to see the glint if anyone under thirty comes into the office. In fact, I'll bet she glinted at that surveyor who managed to get inside the mysterious Tarleton. Was he worth glinting at?'

'I only spoke to him over the phone. He sounded rather nice though.'

'Whatever he sounded like, I'll bet Shona didn't like him borrowing the keys to the Tarleton,' said Judy. 'She doesn't like anyone going in there, does she?'

'No, but to be fair that's because the owner wants it kept firmly closed.'

'Who is the owner?'

'I don't know. I don't think anyone does. There isn't even a name in the file,' said Hilary. 'That's one of the mysteries.'

'I bet Shona knows who it is.'

'If she does, she isn't saying.'

The mysterious Tarleton Music Hall was a bit of an on-going joke at the Harlequin. Every so often somebody came across a new reference to it and started up a line of speculation as to why it had

14

been closed for more than ninety years and who the owner might be. Hilary was always meaning to borrow the keys when no one was around and take a look inside on her own account, but she had never got round to it.

Judy wandered round the office inquisitively, keeping up a running commentary, mostly about the TV programme called *The Edwardians' Dining Table*, which the Harlequin had helped research.

'They're just recording the episode on puddings. Tansy pudding and tipsy cake – Oh, that sheet music you found was terrific, by the way. Exactly right, and they'll definitely use it as backing for that particular episode. Where on earth did you find it?'

'All Because of Too Much Tipsy Cake,' said Hilary, remembering. 'Toby Chance wrote it in the early 1900s. He had some connection with the Tarleton, although I don't know exactly what. I picked the music up in an old bookshop just off St Martins Lane.' In odd moments when there was nothing else going on she was assembling a folder of pre-first world war songs in case they could interest a publisher in bringing out a collection. 'It didn't look as if it had been performed for about a hundred years.'

'I don't think it has, but it sounds marvellous when it's played and sung,' said Judy. 'Saucy, but in a very subtle way. Oh, and they're definitely going ahead with one of those TV-tie-in books for the programme as well. I'll make sure the Harlequin gets a credit, of course.' She found her gloves which were in one corner of the office and her scarf which was over the back of Hilary's chair. 'See you soon, Hilary. Don't let Seymour get her hands on that surveyor and if he vanishes into the Tarleton's mists, send in the SAS.'

Hilary thought about the Tarleton on the way home that evening. It was a place that got under your skin if you wondered about it for too long, it made you want to find out what had plunged it into its long twilight. A violent death? A plot to overthrow the government? Somebody with a sleeping beauty fixation? The real reason was probably that the owner had gone mundanely bankrupt and the bailiffs had moved in.

Her flat was warm and welcoming after the rush hour. It was the upper floor of an old house which had been divided up quite imaginatively, although the plumbing was sometimes a bit peculiar and if two people in the house had a shower at the same time the water was apt to run icily cold without warning. Occasionally they all said they would have to draw up a rota for showering and hair-washing, but they never did.

As she switched on the lights and turned up the heating, she considered whether to phone Gil to see if he would like to share a pizza. It was not a very appealing idea; they had been a bit lukewarm lately and Hilary found herself remembering with annoyance his habit of finding an excuse not to go out if the weather was unfriendly. So instead she made herself a large and substantial sandwich, added a glass of wine, and carried the tray up to the tiny study and the laptop.

One of the things she liked best about her flat was the little twist of six stairs just off the main bedroom which led to an unexpected half-attic room. The shape was too awkward to house a bed so she had all her books up here and a desk with the laptop. It was sufficiently removed from the rest of the house to be a small island of silence and isolation which was great if she brought work home from the office or had the occasional freelance project to deal with. At the moment she did not have any freelance work on, but if she was going to delve into the Tarleton's past tonight – and she thought she was – it would be better to do so out of Shona Seymour's sight and hearing. She would probably not find anything new, but it would be a lot more interesting than listening to Gil's reasons why he could not make the one-stop Tube journey to Hilary's flat and why Hilary need not make her own journey to his house.

The desk lamp cast a soft pool of light over her desk and as the computer screen flickered, Hilary had the sudden feeling she was about to step out of the modern world for a while and reach back into the past. It was a good feeling; it was how research ought to feel and rarely did.

She typed in a search request for 'Tarleton' and 'Southwark' and 'music halls' altogether, which yielded a few pages of more or less standard entries. Hilary worked her way diligently through them, but most were references to music-hall luminaries who had appeared there. This was not really what she was looking for although it was interesting in itself. Marie Lloyd had apparently given a couple of performances on the Tarleton's stage, and several lesser-known names had appeared there over the years. A lady who had been known as the Flowered Fan caught Hilary's attention: she had, it seemed, been one of the Tarleton's stalwarts and had performed a dance involving a very large, feathered, flower-embossed fan and not much else. There was part of a review written about her in 1886 which referred to her dimpled charms and exuberant dancing. It also slyly mentioned that the Fan's admirers had recently expanded to include an eminent Foreign Office official, and the writer wondered, a bit coyly, what Mr Gladstone might think of this.

There was a rather arid reference from a dull-sounding catalogue of London's theatres, saying that the Tarleton was one of the oldest theatres in Bankside, dating back to the late 1700s. It had, however, been closed at the outbreak of the first world war and never reopened.

Hilary, who knew most of this already, was aware of vague disappointment, but she checked the last result, which merely said, 'Theatrical memoirs published circa 1930. CDF, folio 210, University of Durham.' It was probably another dull-as-ditchwater library catalogue with incomprehensible index numbers and no more than a half-line reference to the Tarleton, but it was worth looking at.

The entry was not dull at all. It was a brief extract from memoirs of an unidentified actor and Hilary thought the estimated publication date of 1930 was probably accurate. Whoever the writer had been and whatever his talents as an actor, his writing was very dramatic indeed, and after the first sentence Hilary began to enjoy it very much.

During the years immediately after the Great War, a theatre I often played in was the old Roscius on the Surrey side – a noble house and named for a noble tradition. One piece was *The Suspicious Husband* – a revival, but none the worse for that, and very good it was with My Public cheering me every night.

The touch of unashamed egotism was rather endearing. Hilary, visualizing a fruity-voiced, dear-laddie gentleman whose heyday had been the florid 1890s, grinned and read on.

But the piece closed after two weeks – we could have run longer but the money-grubbing Management had Bunstable [the Cockney Comic from Hoxton] booked to appear – to my mind a shocking waste of money for Bunstable had been past his best for years by then, and I always thought his notorious act with the kippers rather *near the bone*.

There was the impression of the writer dismissing the ageing, near-the-bone Mr Bunstable with a gesture of superb and immense indifference.

However, on the night after our final performance at the Roscius, some of the company suggested we go along to the Pickled Lobster Pot tavern in Southwark. I was still a comparatively young man in those days and always ready for a roistering night out, so I spruced myself up and joined them.

Readers familiar with that part of London will realize that

our way took us past the Tarleton Music Hall. A strange old place, that one, although I played there several times before the War (my Monologues), and always found it a welcoming and happy house. Mr Toby Chance was in management, I recall – my word, he was one who attracted the ladies – bees drawn to a honeycomb had nothing in it when Toby Chance turned on the charm! Still, I think it fair to say I gave him a run for his money on a couple of occasions! The ladies do not always want these pale young men; they often prefer the older, more experienced man and find a well-fleshed, well-tailored, *well-groomed* figure attractive. But I will allow that Mr Chance, though at times resembling a toff in need of a haircut [see photograph on facing page], was a talented young man, albeit given to booking the likes of Bunstable and the kippers for Saturday nights.

It was after the Roscius company had supped, that the talk turned to the Tarleton itself. Several people speculated as to its continuing closure, and old Bob Shilling who was doorman there for many years, and who was somewhat flown on stout by this time, boasted he still had a key to the stage door, but said he would not go inside the place by night for a hundred pounds.

'Why not?' demanded several voices at once.

'Because of the ghost, that's why not,' says Shilling. 'Have none of you heard of the ghost?'

Nobody had although several people pretended they had.

'They say he creeps through the darkness, still clothed in the long overcoat and muffler he always wore in life,' said Shilling, lowering his voice thrillingly. 'Wearing a wide-brimmed hat pulled well down to hide his face. He's not been seen for a while now, but he used to prowl the streets round the Tarleton regularly. He liked the dark and he specially liked the fog.'

'Pea-soupers,' said someone and there was a general groan.

'London Particulars we called them in those days,' said Shilling. 'And there was nothing like a London Particular for hiding folks as didn't want to be seen. People living in the streets around the Tarleton would warn their children not to go there. Misbehave and the ghost will get you, they'd say. I knew all about it for I lived nearby, just off Candle Street, and I saw the ghost – Oh yes, several times I saw him.'

Well! From there, Shilling got firmly into his stride and it became difficult to separate fact from fantasy, and fantasy from the ale that was flowing (although not freely; I had paid for two rounds myself). But Shilling said some people maintained the ghost was a real man – maybe a soldier mutilated in the Great War who dared not show his face for fear of people running screaming from him.

This was received with respectful, if incredulous silence.

'But,' says Shilling, clearly playing to the gallery by this time, 'there were others who said he was a bastard of royalty – one of old Edward VII's most like and the spit image of him, so that they'd paid him to keep his face forever masked, in case he might be used in a plot against the throne.'

This time there were murmurs of 'rubbish' and one or two remarks about Dumas' books and men in iron masks.

'You may well laugh,' says Shilling (several of the younger ones were doing so, very ill-mannered). 'But I've always maintained he'll be seen again one day.' Here he nodded to himself, supped the dregs of his stout and set the empty glass down rather ostentatiously. 'People in these streets have long memories and Candle Street has the longest memory of all,' said Shilling. 'And I saw him for myself several times, that gentleman in the dark overcoat. I saw him stealing through the streets after dark and each time I heard him humming quietly as he went – almost as if he was using a snatch of music to keep himself company. They say he liked to sing to himself, that ghost.'

'Ghost song,' said someone thoughtfully.

'Whatever you call it, I heard it,' said Shilling. 'Although whether it was a ghost or a flesh and blood man I could no more tell than the man in the moon.'

He paused and someone (I think it was one of the girls) asked about the closing down of the Tarleton. Hadn't that been a bit of a mystery on its own account? Was it in any way linked with the ghost story?

'I never knew that,' says Shilling. 'But there were folk who said there'd been a conspiracy of silence, and certain people had taken a solemn vow never to talk. But no one told at the time and no one's told since, and I doubt there's anyone alive now who knows the real story. And the Tarleton kept its secrets.'

So, reader, there is my little ghost story for you! A trifling small banquet, but all mine own.

But in the years that followed that night, I never walked along Candle Street, or went past that theatre, without thinking of old Bob Shilling's story – even (I admit it!), listening for the ghost song. But I never heard it, and I never heard if there was an explanation for the ghost, either. And, as Shilling said, the Tarleton keeps its secrets.

It was not really surprising to find a ghost story in the Tarleton's history. Hilary thought there could not be many theatres that did not have an eerie tale or two to their name.

But the images were remarkably disturbing, the more so because they were not horrific in the conventional, modern sense. The Tarleton's ghost was a gentle one: a dark-clad man, prowling fog-bound London streets, hiding his face as he went, occasionally humming a snatch of song, 'to keep himself company . . .'

Ghost song, thought Hilary. It was probably just an old

21

doorkeeper or a props man who had a bad chest, and liked to totter along to the local pub for a nip of rum, singing a bit drunkenly on the way back! But for a moment she could see the swirling greyness of a London older than the one she lived in, and could hear the rumble of hansom-cab wheels and see the fuzzed discs of light from the gas jets. She could see the man's silhouette, sharply black against the damp fingers of the mist.

She printed out the extract from the memoirs in case the page should vanish into the erratic ether of the internet, switched off the computer and went back down to the main part of the flat to consider her findings. The unknown actor's story unquestionably provided her with more information about the Tarleton – there was the stage manager's name, and also that reference to Toby Chance and his being in management there. Hilary rather liked the sound of Toby. A toff in need of a haircut and attracting the ladies. She remembered the sly sauciness of the song written by Toby she had found for Judy and the TV programme.

But there were no hints as to the ghost's identity or origins, and no suggestion as to why the theatre had closed and had stayed closed for nearly an entire century. An ephemeral, musically inclined gentleman wandering through the fog was hardly a reason for putting what sounded like a fairly prosperous music hall into that twilight sleep.

Yes, but that old stage doorkeeper, Shilling, had believed there had been some kind of conspiracy of silence. That people had taken a vow to keep a secret.

Could that be true? And if so, what had the secret been? Presumably there was a logical explanation somewhere for all this, but at the moment Hilary could not think what it might be.

CHAPTER THREE

Shona Seymour was annoyed to find herself disconcerted when Robert Fallon telephoned to request permission to explore the foundations of the Tarleton.

It was his mention of the underground wall that had thrown her, of course. Underground walls were things to be treated warily: they could hide secrets, memories, things better left undisturbed . . . She had always known that ever since she was a child.

She told Robert Fallon that the Harlequin's instructions regarding the management of the Tarleton were specific and clear. On no account were the foundations or any part of the structure to be disturbed or tampered with.

'Not by anyone,' said Shona, preparing to end the conversation.

But Robert Fallon did not let the conversation end. He was perfectly polite, but he said the wall had prevented him from surveying the place properly and he wanted to remove a section of it.

'It's closing off what I think is quite a large area of the foundations,' he said. 'My concern is that the Tarleton is near enough to the Thames and to some of Joseph Bazalgette's original sewage tunnels to make the foundations vulnerable – in fact there's an old

Victorian pumping station in Candle Square that I think backs onto the Tarleton's land. It's possible that the river – even sewage – has leaked in without anyone realizing it. If so, it could be eroding the foundations. It wouldn't be the whole wall we'd remove, of course, and it could be done quite neatly. Just a small section of bricks knocked out – a good builder could do it in a couple of hours, in fact I could probably do it myself. It would take half a day at the very most. I'd oversee the work and make sure it was properly rebuilt after I'd seen what was on the other side. But I can't do something as radical as that without the owner's permission. Or the permission of the owner's agents – in other words, the Harlequin Society.'

'We don't need to contact the owner,' said Shona at once. 'I – in other words, the Harlequin Society – have complete authority. I'm so sorry.'

'But surely if we explain the situation . . . I could write to the owners, or go to see them—'

'I'm afraid that really isn't possible.' Shona paused, then said, 'This wall – are you sure it isn't just part of the building?'

'Quite sure. It's an old wall but was obviously built long after the original structure.'

A wall built in an old building long after the original structure. An underground wall . . . Shona was aware of an old childhood nightmare stirring again, as if a forgotten bruise had been pressed. She frowned, and said, 'I'm very sorry I can't help you, Mr Fallon. We'd like to have a copy of your report though, if that's possible.'

'I think the Theatres Trust sends one automatically, but I'll make sure,' said Robert.

'Good. It will be useful to have it on file. Thank you.'

'Mr Fallon? My name's Hilary Bryant and I work for the Harlequin Society,' said the voice on Robert's phone. 'You've just surveyed the Tarleton and I wondered if I could possibly talk to you about it. It's a genuine request and I'm genuine as well, but if

24

you prefer to make a polite excuse about pressure of work or an urgent survey required at Highgrove House, and hang up . . .'

Even without the introduction, Robert had recognized the voice as belonging to the Harlequin Society – it was the voice he had spoken to on the phone to arrange to borrow the keys. He had not met the owner of the voice, but he remembered he had assigned to her cropped hair, green eyes, and the kind of short upper lip that created a resemblance to an attractive cat.

He said warily, 'What exactly did you want to talk about?'

'At the risk of sounding melodramatic, I'd rather not say over the phone,' said Hilary Bryant.

Robert remembered Shona Seymour's icy politeness and supposed the call was being made from the Harlequin's office. He said, 'Well, I'm certainly interested in anything to do with the Tarleton at the moment. How about meeting for a drink after work? Would Linkman's Wine Bar do? That's fairly near your office, isn't it?'

'Linkman's would be fine. I could be there about half past six.'

'Good. I'll see you then.'

Hilary was not quite as Robert had imagined from her voice, but he had not been far out. She was a bit younger than he was – probably about twenty-seven or -eight – and he had got quite a lot right about her appearance. He had certainly got the eyes right – they were green, slightly slanting and fringed with black lashes, although that might be due to make-up; Robert never knew how to tell the difference which made it difficult to know when to make a complimentary remark. Her hair was fairly short and a pleasing shade of chestnut brown, and she had the air of expecting life in general to be entertaining. But when she sat down and accepted the glass of wine Robert offered, she said, quite seriously, 'As I said on the phone, this is to do with the Tarleton. I expect you're bound by professional discretion or the surveyors' confessional or something, but I'm not bound by anything at all – I'm not really

25

even bound by loyalty to Shona Seymour, so I can be as indiscreet as I like. But since you've just spent two days in there, I thought you might be someone I could talk to about the place.'

'Well . . .'

'I'd better explain that I haven't got any hidden agendas,' said Hilary firmly. 'I haven't so much as inherited a family vow to preserve the memory of an ancestor who sang saucy songs on the halls, but I like my work and I love old theatres and I think there's something very mysterious about that one.'

Robert did not say that he thought this as well. 'Tell me about the mysteries.'

'For starters, there's an absolute taboo on just about everything to do with it,' said Hilary. 'You're probably the first person who's managed to get the keys and go inside – apart from cleaners who go in once or twice a year because the Harlequin Trustees think that looks efficient, and a *very* cursory inspection for the insurance of the building.'

'I probably only got in because the Theatres Preservation Trust commissioned the survey,' said Robert. 'It's not precisely Home Office controlled – it's partly funded by the government and partly by things like lottery grants – but one of its responsibilities is to organize surveys of disused theatres. But if you've got the Home Office at your back, people don't normally say no to you. Your cleaners do a reasonable job, by the way; everywhere was fairly clean, apart from the underground room – it didn't look as if anyone had been down there for years.' He regarded her thoughtfully. 'Why are you so curious about it?'

'The thing is, Mr Fallon—'

'If we're going to be on mystery and taboo-sharing terms you'd better make it Robert.'

'OK then Robert, I've been looking into the Tarleton's history, and the first thing I've established is that over the past ten years a number of organizations – perfectly genuine and respectable set-ups – have tried to revive its fortunes. To reopen it. They're groups dedicated to the preservation of old theatres in the main, or development projects in this part of London. They've made all kinds of approaches and suggestions: a music-hall museum, rehearsal rooms, a restaurant with bits of memorabilia everywhere – old posters and framed programmes on the walls – even a small conference centre. And any of those things would be great. There's such a buzz in Bankside these days.'

'That's true,' said Robert.

'But Shona's blocked them all,' said Hilary. 'She's done it politely and she's used a whole range of excuses, but she's success-fully repelled every single approach. I don't know if she's the one doing the blocking or if it's the owners. But if it's Shona her-self, that's really odd, because the Harlequin's whole reason for existence is supposed to be the preservation of theatre history in general and Edwardian theatre in particular. And if it's the owners then it's even odder, because anyone keeping a place like that standing empty all these years has got to be pretty flaky.'

'Hasn't anyone ever thought all those refusals a bit peculiar?'

'No, because none of them would have known about the other approaches and refusals. They just accepted the fact that the owner didn't want to negotiate at the moment, or there were other plans for the place, or there were planning restrictions on the street, and so on and so on, and they went away and found somewhere else.' She grinned at him rather engagingly. 'And although Shona had to agree to your survey, it was clear she wasn't very pleased about it,' said Hilary. 'That added another layer to all the mystery, so in the end I thought I'd phone you, although I dithered for a whole day before I made the call.'

Robert, who was starting to enjoy Ms Bryant's mode of con-versation and could not imagine her dithering in any situation at all, said, 'You said that was the first thing you established. Did you find out something else?'

'Well, I did, but I don't know how relevant it is,' said Hilary. Reaching in her bag she handed him two sheets of paper.

'What's this?'

'It's from some old actor's memoirs. I found it on the internet. It's 1930-ish, I should think. It's a bit melodramatic in places, but very interesting. I don't know who the actor was, although I'm hoping I can find out.'

Robert read it carefully, pausing occasionally to go back to an earlier passage to check a detail. When he reached the end, he said, thoughtfully, 'He's saying something happened and there was a cover-up and the Tarleton was closed because of it.'

'Yes.' Hilary read out the quoted words. ' "A conspiracy of silence, and certain people had taken a solemn vow never to talk." '

'It's probably nothing more than an ageing actor trying to spice up his memoirs,' said Robert. 'In any case it's so far back it can't possibly matter now.' But he went on studying the printout. 'You're right about it being intriguing,' he said at last. 'But don't let's get carried away. There's a strange underground wall and it's true Miss Seymour wouldn't give permission for me to look behind it. I couldn't overrule that. In any case, there were no indications of any ominous damage having occurred to the structure. And people do get jittery if you suggest knocking out sections of brick-work – they visualize roofs caving in and all kinds of disasters, so her attitude isn't all that extraordinary. It just means I've had to put a carefully worded disclaimer in my report, explaining that part of the foundations wasn't accessible.'

'How old is the wall?'

'The bricks were machine-made, so it's certainly after about 1870. Until then building bricks were hand-made. I don't like making guesses, but if I had to, I'd say it was built in the early 1900s.'

'Playing devil's advocate for a moment, don't people build walls simply for relaxation?' said Hilary. 'I remember reading Winston Churchill used to do that.'

'Yes, but I don't think Winston Churchill built a wall in the foundations of a Southwark music hall,' said Robert drily. 'But I would have liked to check what was on the other side.'

'The mummified remains of some old actor?'

'Sewer spillage and sluice gates,' said Robert repressively. 'That could be potentially disastrous to the foundations. But what I did find odd was that the wall looked as if it been constructed by somebody who didn't know much about building. Or,' he said, remembering his earlier impression, 'by somebody working in a great hurry.'

'Was there any other means of getting behind that wall?'

'No. At least . . .'

'Yes?'

'There's one of those old trap arrangements in the stage,' said Robert a bit reluctantly. 'At least, I think that's what it is. For ghosts and things to suddenly appear or vanish. It would have to lead straight down to the under-stage area.'

'Yes, it would. Couldn't you open it and put down a ladder? Or even shine a torch?'

'It's got a length of wood nailed over it.'

Hilary looked at him. 'Really?'

'Yes. A very thorough, but very amateurish nailing down. I've been trying to think it was done as a safety measure when the theatre was closed.'

Hilary said carefully, 'Could it be removed? Or levered open?'

'It could probably be levered open,' said Robert. 'But it might result in damage to the stage itself. I can't risk that, not without the owner's permission. If you can't get at certain areas in a survey, you just point that out and make appropriate recommendations.'

'I've always wanted to go inside that theatre,' said Hilary wistfully. 'I've wanted to sneak the keys out and take a look for myself, but the thought of playing hide-and-seek with Shona all along Southwark Street and Burbage Street has always been too daunting, so I never have.'

'Hilary, who really owns it?' said Robert.

'I don't know. Obviously somebody does, but there's nothing on the main file, because I've looked. All the accounts go to a bank, who pay up very promptly but very anonymously. Shona has a locked filing cabinet in her office though, so there might be another file there.' She sipped her wine. 'You know, Robert, we could get in tonight and take another look. We could even see if the cover of the trap could be levered up a couple of inches. There's no security system or anything like that. Not even an old-fashioned night watchman who swings a bull's eye lantern and talks in Cockney rhyming slang. It would just be a question of getting the keys from the office, and I've got my own office keys.'

'Would anyone be in there at this time?'

'No. It's just on half past seven – we could be in and out by half past eight. Nine at the latest.'

Robert thought: I'm contemplating entering a dark deserted old theatre – an historic London building – with a set of stolen keys and a female I've only just met, and hammering out part of a stage that dates back to the nineteenth century, if not earlier, and may have been trodden by some of the luminaries of the English comedy theatre. This is mad. But I can't stop thinking about that place, and perhaps if I just have another look inside . . . I wonder how far I can trust Hilary Bryant? Still, she's only just met me as well, and she seems to be trusting me.

Hilary said, 'I promise you I'm perfectly genuine about all this. I'm not setting some kind of peculiar trap.'

'I didn't think you were. I can't imagine what the purpose of such a trap would be, anyway. To discredit me? To get me drummed out of the Royal Institution of Chartered Surveyors? I'm starting to sound like you.'

'We're only going to lever up a bit of worm-eaten timber.'

'It wasn't worm-eaten. And I'd have to have pliers and things.'

'Have you got them?'

'Well, as a matter of fact there are some in my car.'

'Where is it?'

'In that car park just off Burbage Street.'

'Oh, quite near,' said Hilary innocently.

'All right, we'll get them,' said Robert, with the feeling of throwing discretion and sanity to the winds. 'Let's do it now before I change my mind.'

It was raining when they got outside. The lights from the cars, shop windows and bars were reflected in the shiny pavements, and London was just crossing over the line that separated its daylight identity from the dark, sometimes sinister, face it wore at night. Robert had worked in London for three years now, but he still found it fascinating to see the change from the hurrying, business-suited persona of the city to the night-time mood. He liked seeing the way that people dressed and talked and even moved differently.

Hilary had jammed a twenties-style velour hat over her bright hair. Robert wondered whether he should say it suited her, and then thought he had better not in case she misinterpreted it. She was not wearing any kind of ring but that did not mean a thing.

They collected the small haversack Robert used to tote the impedimenta of his trade, and went along to the Harlequin's offices. The building was in darkness except for a couple of dim security lights. 'I won't put the main lights on,' said Hilary as they went up to the first floor. 'They might be seen from the street. We share a security man with about a dozen other buildings in the row and if he sees lights he might come up to check. There's no reason why I shouldn't be here but I'd rather not have to explain. I'd certainly rather Shona didn't find out.'

'I feel like a house-breaker,' said Robert as she switched on a shaded desk light.

'Yes, it's odd, isn't it, how places change their personalities when they're deserted and it's dark? I sometimes think London itself does that as well.'

'I always think it.'

The dim green light fell across some of the hand-written labels inside the key cupboard. Empire Halls and Palace Theatres and

31

Apollos and Playhouses and Theatre Royals. At the sight of them Robert felt the memories stirring again, as he had in the Tarleton. All of these places were empty or had been turned into bingo halls or cinemas or clubs, but all of them had once been rich with gilt and hung with red velvet, their cornices and caryatids bathed in the incandescent glow of gaslight, if not limelight . . . What would the ghosts think of strobe lighting and computerized number-calling, or the dazzling effects of the cinema-makers? Were they still even around, those ghosts? All those bewhiskered gentlemen, thumbs hooked in waistcoat pockets as they told slightly risqué jokes . . . All those girls with parasols and sweet voices singing about the boy they loved being up in the gallery . . . Older ladies with the formidable S-shaped silhouette of the Edwardian matron, thrusting bust and jutting bustle, majestically singing patriotic songs about Britannia . . . Acrobats and strong-men in leotards and tap-dancers with long shoes, and cheerful Cockney chars who stopped off on the way to have the old half quartern and could not find their way home . . .

With the idea of keeping a hold on the practical world, he said, 'Exactly how far-reaching is the Harlequin's authority? Are you just agents for theatre owners or do you get a kind of power of attorney as well?'

'I have no idea. I don't really have anything to do with the legal side of things – I'm a researcher. But we do look after a number of theatres – most of them belong to big conglomerates. Faceless companies with so many subdivisions they hardly know what they do own. That's why the buildings stand empty for years.'

'No privately owned theatres?'

'I doubt if many theatres are privately owned these days,' said Hilary. 'Not in London anyway. I do know the Harlequin's got a few with long-running legal wrangles over lawful ownership – freehold and leasehold all mixed up together, and people denying ownership or trying to claim ownership. Or cases where title deeds were lost in the Blitz and nobody can trace the real owner. With those, the solicitors hand the caretaking to us while it's being sorted out, although it often takes years. These are the keys.' She dropped them in her jacket pocket and switched off the desk light. 'Ready?'

'No,' said Robert, 'but let's do it anyway.'

He followed her down the stairs, waited for her to lock the street door, and then said, 'I don't think we'd better use the main entrance, it fronts onto quite a busy part of the street and it's a bit noticeable. There's an alley along the side of the building, leading to the old stage door.'

'Platt's Alley,' said Hilary. 'Yes, I know it.'

'I think it would be better to use that. It's narrow, and it's likely to be dark and a bit unsavoury, but—'

'Unsavoury I can cope with,' said Hilary. 'And we've got a torch for the dark. Lead the way.'

CHAPTER FOUR

At this time of evening Platt's Alley was dark and very unwelcoming indeed. The rain lay in oily puddles everywhere, and little heaps of sodden rubbish lay in corners.

'It isn't anywhere near as unsavoury as I thought it would be,' said Hilary, shining the torch.

'It'd be very unsavoury if we were caught trespassing,' said Robert.

'We aren't trespassing. This is a public thoroughfare and we've got the keys to the building.'

'Good. Remember that argument when we're in Bow Street, will you? The stage door's at the far end.'

'Yes, I see it.' Hilary shone the torch. 'There's something carved into the stone over the door – can you see what it says?'

'It says, "Please one and please all, be they great, be they small".'

'Nice,' said Hilary approvingly. 'I wonder where it's from and who put it there.'

'Your ghost, perhaps.'

'Somehow I think it's older than the ghost. Or are ghosts ageless?'

'Whatever they are, let's hope we don't meet any tonight.'

'What's beyond the alley?'

'A ten-foot-high wall. It separates this plot from Candle Square and all those little streets leading off.'

As Robert opened the stage door, Hilary did not exactly shiver, but as they stepped inside she hunched her shoulders as if suddenly cold, and dug her hands deeper into the pockets of her jacket. He locked the door, and shone the torch into the swirling darkness. 'The room on the right would have been for a porter or a doorman, I think,' he said.

'It was a doorman who told the ghost story to the old actor,' said Hilary. 'Bob Shilling. He said he wouldn't come in here by night for a hundred pounds.'

'I'd rather you hadn't reminded me of that. Further along this corridor there's a side passage with stone steps leading down to the cellars.'

'Which is where the mysterious wall is?'

'Yes. I'm assuming you don't actually want to see it tonight?'

'Well, perhaps we could do that in daylight,' said Hilary, glancing to where the steps went down into a well of blackness.

'We can get through to the foyer this way,' said Robert. 'It takes us along past cloakrooms and the old Oyster Bar.'

'That's evocative, isn't it? Oyster Bar. Gentlemen in evening dress wolfing down oysters, and making a play for chorus girls. Very 1890s.'

If the Tarleton's ghosts had been mildly inquisitive when Robert carried out his survey, on a dark rainy night with only a couple of torches for light and semi-stolen keys for access, they were very nearly aggressive. They're not liking this, he thought as they walked along, their footsteps echoing. They're used to people coming in occasionally in daylight, but if they're disturbed when night falls they close ranks because of guarding the secrets . . .

'I thought the foyer would be bigger,' said Hilary as they went through a heavy swing door, the torch creating a triangle of light.

'But then Drury Lane's foyer isn't very big, so if it's good enough for— What's up there?'

'Stairs to the dress circle. Over there, on the left, is the equivalent of the box office, and the door to the main auditorium's straight ahead. Sorry if I'm starting to sound like a coach-tour operator.'

Robert pushed the auditorium door open; it was on a swing mechanism which protested a bit but opened reasonably easily. Hilary went through, then stopped just inside, staring at the rows of tip-up seats still in place and at the faded gilt paintwork.

'Is it as you imagined it?' said Robert after a moment.

'I don't know. I don't really know what I expected – well, other than finding the Glamis monster or Bluebeard's murder chamber.' This was said with a fair attempt at flippancy. 'But that's Shona's fault, of course. "You can go anywhere you like in the castle, but whatever you do, don't open the seventh door ..." And so you instantly want to open that door more than anything.'

'Or in this case demolish a wall.'

'We aren't going to do that, are we?'

'Not yet,' said Robert.

'I hope that's a joke.'

'So do I.'

'But now I'm here,' said Hilary, still staring about her, 'I don't think the Tarleton's got a monster to its name.'

'No monsters at all,' said Robert, and then, to see how she would respond, said, 'There are maybe a few ghosts,' and was absurdly pleased when she said, 'Yes, the ghosts are definitely here, aren't they? All those singers and musicians and dancers and backstage people ...' She glanced at Robert. 'And the man who prowled the streets and hid inside the old London fog. Whoever he was, I have a feeling he's still here sometimes.' She frowned. 'Can we get onto the stage from here?'

'Yes, there are steps on the right. You'd better have the spare torch.'

Hilary took the torch and walked down the centre aisle, occasionally reaching out to touch the worn surface of a chair. Halfway down she looked up at the boxes at the side of the stage, and stopped abruptly. Robert saw her expression alter, and said, 'Hilary? Is something wrong?'

Hilary was shining the torch onto the box. For a moment she did not speak, and then, in a low voice, she said, 'I think there's someone up there.'

Robert's heart skipped several beats and although he was not aware of having moved, he discovered he was standing next to her, holding her arm protectively. 'There's no one there,' he said, peering into the shadows. 'The place is empty.'

'There *is* someone there.' She moved the torch. 'He's stepped back, but he's still there. He's watching us.'

Robert shone his own torch onto the box and for the fraction of a second thought he saw the shadowy figure of a man wearing a long coat and a deep-brimmed hat pulled well down to hide his face . . .

He moved the torch again and then, with a gasp of relief, said, 'It's all right – it's just the fall of the curtains inside the box. Can you see how they sort of bunch together on the right? It does look like a man's figure. That's what you saw.'

They were not exactly whispering, but they were speaking in low voices as if afraid of being overheard. Robert was aware of a stir of unease, because when he left the theatre after his survey, those curtains had been pushed so far back against the wall they had been barely visible. He had noticed it particularly, because he had gone into the box to inspect the timberwork. But now those same curtains were in a different position: three quarters drawn and hiding most of the box's interior. Had someone been in since the survey and moved them? But Hilary said no one ever had the keys.

To say any of this would only frighten her, so in an ordinary voice, he said, 'It's an optical illusion. Like when you see faces in cloud formations or cracks in a ceiling that look like a map of the world.'

Hilary said, in a very soft whisper, 'But what about the shadow?'

The shadow. Robert saw it then: a blurred outline fell on the wall of the box nearest the stage and was unmistakably man-shaped. Exactly as if someone really was standing there, looking down at them. And curtains, surely, did not cast shadows . . .

To dispel the sudden apprehension, in a challenging voice he called out, 'Hello? Is someone there?'

The echoes picked up his voice and bounced it round the empty auditorium, and Robert waited, his eyes still on the box, but nothing stirred. It was impossible to see more than a small portion of the interior, but when he shone the torch again he thought there was a flicker of movement, as if someone might have dodged back out of sight. He remembered the boxes were quite deep; it would be possible for one person – for two or three people – to stand up there unseen. But whatever the shadow had been, it had vanished.

'I'm sure there's no one there,' he said at last. 'All the doors are locked, and we locked the stage door behind us when we came in – unless someone's got another set of keys no one knows about?'

'I don't think that's very likely,' said Hilary, looking round a bit uneasily. 'I think we'd know if anyone was going in and out and we keep a careful record of anyone borrowing the keys. We do have quite a lot of freelancers who come and go all the time, and there're three or four locals who come in to help with mailings and exhibitions and things like that – mostly retired people who want to earn a few pounds and enjoy the contact. But I don't think any of them would be able to take the keys without it being noticed.'

'What about the owner?'

'Yes, the owner must have keys, but I can't see him – or her – creeping round the place in the dark,' said Hilary. 'Other than that, there's no way anyone could get in here.'

But supposing someone was in here all along? Or supposing what we've just seen doesn't need keys to get in? Stop it, thought Robert, angrily.

'I expect you're right about it being an optical illusion,' went on Hilary a bit shakily. She did not sound entirely convinced of this; she sounded more as if she was seizing gratefully on a just about credible explanation. 'There's also the point that this place reverberates like the inside of a drum which means we'd have heard doors opening or footsteps. I'm sorry I spooked you like that, Robert. It'll teach me not to read melodramatic memoirs. I'll bet he was a closet ghost-story writer, that old actor.'

'This place is enough to conjure up any amount of imaginary ghosts anyway,' said Robert. 'Hilary, I was thinking – if this place was really closed in 1914, are you sure it wasn't simply because of the outbreak of war?'

'Not absolutely sure, but it's not very likely,' said Hilary. 'People wanted the theatres to stay open, in fact the government took measures to keep them going as much as possible. It brought an air of normality to life and it was good for morale. Some of the theatres were turned into Red Cross centres or army clubs, but that was a good while after 1914. And quite a lot of the performers put on shows to encourage the young men to enlist. I've got a few recordings from that era – they're on vinyl and dreadfully scratchy, but hearing them gives you the most marvellous feeling of touching the past.'

Robert suddenly wanted very much to listen to these scratchy old recordings with Hilary. He said, cautiously, that he would like to hear them.

'Yes, of course,' she said at once, sounding pleased. 'Are those steps safe?'

'Yes, but they protest a bit.'

'I don't know about protesting, they creak like the crack of doom,' said Hilary, going cautiously up onto the stage and peering into the dark void of the auditorium. 'I wish I could see it as it was

39

a hundred years ago,' she said. 'Lit up and filled with people and music and noise. Is this the trap? Oh yes, I see. I suppose it is a trap, is it? It isn't just a makeshift repair over a bit of damaged stage?'

'It's a bit too contained for that,' said Robert, following her onto the stage and putting the haversack down near the trap's outline. 'And there's a pulley mechanism with a hand winch in the wings that I'm fairly sure would have operated it.'

'It's bigger than I was visualizing,' said Hilary, still studying the outline at her feet. 'But the name's the clue, of course. Anyone being taken down by it would be lying prone. How are we going to get it open?'

'It'll just be a question of getting the nails out and then lifting it clear,' he said. 'Could you hold my torch as well as your own? Just shine both beams straight onto the section of wood.'

He was aware of a mounting apprehension, but he laid out chisels and hammers and, without looking over his shoulder, applied himself to levering out the nails. It was more difficult than he had expected and it took longer than he had bargained for. The nails had rusted into place and several of them broke and had to be dug out with pliers. Robert swore several times and each time he did so the old building picked up his voice and bounced the words back at him as if mischievously enjoying them. He found himself wanting to look back into the box – they were much nearer to it here, of course – but when he did so there were only shadows and an old chair no one had bothered to tidy away. And the curtains, he said to himself. The curtains that somebody's moved since I was here two days ago and cast that man-shaped shadow.

In the end, he managed to get enough nails free to force the section of timber partly up and slide the chisel into place to form a lever. He was not sure he could have done all this on his own; the sound of the pliers scraping on the old timbers echoed eerily through the auditorium and several times Hilary glanced nervously into the darkness of the theatre. The ghosts really don't like what we're doing, he thought. If it comes to that, *I* don't like what we're doing.

The wood came away suddenly, splintering slightly as it did so, showering fragments everywhere, and Hilary, who had been kneeling on the stage, holding the torches, crawled nearer to have a better look.

For a moment neither of them spoke, and then Hilary said, 'That's not quite what we were expecting, is it?'

'No,' said Robert, staring down.

Directly beneath the rectangle of wood was a heavy steel plate, almost flush with the stage's surface. Robert tapped the steel with the chisel and the sound reverberated dully but the steel plate did not move.

He said, 'I thought we'd see a sort of wide shaft going all the way down below the stage.'

'So did I. Won't this be part of the trap's mechanism? The floor – the bit the actor actually lay on before being sent down to the depths?'

'I think it must be,' said Robert, still frowning at the thing. 'Yes, it would have to be, wouldn't it? Like a long platform. They'd leave it up here in place.'

'Is there any means of operating it?' said Hilary hopefully. 'Winding it down? You said there was a pulley or something?'

'Yes, but . . .' Robert took one of the torches and shone it onto the sides of the steel oblong.

'What is it?'

'If you look closely you can see where an L-shaped bolt has been put on each side, and then hammered into place.'

'Yes, I do see it,' said Hilary, having peered more closely. 'We can't get that out, can we?'

'Not without an oxyacetylene welder, or smashing up half the stage.' He sat back on his heels. 'At some time in its history somebody was very determined indeed to seal up every possible access to the vault below the stage.'

At once there was the sensation that the ghosts had crept nearer and were peering over the shoulders of the two intruders, and were nodding their heads wisely to one another, saying, 'Yes, that's what happened all those years ago. The stage vault was sealed and never meant to be reopened. We saw it all, we know why it was done . . .'

Hilary shivered. 'Have we seen enough, d'you think?'

'Yes. Wait while I hammer this back into place.' He did this with new nails from the haversack, gathering up the original ones and putting them into a side pocket. It was not difficult to realign the splintered sections of wood: a close inspection would show the new nails and the slight damage, but anyone examining the trap would probably assume it was a small repair recently found necessary.

They went back down the creaking old steps to the back of the auditorium. Robert had just reached for the handle on the foyer door when Hilary looked back. 'Listen.'

But Robert had already heard it. Footsteps. Somewhere in the empty theatre someone was walking about. The sounds were soft but unmistakable.

Keeping his voice low, he said, 'It's coming from the dress circle.' He opened the foyer door and they stepped out of the auditorium. The old mechanism of the door sounded shockingly loud.

'Do we make a run for it or stand our ground?' said Hilary softly.

'It might be someone with a perfectly lawful reason for being here,' said Robert, knowing they were both remembering the half-glimpsed figure in the box. 'Are you sure there isn't a night watchman?'

'Positive. And anyway a night watchman would have challenged us by now. We've made enough noise for an army.'

'True. Then I think discretion is the better part of valour on this occasion. But there's no need for stealth, he already knows we're here.'

They crossed the foyer and opened the door leading to the stone corridors. As they went towards the stage door they heard the footsteps coming down from the dress circle. Keeping his voice very low, Robert said, 'I'll let you out and lock the door after you. He should hear that and he'll assume we've both left. But I'm staying to see who he is. We'll meet up at Linkman's Wine Bar.'

'I'll stay,' said Hilary at once.

'No. Wait for me at Linkman's. He might be drunk or on drugs. Even violent.'

'All the more reason for me to stay. There isn't time to argue. We can hide in the doorman's room. Where are the keys?'

Robert produced the keys from his jacket pocket. He unlocked the stage door and made a play of opening it and then banging it shut quite loudly and relocking it. Then he pocketed the keys and took Hilary's hand, pulling her with him into the doorman's room, leaving the door slightly ajar.

The room was musty and there were no windows, but after a moment Robert's eyes adjusted to the dimness and he made out the shape of a large desk in one corner and of an old-fashioned pigeon-hole rack for letters still nailed to the wall. He imagined the performers coming in here each evening, calling out to the doorman to know if there were any messages for them.

The chink in the door gave a rather narrow view of the passage, but Robert thought he could see enough. His heart was pounding and he was aware of Hilary trying not to shiver. And then, as the footsteps came nearer, he became aware of another sound. A soft humming, was it? Singing? It *is* singing, thought Robert incredulously. He's singing to himself. He glanced at Hilary and saw her eyes were wide with horror and he knew they were both remembering the words of the old doorkeeper again. 'I heard him humming quietly as he went – almost as if he was using a snatch of music to keep himself company . . .'

He thought he had never heard anything quite so eerie as this soft wordless singing. No torchlight showed anywhere and the footsteps were not hesitant or fumbling. Whoever this was, he knew the way without needing lights – he was walking surely and firmly. Robert tried to work out what they would do if the door was pushed open and the figure described in the old memoirs really was standing there.

There was the impression of movement in the unlit passageway, and the footsteps paused. Robert was annoyed to find that all he could make out was a cluster of shadows. Had the figure stopped? No, it was going back down the passage. There was the sound of the foyer door closing and the footsteps fading. The soft singing was no longer audible.

Robert realized he had been holding his breath and let it out in a gasp of relief.

'He's gone?' said Hilary softly, only making it half a question.

'Yes. I don't know where, but I don't feel inclined to play hide and seek with him. It looked – and sounded – as if he knows this place inside out. I'm not sure if he realized we were here or not, are you?'

'No. But let's beat that retreat now.'

They stepped into Platt's Alley and Robert relocked the stage door.

'You're locking him in?' said Hilary.

'I want to see what he does, and if he comes out,' said Robert. 'Are you all right?'

'Perfectly. You do know how to give a girl an unusual evening.'

They reached the end of Platt's Alley, and walked a little way along the street, stopping in the semi-shelter of a shop doorway, where they could see the opening of the alley. It was still raining and people with umbrellas hurried along, collars turned up.

'It's difficult to see who's who and what's what in this,' said Robert after a moment. 'I don't think anyone's come out of the alley though, do you?'

'No. It looks as if we really have locked him in.'

'Unless he went out through the main street doors. Damn, yes, he might have done that, and I don't think we'd have heard that from the doorman's room. Not through those stone passages. And the street doors are one-way arrangements – a horizontal bar you lift and push, and then it locks itself after you.'

'Hold on,' said Hilary suddenly, 'isn't that someone now?'

Robert peered through the rain. 'I can't tell,' he said.

'Neither can I. The trouble is everyone's wrapped up against the rain tonight – almost any of them could be our man. No, I think it was someone coming out of the wine bar on the other side of Platt's. Or is it? Should we follow him to find out?'

But the figure they had both seen had already melted into the crowds.

'No point,' said Robert. 'And we aren't even sure if it was the right man.' As they walked back to Linkman's, he said, 'Hilary, I think one of us will have to find a reason to go back tomorrow. I mean an official reason. To make sure we haven't shut anyone in. What was that he was singing? Did you recognize the tune?'

'No,' said Hilary. 'Did you?'

'No. But I'd know it again if I heard it.'

'So would I.'

Linkman's was blessedly warm, noisy and normal, and drinking coffee gratefully, Hilary said, 'You know, Robert, anyone listening to some of the things we've said tonight might almost believe we really do think the Tarleton's haunted. I don't mean just enjoying the atmosphere and the echoes – I mean really haunted.'

'I do think it's haunted,' said Robert. 'So do you. All old buildings are haunted, to some extent anyway. I don't know what we encountered tonight, but whatever it was, I don't think that what's sealed beneath that stage is a ghost.'

CHAPTER FIVE

May 1914

After all it had not been a ghost Toby had heard in the Tarleton when he came in early to rehearse his song, and it had not even been the rain. It had been Alicia Darke, she of the crimson silk gloves and questing hands.

She had walked down the central aisle of the stalls, her skirts swishing over the ground, and Toby, who was still on stage, thought: damn, another three minutes and I'd have been in the green room and she wouldn't have seen me. And now I've lost that beautiful hour being here on my own.

'I'm truly not here to disturb you, Toby,' said Alicia, mounting the steps to the stage. 'This is your time before the performance – I do understand that's important to you.' She had the knack of saying what people wanted to hear, and once or twice it had occurred to Toby that born into a slightly different social stratum she might have become a very successful, very high-class courtesan.

He murmured something about needing an extra rehearsal before the evening.

'Yes, of course. Your new song. I shall be watching from my box,' she said, and a different, less attractive image came uppermost: that of the female counterpart of the stage-door Johnnie. Is she just slumming? thought Toby. Is that what this is?

'But,' said Alicia, 'I have an invitation for you, and I wanted to issue it before the performance.'

It would be supper at her house most likely, and the meal would start in the small elegant dining room and finish in the perfumed bedroom looking out over the park. Toby had twice been invited into Alicia's bedroom and both times had found it a remarkable experience, visually as well as sexually. In her own way Alicia was something of an actress: she liked to set branched candlesticks in front of the mirrors to create the impression of an amber-lit cave, and to offer her guest a sensual meal in which dainty morsels of chicken, petits buerres, or grapes dipped in chocolate could be erotically shared. Toby had no objection to any of this, but at the moment he could not really think any further than eight o'clock this evening, with the Tarleton packed full of people. (Would Frank get that second set of chords right so that it suggested the butler being so drunk he tripped over his own feet? Would Toby himself make a sufficiently descriptive gesture to indicate tipping the bottle into the mixing bowl in the first verse? Would an audience even turn up to listen?)

But it was not supper at Alicia's house she had in mind at all.

'I wondered,' she said, 'if, after the show, you would care to come to a meeting of a small society I occasionally patronize. All rather secret, you know, which is why I didn't want to ask you in front of anyone else. But I think you might find it interesting. A small group of friends who have similar tastes and aims in life. It will began at half past eleven this evening.'

'Secret society? Half past eleven?' Half past eleven was not particularly late for Toby's theatre friends, but it was rather late for most other people.

'Do come, Toby. They're all longing to meet you.'

They're all longing to meet you . . .

For some reason the words sent a faint chill through Toby's

mind, but he murmured a vague acceptance – it did not seem as if Alicia was going to brook a refusal anyway – and then escorted her to the stage door. It was raining in earnest now, and the thunder was unmistakably closer. Toby asked Shilling, the stage doorman, to get a cab for her, then went back to his preparations for the evening.

But her words stayed with him. *They're all longing to meet you . . .*

Who were they, these unknown people who were longing to meet him at this secret-sounding meeting? Wild visions of devil worship and bacchanalian orgies nudged at his consciousness, which was irritating when he wanted to concentrate on 'Tipsy Cake'.

By now the other performers had arrived, grumbling about the heavy rain which had turned Platt's Alley into a river of mud, ruining people's shoes and coiffures. The musicians were in a bad temper – the flute player had dropped his music in the gutter and would have to dry it over the gas ring in this flippin' heat. The Rose Romain dancers had all had their hair dressed by Monsieur that very day and said it was a bleedin' nuisance, pardon their language, dear, it was a shocking inconvenience when you had paid two and sixpence a go, and then had to walk along a rain-sodden alley with no umbrella. You would have thought the Tarleton might have had a better approach to the stage door, wouldn't you?

They wandered round the stage, criticizing the placement of curtains and properties, picking up the threads of long-running quarrels with one another and getting in the way of Rinaldi, the stage manager, who had been at the Tarleton since he was eight, learning his trade from his father who had been call-boy and pot-boy combined and had lived in a sliver of a room in Candle Street along with six others, and been grateful for the pork pie given him each evening as part of his wages. The present Rinaldi lived in the same house, but now owned it, and his wages were considerably more than a pork pie. He was the mainstay and prop of the theatre; Toby held him in considerable affection and could not imagine life without him.

It was one of the theatre's gentler legends that Rinaldi had been devotedly and blamelessly in love with Toby's mother since he was eighteen when she was a famous music-hall dancer, performing to London audiences wearing a few feathers and sequins and plying the enormous fan that had been her trademark. It was a good twenty years since Flora's marriage to Sir Hal Chance had sent tremors of shock through the Foreign Office, but people still occasionally told how Mr Gladstone himself had sent for Hal, and said, 'Now look here, Chance, you can't possibly marry a music-hall performer who calls herself the Flowered Fan.' Toby had no idea if this had actually happened and he had never been able to ask either of his parents about it, but he always hoped the story was true.

Tonight's dancers were complaining vociferously about the dressing room allotted to them, and reminded Toby, solo and in concert, that they had been headliners on several of the halls. Elise Le Brun, who had been born plain Elsie Brown but did not believe in letting one's origins get in the way and was the leading Romain dancer, said it was not good enough, it reely was not. They had played Holborn Empire last winter and Collins's Music Hall in the spring. They had been called the new Gaiety Girls more than once, which just went to show.

The lugubrious comedian was drunk, and the sharp-witted Cockney, whose name was Bunstable, was cheerfully toasting kippers over the gas ring in the green room. The smell would probably reach the first six rows of the stalls. Remonstrated with, Bunstable said, peaceably, that he could never do a show on an empty stomach, and added that he was partial to a kipper for his tea and was in fact developing a whole new comic routine in which the kippers assumed a significant part. He offered Toby and the flute player a share in the repast by way of appeasement. The flute player, who was trying to dry his music over the gas ring, accepted, but Toby refused and told Bunstable to open all the windows.

After this, he asked Bob Shilling, who had been leering at the Rose Romains, to make black coffee for the drunken comedian. He told Le Brun that the Tarleton was so old it was impossible to have the dressing rooms made any larger and offered to release her from the evening's engagement, although it was a pity if she and the other girls did not stay, said Toby artfully, what with the agent for Drury Lane coming in tonight, touting for possible acts for pantomime. Le Brun's eager cat-like face sharpened, and she said, Oh well, if that was the case, she had not perfectly understood, and they might squeeze in one of their extras as a favour.

May God forgive me for lying! thought Toby and went up into the flies to make sure the backcloth for his song was in place. He and Rinaldi had explored the under-stage storage rooms the previous day: he had asked Rinaldi to come with him, partly because Rinaldi would know what was to be found down there, but also because Toby always found the underground rooms uncomfortably sinister. He knew, logically, that it was simply that the rooms were dark and dismal and had shadowy corners and odd echoes, but he could never rid himself of the feeling that something menacing stood unseen in the shadows, watching him.

He had been an inquisitive five year old when he first came down here, wanting to explore everywhere about this marvellous place where his mamma somehow belonged and where nothing was quite what it seemed – where people changed themselves into all kinds of exciting beings purely by painting their faces, or playing music, or by standing in a coloured ray of light like the snipped-off piece of a rainbow. In those days he thought the Tarleton was filled with magic – he still thought it now he was grown up, but it was a different kind of magic. But he clearly remembered how he had found the heavy old door at the head of the steps and had gone down them without anyone realizing. At first it had been spookily dark, but Mr Shilling who watched the door for people coming in and out and gave out letters to them, had lit a box lantern inside his own room on account of it being a dark January day. Toby was not really supposed to touch anything to do with burning candles and he was probably not supposed to borrow Mr Shilling's lantern either, but Mr Shilling was not in his room to ask permission, and Toby thought if he was very careful and very quick . . .

Going down the steps was like going down into a magic cave. He had been taken to see *Aladdin* at Drury Lane at Christmas so he knew about caves that were filled with treasure and it was all very exciting. But the flickering lantern light, instead of making it exciting, made it frightening. Toby began not to like the huddled outlines of scenery and furniture, and he began to wish he had not come down here.

He was found some immeasurable time later, huddled in a corner, his fists crammed into his eyes to stop himself crying, shaking and white-faced. It was a bad old place, he said sobbingly when he was back upstairs and starting to feel safe again. A bad *bad* old place and he had not liked it one bit.

'It's only because it's dark and dusty,' said Rinaldi – Mr Rinaldi, Toby had called him in those days. 'We'll take a lot of lanterns down there one day, Master Toby, and light everywhere properly, then you'll see how it's really a very interesting place.'

Toby had not wanted to go back into the cellar ever again, even if Mr Rinaldi took a hundred lanterns, but he said thank you very much and secretly hoped Mr Rinaldi would forget or not have time.

His mamma said afterwards, 'But Toby, darling, why on earth didn't you just run back up the stairs?' and Toby mumbled that he did not know, but he 'spected he had got a bit lost. He never told his mother or anyone else that he had thought there was someone in the underground rooms with him – someone he could not see but whom he knew was there, like an invisible person in a story. Grown-ups did not believe in invisible people and they would probably pat him on the head and say he was imagining it. Toby did not think he had imagined it at all: he was as sure as sure that someone had been standing at the foot of the steps watching him, stopping him from going back up the steps.

CHAPTER SIX

Toby did not precisely forget his experience that day, but he managed to push it to the back of his mind. But something of it stayed with him, and even now, all these years later, he did not like going into the underground rooms.

But yesterday Rinaldi had trundled down there with him, pleased that he could help his beloved Mr Toby, talking about what they might find and happily identifying this bit of scenery or that bit of furniture, as they searched: 'We used that cottage flat for *Jack and the Beanstalk* in 1910, Mr Toby.' 'Those were the curtains we had for the old Queen's Diamond Jubilee celebrations,' and in Rinaldi's company Toby did not mind the rooms at all. And it was a useful trip; they found a scullery backcloth used when the Tarleton put on *Cinderella* many years ago. 'Mr Prospero Garrick played Baron Hard-up as I recall,' said Rinaldi. 'Although he'll never admit to it now, for he likes everyone to think he only does Shakespearean roles. Shocking old ham.'

'I expect he needed the money that year,' said Toby charitably, and because he rather liked old Prospero.

'It was a long time ago, Mr Toby – My word, I think it might even have been in your mother's day.'

'I'll ask her if she remembers,' promised Toby before Rinaldi could go off into one of his trips of memory, recalling how Flora the Flowered Fan had dazzled audiences, and how Toby's father had fallen in love with her from the front row of the stalls, so to speak. A great scandal at the time it had been, Rinaldi always said with happy nostalgia, what with Toby's father being Sir Hal Chance, highly respectable and not at all the kind of man you would expect to marry a music-hall performer.

Toby had been pleased to find the *Cinderella* backcloth which would nicely suggest the kitchens of the big house in which the cook was making tipsy cake. Rinaldi was pleased as well; it had been a nuisance to lug the backcloths all the way down to the cellar rooms after the pantomime, but he had said at the time it would be worth the trouble. The canvas was slightly cracked at the edges but they could repair that this afternoon and put a lick of paint on it. It could be hung from the grid and, even from the front row, it would look as good as new.

'I remember my old father saying to me you should never waste anything in the theatre, Mr Toby. He used to tell me stories about how he worked his way up. I loved hearing them, those stories. All the memories.'

'Including the ghost?' said Toby, as they carried the backcloth upstairs. 'The cloaked man who slinks along Platt's Alley, hiding his face?'

'I don't recall anything about the ghost,' said Rinaldi rather shortly, and Toby glanced at him in slight surprise because there had been an unusually abrupt note in his voice. He was not normally abrupt about anything to do with the theatre, which was his entire life. Toby's mother had once said the Rinaldis were a theatrical institution all by themselves; they had sawdust and glue-size in their veins instead of blood.

The backcloth was in place tonight, waiting to be winched down from the gridiron framework under the roof. Having checked this,

Toby retreated to his own small dressing room. Performing a quick change into the slightly raffish evening clothes he normally wore for his act, he heard music flooding the theatre and hoped that meant the flute player had dried out his music. Now Bunstable was on from the sound of it – there was a roar of appreciation from the audience who liked Bunstable because he came from Hoxton and was regarded as one of their own. It's going all right, thought Toby.

He surveyed himself one last time in the fly-blown mirror. Loosened evening tie, coat unbuttoned, silk hat tilted at a disreputable angle, hands stuck in trouser pockets ... Not precisely drunk-looking, but a bit the worse for wear. 'Mr Chance looks like a toff after a night on the tiles,' one critic had said, which had pleased Toby immensely.

One last check – which was, in the words of the old Victorian turns, a question of, 'All right behind?' He twisted his head over one shoulder to look backwards in the mirror. Yes, he was all right from all angles. He went out to the side of the stage to wait for his cue, and panic welled up. I'm not getting the surge of power, thought Toby. I'm not filling up with that thousand-candle-power energy and I should be; in fact, I should be crackling like a cat's fur in a thunderstorm by now – *Bloody* Alicia Darke and her sinister alluring secret societies ...

Rinaldi was winching the backcloth down. From here Toby could see the repairs he had made to its edge. They looked very good and they would certainly not show from the front.

Sheer terror had him by the throat now and he knew he would not be able to sing a note. And even if I do, they won't hear me for the thunder, he thought. Oh God, this is the night I always knew would come – it's the night I'm going to fail. They'll boo me, they'll hate the song, they'll give me the bird, I'll die the death. I'll have to live out the rest of my life in squalid obscurity, busking outside the theatres. And if they write any histories of music halls in the future, and if they include the Tarleton, they'll say, 'During a night in May 1914, Mr Toby Chance was jeered from the stage during a thunderstorm and disappeared into obscurity ...'

Oh, for pity's sake, he said sharply to himself, you're not Irving or Garrick – you're not even that shocking old ham Prospero Garrick who does monologues on Monday nights if we can't get anyone else, and is always threatening to write his memoirs. You're just here to sing a couple of tunes and cheer people up, and if you're letting a bloody thunderstorm and a deliberately mysterious female get to you, then busking in the street's about what you deserve.

'Mr Toby, you're *on*,' said Rinaldi's frantic voice, and Toby realized that Frank had reached the end of the opening bars and was looking across to the wings.

He took a deep breath and walked forward into the lighted well of the stage. The footlights flared, hissing slightly, and the heat and lights and scents of the theatre closed round him. There was a delighted cheer from the stalls and whistles from the gallery, and the sizzling energy he had sought was suddenly there, pouring into his whole body. In that moment he loved everyone inside the Tarleton, extravagantly and indiscriminately. It was going to be all right – the song really was going to be the best thing he had ever written, and Frank's music was already tripping slyly across the keys exactly as they had rehearsed, and the audience was already shouting in time to it.

We're almost there, thought Toby. Look at the audience now – look at *all* the audience. That was his mother's dictum, of course: use your eyes, Flora always said. Stalls, dress circle, gallery, and don't forget the poor so-and-sos behind that pillar on the far left, because they've paid as well ...

I'm not forgetting a single one of them, thought Toby. Here we go ...

> '*In the Maida Vale kitchens of the house*
> *The maids were stirring soup and roasting grouse.*
> *They were baking bread and cakes and boiling ham.*
> *And the cook was feeling merry, just a-tasting of the sherry.*
> *Making tipsy cake with sheets of sponge and sweetest strawberry*
>   *jam . . .*'

Pause. Let Frank play the four bars of footstep stumbling music. Now the orchestra was coming in as they had rehearsed, and this was the verse about the butler getting frisky, having drunk the master's whisky, and the confusion about the sheets of sponge cake and the sheets on the cook's bed. Had the audience picked that up? Yes, of course they had, trust a Tarleton audience for that. Toby grinned and took off his silk hat in a mock bow to the house, who shouted their appreciation, and when he sang the chorus for the second time, they roared it with him.

> '*She'd just tipped up the bottle for the smallest taster*
> *When the butler said, "Let's have another glass."*'

The cheers were still ringing in Toby's ears and the music was still running in his mind when he finally left the theatre. He thanked Rinaldi, looked in on Bob Shilling to see if there were any messages in his pigeon-hole, and then went out, walking briskly down Platt's Alley.

He was delighted with the response to the song; he thought the errand boys would undoubtedly be whistling it tomorrow morning. He might come down here early and walk along Southwark Street just to listen to them. Was that being vain? Who cared if it was, he would do it anyway.

It was a little after eleven o'clock, and the storm had blown itself out. It had not cleared the air though: the night was still hot and close. Toby would have preferred to go straight home and take a cool bath and eat whatever Minnie Bean would have left out for him by way of supper, but there was the hansom at the end of Platt's Alley as Alicia had promised, and Alicia herself would be tucked sinuously inside it. No escape, thought Toby. But I'm not sure I want to escape, because whatever this is, it sounds quite adventurous. Even a bit risky, maybe. Shall I bet my virtue (ha!) on it being a plot to topple the house of Saxe Coburg Gotha in favour of some bizarre claimant? After all this anticipation, it would be an anticlimax if it was just another outré drinking club.

As the cab rattled through the streets, he said, 'You still haven't told me what this is all about or where we're going.'

'It's in Bloomsbury,' said Alicia. 'That's where we're going.'

Then it was unlikely to involve Hellfire Clubs or Jacobite Pretenders. It would more likely be earnest writers and painters, which might be deeply interesting or stultifyingly dull.

'A group of like-minded people,' Alicia was saying. 'We meet to discuss the situation in the world.'

'A political meeting?' said Toby sharply, suddenly seeing several different and slightly worrying possibilities.

'Well, I would not use quite such a dull term as *political*,' she said, and gave him the smile that one of her admirers had likened to a very patrician cat, but that at the moment reminded Toby more of a snake contemplating its prey.

'What name would you put to it?' he said.

'It has a number of names,' she said. 'It was formed from a larger organization called Narodna Odbrana.' She glanced at him, and then said, 'That's Serbian, and literally translated it means the People's Defence.' She paused, clearly waiting for a reaction, and when Toby did not speak, went on, 'Tonight's meeting is a splinter group from that. It is called Tranz.'

Tranz. The name dropped into the dark stuffiness of the hansom like a heavy stone. After a moment, Toby said, 'And its purpose?'

'It has several purposes. You will understand better when you meet the others and hear the discussion. They can explain it better than I.'

The cab rumbled its way forward, and although she continued to talk, lightly and almost flippantly about the meeting ahead of them, Toby scarcely heard her.

His mind was in turmoil. He had heard the names of Narodna Odbrana and Tranz because of his father's position within the Foreign Office.

'Dangerous nest of rebels and trouble-makers, Narodna Odbrana,' Sir Hal had said one night, when he had had a drop too much to drink and for once had opened up to Toby about his work. 'At ground level it's a cluster of grubby little secret societies – groups of a dozen or so people – but the higher you go the bigger it gets and the more important it seems to become. It has government officials and high-ranking army officers, and goodness knows who else in its ranks.'

Toby had asked what this partly grubby, partly important society actually did.

'That's open to question,' said Hal. 'They'd tell you they're promoting a greater Serbia and breaking down barriers between countries. Hence this splinter group, Tranz.'

'Tranz,' said Toby thoughtfully. 'Translating as "to cross barriers"?'

'Exactly that.' Hal shot his son an appreciative glance. 'And I'd have to say it all sounds very fine on the face of it.'

'Isn't it?' It was not often Toby's father talked to him like this and he was interested.

'No, it's not,' said Hal impatiently. 'Boiled down to the bones, it's a breeding ground for saboteurs and spies. A machine to promote war between Serbia and Austria.'

'So there really is going to be a war?' said Toby.

'My dear boy, there's going to be one hell of a war before the year's out. Serbia, Austria, Germany, Russia. They'll all go into it. It's a seething cauldron, and the lid's about to come off it.'

'And this country? Will we go into the cauldron as well?'

'Oh, we'll be in it up to our necks, there's no doubt about that.

I'm not an especially pious man and it's not often I thank God for being the age I am,' said Hal, 'but when I contemplate what's brewing up in the world, I thank Him very sincerely for that.' He sent Toby a sudden sharp look. 'It'll be a bloodbath, Toby. It'll sound mightily heroic at first but when it comes to the reality, it'll be the grimmest thing we've ever known.' He did not say, so stay out of it, but Toby knew his father was thinking it.

As the cab took him and Alicia through the streets, that conversation came back to him, and most vivid of all was his father's final remark.

'We've never proved it,' Hal had said, 'but we suspect Narodna Odbrana – and therefore Tranz as well – of arranging political murders.' And then he had said, 'My lord, I must be squiffy to talk like this; I hope you will be discreet about this conversation.'

'State secrets?' Toby had said, trying for a lighter note, and Hal had said, 'For the moment they're secret. Pray they stay that way. In any case, I'm most likely wrong about Tranz.' On which note he had gone a bit unevenly to bed.

And now, according to Alicia Darke, this group of people – Tranz – who were suspected of training saboteurs and committing murder, were longing to meet Toby.

Why? Because of his father's Foreign Office work and connections? That was surely the likeliest answer. But what if it was not? Toby thought of himself as a singer and writer of music-hall songs, but he was also part of – part-owner of – an extremely successful theatre. He could not see why a group of political agitators might be interested in a theatre, but he supposed anything was possible.

CHAPTER SEVEN

The Present

Shona Seymour had always had the feeling that when it came to the Tarleton, anything was possible.

Since she had started to work for the Harlequin Society she had come to know quite a lot about the old theatre's history. Anyone who was at all interested in that branch of Edwardian theatre knew in a general way that in 1914, when the lights went out all over Europe, they went out at the Tarleton as well. But what very few of them knew was at the same time a strange restriction had come into being – a restriction that turned the place into a curious half world, almost a twilight sleep.

It had not been until Shona was promoted that she had found out a little more. This was the late 1980s and, although the era of Thatcherism was drawing to a close, it was still a good time to be working your way up in London or anywhere else for that matter, because people were conscientious about equal opportunities. Shona's boss, preparing for his retirement, had been very pleased to hand over the reins to the assistant who had worked so hard and so devotedly for the last five years. But one of the things he had said was that Shona needed to know about the Tarleton. 'We haven't a great deal of information,' he said, 'but you'll have to keep what there is to yourself – that's a condition imposed on us. You'll have to agree not to talk to anyone about it.'

'Of course,' said Shona. 'You know I don't gossip. You know how discreet I am,' and her boss, who had very good cause indeed to know the truth of this, nodded.

'It's years before you'll actually need to do anything about it,' he said, 'but make sure you read the file thoroughly. We've never been given all the facts and we probably never will be, but we're being paid to keep the place in mothballs until – well, until the restraint ends. You'll see the dates on the file for yourself.'

Shona had read the file which was just about the oldest one the Harlequin Society possessed, absorbed the rather sparse information it contained, and noted the dates. As her boss said, it would be many years before anything could happen – years of silent darkness. Twelve years, ten, plenty of time left. As the eighties slid smoothly into the nineties, Shona worked hard to make the Harlequin Society respected and profitable, choosing permanent staff carefully and building up a reliable register of freelancers. It was interesting work and the members of the governing trust – in the main distant figures whose involvement did not amount to much more than attending committee meetings twice a year – were pleased with the results and with Shona herself.

Shona was pleased as well; she found her work rewarding and later on, when Bankside and Southwark underwent their own renaissance and came into the public eye, the Harlequin became quite well known and Shona was regarded as a sharp business-woman. She enjoyed the social life all this brought her: the lunches and dinners, and the requests to speak at various functions. It all funded her smart flat, exotic holidays, designer clothes and first-class travel. The lovers. She was careful to spend the occasional night with her former boss, however; it was a bit of a nuisance but one of the things she had learned quite early on was that it was as well to keep sweet the people who had helped you. That did not prevent her from enjoying the company and the beds of others.

Twice a year she went briskly and unemotionally into the Tarleton, carrying out a businesslike check of all the floors. She had to force herself to do it, however she never allowed anyone else to go inside, except the contract cleaners and the surveyor from the insurance company who inspected the fabric once a year. One day the restraint would come to an end, but that day seemed so far into the future that Shona did not think about it very much. It was a long way ahead. Eight years. Five. The millennium with all its hype and glitz came and went and the Tarleton remained undisturbed.

And then, just under a year ago, the date the theatre could reopen arrived. Shona had waited, expecting a letter or a phone call from the bank – even some contact from the unknown owner.

There was nothing. The mystery had stayed as closed as it had always been, and the Tarleton had stayed closed as well. Somebody's forgotten, thought Shona. Nothing's going to happen. Whoever it is has simply decided it's all too much trouble. (Too much trouble to realize the potential of a dormant London music hall? she said to herself incredulously. Too much trouble, even to engage a good estate agent who will put the place on the open market or set up an auction? Doesn't the owner know if that were to happen there would be a queue halfway to Blackfriars?) The bank continued to settle the bills for the odds and ends of upkeep, and the insurance for the fabric was renewed, and after a time Shona came to the conclusion that the owner must be some rich eccentric: some unaccountable old recluse who did not want his – or even her – ordered life disturbed and did not care about the money.

But the Theatres Preservation Trust and the surveyor, Robert Fallon, between them had worried Shona. It did not really matter what was done to the Tarleton or who looked behind the subterranean wall, but the thought of that underground wall being demolished – even partly – stirred a deep unease in her mind. Every time she went into the theatre, to check that everywhere was sound and safe and make sure the twice yearly cleaners had done their job thoroughly, it was as if an old nightmare uncurled and fastened its claws in her mind. It was impossible not to sense the secrets in the brooding old building: they might be perfectly innocent secrets – but they might not. And you have to keep secrets buried, said a sly voice in Shona's mind. No matter what they might be, they're better left alone, especially secrets that lie behind cellar walls – you know that, don't you, Shona . . . *Don't you?*

And so Shona, who did know it, resolved to block all attempts to demolish the underground wall. It was annoying that Robert Fallon was so thorough about all this. She considered him thoughtfully. Might it be useful to seduce him? It certainly might be interesting; he was quite a bit younger than she was but that had never mattered to her, in fact rather the reverse.

Probably one day a directive would come to reopen the Tarleton – or simply to hand over the keys and close the account. If so, Shona would try to retain some degree of involvement. She would put forward plans and proposals for the place's future: this was something the Harlequin did very well. Shona was not an ideas person herself, but Hilary Bryant was. Hilary could probably head a small team for the project and the Harlequin could even mount a small exhibition about it: the exhibition side was something Shona had developed over the last few years, mostly using freelancers and local people.

One of the most frequent of the casual workers was Caley Merrick, although Shona had hesitated about employing him three or four years ago. He was a quenched-looking little man with an old-fashioned walrus moustache. He had been a clerk at Southwark Council, he had said with rather touching pride. He had worked there since he left school, but ill-health had forced him into early retirement a few years ago. He tapped his chest by way of illustration and Shona supposed he suffered with heart problems and wondered how reliable he would be. But he had turned out to be conscientious and always prepared to help out with whatever casual work was needed, or to cover for people on holiday and answer the phones. He seemed to like the tenuous contact with the theatrical world and Shona had concluded he was slightly stage-struck. But whatever he was, he was polite to everyone, which Shona liked because she had been brought up to be polite herself.

'You must always be polite,' her mother used to say to her when she was small, all those years ago in Grith House, the dark house on the edge of Moil Moor in Yorkshire. 'You must remember that, Shona. You must be polite to everyone, of course, but you must be especially polite to your grandfather.'

Grith was Grandfather's house and Shona and her mother were allowed to live with him after Shona's father went away. ('But we never talk about that,' her mother always said.)

Grandfather said Shona must be diligent and work hard, never mind that she did not go to some fine-sounding school or college in York or Durham. Grith House and the school in Moil was good enough for anyone, said her grandfather, and Shona must be conscientious and pious and strive to keep out all wickedness. They had to be forever on the watch for wickedness, and work was one of the best deterrents.

The much younger Shona had not known what a deterrent was but she did as she was told and worked hard, mostly because there was not much else to do. Every day she went to the village school which looked out over Moil Moor, and every afternoon at half past three Mother was at the gates to collect her. If it was sunny they walked because Grandfather believed in the benefits of good Yorkshire air, but if it was very cold or if what they called the Moil mist had come down, her mother drove the battered station wagon which was quite good enough for jolting around the moor roads.

They were certainly not going to spend good money on a smart shiny car whose paintwork would be splattered with mud and whose suspension would be ruined inside of a week.

After school there was usually homework which Shona did in the dining room with the lights on, because all the windows at Grith were tiny and most of the rooms were dark. The two Cheesewright sisters, who came to help with the cleaning every Wednesday and the washing every Monday, said Grith was the darkest and gloomiest house in the world, and told how you could get smart windows with white frames and double-glazing, but Grandfather would not have any truck with such gimcrack nonsense and the windows stayed as they were.

When the mist came in from Moil Moor, Grith became wrapped in a thick silence. All the mirrors fogged up and sometimes there was what Mother called a bloom on the furniture. Edna Cheesewright polished everything for all she was worth every Wednesday, using soft cloths and beeswax, but it did not make much difference.

There was often a bloom on the dining table which was big and heavy, so that Shona had to put two volumes of the encyclopedia on her chair to be high enough to reach the table. Other girls had desks in their bedrooms which had been made into little studies. Shona would have liked a desk in her bedroom as well, but even though there were several spare rooms at Grith her mother and grandfather did not seem to think it a good idea. Most unhealthy to be shut away, said her grandfather. Shona would do better to be down in the everyday part of the house. There were plenty of things for her to do, he said. She had her studies, and could do needlework – embroidery and the like. In his day, embroidery had been what little girls did. Traycloths and handkerchiefs. Quiet things. Pressing wildflowers in a book – Moil Moor was a grand place for wildflowers, you could not find a better if you travelled the length and breadth of England, not that he himself had ever felt the need to do so.

No one Shona knew had to sit at a dining-room table on two volumes of encyclopedia and press wildflowers or embroider for a hobby. People had music centres and their own televisions, and they saw things like *Jaws* at the cinema. The older girls went to see *The Godfather* and said Marlon Brando must have been a knock-out as a young man, and boasted that they had got in to see *The Exorcist*. They sang pop songs and read *Lord of the Rings* (or at least, they read *The Hobbit*, which they said got you started). The older girls tried to look like Abba, and the boys they giggled over tried to look like the BeeGees. None of the girls embroidered traycloths; Shona thought most of them probably did not even know what a traycloth was.

Once, when Grandfather thought Shona was not listening, he said to her mother that they were coping very well; all that was needed was a quiet life. Nothing to excite or stimulate. It was already working, did not Margaret see that it was?

'I do. And you're very good to us, Father,' said Shona's mother, in the snuffly voice that usually meant she was trying not to cry. 'I'll never be able to repay you for what you've done.' Shona's grandfather h'rrmphed and said, now then, lass, there was no call to be getting emotional, family was family; there were loyalties and obligations.

At eight years old Shona did not know what loyalties and obligations were, but she knew about having to be quiet all the time. Even if she was asked to a birthday party or a picnic, or to join in the little trips and expeditions the school sometimes arranged, there were always reasons against it.

'Best not,' Mother said, and when the other girls were talking about what they would wear for the party, or what they would eat at the picnic or the play, Shona's mother would be at the school gates and Shona would go home to Grith and the silent dining room and the cold kitchen with the stone floor and the smell of onions if it was Wednesday when Edna Cheesewright made a big hotpot which stank out the house almost until the following week.

But it might have been worse. It was a large house, and her grandfather was in his study quite a lot. Shona always knew when he came out, because he hummed snatches of old songs to himself: you often heard the humming before you heard his footsteps. He liked the old songs. Occasionally he sat down at the jangly old piano in what used to be the morning room and tried to play them. The morning room was the dampest room in the house and no one ever used it. The music in the tapestry-covered brass box was spotted with damp and the piano strings were warped and her grandfather's fingers were no longer supple because of rheumatism, but sometimes he still liked to play.

'Caterwauling sound,' Edna Cheesewright said dismissively, although her sister, Mona, thought it was grand to hear the old piano coming to life and was apt to become sentimental about her own childhood when families gathered round a piano and sang. You did not get that any longer, music was all thumping rubbish from modern radios.

It was shortly after Shona's ninth birthday that she began to think the wickedness – the wickedness her grandfather was always saying they must watch for – might have something to do with Anna.

Anna. It was curious how the name had got into Shona's mind and it was even more curious that she had not noticed it getting in. One minute it was not there at all, and the next it seemed to have been there very firmly for a long time. When Shona looked properly at this name, this *Anna*, she saw she knew quite a lot about her and one of the things she knew was that Anna had lived at Grith House. But when she asked Mother about Anna, Mother stared at her as if suddenly confronted with something terrible. Then, in a tight high voice quite unlike her usual one, she asked wherever Shona had heard the name.

'It was just something someone said in the village,' mumbled Shona, letting her eyes slide away from her mother's stare, because eyes were the things that could give you away. 'I 'spect I got it wrong, though.'

'I think you must have done,' said Mother.

This seemed to mean that no one called Anna had ever lived here, which Shona found puzzling because Anna seemed to understand so much about Grith. She said she had hated the things Shona hated about it: gardening and helping with church fêtes and being quiet and well mannered all the time. Boring, said Anna.

When Shona lay in bed at night she could hear Anna whispering to her – she could not hear everything Anna said, but if she concentrated very hard she could hear most of it.

At first it was quite scary to have this whispery person around, but after a while Shona got used to it. Sometimes she tried to work out when Anna had first started whispering to her and peering out from the mirrors that fogged over when Moil Moor overflowed, but she could not. She was fairly sure, though, that Anna had not been around until after Shona's own ninth birthday.

CHAPTER EIGHT

———◆———

Shona had looked forward to her ninth birthday. Nine was nearly grown up, almost double figures. She tried to imagine the presents she would get. Grandfather usually gave things like new pyjamas or gloves but sometimes he gave a book token which was better, except that he had to be shown the book Shona bought with it. It never mattered what it was, because he always thought it a poor choice, and wanted to know why she could not read the good old classics of his own youth. *Aesop's Fables* or *The Water Babies*. He had enjoyed *The Water Babies* as a boy: a very improving tale, it was.

It was the middle of the 1970s and people in Shona's class were reading things like *Charlie and the Chocolate Factory* and *The Ghost of Thomas Kemp*. If Shona was given a book token, that was what she would buy, but she was not going to say this until she had actually got the book and it was too late for grandfather to do anything about it.

She liked to lie in bed for as long as she could stay awake, and think about her birthday. So, about a week before the day, she did not in the least mind being told to go to bed earlier than usual, even though it was Friday, with no school tomorrow. She was, in fact, feeling a bit tired.

'Early bed, I think,' her mother said, as Shona drooped over her supper, and for once Shona did not try to argue that the girls at school were allowed to stay up much later.

She lay in bed thinking about her birthday. Mother had said there could be a small party and Shona must make a list of her school friends so they could be sent an invitation. She could ask eight children which grandfather thought quite enough. They would be given a nice tea and could stay until six o'clock. It would be dark then but their parents would collect them. Mother wondered rather tentatively whether they might not offer the parents a glass of sherry, and Grandfather, when consulted, was agreeable. He dared say folk would not stay all that long anyway.

It was an odd thing about parents. Everybody Shona knew had a father as well as a mother, except for one or two whose fathers had died young. But when Shona asked about her own father, her mother became tight-lipped and frosty, and would not discuss it. Not a subject to talk about, she said. Certainly it was very sad for Shona not to have a father like other girls – it was very unfair for her – but life could be unfair at times. No, he was not dead, he had just gone away and that was an end to the subject.

Shona would have liked to have a father who came to things like other girls' fathers did. To clap at school concerts if she had a poem to recite, or to run in the fathers' race at sports day. He would have been at her birthday party as well; he might have made people laugh, and he would have joined in the games. You could not imagine Grandfather joining in Pin the Tail on the Donkey, or Squeak Piggy Squeak.

She had fallen asleep thinking about all this, and she had thought, on the way down into sleep, that she would not wake until morning, so it was a surprise to find herself wide awake in the pitch dark, and to look at her little bedside clock which said two a.m. Two a.m. was the middle of the night, Shona knew that. Usually she liked being awake when everyone else was asleep, and feeling warm and safe in the darkness, but tonight the darkness did not feel safe at all. Shona began to feel as if something was wrong somewhere. Was someone moving round the house, perhaps? She listened carefully. There might be a bird fluttering in the eaves outside her window – the house martins liked to build nests at Grith – but a bird would not make her feel frightened like this. Perhaps it was just Grith itself, creaking in the cold night air. Grandfather had explained about that to Shona; he said things got a bit clattery and creaky when they were older and it all sounded different in the dark. Grith was quite old and had doors that rattled in the wind and pipes that clanked. He probably creaked and clanked a bit himself, he said with one of his rare smiles. Shona had not minded hearing the creakings after that; she had thought of them as being like Grandfather's legs which he said were a tribulation to him, especially when it rained and Moil Moor became sodden and the mist came creeping into the house.

But it was not the house creaking tonight. It was someone walking about. Yes, there it went again. Someone had walked along the short corridor outside her room and was going downstairs. There was the creak of the fourth stair which was always quite loud if you did not remember to skip over it, and now she could hear a door being opened and closed. She sat up in bed, shivering a bit in the cool air. Who was walking round downstairs? The clock had moved to half past two, which was surely very late for Mother or Grandfather to be around. It was to be hoped neither of them was ill. Or might it be a burglar? This was a very scary idea indeed; Shona did not want to stay in her room on her own in case the burglar came in. She would get up and creep along the passage to her mother's bedroom, but she would be very quiet about it and if she saw a burglar she would run as fast as she could and once in Mother's room they would bolt the door and telephone the police from the phone by the bed.

She put on her dark blue dressing gown which would look like part of the shadows and went cautiously out. But when she got to the head of the staircase she saw lights downstairs. Burglars did not put lights on: they had torches and moved around in the dark. Shona crept part way down the stairs until she reached the half-landing where she could look down into the hall. She sank down onto the stairs and peered through the banisters.

This was becoming odder and odder. The little door in a corner of the hall – the door to the cellar that was hardly ever opened – was propped wide by a chair. It was not the main lights that were on, but the two table lamps. In the dim glow from them she could see that the door leading through to the kitchen was propped open by another chair. Shona stayed where she was and waited to see what happened.

What happened was that Mother, wearing her gardening things, came in from the kitchen – she must have been outside because there was a spattering of rain across her shoulders – Shona could see the little drops in the lamplight. She was trundling a large wheelbarrow piled with bricks – the bricks and the barrow were leaving a trail of dust all over the nice oak floor – Edna Cheesewright was not going to like *that* when she came in on Wednesday! – but Mother did not seem to care about the brick dust or even notice it. She stopped just inside the propped-open door, and a man came up from the cellar below. At first Shona shrank back in panic because it *was* a burglar after all – it was certainly a stranger – and then she saw with a shock that the man was wearing Grandfather's old tweed jacket and the chewed-up hat he kept for bad weather. Mother always said the jacket and the hat were a disgrace and Father should think shame to be seen in them and she would put them on a bonfire one of these days.

It was Grandfather, it really *was*, but his eyes were like little black pits and his expression was so dour and grim that Shona began to be frightened in a different way. It was as if something else had put on the old jacket and the battered hat and was pretending to be her grandfather, like when the wolf dressed up in frilly nightclothes and lay in wait for Red Riding Hood. Would

73

Grandfather suddenly snarl and pounce and slaver, as the wolf had done in the woodland cottage?

But he seemed intent on helping her mother get the wheelbarrow with its heap of bricks down the steps inside the door. Shona could not see them but she could hear the wheelbarrow bumping and scraping as it went down. She heard her mother say, 'The last load, I think,' and her grandfather reply, 'Yes, we've enough now, but it's taken longer than I expected.'

What had taken longer than expected? What was this about? Greatly daring, Shona crept down the stairs, and crossed the hall.

A dull light came up from the cellar and, as she peeped down, Shona saw they had lit the storm-lanterns that were kept for power cuts. There were three lanterns, set on the floor, and in their light she could see the mound of old bricks in one corner – masses and masses of bricks, all lying higgledy-piggledy. There was a tub of something grey and sloshily wet nearby, and a little clutter of gardening things: a trowel and a small spade. The person who was so scarily unlike her grandfather but who still had his face was moving about. He was lit from below by the storm-lanterns – perhaps it was just the light that was making him look so strange. Shona hoped so.

He bent down and lifted something that had been lying in a corner. Shona saw it was a woman of about twenty-five with long brown hair. Her face was a mottled blue-grey and Shona had a feeling she ought to know who she was, but although she looked very hard, she did not recognize her at all. Whoever she was, she was so still Shona thought she must be dead. It was how dead people looked in comics – she had seen them at school. This was very bad indeed. Shona would not have picked up a horrid dead body in her arms, but her grandfather did not seem to care. He did not look scary now, he looked as if he might be trying not to cry and he stood quite still for a moment, holding the woman in his arms. Shona felt a sudden surge of loathing for the brown-haired woman because her grandfather and mother were both looking

74

down at the horrid dead face with such immense love. They had never looked at Shona like that, not ever! She thought nobody had ever looked at her like that in her whole life. Her mother always had lots of things to do in the house and garden, and her grandfather was only ever disapproving, telling her to be quiet, or to do her homework, and wanting to know why she could not occupy her time with boring old embroidery and pressing wild-flowers. Remembering that, Shona found herself hating the brown-haired woman who made Grandfather's face go all soft and silly, and Mother's eyes fill with tears.

Grandfather put the woman in a little recess at the back of the cellar. It was the tiniest space imaginable and there was not room to lay her down on the ground so he propped her against the wall and the black pipes immediately behind it. Twice she flopped forward, falling onto his chest, and Shona saw her mother shudder. But at the third attempt the woman stayed upright, wedged between the thick pipes, her head lolling forward. Grandfather glanced at Shona's mother, then leaned forward and cupped the dead face in his hands, and kissed the forehead. After a moment, her mother stepped forward and did the same. This was disgusting. Shona felt sick to see them kissing this woman, sick with jealousy.

Grandfather squared his shoulders as if he had to take on an immensely heavy burden, and began to build up the bricks to hide the woman. His face had the scary expression again, as if the wolf might be about to throw off the disguise and leap forward.

Her mother did not seem to see this. She helped him lay the bricks and put on the wet cement. Once Grandfather said, half to himself, 'Such wickedness, Margaret,' and Mother let out a half sob, and then said, 'The wickedness was never meant, Father. You do know that.'

'Of course I know.' His hands, a bit twisted with arthritis, reached out to hers and enclosed them for a moment.

'I can hardly believe you're doing this for me.'

'I look to my own,' he said gruffly.

'But the risk. If it's ever discovered—'

'It won't be discovered,' he said. 'We'll do what has to be done, and then it'll never be spoken of. The wall will look like part of the cellar. No one else need ever know.'

'No one must ever know,' said Mother. 'Never.'

Neither of them said anything after this, and for a long time the only sound was the wet slapping of the cement and the scraping of the bricks, and the laboured breathing as Shona's grandfather worked.

Shona watched, seeing they were building the wall all the way up to the ceiling, seeing that this woman was going to be so well hidden no one would ever guess she was there – as Grandfather said, the wall would just look like part of the cellar. It would be horrid behind the wall: the water pipes would clank and hiss to themselves in the dark, and spiders and black beetles would come out when it was quiet and scuttle over the woman's feet.

It seemed to take for ever to lay the bricks in neat rows and cement them into place, but eventually they reached the ceiling. Shona watched for a bit longer, then went quietly back to bed. She could not sleep and lay awake for a long time, going over and over what she had seen. Who had she been, that woman, and why were Mother and Grandfather hiding her body?

The really strange thing was that when Shona woke up next morning, it all seemed so unreal she was not entirely certain it had actually happened. Her mother and grandfather could surely not have put an unknown lady behind a wall and left her there in the dark. The more Shona thought about it, the more unlikely it seemed. It must have been another nightmare; she would forget it and look forward to her birthday.

But she did not forget completely. She dreamed about it, often for four or five nights in a row. Sometimes she dreamed she was in the cellar on her own, listening to her grandfather walking about the house, humming his songs as he went. For some reason this was very frightening indeed, because she knew her grandfather must not find her. But, just as his shadow appeared on the stairs, huge and terrifying in the darkness, she woke up. She was always sticky with sweat and gasping after these dreams, and once she had to get out of bed to be sick, doing it in the basin on the old-fashioned washstand because she dare not let anyone hear her going to the bathroom at the end of the corridor.

On the mornings after the dream came, her mother sometimes said at breakfast that Shona looked pale and asked if she felt all right. Shona always said she felt quite all right, thank you. Once or twice she wondered whether to tell her mother about the dream and see what she said, but she never did.

It seemed that after all there was not to be a ninth birthday party. Her mother thought it would cause too much disruption; it would mean a lot of work, she said, and Shona's grandfather did not really like being disturbed. Better if they just had a little celebration by themselves. Shona could have her presents and she would ask Mona Cheesewright to bake a special cake with candles. There was not much point in arguing so Shona did not bother. One day she would find a way of getting all the things her mother and grandfather were not letting her have now.

Life at Grith was somehow different after her ninth birthday; it was quieter and Grandfather hardly ever hummed little songs to himself as he went about. He spent a lot of time shut in his study, although Shona did not think he actually studied anything there. Mother sat staring into space for hours, not saying anything and not seeming to be aware of what was around her. Quite often in the evenings she said in a rather unfamiliar voice that she would take a little nip of sherry; it was good for the digestion, sherry. When she came up to kiss Shona goodnight, the kiss smelt quite strongly of sherry. Some nights she did not come up at all and Shona knew there had been several quite big nips of sherry and maybe of whisky as well, and that her mother had fallen asleep in her chair and forgotten about the goodnight kiss.

When Shona and her mother went away for their usual little holiday at Shona's half term which grandfather liked them to do each autumn on account of it giving them a rest from each other, the walks they normally took together along Robin Hood's Bay did not happen. After lunch Mother always said she was tired, but Shona knew it was because she had drunk too much of the whisky she had hidden in her suitcase. Shona did not miss the walks very much, but it was just one more thing that was different about her life.

The other thing that seemed different was that her mother said she must remember never to go through the door behind the hall screen. 'You can go anywhere else in the house,' she said, 'but not down there.'

When Shona asked why not, her mother said, 'Because it's dangerous. It goes down into the foundations of the house.'

Her grandfather added something about damp seeping in from the moor. 'Moil Moor sometimes overflows a bit after heavy rain. It's likely that the cellar occasionally gets flooded.'

'Oh, I see,' said Shona.

Grandfather put a carved screen across the cellar door, which he said was a rood screen and had come from a church. It partly hid the door so that it was not very noticeable, except that Shona always noticed it because of the dream and because of having a vague memory that there was something very bad and very frightening on the other side of the door. When they ate Sunday dinner in the hall, which her grandfather liked to do on account of it being a tradition at Grith, her eyes kept going to the screen. There were secrets behind that door. Over the years, secrets came to taste of roast beef and the thick gravy her mother always made on Sundays.

CHAPTER NINE

———◆◆◆———

Grandfather died just before Shona's thirteenth birthday.

He had been ill for several weeks, and had sent for a distant cousin to come to Grith House to help nurse him. Her name was Elspeth Ross and Mother told Shona that Elspeth would most probably be living with them at Grith House. It was what Shona's grandfather wanted, said her mother; he had said they must look to their own.

'I look to my own.' That was what the figure in the dream had said – what he still said when the dream came. 'I look to my own ... We'll do what has to be done ... No one else need ever know.'

Shona had never heard of Cousin Elspeth, who was a slab-faced female a few years older than her mother. She wore granite-coloured jumpers and tweed skirts and clumpy shoes. Shona, who was noticing things like clothes more and more, could not imagine where Elspeth found such things or how she could bring herself to wear them. When she said this to Anna, she had the impression that Anna tossed her head and said, Oh, you saw all kinds of frumps in the Ross family, hadn't Shona realized that by now? This again seemed to indicate that Anna knew, or had known, some of the family.

Mother said Elspeth had fallen on hard times, poor soul, but Shona was not sure if she had got this right, because a lot of things seemed to get done to Grith after her arrival. One of these was the fitting of new locks on all the doors and some of the windows. Cousin Elspeth told Shona she liked to be secure in any house where she lived. You could not be too careful, she said, in fact she always locked her bedroom door at night. It was a good thing to do and Shona should remember it and lock her own door.

Grandfather died at the height of that summer which was a particularly humid one. A lot of people were away on holiday and the wearing of black was stickily uncomfortable. When they drove past Moil Moor on the way to the funeral, the undertaker had to close all the car windows because Moil always smelt bad in the hot weather. The church smelt of clogged-up drains and the vicar did not seem to have washed his cassock for about a year because when he came to talk to them after the service, he smelt of clogged-up drains as well.

A few people were invited to Grith for a glass of sherry and ham sandwiches afterwards. Edna Cheesewright had baked the ham and Cousin Elspeth had supervised it even though Edna had been baking hams for years and did not need telling how you rubbed brown sugar onto the outside and studded it with cloves. Mona had made plain scones and there were wedges of veal and ham pie.

All the mourners were polite and soft-voiced and said what a sad day it was, but Shona noticed most of them kept sneaking furtive looks round the big drawing room which had been opened up for the occasion. People did not often get asked to Grith and she thought most of them were only there from curiosity.

Shona's mother sat down and cried when everyone had gone, and said it was too much for a body to bear – all those folk coming to gloat. People could be very cruel and very critical, Shona must always remember that.

Shona was about to ask why people should gloat or be critical, when Elspeth came bustling in and said it would not help anyone if Margaret wilted and drooped all over the house. Life went on, said Elspeth briskly, and Mother sat up a bit straighter and said Elspeth was perfectly right, and she would have a small drop of whisky to put new heart into her, never mind it being four o'clock in the afternoon. After the small drop, she said it was all very sad, but they had to remember Grith House was now theirs, and they were lucky to have such a lovely home. When they got used to not missing Father so much, said Margaret Seymour taking a second small drop of whisky, things would be just as they had been before.

Shona did not much miss her grandfather who had been strict and old-fashioned, and things were not in the least as they had always been. One of things that was different, was having Elspeth here. She seemed to have fallen into place at Grith, but it was a rather odd place, midway between a guest and a housekeeper. Mother said Elspeth was useful in helping to run the house – Shona did not realize what a lot of work there was in a house this size – but Shona could not see there was all that much to do with just the three of them. Hardly anyone ever came to Grith; her grandfather had not much liked visitors – 'Poking and prying into folk's private business,' he always said – and her mother had never seemed to like them either.

Elspeth undertook some of the cooking, which these days seemed to be too much for Shona's mother, and oversaw the Cheesewrights when they did the cleaning. Edna Cheesewright said that Miss Ross was downright rude at times: she and Mona were not skivvies to be spoken to like that and they only came to Grith to oblige. Shona's mother promised Elspeth would not be so outspoken in the future, but Edna said they were hurt in their feelings and might have to consider their position. They were neither of them as young as they had been. Shona heard Mona say afterwards that happen Mrs Seymour would be selling the rickety old house now Mr Ross had died – a shocking condition it was in, wasn't it? But likely it would fetch a good price and then

Mrs Seymour could get a neat little bungalow, said Mona. You could go further and fare worse than a neat little bungalow.

Shona was beginning to have some sympathy with what her grandfather had said about people poking and prying, because Elspeth poked and pried a lot and most of it was into what Shona did. She was often the one who took Shona to and from school: she had learned to drive the old station wagon and was always outside the school gates on the dot of half past three.

Outside school hours she watched Shona a good deal, which was annoying. If Shona went for a walk to the village, like as not she would hear Elspeth's loud voice hailing her cheerily – Elspeth was always cheery, Mother said it was as good as a tonic having her in the house – but Shona found it very wearing at times. There was always a good reason for her to be following Shona: Elspeth had just discovered they were out of butter, or scouring powder, or black sewing thread, and she had said to Margaret she would just nip along to the village to get some. Or she had found it stuffy in the house, and had just nipped out to get a breath of air. She was always just nipping somewhere and most of the nipping seemed to take her in the same direction as Shona. She was a frumpy old nuisance and if Shona had been able to think of a way of getting rid of her without getting caught and punished, she would have done it.

The old dream about the cellar came back occasionally, which Shona hated, but it was her first year of being a teenager and there were more important things to think about than stupid childish nightmares. You were almost grown up when you were a teenager – everybody at school said so – and Shona hoped things at Grith would change at last, and she would be allowed to go out and do the things other girls did: youth clubs and parties with cider to drink, and giggly shopping trips into the nearest town with a group of girls.

But things did not change at all and the nearest she got to shopping trips was if Cousin Elspeth drove them into Norton or

Scagglethorpe. Twice they took the train to York and went into Marks & Spencer and had lunch in a tea room on the top floor of C&A. Cousin Elspeth said this was a great treat. Shona thought she could hear Anna laughing at this.

Shona finally left Moil and Grith House three weeks after her eighteenth birthday. She went quietly and unobtrusively, and without any regrets. She had been born there and had lived there all her life, but she would not miss any of it – not the place or the people or the memories.

She knew all the stories about naive trusting girls who went to London thinking they were going to become actresses or film stars or models, and who ended up living in dreadful bedsits or even sleeping rough on the streets, but she did not particularly want to be an actress or a model. She thought she was being practical and sensible about the whole thing. She was prepared to take almost any job she could find, and she had money on which to live for a reasonable length of time.

It was as simple as getting a taxi to York, then boarding the London train and getting out again at King's Cross. She stood for a moment on the platform, clutching her suitcases, momentarily bewildered by the sheer size and noise of everything, and by the volume of people all rushing to and fro so purposefully, but she was determined not to panic at any of it. Wasn't this what she had wanted?

Despite her resolve, she found London frightening at first and what she found even more frightening was the realization that her money might not last as long as she had thought. Rents for even the pokiest of places were astronomical and the cost of quite ordinary things appalled her, but eventually she got a tiny flat south of the river, in a house overlooking Tabard Gardens. She furnished the two rooms carefully, because she might have to stay there for several years.

Finding a job was a bit more difficult than finding a flat. It was the mid-eighties, still the era of the yuppies, but the effects of the boom and bust years were starting to bite and employment was becoming uncertain. In the end she got a very junior position with a company managing theatres for absentee landlords or owners, and specializing in research into Victorian and Edwardian theatre. It was not precisely the kind of job she had imagined, but for the time being she did not mind performing lowly but necessary tasks such as answering telephones, making coffee and filing. A gofer, they called it – Shona had never heard the word before, but she understood it was what her grandfather would have called a dogs-body. It did not much matter what it was called because it was a job with a salary and the office was in Southwark, reassuringly near her flat – she could not afford to live in Central London which still bewildered her. She did not know very much about theatre in any form, but she could learn and it seemed to be the kind of set-up where you could get noticed.

It certainly looked as if her boss was going to notice her; Shona had dressed carefully for the initial interview and after she got the job, she bought smart but subtly sexy outfits to wear each day. She was not very knowledgeable about clothes – she had already realized that Moil was about fifty years behind the fashions – but she studied people in the street and the displays in the better-class shops. The money she had brought from Moil was already deposited in the bank to earn interest – her grandfather would have approved of that! – but Shona thought she was justified in using some of it for clothes. She bought well-cut suits with narrow skirts or trousers and expensive shoes or boots, and she had her hair done every week and learned about make-up. Without telling anyone at the office, she took evening classes in management and book-keeping. Attending the classes and completing the various assignments filled her evenings, which might otherwise have been lonely. When she had the qualifications she intended to mention them casually to her boss. Between classes she read up on Edwardian and Victorian theatre, and went to lectures and exhibitions. She made a few rather tepid friendships and determinedly lost her virginity to a fellow student on the book-keeping course, in order to learn the rudiments of love-making. After this she progressed to one of the lecturers who was older and more experienced and from whom she was able to learn considerably more than just the rudiments. It was amazing what two human bodies could achieve, although some of the positions were surprising.

She had worked for the Harlequin Society for four years, gradually learning about the administration of the place, and was starting to be given slightly more responsible work, when she was trusted with checking the inventory of a couple of the theatres. 'Good training,' said Shona's boss, who had not missed the fact that this attractive member of his staff worked hard and often stayed after hours or skipped her lunch hour. 'A straightforward job and it needn't take you much more than a couple of hours for each one, but it's something we have to do.'

One of the theatres in question was a small concert hall, tucked between two warehouses, and mostly used for amateur shows and choral societies. It only took Shona an hour and a half to go through the list of contents, and by four o'clock she had typed up the report, although she was careful to be seen still diligently working on it when everyone left at five thirty.

The other theatre was the old Tarleton Music Hall. Her boss had said he would not normally suggest she go into this one by herself because it was quite a big place and a bit more of a target for vandals and drop-outs, but the cleaning company had just yesterday finished the six-monthly spruce-up, so she would be perfectly safe.

'The electricity's been switched on for the week for the cleaners, so it'll still be on now,' he said. 'But you'd better take a torch in case any bulbs have blown. You really only need to check the auditorium, the supper room and the dressing rooms anyway – Oh, and the green room. Don't bother about the dress circle or the boxes – they've been empty of everything for years. And we leave the lower levels to the annual survey – in fact it would be better not to go through the door leading down to the cellars at all; it'll be dark and possibly dangerous.'

It's dangerous Shona . . . You can go anywhere else, but not down there . . . In the depths of Shona's mind something stirred, but she pushed it away, and said of course she would not go into the underground sections. Was there something structurally wrong with the place? She had been secretly trying to study some of the basic points of building construction, but it was not a thing you could do properly without practical experience and someone to explain things to you along the way. 'Has it got settlement?' she said tentatively, not exactly plucking the word at random from her gleanings, but hoping it was a sufficiently general term to be appropriate. 'That area's had problems in the past, hasn't it?'

Her boss glanced at her, plainly surprised, and then with more attention, which was exactly what she had been hoping for. He said, 'I don't think there's any actual settlement, in fact on the whole the fabric's very stable and sound. But there's an old pumping station in Candle Square and I shouldn't be surprised if the Thames doesn't occasionally slop over its sluice gates round that neighbourhood; so it's possible the Tarleton's foundations occasionally get flooded.'

The memories stirred again. *Moil Moor sometimes overflows a bit after heavy rain*, her grandfather had said. *It's likely that the cellar occasionally gets flooded.* The words came into Shona's mind like thin fog, like the will o' the wisp lights people said flickered over Moil Moor itself. She frowned and forced her mind to concentrate on what had to be done, getting the file from the cabinet, studying the list of contents she would have to check. It would probably not take long: it sounded as if anything not actually nailed down had long since been removed.

She went to the Tarleton the following day, arming herself with a good torch and making sure to take the office mobile phone with her. Mobile phones were becoming more common but they were still quite expensive. Even so, Shona's boss had invested in one for general use; people going into deserted buildings as his staff often had to do, should be able to summon help in the event of the unexpected, he said. Walking along Southwark Street, the file in her bag, the phone in her coat pocket, Shona was aware of a sudden surge of well-being. For the first time she felt she was really part of London and of the people who scurried importantly to and fro.

She turned off Southwark Street and into Burbage Street, and from there went along the narrow passage called Platt's Alley at the side of the theatre. The old lantern with the legend 'Stage Door' engraved on it was still over the door; Shona glanced up at it and tried to imagine how it must have looked nearly a hundred years ago with the gas light flaring.

The lock was not exactly stiff, but it resisted the key before the door finally opened. Shona had been braced for the smell of dirt and age, but there was a sense of newly cleaned walls and floors. There was a fairly wide passage beyond the door, with a small hatch and a counter on the right, a bit like a cloakroom hatch in an old-fashioned hotel. Over the hatch was faded lettering – 'Stage Doorkeeper'. Shona looked inside and saw the battered desk and chair, and the large pigeon-hole rack on the wall for letters.

Once inside the main part of the theatre she went through the ground level methodically, checking the list of contents, noting that a light fitting had fallen down in the supper room, seeing that there were only eight chairs in the green room when the inventory stated ten. Could one of the cleaners have filched a couple? If they were anything like the chairs still here they had probably not been worth anyone's while to take, but she would check tactfully, although she would be firm. Her grandfather had always said you should be firm with servants, 'Or they will ride roughshod over you.' Her grandfather would probably have been lynched in today's classless society.

Everywhere was spick and span and pleasantly scented with

polish and soap. Shona could report this and her boss would be pleased with the cleaning company and with Shona herself for being so efficient and thorough. She might create an opportunity to talk a bit more to him about how she was studying theatre history in her spare time: it might develop a spark between them. She would quite like to stay with the Harlequin Society, but she did not intend to answer phones and file reports for much longer and she would do whatever it took to move up the ladder. Her grandfather would have drawn down his brows at that, and said she was selling herself like a cheap tart, but Shona was not going to be cheap, in fact she was going to be very expensive indeed.

For the time being, she focussed on her work, sitting down in a corner of the auditorium to check the inventory again. She thought she had not missed anything and closed the file and went back through the foyer and along to the stage door. If she left now she would be back at the office before they locked the street door. It was then that she saw the secondary passage, almost opposite the doorkeeper's room. Did it lead to the underground rooms? She hesitated, remembering her boss's offhand warning, wondering if he would be pleased if she reported making a quick check of the cellars or if he would be annoyed with her for ignoring his instructions. Perhaps she could just go to the end of the passage and see what the layout was.

It did not look as if electricity had been extended down here, and when Shona switched on the torch it was clear that the cleaners had not extended their attentions here either. The brick walls were draped with cobwebs and the ground felt gritty with dirt.

As she went cautiously forward, she could hear timbers creaking overhead which made her think of her grandfather saying Grith House creaked because it was old. But the creakings in here were not just an old building's joists and timbers; they were more rhythmic. Almost like footsteps. Shona's heart started to beat a bit faster. Could it possibly be footsteps she was hearing? She remained where she was, listening intently, hearing faint sighings.

Probably the sighings were just little gusts of wind getting in through a badly fitting window somewhere. Grith House had sighed and creaked in the same way.

The creakings came again, louder this time, and with a definite pattern to them. Footsteps? No, it was her imagination. But it really did sound as if someone was walking round inside the theatre. Supposing someone had got in and was hiding somewhere in the darkness, watching her? Shona was becoming quite frightened by this time, but tried to remember if she had locked the stage door when she came in. Yes, she had. Then there could not be anyone in here. She turned to retrace her steps, intending to get out of this place as quickly as possible and into the safe, crowded London streets.

The door from the foyer opened and the footsteps came along the corridor towards her.

There was no longer any question of getting out. The footsteps were already coming along the corridor and whoever the owner of those footsteps was, Shona would run smack into him. Even if she could beat him to the stage door, the old lock would take a minute or two to unfasten. She supposed it was just about possible this was someone with a reasonable right to be here, but as far as she knew the Harlequin Society had the only set of keys and she was not prepared to take any chances.

She switched off the torch, and moved back into the musty shadows of the brick tunnel. It was not pitch dark, there was just enough spill of light from the corridor to see the way, but it was dark enough to be cautious. With luck he would not know she was here and once he had gone she could get out. She pressed back against the cobwebby wall, her head turned. Would he go past? But unless he had his own keys, she was locked in with him. And then she heard something else – something that caused one of her old nightmares to stir uneasily.

Whoever was out there was singing quietly to himself as he walked through the darkness.

At the sound of that soft singing, Shona felt absolute terror scald through her, and for a frightening, shutter-flash of a second the nightmare was with her – it was all round her, and it was the dark night, the *bad* nightmare, the one in which she crouched in the darkness, listening for footsteps and for the soft singing that would mean her grandfather was coming and might find her . . .

She pushed the nightmare away and stayed where she was, not daring to move. The singing stopped and the footsteps paused, as if their owner was looking round. Had he realized she was here? If he looked into this passageway would he be able to see her? She risked turning her head to look deeper into the shadows and now that her eyes had adjusted to the dimness, she saw the little recess in the bricks on her left, about five feet high. Was it deep enough to hide in? Making as little noise as possible, she moved along to it. It was not a recess after all, but a door set deep into the brickwork: a door with a scarred oak surface and an iron handle.

A thick oak door, worn and scarred with age. A door that had been hidden behind an old rood screen and was never opened. But it was all right, because this was not Grith, this was the Tarleton.

This door was not locked. It made a rusty protest which Shona thought was not loud enough to be heard beyond the passage, and when she turned the handle it swung inwards with only the faintest scrape. She glanced back towards the main passageway, listening, but nothing happened and she could no longer hear that soft, eerie singing. She looked back at the partly open door.

It would be better not to go through the door leading down to the cellars, her boss had said. *It'll be dark and possibly dangerous.* And, *Don't go through the cellar door, Shona,* her mother and grandfather used to say. *It's dark and dangerous down there . . .*

Shona's surroundings blurred and the scents of dust and age were no longer those of an old music hall in London's Bankside: they were unmistakably and terrifyingly the scents of Grith House. But this was London, not Moil, and she was in the Tarleton and the ghosts had been left behind at Grith House.

Are you sure about that, Shona? You might have left me, but perhaps I never really left you – perhaps I came with you all the way to London and your splendid new life. Perhaps I'm here with you now.

You're not here, said Shona to the sly voice. You're at Grith.

Beyond the door was a flight of steps – old stone steps, worn away at the centre, winding down into a thick blackness. A faint stale breath of air gusted out to meet her like bad drains, like something walled up in an old cellar, like the Thames slopping over its sluice gates, or Moil Moor overflowing after heavy rain.

Shona could no longer hear the soft singing or the footsteps, but she could hear the whispering inside her head.

Are you going down there, Shona?

She could ignore the whispering voice; the vital thing was to stay out of the way until the intruder had gone. There was no real need to worry, and she had the mobile phone if she had to call someone for help. But it would be better if the intruder did not know she was here. She would go down the steps, just a little way.

It was very dark but Shona could see her way and there was a narrow handrail. Halfway down she remembered the torch and switched it on; its light would not be seen from here. Her grandfather would not know she was here; he would not catch her down here— No, Grandfather was not here, he was at Moil and had been dead for years. Keep hold of the present, Shona. Yes, but someone had walked through this place with Grandfather's tread, humming softly in the way Grandfather always did ... Shona glanced back up the steps uneasily, but nothing stirred.

The steps ended in a large, low-ceilinged room – probably it had once been used as a general storage area, but there was nothing much in it now except some pieces of scenery stacked at one end, and a couple of old skips, their lids open to show old stage costumes and folded lengths of cloth, all thick with dust and grey with age. She moved the torch beam round the cellar. There was nothing much down here, except dust and dirt, and—

And a flat brick wall. A wall that was grimed with dirt and

cobwebs, but that looked different from the rest of the cellar. Newer? Because someone had built it secretly and privately, in the middle of the night. Someone who had had to work by lantern light and candlelight.

Something seemed to move deep within Shona's mind, like a deep fissure in a cliff widening, and this time the flare of memory was stronger, it was like a scalding tide of acid. She sank to her knees on the lowest step, and crouched there, hugging her knees in her arms, the sinister footsteps that had driven her to hide forgotten. She had no idea how long she sat like that, but she thought it was a long time before she finally managed to thrust the memories down and shakily stand up again.

There was no sound of movement from above. She looked back at the brick wall, then, moving warily, went back up the steps and closed the cellar door. The sly voice came again then, asking if she really thought she could shut the ghosts away so easily, but she managed to ignore it.

She stood at the entrance to the passage, listening, but the theatre seemed to be silent and unthreatening and she went out into Platt's Alley, and back through the safe anonymous London streets to the office.

Her boss was pleased with the careful, detailed inventory she presented. He wanted to know if she had been all right inside the Tarleton on her own. She said yes, of course, she had been all right, and what an interesting old place, and how sad it had been dark and sealed for so many years.

'Those years will pass,' her boss said.

And the years had passed and for most of the time Shona was able to forget the memories and the ghosts. But every time she thought about the Tarleton, there was a deep twisting inside her mind, like cramp from eating too many unripe apples or the sickening pain when you catch a fingernail and tear it back from its bed.

She did not think anyone realized this.

CHAPTER TEN

Caley Merrick hoped Shona Seymour had never realized how much he had wanted to create some kind of connection to the Harlequin Society.

He had heard, in a general way, that the society occasionally made use of local people to help with small exhibitions and mailings and the like, and he had requested an interview to see if he might be considered for this. When he explained about living in Candle Street, barely five minutes away, Miss Seymour had seemed pleased; she said they liked to use local people whenever they could, although Mr Merrick must understand it would only be an odd few days here and there. Envelope folding in the main, or help with their exhibitions. What the Americans called grunt work, said Miss Seymour, but useful and necessary, and they paid an hourly rate. But it really was casual, infrequent work. Caley had not said he did not care how casual or how infrequent the work was.

He had not, in fact, liked Shona Seymour much. He had found her shrewd and sharp – exactly the kind of woman who made him nervous and unsure of himself. Once or twice during the interview he thought she looked at him very searchingly, but he reminded himself that she could not possibly know who he was, or how he had waited and watched for the right moment to make his approach.

He thanked her profusely when she said they would add him to their register, and if he was free he could come in at the end of the month to help with setting up a small display they were having of Edwardian theatre posters. She had seemed faintly amused at his gratitude and Caley had realized, too late, that as usual he had been apologetic and humble.

It had always been the way. 'You're too apologetic,' he had been told as a child. 'Too easily put off. You should be more pushy – you'll never get anywhere if you don't develop a bit of push.'

But he never had. When, at seventeen, he went to work at Southwark Council, his bosses said much the same thing. 'Promotion for young Merrick?' they said. 'Oh, he's much too quiet. Far too meek.' And the promotion or the salary rise or the training opportunity always went to someone else.

Later, they changed it to: 'Old Merrick? Bit of a has-been now. Better go for somebody younger. Somebody with a bit more go.' None of this was ever said in Caley's hearing, but he knew.

In an odd way the asthma he had suffered since he was eighteen had rescued him. It had meant semi-retirement on his mid-forties and then full retirement when he was just fifty. How sad, people said, but to Caley it had provided him with excuses. He could say that but for his asthma he might have done so much more with his life: he might have achieved promotion at work, afforded a smart car, exotic foreign holidays, a nicer house perhaps, although he would not have wanted to leave this area. Mary had not wanted to leave it either; she had always been nervous at the thought of moving away from the familiar streets. She had liked being married and having her own house, but Caley had known from the first night that she did not like the physical side of marriage. She endured it patiently though, because it was what you had to do in marriage. They never talked about the fact that the years slid by without children being born to them; Caley supposed it was a sadness to her, but she did not refer to it and he found it difficult to broach the subject.

And then, entirely without warning and certainly without intention, had come the pregnancy when Mary was thirty-eight. Oh dear, not an ideal age, the doctors had said, pursing their lips. There could be all kinds of difficulties with such an elderly birth. Mary's sister said it was a downright disgrace and Caley ought to have had more self-control. Caley did not, of course, tell her their sex life had been practically non-existent for years, but that there had been an isolated incident after that year's office Christmas party. He did not much like Mary's sister and she did not like him. She had once told Mary she thought him very la-di-da. Who did he think he was, coming on so toffee-nosed, when he was only a council clerk?

When Mary died giving birth to the baby who died with her, her sister said it was entirely Caley's fault and she would never forgive him. She would be polite to him if they happened to meet in the street, but that was all.

It was all very sad, but one of the really sad things – the thing that caused Caley so much guilt – was the discovery that Mary's death was rather a relief. He was free of the gentle nagging, the preoccupation with domesticity to the exclusion of all else, and he could do whatever he wanted – he could read all day and all night if he wished. With a thump of excitement it occurred to him that he could take up the threads of an old dream – a dream he had reluctantly put aside years earlier.

The dream centred on the Tarleton, the ugly old music hall that had been locked and silent ever since anyone in this part of London could remember. Caley had grown up in the streets surrounding it and had walked past it hundreds – probably thousands – of times. Its facade was peeling and the stonework was grimy with years of London dirt, but it was a bit of a legend in this

95

part of Southwark. People referring to an empty building said, 'It's as empty as the Tarleton.' Or, talking about something that no longer had any application in the modern age, 'As redundant as the Tarleton.'

But by the time he went to work for the Harlequin Society, Caley Merrick thought he knew as much about the Tarleton as anyone living. This was not being conceited; it was simply that he had read almost everything there was about it – not absolutely everything, because nobody could read absolutely everything about any subject, but a very great deal. The people who had worked and performed on its stage were familiar to him – they were sometimes more real than the people he met on buses or the underground or in shops.

Walking along Burbage Street, turning into Candle Square, over the years it often seemed to Caley that his mind was opening up to receive the colour and light those long-ago people had carried with them and the music that surrounded them like cloaks. Once or twice, moving from bookshop to library, and from library to archive departments and back again in his beloved quest for information, he wondered if he might be becoming just a bit unbalanced about the Tarleton. This worried him for a while, but then he thought that a lot of people had an area in their minds that was very slightly out of kilter with the normal world.

Sometimes, when he was on his own, he caught himself murmuring those performers' names to himself like a litany. The Flowered Fan with her incorrigibly saucy dancing – Caley had vowed to one day find out her real name and discover what had happened to her. And there was Marie Lloyd, of course, who had been so famous she was still remembered today. Bunstable the Cockney comic who sang songs and performed sketches. There were lesser names as well: dancers and jugglers and strong men; Shilling, the doorkeeper, and Rinaldi, the stage manager.

And there was a hammy-sounding actor called Prospero Garrick, who had apparently performed monologues and Shakespearean speeches. Caley had found Prospero's memoirs years earlier in the small library near Candle Square. 'Prospero Garrick' would be a made-up name, of course – theatre people used all kinds of flowery names, and the Victorians and Edwardians had been particularly flamboyant on that count. Even so, Caley rather liked the sound of Prospero, who came over as having been outrageously vain and unquenchably conceited, but very amiable. He visualized the old boy wearing a swirling opera cloak and a silk hat, carrying a silver-topped cane and eyeing the ladies with a knowing wink. What used to be called, in the vernacular of the day, a howling swell.

But above all of these people was the most memorable one. The charismatic young man who, according to everything Caley had read, had been able to light up the entire theatre purely by walking out onto the stage and smiling at his audiences.

Toby Chance.

May 1914

As the hansom jolted across the river and turned towards Bloomsbury, Toby was already starting to question the wisdom of what he was doing. This secret society, this Tranz, might turn out to be nothing but a group of people genuinely working towards peace in Austria and Serbia – which was no doubt very worthy, but which Toby would probably find extremely boring.

But it might be something quite different, and if so, that might be a bit more exciting. It might even be what his father suspected: a gang of agitators and ruffians, hell-bent on stirring up a European war. Toby glanced at the figure seated beside him and revised this last opinion slightly, because it was impossible to imagine Alicia Darke associating with ruffians. If Tranz did turn out to be a bunch of war-mongers they would be gentlemanly war-mongers. The kind who apologized courteously before they let slip the dogs of war. According to his father, those particular war dogs would rampage across most of Europe, and Britain would be up to her neck in the fight.

The thunder had stopped, but the air was not any fresher for the small storm. We'll remember this hot summer, thought Toby. If war does come as my father thinks it must, we'll all say, afterwards, that we felt its approach in this stifling heat. We'll tell each other it was a portent.

He glanced out of the window. They were in Bloomsbury now – he caught a glimpse of the British Museum, but then the hansom took two or three turns into side streets and across a couple of small squares and Toby's sense of direction became confused, although he could see that the houses no longer looked quite so smart and well cared for. But presumably Bloomsbury had its seedier pockets like anywhere else. One of the fascinations of London was that just when you thought you had identified an area as being prosperous, you turned a corner and within a dozen steps found yourself among shabbiness or outright poverty.

The cab came to a halt and Toby got out and helped Alicia down. They were in front of a dingy house whose facade had once been white but was now a leprous-looking grey. The house was not precisely dilapidated but it was certainly a bit shabby, although shabbiness did not automatically mean shadiness – you had only to look at a lot of theatre people on the morning after a performance, in fact you had only to look at Toby himself on some mornings. And the man who opened the door to them looked completely ordinary. He nodded to Alicia, considered Toby for a moment, and then indicated to them to follow him.

'No secret password?' murmured Toby to Alicia as they were led through to the back of the house.

'Not even a series of pre-arranged knocks on the door,' she said.

They were shown into a long room which Toby thought might originally have been two separate rooms – or even three. An assortment of wooden chairs had been set in rows and there was a small dais at the far end. The room was filled with people, most of whom were seated, with the rest standing in groups, all of them talking excitedly and with an air of expectancy. Toby, pausing in the doorway and looking about him, thought their eager anticipation was so strong it was almost visible. There were probably thirty or so people present, with about the same number of men as women. Most of them were quite young, although there were three patriarchal-looking gentlemen, two with beards of almost biblical length and one who had several weighty-looking books under his arm and looked like a Jewish scholar. In a corner, a straight-backed old lady wearing a diamond choker that needed cleaning and imperious but rusty-looking black draperies, sat on the only chair with cushions, and held court to half a dozen avid young men who sat cross-legged on the floor in front of her.

Apart from the black-clad lady who might have been a duchess, the women were rather sloppily dressed. Most of them sounded English, but some spoke a language Toby could not recognize; it certainly had no relationship to the smattering of German and Italian he had himself. Russian? Romanian? They had the distinctive slanting cheekbones and dark eyes he associated with those parts of the world. They might be Russian, or they might be Middle European – perhaps from Czechoslovakia or Bosnia or Herzegovina. The places his father had called a seething cauldron.

A young woman pushed her way through the crowd, eyed Toby with aggressive curiosity, and said, 'Alicia, is this the guest you promised us?'

'It is. Mr Toby Chance,' said Alicia smoothly. 'Toby, may I present the Honourable Sonja Kaplen.'

'No honourables,' said the young woman at once. 'Plain Sonja Kaplen,' and Alicia stared at her coldly, as if thinking anyone disassociating herself from a title – even a mere honourable – must be a little mad.

'How do you do,' said Toby.

'Oh, God, a gentlemanly one,' said Miss Kaplen with a faint air of exasperation. Toby noticed she was one of the better-dressed females, although her clothes had an impatient look about them, as if she had merely grabbed whatever had been nearest to hand in her wardrobe and put it on. She had dark glossy hair and a slightly too wide mouth which either made her strikingly beautiful or very nearly plain; Toby found this rather intriguing. 'Alicia, I do wish you'd bring us people likely to be of use to the cause,' said this unusual-looking young woman, glaring at Toby.

He said, 'But looks are deceptive, Miss Kaplen. Given the right circumstances I can be very useful indeed.'

'Are you trying to *flirt* with me?' demanded Miss Kaplen. 'Because if so, I should warn you I never—'

'Heaven forefend that I should stoop so low,' said Toby, starting to enjoy himself. 'A very bourgeois convention, flirting.'

She looked at him suspiciously, then said, 'I suppose since you are here ... And if Alicia vouches for you ...' She made a brisk gesture, indicating the crowded room. 'All the seats have been taken by this time. If you'd got here half an hour ago you might have got one.' There was a faint air of reproach. 'They're all here early because Petrovnic is coming. If you don't mind a windowsill there are a couple left.'

'Never let it be said that I disdained a humble windowsill,' said Toby. 'And it's entirely my fault we're late; I had to entertain a few people for a while. If that's wine in that jug being offered round, I hope it's going to be offered over here.'

'It isn't wine,' said Sonja Kaplen scornfully. 'We can't afford to give wine to our members. All the money we have goes towards the cause. It's lemonade.'

'What could be better on a hot summer's night?' said Toby. 'As a matter of fact—' He broke off as a stir went through the assembly, and people who were still standing moved back to allow someone to walk up to the dais.

'That's Petrovnic arriving now,' said Sonja, turning to look at the newcomer, a touch of reverence in her voice.

'A striking-looking gentleman,' said Toby.

100

'Looks do not matter,' said Sonja scornfully. 'It's personality that counts.'

'Oh, every time.'

'Do hush. Petrovnic's about to begin.'

'I shall be as silent as a midnight grave. Lead me to your windowsill. Alicia, you're coming as well, aren't you? Do you prefer plain wood with a south-facing view or will you have tiles and an outlook over a dustbin yard? There appears to be a choice.'

To Toby's slight surprise Alicia appeared tolerant of the shabby room and the eclectic mix of people and sat down gracefully. It occurred to him that she was regarding the evening as a game and the people as curios who might provide her with an hour or two's amusement, and he realized with slight annoyance that he was doing more or less the same thing. Then he remembered his father's words about Tranz and the amusement gave way to unease. I shouldn't have come, he thought. But I want to know what this is about and why, according to Alicia, these people wanted to meet me.

The wooden windowsill might have become very uncomfortable in the hour that followed because Petrovnic held the floor for a remarkably long time, but Toby was so fascinated he forgot about being perched on a ledge barely six inches deep, and forgot that the room was overcrowded and too hot for comfort. He even forgot the presence of Sonja Kaplen on his left and Alicia Darke on his right which, as he admitted to himself later, was not like him.

It was a relief to discover that Petrovnic spoke in English, although he had a marked accent. He was a thin man, of perhaps fifty-four or -five, with hair the colour of polished mahogany, high cheekbones, and fiery, intelligent eyes. The women were regarding him almost adoringly and even Alicia was staring at him with relish. Oh my, oh my, thought Toby, glancing at her. What big eyes you have, my dear Alicia, and what a voracious appetite for gentlemen. I suppose you've marked Petrovnic for your next adventure. He's a bit old for you, I should have thought, but even I can see that he's attractive.

The men were almost as enraptured by Petrovnic as the women, although Petrovnic himself seemed unaware of any of it. Either he was so genuinely engrossed in his subject that his audience's devotion did not touch him, or he was so used to people gazing at him as if he were a god he no longer noticed it. Whichever it is, it's very effective, thought Toby, studying him critically. I wouldn't mind having a touch of it myself; it would be very useful on a rowdy Saturday night at the Tarleton.

Petrovnic had launched straight into an impassioned plea to the members of Tranz to gather their strength and stand fast to the cause. A number of the younger ones gave soft cheers at this, and when he said, 'I need you all – I need *all* of you, body and soul,' two ladies sitting near to Toby sighed and hugged their arms round their upper bodies.

As they all knew, said Petrovnic, the old Austro-Hungarian Empire had been built by conquest and intrigues and above all by treacheries, and one of those treacheries was the annexing of Bosnia and Herzegovina a few years earlier.

'It was an act of imperialistic greed at its worst. It was the arrogant high-handedness of the Habsburgs who feel the need to show they are still Europe's overlords.' He looked round the room. 'They must not be permitted to behave in such a fashion any longer. We must make our protests – the Serb races, the people of Bosnia and of Herzegovina, must be allowed their independence.

'His Imperial Highness, Franz-Ferdinand von Habsburg-Lothringen,' said Petrovnic, practically spitting the name and title out, 'is to visit the capital of Bosnia at the end of June, to direct army manoeuvres in the neighbouring mountains. And, my dear friends, when Franz-Ferdinand gets there, Tranz will be there also. Tranz will seize its opportunity, and it will demonstrate its anger.'

Franz-Ferdinand, thought Toby, his eyes on the speaker. What do I know about him? Not very much – they're a complex family, those Habsburgs. But I think the Franz-Ferdinand Petrovnic's talking about is heir apparent to the Austro-Hungarian throne. I don't like this. I think there's something a bit sinister behind it.

But despite the sense of dark undercurrents, he was swept along by the allure of Tranz's ideals. Was it possible that his father had got them wrong? Everything Petrovnic was saying about the regaining of independence, the sweeping away of the old Austrian imperial rule, was finding a strong response in Toby. Why should Bosnia and Serbia not have their independence and their country? Why should Austria be allowed to arrogantly march in and take them over?

When Petrovnic, his voice rising to a near shout, cried that the Austro-Hungarian Empire was corrupt – that it had been built by conquest and intrigue and treachery – half the audience leapt to their feet, cheering their agreement, and Toby found himself on his feet with them.

'A protest march!' cried Petrovnic, his hair dishevelled, his face flushed and his eyes blazing. 'A protest such as no one has ever known before! That is what we shall stage for this decadent imperialist line! Our friends will come from other countries – the Czechs long to be independent of Austrian rule and the Romanians live under Hungarian administration in the protection of the Romanian crown. So we must make the voice of Tranz and the voice of the people heard. And the Archduke Franz-Ferdinand—' He stopped very deliberately and looked round the room. No one moved or spoke. 'The Archduke,' said Petrovnic, almost in a whisper now, 'will have no choice but to listen. Governments will have no choice but to listen. And if we are steadfast, the people of Bosnia and Herzegovina will be free.' He looked round the room. 'Well, my friends? Who will accompany me on this quest for justice? For freedom? Who will come to Sarajevo for the twenty-eighth day of June? Who will be there? A show of hands, please! Volunteers!'

Toby was aware of five or six people raising their hands and of most of the others nodding and cheering. They won't all go, he thought. I don't suppose they can – most of them will have families and work, and the cost of the journey will probably be beyond their means. He saw that the straight-backed old lady was one of the people who had raised a hand, and that Sonja had done so as well. Her eyes were shining and her lips were parted with excitement, and as if sensing his regard she turned to look at him.

'Not joining us, Mr Chance?' she said, challengingly. 'Or don't you care about the oppressed nations of the world? Doesn't that kind of thing reach Kensington or the artificial world of the theatre?'

Toby was about to reply angrily that he was damned if he was going to go mad-rabbiting across an entire continent, simply to wave a few flags against imperialism and shout slogans at a Habsburg archduke, but Sonja was already saying, dismissively, that she supposed the journey would be too difficult for him.

'Most of it's by train and the conditions won't be in the least what you're used to, anyway. No grand hotels or first-class railway compartments. Certainly not the Orient-Express.'

'But,' said Toby, 'I don't suppose there are many places in the world Thomas Cook's can't reach.'

He saw that he had disconcerted her, and was aware that Alicia had turned to look at him. Sonja said, 'You surely don't mean you'd come with us to Sarajevo?'

She sounded so incredulous that Toby was furious with her. 'If your friend with the gift for oratory will take me, I'll certainly come with you.'

CHAPTER ELEVEN

He saw Alicia home, but managed to avoid going into the elegant little house with her, pleading the extreme lateness of the hour and the demands of his performance earlier at the Tarleton. For once he could not have coped with Alicia's silken bedroom and her silken love-making; he needed to be alone, because he was starting to feel horrified at what he had done, although he was determined to show that scornful opinionated Sonja Kaplen that he cared just as deeply about oppression as anyone else.

As yet he had no idea what he would say to his father, but he would think of something. Preparing for bed in his own room, he made a mental review of his appearances at the Tarleton for the forthcoming month. There were only two and one was in four days' time, the other in two weeks'. After that, there was nothing that could not be postponed. In any case, the theatre put on very few shows at the end of June – 'People don't want to sit in hot theatres in the summer months,' Flora Chance always said. 'So it's a good opportunity for us to give the old place a lick of paint and a bit of a spruce-up.'

He slept fitfully and woke at four. What had he done? Bosnia, for pity's sake! Half a world away. Unknown language, unfamiliar people, appalling travelling conditions, all in company with people he had only just met ... And simply because that infuriating Sonja Kaplen had taunted him with being too wrapped in a soft Kensington life to care about suffering and deprivation! No, be fair, it was as much that he had been attracted by the idea of righting wrongs inflicted by a decadent Austrian Empire and helping an oppressed nation regain its independence and identity. At midnight in a roomful of eager people – some of them persuasive and attractive – this had been an alluring idea, the stuff dreams were made of and from which stirring adventures were woven. In the dawn of a stuffy bedroom by himself, it was annoying and even vaguely sinister.

By half past five he began to feel irritated with the whole thing. It ought not to be Tranz keeping him awake in this too-hot dawn; it ought to be the pleasing memory of how well the new song had been received, and of how he would sing it again that night.

At six he got up and found his old school atlas, turning the pages until he came to Bosnia. There it was, rather like an inverted triangle. South of Hungary, west of Romania. It was considerably further east than he had been thinking, in fact alarmingly so – you only had to cross the Aegean Sea to be in Turkey. Persian carpets and Scheherezade spinning stories, thought Toby. Caliphs and grand viziers and the Ottoman Empire. And if you went north, across the Black Sea, you would be in Russia: tzars and troikas and wolves in the forests and Fabergé eggs. He considered all of this and thought if he really did make this journey, then plainly he was madder than anyone had yet suspected.

He tried going back to bed but at seven o'clock gave up the attempt to sleep and got up again, splashing cold water on his face and pulling on the nearest clothes. As he slipped out of the house everywhere was silent, and Toby walked round the square, enjoying the early-morning quiet. Even at this hour, there was a haze across the park, suggesting insufferable heat would build up as the morning progressed.

He got back to the house in time to see Minnie setting out breakfast in the small morning room at the back. He smiled and said good morning to her, at which she grunted something unintelligible, and stumped out.

Toby helped himself to eggs and bacon and a large cup of coffee, and when his mother came in, he said, 'It looks as if Minnie was in the Sailor's Retreat again last night.'

'She was and she said they were singing "Tipsy Cake" in there by half past ten, and doing so with great relish,' said Flora, and Toby experienced a rush of undiluted delight. That's what my life really is, he thought. Writing songs and singing them, and trying to make the Tarleton as prosperous as possible. Not gadding off to bizarre countries to shout rude slogans at archdukes and annoy emperors. Yes, but I gave my word. How will I back out of it?

'Some of the regulars at the Sailor's Retreat had been to the performance,' Flora was saying.

'And they went back there afterwards to eat,' said Toby. 'Mutton pie and ale. I keep telling you the Oyster Bar charges too much for at least half our audiences. Serve them jellied eels and stout or one of the old sixpenny ordinaries and they'd eat there.'

'I'm certainly going to see if we can serve tipsy cake tomorrow night,' said Flora, pouring coffee, and Toby looked up quickly, pleased at the idea and annoyed for not having thought of it himself. 'It's a fairly easy thing to assemble anyway,' said Flora. 'Layers of sponge cake soaked in sherry, with jam and cream. But whatever we give them to eat, they like your song. It sounds as if it's one of your best yet.'

'Moderately reasonable,' mumbled Toby. 'It's going to the printers today to be engraved for the song sheets.'

'It sounds as if it's a bit more than reasonable,' said Flora. 'I thought I'd come in tomorrow to hear it.'

'Did you? Good.'

'Toby are you really going to eat a second helping of eggs and bacon?'

'I am,' said Toby and grinned at her with affection and approval. She must be approaching fifty and the slender girl who had plied that infamous fan for the delight of half the male population of London's halls had vanished beneath a degree of unashamed plumpness. But it was an attractive plumpness, satin-skinned and firm, and her hair was still glossy and becomingly dressed. She wore a discreet touch of rice powder on her nose, and her outfit that morning was a well-cut moss-green silk costume. Even after all these years, Toby had seen his father look at her with love and pride. He wondered if he would ever feel like that about someone himself. On present showing it did not seem very likely.

'Are you working here today, or are you at the theatre?' enquired Flora.

'What? Oh, I think I'll work here after I've seen the printers,' said Toby. 'I've got an idea for a new song about a theatre ghost.'

'The Tarleton's ghost?' There was an unusually sharp note in her voice.

'No, it's the old saying about the ghost paying the wages,' said Toby. He glanced at her. 'I've never asked if you ever saw the Tarleton's ghost?' He was quite surprised to hear himself asking this question. But she'll laugh and say that of course she never saw it, he thought. And that there are no such things.

'Yes,' said Flora. 'Yes, I did see it once.'

Toby looked at her in surprise. 'You've never mentioned it before.'

'It was a long time ago,' said Flora. 'Before I married your father. And I was never actually sure what I had seen: it was one of those fog-ridden nights, so afterwards I thought I might have been mistaken.'

'That's part of the legend, though. He's only ever been seen walking through the fog.'

'Has he? I didn't know that. I daresay it's just that fog makes the story sound more eerie,' said Flora rather indifferently. Then she smiled, said something about hoping he would not work too hard in this killing heat, and went out of the room before he could ask any more questions. Toby could not decide if his reference to the ghost had upset her. Perhaps it had reminded her of her youth and made her feel a bit wistful. He thought he would not mention it again, and in any case he did not really want to know the ghost's provenance. He would rather keep it mysterious and timeless, so he could slot it into whatever century he liked, and allot to it whatever tragedy or melodrama or romance occurred to him. He wondered if this made him a thwarted romantic, or a ghost story writer manqué?

He saw the printers – there was going to be a rather good cover on this song sheet: a leery, beery gentleman in butler's attire winking at a mob-capped cook, with an improbably lush, cream-topped confection of the chef's art set between them. Toby approved the cover, and went back to the house to work on his new song. There was a large empty room next to his bedroom which he had turned into a study, importing a big oak desk, two comfortably battered chairs and most of his books.

After lunch, he heard his mother come upstairs and go into her own bedroom and close the door. It was quite unusual for her to retire to her room during the day, but the heat this summer was enough to drain anyone's energy. Toby carried on working and at six o'clock went out to Frank Douglas's comfortable, slightly battered rooms in Earls Court to see if they could fit music to his lyrics.

Frank was pleased with the proposed cover for 'Tipsy Cake', and he loved the concept of the salary distributing ghost in Toby's new lyrics. He adored making people laugh and he immediately sat down to improvise some beautifully semi-eerie, semi-comic music. They spent the evening polishing this and rehearsing the song, sending out for beer and hot steak pies halfway through. By midnight they were agreed that the song would be ready for Saturday night.

Toby had kept the first few lines exactly as they had formed in

his head that evening in the theatre when he had heard Alicia
walking about.

> On Friday nights the ghost walks
> Rattling its chains to itself;
> Because that's the night the ghost hands out the pelf.

They agreed they would ask Rinaldi to turn down some of
the footlights at that point, and Toby thought they might even
have something clanked loudly off-stage to indicate chains, or even
create echoing footsteps. Filling the rain-box with lead shot ought
to work very effectively.

Two more lines followed the opening chorus, describing how
the ghost shook its head mournfully at the amounts it had to pay
out and bewailing the fact that it had never been paid half as much
in its own heyday. Then came a verse listing the tribulations of
the actors themselves as they waited for wages night.

> There's sweet Daisy Croker who dances the polka
> By Thursday she's gone to the nearest pawnbroker . . .
> There's young Johnnie Smart Heels who turns fifty cartwheels
> And adds a few tumbles to hide stomach rumbles . . .
> And Leo the Strong Arm who don't come to much harm
> Until he's deprived of his nightly half quartern . . .
>
> But on Friday night the ghost walks,
> Always as white as a sheet
> Cheerless as sin, so they buy it some gin,
> And some bedsocks for its feet.

Frank said the Saturday night audience would love it; almost
all of them would understand about running out of money by
Thursday and resorting to pawning things, and about enjoying a
drink in the pub no matter how broke they might be.

By this time Toby was more or less resigned to the journey to Bosnia with Tranz. He had tried to think of a way to renege on it and had thought of at least three excuses that would hold water. The trouble was that he kept seeing Sonja Kaplen's contemptuous expression if he broke his word.

Flora Chance's bedroom overlooked the garden, and someone, probably Minnie, had opened the windows earlier on so the room was cool. The scent of lavender and lilac drifted in, mingling with the tang of herbs from the little kitchen garden. Parsley and thyme like the old song, and the cool sharpness of the mint. Fennel and rosemary. Rosemary was for remembrance, of course, everyone knew that old line, although Flora could never remember where it was from. Toby would probably know, she would ask him later.

She could hear a faint clatter of crockery from the kitchen – she and Hal were going to the theatre with some of his Foreign Office colleagues tonight and then entertaining them to supper here afterwards, so Flora would shortly have to make sure the preparations were all in hand. It would be what cook called an informal summer meal, but there would still be panics about whether the salmon mousse was setting and if the iced pudding would stay properly iced in the current heat. Flora would help the kitchen staff to solve these problems and it would be one of the many times when she would be secretly amused to think the girl from the East End could these days coolly give orders to a cook and supervise the correct laying of a table for ten people. I've come a long way, she thought with the self-deprecatory amusement this knowledge always gave her.

But only a small part of her heard these ordinary household sounds because the memories and ghosts were crowding in, blotting out everything else. Ghosts . . . One ghost in particular . . .

'I've never asked if you ever saw the Tarleton's ghost?' Toby had said, and Flora had managed a light-hearted reply. She had seen it more than just once, that figure. And she had known who it was and what its purpose was, and that was the really dreadful part of those memories.

She leaned her face against the coolness of the windowpane. From Toby's room came the occasional snatch of piano music; he was no pianist, but he had a small upright piano in his room and he could play enough to help with the initial shaping of his lyrics. Busking it, he called it, smiling with his father's smile. Flora loved it when he looked like that. Toby was one of the very best things in her life: one of the shining things. He had said the new song was something to do with the hoary theatrical expression about the ghost walking – meaning the paying of wages to the actors at the end of the week.

The ghost ... Memory looped back to the past once again, to a world very different to this present one. Twenty-seven years should not, realistically, make much of a difference to a city, but the London Flora had known then seemed nothing like it was today. That's a sign of increasing age if ever there was one, she thought wryly. But that London had been full of excitement and promise, of colour and discovery. There was new electric light and horseless carriages ... Celebrations were in full swing for Queen Victoria's Golden Jubilee ... Cumbersome bustles were giving way to a sleeker, more seductive cut for ladies' skirts ...

And a rising young dancer called the Flowered Fan, appearing at the Tarleton Music Hall, was being pursued by two brothers – twins lately come to England from somewhere in Central Europe – who had both fallen obsessively and dangerously in love with her.

1887

Flora was twenty-one, dancing her insouciant way through London music halls and starting to achieve a modest but gratifying success.

The Prince of Wales had seen her perform on two occasions

and was known to have remarked that he considered her a very alluring lady, and there were admirers who sent flowers and who came to the stage door to take her to supper.

'But don't bestow any favours, madam,' Minnie Bean said firmly. 'Not until there's the sound of wedding bells.'

'You're a fine one to talk,' said Flora. 'You've bestowed a few favours in your time.'

In fact she did not intend to bestow any favours at all, but she enjoyed the suppers in the West End and the picnics and the days at race meetings. She accepted the gifts of flowers and chocolates, but always returned jewellery or clothes and on two occasions was known to have directed an extremely frosty stare at gentlemen who tried to give her money. This caused a rumour to start up that the Flowered Fan was cold-hearted, and a gentleman who had sent a cobweb-fine silk chemise along with a ten-pound note and a suggestive little message, used an uglier word.

Flora did not really mind. She would rather be considered cold-hearted or a cock-tease, than be thought of as a Piccadilly tart, and in fact the ardent attentions of some of her admirers really did leave her unmoved – so much so that she sometimes wondered if the accusation of cold-heartedness might be true. At the very least she seemed wholly unresponsive to any kind of love-making. She did not admit this to anyone because she felt it to be vaguely shameful, and she accepted the kisses – never anything more intimate than kisses – with suitably restrained appreciation.

For the rest of the time she worked hard at perfecting her dancing routines, helping to design her costumes and fans, and toying with the idea of taking singing lessons.

Minnie disapproved of this last idea ('Stick to what you know you can do, madam'), but Minnie disapproved of most things on principle. One of things she disapproved of most strongly that autumn, was the presence of Anton and Stefan Reznik, who some people said were Romanian or Hungarian or even Russian, and others said hailed from Macedonia or Bulgaria or one of those confusing European countries. Although their English was excellent, everyone agreed, you had to say that for them. And they appeared to be acceptably wealthy and to possess *very* agreeable manners.

Whatever the Reznik twins' true nationality, they were in the front row to see the Flowered Fan dance on every possible occasion. Flora thought them both rather immature and somewhat intense, but for a while she quite enjoyed being seen with two such dramatic young men who were startlingly alike in appearance and could afford to take her to Simpsons and Rules, and introduce her to some of the raffish attractive people who frequented the Café Royale. They both declared their passionate love for her on every occasion they met, sometimes singly, but more usually in chorus, neither seeming to mind if the other twin was present to hear these avowals. Flora several times had the strong impression that they found one another's passion secretly arousing. This was disconcerting.

'I don't know about disconcerting,' said Minnie. 'What I do know is that four bare legs in a bed is natural, but six legs is a bit questionable.'

'It happens, though,' said Flora. 'Three in a bed.'

'Yes, but if two of the three are brothers, then to my mind it's unnatural, in fact, not to mince words, I'd say it's downright perverted. Mind you aren't heading for trouble.'

'I can deal with those two,' said Flora, although she was beginning to wonder if she could.

Still, she seemed to be dealing with them quite well until the night their shared passion erupted into something very dangerous indeed.

Flora had not seen the twins for over a week – 'Because you've been too taken up with that political one,' Minnie had said. Minnie liked to pretend she could never remember the names of Flora's various admirers.

114

The 'political one' was Sir Harold Chance, whom Flora had already learned to call Hal, and who had walked into her dressing room a fortnight earlier, and said, 'I haven't brought flowers or anything like that, but if you're free for supper tonight or tomorrow, or any night from now until the opening of the twentieth century . . .'

It had been like tumbling down a well, like being knocked over by a carriage and left gasping and breathless, so that you scarcely saw anyone else in the whole world, and you certainly did not hear the bleatings of other young men no matter their romantic natures and nationalities, no matter how much they swore undying devotion or threatened suicide if one did not return their passion. Flora was daring to believe it had been the same for Hal, although she did not yet know what he intended to do about it.

'It's plain to *me* what he intends to do about it,' Minnie said. 'He'll be out for what he can get. Out for a spot of bed. Are you going to wear this green costume tonight? I should say are you ever going to wear it again, because in my opinion it's ready for the dustbin. It moulted all over Collins's stage on Monday – don't laugh like that, it's quite true, they had to sweep the boards after you went off, I saw them. It's worse than a plucked chicken, that costume, and I'm not having you cavorting across the Tarleton's stage looking like a plucked chicken. I'll cut it up for curtains, shall I? Nice bit of brocade, that is.'

It was the fourth or fifth time Flora had appeared at the Tarleton, so it felt pleasantly familiar by now. Tonight was something of a gala occasion as it would be closed for the whole of November for refurbishment, so the evening was being billed as a Grand Autumn Finale and there were some quite famous people on the bill. The theatre was going to be electrified which was a considerable event in its history, and it would reopen at the end of December with a run of Christmas shows. Flora had been approached to see if she would take part in the pantomime which was to be a fairly robust version of Cinderella. It had apparently been thought that she might play the part of the fairy godmother. 'Not the traditional sequins and tutu,' the theatre manager said to her. 'We're thinking of something a bit livelier, just by way of a change. We'd very much like you to do it.' He added what had been a phrase on everyone's lips for the past week. 'It'll be electric lights, remember.'

Electric lights aside, this would be a new and rather exciting direction for her career to take, but she said she would think about it, which infuriated Minnie who accused her of playing for time in case Sir Hal proposed.

'And he won't do it, not in a pig's eye he won't. The likes of him don't marry the likes of us, so think on. He may be very gentlemanly, with his Kensington house and his title and the Foreign Office, but it'll come down to him wanting four legs in a bed and no marriage lines on the mantelpiece.'

'Minnie, you're becoming preoccupied with this business of legs in a bed.'

'That's because men are all alike,' said Minnie, fluffing up Flora's costume before the call. 'They have to be watched and guarded against. And where is Sir Hal tonight, I'd like to know. If he's so smitten he should be in the front row applauding your act.'

'Late meetings at Westminster,' said Flora, to which Minnie retorted he was more likely at home with a lawful wife and children, or engaged in some disgraceful debauchery somewhere.

'No, he isn't.'

Minnie said time would tell and stumped crossly off to tell that jumped-up young stage manager Rinaldi that madam's music was not to be played so fast tonight. Did they think she was one of those Frenchified dancers, all black stockings and frilled drawers? Madam's act was art, said Minnie, and pretended not to hear the hoots of derision.

CHAPTER TWELVE

But if Hal Chance was not in the front row, Anton and Stefan Reznik were, and they were waiting for Flora in her dressing room when she came off. They had booked a table for supper at Kettners, they announced.

This cool appropriation of the rest of her evening annoyed Flora, who said, as politely as possible, that she was too tired to go out to supper that night.

'You will come,' stated Anton. 'It is all arranged.'

'And we shall invigorate you.'

One of the increasingly disconcerting things about them was the way they seemed to finish each other's thoughts. Flora would normally have found this rather attractive in twins, but with these two it was becoming slightly scary.

She said, 'Perhaps another night. I'm going straight home.' She was genuinely tired and was looking forward to putting her feet up and eating the supper Minnie would cook. She did not tell the twins that if she could not spend her after show time with Hal Chance she did not want to spend it with anyone these days.

They would not accept the refusal. They stayed obstinately in the dressing room, oblivious to all Flora's hints. Anton perched on

117

the arm of a chair, Stefan lounged in the chair itself. They were imperiously monosyllabic with people who looked in to say how well the evening had gone and how much they were looking forward to panto, and asked if it was true that Flora was going to be in *Cinderella*, which would be rather fun, because Freddie was playing Buttons and that young actor, Prospero somebody-or-other, was Baron Hard-up.

None of this was well received by the twins. Anton affected to find it boring and Stefan sent smoulderingly jealous looks at everyone and took frequent swigs from a silver flask. Flora hoped they were not heading for a difficult situation and wondered if she ought to call the helpful Mr Rinaldi, or even the doorkeeper, Bob Shilling, whom she did not much like but who could certainly sort out trouble-makers and drunks. Anton was not drunk but she did not think he was entirely sober.

Minnie left shortly after eleven, talking pointedly about lighting a nice fire against the chilly night and getting some supper for Flora – 'I daresay you'll be along soon, will you, madam?' – but it was twenty past eleven before Flora finally went out of the dressing room with the twins on each side of her. It was faintly worrying to discover that everyone else seemed to have gone home and the theatre was in semi-darkness.

'We are locked in?' said Anton.

'I shouldn't think so,' said Flora at once, not liking the sudden predatory note in his voice or the way Stefan was standing so close to her. 'Bob Shilling will still be on duty at the stage door, and even if he's not there and it's locked, he'll be back at midnight. He always does a midnight round, it's one of the eternal jokes about this theatre, Shilling and the midnight round.'

She wanted to see if there were any messages for her in the doorman's room: it was just possible that Hal had sent a note to say his meeting was finishing early and asking if they could meet at one of the little restaurants near the theatre for a late drink or even a bite of supper. The Linkman, perhaps – they had been there twice after a Tarleton night and Hal had liked it. He had liked meeting the scattering of theatre people who had drifted in after their respective shows. Flora had introduced some of them and Hal had seemed to find it easy to fall into conversation and to be genuinely interested in them. This was not something Flora had expected and it had pleased her. On the second occasion, Hal had said, 'Would you like to see round Westminster, Flora? Then you can meet some of the people I work with.' Flora had said she would love to, but perhaps his colleagues would not think it suitable.

'Why on earth not?'

'Because you can't take a music-hall dancer into those hallowed halls,' she had said, trying to keep the tone light.

'I'll take whomever I want into any number of hallowed halls,' he said, and smiled and reached for her hand across the table, and they had arranged that he would take her to Westminster the following week and on to afternoon tea somewhere.

As Flora went through the auditorium with the twins, she found the darkness unnerving; she was used to seeing a theatre – any theatre – blazing with light and filled with people and music. There were two low gaslights burning – one near the main exit and another by the stage box – casting slightly eerie shadows. As they went through to the stone passage with Bob Shilling's room at the far end, she began to wonder if it was the twins who were making her nervous, rather than the shadowy theatre. Stefan was very drunk, but he was not unsteady on his feet or likely to be sick. If Shilling was around she would ask him to get them a cab: she thought the twins lived somewhere in Bloomsbury. Or would they see that as an insult?

There were a couple of gas jets burning in the corridors, and Flora began to feel safer, because no one would leave gas jets burning unattended. But Shilling's room was in darkness.

At her side, Anton said, 'The doorman is not there.'

'Are you sure?' said Flora, and moved along the passage. But it looked as if he was right; Shilling's room was empty and no coat was hanging on the usual hook. She glanced at the pigeon-holes, but there was nothing in her box. Then it was to be supper on a tray in her dressing gown after all.

She walked towards the stage door, aware that the twins were watching her. Please let the door be unlocked, she thought. It looks as if Shilling's gone out to the Linkman or the Sailor's Retreat for a couple of drinks, but please let this be the one night he forgot to lock the stage door. Let me be able to open it and step outside into Platt's Alley . . . Her hand closed over the handle, but even before she tried to turn it, she felt the stiff resistance. Locked.

In the uncertain light, the twins suddenly seemed taller and menacing. As Flora walked up to them, Anton said, softly, 'So, Flora, your doorman is not here and we are locked in together,' and before Flora could say anything he put his arm round her waist, pulling her backwards against him, his other hand closing over her breast. Flora gasped and tried to push him away, but Stefan moved in and bent to kiss her, forcing her lips open. The whisky he had been drinking tainted his breath unpleasantly. Flora was by now very frightened, but within the fear was a tiny speck of anger. She tried to hold on to this anger because it gave her courage, and twisting her mouth free she said, 'Stop it both of you. Let me go or I'll yell for help.'

'Yell as loudly as you wish,' said Anton. 'There's no one to hear you.' He pulled her back to him again and thrust his body against her so that she felt the hot hard masculinity between his thighs. Fear welled up all over again, and she shouted for help, the sound echoing hollowly in the narrow passage.

Stefan laughed. 'Everyone has gone to the Linkman,' he said. 'The performers and the people who work backstage. I heard them planning it.'

'We were asked, also, and we said we would be there and you with us.'

'Then they'll wonder where we are,' said Flora eagerly.

'They will not wonder,' said Anton. 'They will think we have

120

taken you to our house, and they will laugh and exchange winks and the men will whisper to one another about what we are doing, the three of us in a bed ... First one then the other, they will say ...'

'We shall be envied,' said Stefan. 'They all want you, but we want you more than they do. We have wanted you ever since we met you.'

'It would be better in a bed,' said Anton. 'But we could be very comfortable in this theatre. There is a couch on the stage they used for the small play earlier.'

'And if we are on the stage we can close the curtains.'

What was beginning to terrify Flora almost as much as the prospect of being raped, was their unity of speech. It was as if only one person was talking to her – one person who somehow inhabited two separate bodies.

But she said, 'I think you must be mad – both of you.'

'Perhaps,' said Stefan. 'But it is a very sweet madness.'

He picked her up bodily and began to carry her back to the main part of the theatre. Flora shouted again and fought to get free, but he held her too tightly. Anton went ahead, opening the door to the auditorium and leading the way between the seats and up the stage steps. The curtains were partly open, but as Stefan laid her on the wide elaborate chaise longue that had formed part of the sketch earlier, Anton went into the wings. After a moment there was the sound of the massive winch being turned and with a slow rattling scrape the curtains drew across, shutting the three of them in.

Flora thought this could not really be happening; it was a nightmare and at any minute she would wake up. Even if it were real, she could not possibly be raped by these two men, here on the stage, on the rubbed velvet of the chaise longue. At any minute there would be the sound of footsteps and a voice calling out to know if everything was all right. It was half past eleven already, which meant Shilling would be back within half an hour. But even half an hour might be too late.

Stefan lay down next to her, already moving urgently against her, and Anton leaned over from the other side and grasped the bodice of her gown as if to unfasten it. Flora jerked away from him, and the thin silk tore and fell forward, revealing the flimsy camisole beneath. Stefan gave a low half-moan of pleasure and thrust his hands inside her bodice, his fingers closing round her breast.

'If you don't let me go I shall kill you both,' said Flora, struggling and starting to feel sick at the probing hands. 'Someone will be here at any minute anyway – you'll be charged with rape – you'll go to prison!' But her voice sounded thin and desperate, even to her own ears.

'We shall not go to any prison,' said Stefan. 'Although at the moment I do not care.'

'Prison would be worth it,' said Anton. 'If you are willing, Flora, so much the better. So much more enjoyable for all. But if not, no matter. We no longer care.' Again there was the sudden lowering of his voice. 'Oh Flora, if you knew how I have ached for you.'

'You make us so strong,' said Stefan. 'Feel with your hand how strong I am for you.' He grabbed her hand and pulled it down between his legs. 'Feel how strong Anton is.' He tried to pull her hand between Anton's thighs. Flora snatched it away and tried to hit out at him, but she was shaking so badly that he dodged the blow easily and grabbed her hands. Anton pulled off the silk necktie he wore and bound her wrists with it. When he pushed her skirts up Flora kicked out and landed a hard blow on his shin and Anton recoiled, spat out a word in his own language that was clearly an oath, then hit her hard across the face. Flora gasped and tears sprang to her eyes. But she would not give way to panic, she would *not* . . .

'You are such a bitch, Flora,' said Anton. 'But you are the most exciting beautiful bitch I have ever known. And tonight is when you pay us back for all the money we have spent. The suppers, the concerts, the flowers.'

'I'm not a piece of merchandise to be bought!' said Flora. That sounded better; it sounded as if she was angry instead of sick with fear.

'But everyone can be bought at some price,' said Stefan.

Anton lay down on her other side, and Flora felt both their hands beneath her gown, exploring, peeling back the silk underwear she was wearing. Twice she was aware of their hands linking with one another, and there was the unmistakable impression of a bizarre caress passing between the two of them. Then Stefan removed his right hand and she realized with horror that he was unbuttoning his trousers. There was the feel of a hot hard stalk of flesh against her bare thighs, and this time the panic and the fear were so intense she thought she might faint. She sought frantically for the tiny burning flame of anger – only it's barely there now, thought Flora in despair, and they're going to rape me; they really are. Oh God, I've never done it – I wanted to wait until there was someone I really loved – and now the first time will be in this dark place with these two madmen forcing me ... Oh, why isn't there anyone here ...

Somewhere in the deserted theatre came the click of a door either being opened or closed, and then – incredibly – the sound of someone singing softly in the darkness. Flora heard it, and it was instantly clear that the twins heard it as well. Stefan jerked back from her and Anton half sat up, staring into the shadows as if trying to see through the stifling velvet curtains. Flora drew breath to yell for help but Anton clapped his hand over her mouth. Stefan snatched his own necktie off, and when Anton removed his hand he tied it over Flora's mouth.

'Tie her legs,' hissed Stefan.

'No time. Someone's out there. We can't be caught like this.'

The two of them went like dark wraiths across the stage and were swallowed up by the shadows.

After a moment Flora managed to sit up. She was shaking violently and her heart was pounding, but she was not hurt. She listened carefully, but there was only the silence of the old theatre.

Had the singer gone? It was possible it might have been Shilling she had heard, although his discordant singing voice was almost as much of a joke as his midnight round was a legend. But whoever it had been could not be far away and if only she could get this suffocating gag away from her mouth, she could call for help. Could she make a noise – overturn a piece of scenery or something – to alert whoever it was? But the twins were still somewhere around and if it came to a fight with the unknown singer, Flora would not like to chance one unaware unprepared man against those two. She got off the couch a bit awkwardly and began to edge her way to the wings, every nerve in her body tensed, expecting at any second that Stefan or Anton would step out of the darkness and seize her. Once she thought she heard the soft singing again, this time coming from the direction of the stage box, but the theatre was filled with such mysterious creakings, it was difficult to be sure.

It was much darker in the wings – the kind of darkness where you wanted to put both hands out in front of you to feel your way. She tugged at the silk round her wrists, but although it gave slightly, the knots stayed firm.

Flora stood still, trying to decide what to do. Could she possibly hide from the twins until Bob Shilling's midnight round? *Could* it have been Shilling she had heard? But if so, where was he now? If she could get to his room without the twins catching her, she might be able to barricade herself in. There was a lock on the door because Shilling sometimes had to keep people's jewellery or money in a small safe, and Flora thought even with her hands bound she could turn a key in a lock. If there was no key, she might be able to drag his heavy desk against the door. She would try that – she could go through the green room and the small costume area which would avoid the auditorium.

She worked her way behind the stage and towards the green room. The door was slightly ajar and she managed to nudge it open with one shoulder and slip through. The room contained the usual friendly untidiness: battered comfortable chairs, and a few pieces of scenery propped against one wall – bits of castles and gardens and park gates made of ply and canvas. There was the scent of glue-size used on the flats, and Flora paused, finding the scent familiar and reassuring. She went through to the wardrobe room which was not much more than a wide section of corridor opening off the green room, linking it with the stone passageways at the side. Most of the acts brought their own costumes, so not much was stored here, although a jumble of brocades and velvets hung from the rails along one side. She walked past them, her heart bumping with apprehension, tugging at the bonds round her wrists again and wishing the gag over her mouth was not so tight.

Opening the green room door must have disturbed a current of air because some of the costumes stirred slightly as she walked past. At the end of the rail, by the door, was a long dark military-style coat hanging from a hook: the brass buttons winked in the glimmering gas jets. Or was it the gaslight? Might someone be inside the coat, and might that someone be getting ready to jump out? Flora stopped, then realized she would either have to keep going or retrace her steps to the stage where the twins might still be lurking. Or were they hiding from the singer? Even worse – had they pounced on the singer and silenced him?

But she was determined to stay with her plan of getting to the doorman's room, and so moving as quietly as she could, she went on again. And it was all right, nothing stirred, and she reached the stone passage safely.

There were discarded props lying about outside the wardrobe area: odds and ends people had not bothered to tidy away – cardboard swords and paper flowers painted in vivid colours so they would not fade to grey under the limelight. It was necessary to skirt carefully round these for fear of making a noise.

Ahead of her was the corridor leading to the stage door; gas jets burned here as well. This time when Flora dragged at the bonds on her wrists, the silk gave slightly. This was encouraging, and she went more confidently into the gaslit corridor, stepping round a tumble of costumes that had been dropped carelessly in a corner – a flower-trimmed hat and some long silk gloves and a mask on a holder, the kind people had once carried at grand masquerade balls – and a long dark cloak hung on a nail, falling in thick folds to the ground . . .

She was level with the cloak when it suddenly billowed out and took on substance, and in the flickering gaslight Flora saw with terror that it had two faces in its depths. Two faces, uncannily and evilly alike, staring out at her. And, oh God, oh God, there were two bodies beneath the thick blackness, and four hands reaching out to her. For several wild seconds the darkened theatre whirled away from Flora, then through the dizzy mists she heard the soft whisper of the cloak being discarded and one of the twins scooped her up in his arms, and turned to carry her back into the main part of the theatre. Anton's voice said something about keeping quiet and hiding somewhere until they could get out. They're still trying to avoid that unknown singer and they're remembering about Shilling coming back, thought Flora. Oh God, if I could just get this silk off my hands I could at least make a fight for it . . .

It was then that she heard, quite distinctly, the sound of the stage door being unlocked and opened, and Rinaldi's voice saying, 'I think she's left, sir. They were all going along to the Linkman or the Sailor's Retreat. But we can go through to her dressing room to make sure.'

And then a voice – the one voice Flora had prayed to hear – said, 'I'd be most grateful if we could do that, Rinaldi. I hoped to get here before the performance ended, but I was delayed. It was a bit of luck running into you in Burbage Street.'

'Just on my way home, sir. Always go that way, along Burbage Street and then through to Candle Square.'

There was the sound of them stepping inside and closing the door, and whichever twin was holding Flora – she thought it was Anton – moved deeper back into the narrow side passage. Flora

126

was not sure where it led, although she thought it might be to the under-stage area. It was very dark, but there was a faint overspill of light from the main passage, and Flora, still fighting to get free, dragging against the silk round her wrists, saw the other twin reach for the handle of a thick door set deep into the wall. This time she saw it was Stefan.

There was the creak of hinges swinging open and a faint breath of cold stale air. They know this place better than I do, thought Flora wildly. How? Did one of them explore beforehand? Wherever it is, they're going hide down there, and take me with them. Did the knots of the silk loosen just then? With sudden excitement she realized that although the knot had not loosened, the silk itself had torn.

'There are lights still on,' said Hal's voice from the main passageway, 'but it does look as if you're right and everyone's gone. Still, I'll just go along to the dressing rooms to make sure, if I may?'

'Yes, of course, sir. I'd best come with you. It'll be a bit dark.'

'It's odd to see the place without lights everywhere, although I daresay you're used to it, so— What was that?'

Their footsteps stopped and Flora visualized the two men, Hal and Rinaldi, standing still, listening. She struggled against Anton again, trying to make some noise and achieving a stifled cry against the silk gag. The silk round her wrists tore again.

'I didn't hear anything,' said Rinaldi at last.

'No. I expect I imagined it.'

'This is a very old building, sir. All kinds of creaks and groans.'

'And ghosts?' said Hal's voice, lightly. Flora could tell he was smiling.

'I've never seen any or heard tell of them, sir, but I wouldn't swear there aren't one or two.'

'I suppose all theatres are a little haunted,' said Hal. 'Through here, isn't it?'

The footsteps were just passing the entrance to this passage when Flora finally managed to snap the thin silk binding her wrists. Before Anton could do anything to silence her, she tore the gag from her mouth and shouted for help.

At the sound of her voice, Hal Chance said, 'Flora?' and ran straight along the passage towards her, with Rinaldi pounding after him. Flora heard him shout her name again – louder this time and more urgently – and even though the darkness must have seemed like a thick black curtain to both men, Hal seemed to take in the situation instantly. He cried out, 'Let go of her, Reznik!' and grabbed Flora's arm, pulling her away from Anton and thrusting her behind him so that he was between her and the twins. Stefan let out a cry of fury, but Anton put out a hand as if to hush him.

'Are you all right?' said Hal, and Flora said, in a gasping voice, 'Yes, I am,' although she was not at all sure she was.

Stefan might be drunk, but he was fighting drunk and furious at being cornered. He swung a blow at Hal who parried it and hit him hard, sending him reeling back. For a moment Flora thought Stefan would fall against the stone wall and smash his head, but somehow he recovered himself, although he did not immediately get up.

'Too drunk to stand,' said Hal, disgustedly. 'We'd better find a way of getting him home. Where's the other one – Oh, you're there. Your brother's in no fit state for anyone's company and from the look of you, you aren't much better.'

Either the words or the tone, or perhaps both, acted like the striking of a tinder on Anton. He whirled round and aimed a blow at Hal, and Hal, although not entirely prepared, somehow dodged it by about a quarter of an inch, and turned back to defend himself. Flora gasped, wondering frantically if she could dart out to the doorman's room and find something to use as a weapon, but Rinaldi had grabbed Anton's arms and was dragging him away from Hal. Stefan staggered up, and hurled himself at Hal and the two of them fell to the ground, struggling together. Stefan suddenly broke away, half falling backwards, skidding across the ground in a semi-huddle, half on his knees. Flora had no idea if it was a deliberate defensive move on Stefan's part or if Hal had hit him hard enough to send him skittering across the ground, but whichever it was, the force of it took him at top-speed towards the half-open oak door. He scrabbled at the stone floor as he went, clearly trying to stop himself, but the stones were too smooth and old. For the first time Flora saw the deep steps immediately beyond the door and saw that Stefan was hurtling straight towards them. Hal saw it as well; he shouted, 'Reznik!' and scrambling to his feet, lunged forward, his hands outstretched to grab Stefan. But it was already too late; Stefan tumbled down the steps in a confusion of flailing arms and legs and the sickening sound of dull thuds.

Anton pulled away from Rinaldi and bounded to the top of the steps, clearly no longer caring about fighting anyone.

'You have killed my brother,' he said through clenched teeth.

'No, I haven't,' said Hal, standing beside him, peering down into the gloom. 'It's quite a long flight of steps and he seems to have fallen all the way to the bottom, but I can hear him cursing fairly robustly. Drunks usually fall soft, anyway.'

'It is no thanks to you if he is not dead,' said Anton angrily.

Hal said, furiously, 'It is no thanks to *you* if Miss Jones is not dead as well. What the devil were you intending to do to her? A little dilettante rape, perhaps?'

'Nothing she was not willing to give.'

'Really?' said Hal disbelievingly. 'Then why were her hands bound and why was a scarf tied over her mouth? Attacking a lady in that way is a very serious offence in this country – it's punishable by a gaol sentence I'm happy to say. And I could add a beating to that without too much persuasion. Or would you like to join your brother down there, because I will happily knock you down these steps here and now.'

'Do not trouble. I am going down there anyway.' Anton began to cautiously descend the dark steps, and Hal said, 'Don't be absurd, man – it's as black as night down there. At least let me get a light.' But Anton ignored him and Hal shrugged and turned back, pulling Flora into his arms.

'My dearest girl, are you sure you're not hurt?'

His hair was tousled, his tie had loosened in the fray and his face was beaded with sweat and dust. He looked far tougher and far less urbane than Flora had ever seen him – more like a street ruffian than a wealthy young man beginning to carve out a dignified and distinguished career in Her Majesty's Foreign Office. She thought he had never been more attractive and as she leaned thankfully against the broadcloth of his overcoat she was aware of the pleasing masculine scents of hair and fresh sweat and clean linen. As if tonight's violence and fear had stripped something away, she felt a bolt of emotion crackle through her entire body like lightning. Not cold-hearted after all then! Not in the least unresponsive!

But even when one had suddenly been sent boneless and dizzy with longing, there were still other concerns, so she said, 'I'm truly all right. Hadn't we better do something about those two villains down there?' But then, because he had always seemed to like it when she displayed irony, said, 'I should add that you and Mr Rinaldi have a very fine sense of timing and drama. You made your entrance just as they were about to – um – have their wicked way with the heroine.'

She thought he smiled and his arms tightened round her, but he only said lightly, 'I'm very glad to hear we were in time. But you're right about making sure the villains are all right. I'd hate to have murder set against me, even if it was the murder of one of those blackguards. Rinaldi, you and I had better go down there while Flora stays here.'

Flora wanted nothing better than to stay here, preferably with Hal still holding her against him, but she said firmly, 'I have no intention of staying up here. If you go down there they might leap on you all over again. I'll come with you.'

'It's pitch black.'

'There'll be matches in Shilling's room,' offered Rinaldi. 'We can light a couple more gas jets. And there's usually a lantern – wait a moment and I'll get them.'

He sped off, and Hal said, 'You'd better have my jacket, Flora. I'll take you home in a minute, but we might have to walk to Blackfriars Road before we get a cab, and you can't do that looking like a bedraggled urchin.'

The jacket swamped Flora but it was warm and safe, like wearing velvet armour.

'Are you really all right?' said Hal, looking down at her.

'Yes. They carried me onto the stage and they were certainly going to rape me, but then we heard something – as if someone had come in – and I got away—' Flora broke off, wondering again what had happened to the elusive person they had heard. Surely he had heard the scuffle out here? She said, 'I was going to shut myself in Shilling's room, but they caught up with me.'

'Flora, were *both* of them going to rape you? Both the brothers?'

'It seemed so,' said Flora rather shortly.

'D'you know, I think I will risk that murder charge after all.' His arms came round her again and his hair brushed her cheek and there was something so extraordinarily sweet and intimate about the feel of his hair against her skin that Flora wished she could stay there for ever.

But Rinaldi was returning, calling out that he had got the lantern and a box of safety matches, and Hal released Flora, and went to help him with the lantern.

'Now for your assailants,' he said, and led the way down the stone steps, holding up the lantern. It was what people used to call a bull's eye lantern and it cast a sharp circle of warmth that Flora thought emphasized the darkness that lay beyond it.

Stefan was half-sprawled against a wall with Anton standing next to him.

'Reznik?' said Hal sharply. 'How badly hurt are you?'

'Nothing broken,' said Stefan. 'But my leg is badly bruised, also

my arm. It is no thanks to you I am not dead of a broken neck.'
He glared at Flora. 'The fall was your fault, you bitch.'

'If you call Miss Jones that name again you will find you really
do have a broken leg,' said Hal icily. 'Perhaps a lot more than just
a broken leg.'

'I do not care. She led us both on. We were entitled to believe
she was willing.'

'Oh, how dare you tell such lies—' began Flora.

'And then, when we accepted your invitation, you laughed,' said
Anton, directly to Flora. 'You are a cock-tease.'

'Reznik, you'll moderate your language!'

'I didn't lead anyone on!' said Flora, breaking in on this. 'I've
never led anyone on! And I certainly made no kind of invitation
to – to anything at all! And,' she said crossly, 'I'm extremely sorry
you didn't break both legs and all your ribs as well when you fell
down here, Stefan, because it would serve you right!'

'Termagant,' said Hal. 'But there are other ways of inflicting
damage. You can lay charges against them at Vine Street in the
morning.'

Before Flora could answer this, Rinaldi said, apologetically,
'Unpleasant for Miss Jones that would be, sir.'

'Flora?'

'I'd rather forget the whole thing,' said Flora, daunted at the
prospect of the police and perhaps a court hearing and avid people
listening to the entire sorry story.

'Much as it pains me, I think you're right,' said Hal. 'Well, then,
Stefan Reznik, you're a black villain and so is your brother, and if
either of you approaches her or enters this theatre again, I shall
make sure you're both thrown into prison for a very long time. For
now, Rinaldi and I will help you back up the stairs and decant you
both into a cab.'

'I would rather stay here all night with the rats for company
than walk one step with you,' said Stefan sullenly.

'Don't be ridiculous. You'll have to be helped up the steps anyway.'

'And there aren't any rats,' said Flora, managing not to glance nervously into the corners. The room seemed to be lined with black brick and there was a jumble of scenery and stage props. At the far end, was the outline of the grave trap's shaft.

'Well, we can't leave you here,' said Hal. 'Apart from anything, you'd probably try to burn the place down out of spite.'

'But we could leave them, sir,' put in Rinaldi eagerly. 'There's one of those new doors in the foyer. A one-way arrangement. It locks itself after you go through it. They could go out that way when they're ready. And Shilling will be back at midnight, anyway. He can throw them out.'

'We will not be thrown out by anyone,' said Anton grandly. 'We will leave after you have gone by ourselves. We will walk out through your stupid door.'

'I suppose,' said Hal slowly, 'we could leave a note in Shilling's room. We could say we've had to leave a couple of drunks down here, and warn him that it might be better to call the peelers to help out.'

'We are not a couple of drunks—'

'I can think of worse names to call you than that,' said Hal challengingly.

'There's a constable who usually stands on the corner of Candle Square,' said Rinaldi with the air of one pouring balm on stormy waters. 'I can tell him what's happened on my way home. I know him by sight and he knows me. I'll warn him to look out for Shilling and perhaps come inside with him.'

'A very good idea,' said Hal. 'And I'll put a half-sovereign in the note for Shilling – that will cover the cost of a cab.'

As Hal picked up the lantern, Flora said, 'We should leave that for them.'

'I'm not trusting this precious pair with a set of matches and a lamp,' said Hal. 'You're too tender-hearted, Flora. Half an hour in the dark won't kill them.'

They said goodnight to Rinaldi on the edge of Candle Square. Hal advised him to go home and take a good tot of something to help him sleep. 'And perhaps you'd have that tot on me, Rinaldi,' he had said, and there had been the chink of coins, and Rinaldi's words of thanks. There had also been a final light-hearted exchange about the forthcoming electrification of the Tarleton and how dazzling it would make the Christmas pantomime.

Hal had paused for a moment outside the theatre, looking up at it.

'It's a shockingly ugly place, isn't it?' he said. 'But it's unashamedly ugly. And it's got a lot of character.'

'That's very perceptive of you,' said Flora.

'D'you know how old it is?'

'I don't think anyone knows, not exactly. But that inscription over the stage door—'

'Please one, please all, be they great or be they small.'

'Yes.' It was nice that he had noticed this; not many people did. 'It's supposed to have been said or written by a man called Richard Tarleton – an Elizabethan clown actor. The theatre doesn't go back that far, of course, or anything like it, but it might mean the site has theatrical associations.'

'It'd be nice to think so.'

As they turned to walk along to get a cab, Flora suddenly looked back.

'Something wrong?'

'It's just that I thought I saw someone going into Platt's Alley. But it's difficult to see properly in this weather.'

'Creeping fog from the river,' said Hal, peering through the greyness. 'It'll probably hang around for days. I can't see anything.'

'It looked as if whoever it was, was wearing one of those deep-brimmed hats and a long coat. But the fog plays peculiar tricks.'

'I expect it was Bob Shilling you saw or even Rinaldi's constable taking a look round.'

'Yes, of course. Should we go back, though?'

'I think you've had enough of that place for one night,' he said.

But as they walked towards Blackfriars Bridge Flora was remembering the soft footsteps inside the theatre and the just-audible humming. I probably imagined it, she thought, or perhaps it was wind sighing in the old brickwork or the roof, or even a trapped animal somewhere.

They picked up a cab near the bridge. The lights along the bank were blurry because of the fog and they reflected smudgily in the river. Inside the cab, Hal put his arm round her and Flora no longer cared what had happened earlier, because she wanted to trap this moment and fold it away somewhere safe, so that when she was old she would be able to unwrap it and remember the feeling. Would she be able to smile because Hal was still in her life to share it, or would she have a stab of pain, and think, ah yes, *that* was the night when I was *really* happy.

When they reached her flat, Minnie cooked a belated supper while Flora washed and put on fresh clothes. Thankfully there was a bottle of reasonably good wine which had been a present from someone; Hal opened it and stayed to eat the supper which Minnie laid on the round cherrywood table in the window. The fire burned up brightly and the room was warm and safe.

They did not talk much about what had just happened. Flora thought this might be because it was the first time Hal had been in her flat and neither of them wanted to spoil it. He seemed to like it, and she was pleased when he wanted to know about the evening's performance. When she told him about the offer of *Cinderella*, he said it sounded like a great compliment and certainly a step forward in her career. Then he paused, and asked if she was wedded to the theatre for life.

'I hadn't thought about it,' said Flora carefully.

'No? I just wondered if there might be other possibilities – other

135

proposals for the future – for your future – that you would consider?'

Flora stared at him and felt a huge delight unfolding inside her. But it seemed important not to be too intense – not yet, at any rate – so she simply said, yes, she would consider certain proposals, very definitely she would consider them.

Hal smiled and said perhaps they could talk more about that quite soon, and in the meantime could he pour her another glass of wine to go with Minnie Bean's excellent supper?

Flora accepted the wine, and wished all over again that these moments of pure happiness could be captured and stored in tissue paper and lavender, and re-lived somewhere in the future.

CHAPTER THIRTEEN

The Present

'I'm so sorry to bother you again, Miss Seymour,' said Robert, speaking into the phone as off-handedly as he could. 'But I've just realized I've left my damp meter in the Tarleton. I need it on a daily basis for work, so I wondered if I could borrow the keys again, just to go in to get it?'

There was a perceptible pause before Shona Seymour answered, during which Robert had time to think that surely she could not refuse. Or would she offer to go and look for the damp meter herself? If so, she would have a long and fruitless search because this was merely a ploy to get back in and see if there was any evidence of the figure he and Hilary had seen the previous night.

But Shona said, 'That would be all right, Mr Fallon. Do you want to call in for the keys this morning? Or can I send someone over to you with them?'

'If someone could bring them to my office that would be very helpful,' said Robert, instantly hoping it would be Hilary. 'I've got a couple of surveys booked today, both in Blackfriars, so I can call at the Tarleton on my way from one to the other. Oh, and would tomorrow be all right for returning the keys? I don't think I'll be

137

free much before half past six today and your office would be closed by then, wouldn't it?' He was hoping she would agree to this, because he wanted the keys overnight and did not want to risk Hilary sneaking them out after hours a second time.

'Yes, we would be closed by then,' said Shona. 'But unfortunately the owner's instructions are very specific and the keys are never to be out overnight.'

'Couldn't I put them through the letter box?'

'We don't have a letter box on the street door – mostly for security reasons – and that door will be locked at six.' She paused, then while Robert was trying to think of another suggestion, said, 'Half past six isn't so very late, though. How about meeting me somewhere to hand the keys back?'

This was the last thing Robert had expected, but he said firmly, 'I wouldn't dream of putting you to so much trouble.'

'It wouldn't be any trouble. This isn't exactly a nine to five job, you know.' Even over the phone it was apparent she was smiling. 'Shall we make it that place on the corner by the Tarleton itself?' She named the wine bar Robert remembered from his nocturnal visit with Hilary: a man had come out of it while they were watching and they had not been sure if he was their ghost-figure. He was rather relieved Shona had not suggested Linkman's which he already associated with Hilary, so he said the wine bar would be fine.

'I'll expect you any time between half past six and seven,' she said. 'We can have a drink together.' Her voice slid several octaves lower. 'Perhaps even dinner,' said Shona softly. 'Goodbye, Robert.'

'Shona Seymour inviting a young man to have dinner with her is tantamount to Messalina inspecting a new consignment of slaves,' said Hilary, when she delivered the keys to Robert's office halfway through the morning. 'You'd better wear combat gear. I like your office, by the way – I love all these old maps you've got on the

138

walls. Medieval and Elizabethan London all the way to the twenty-first century complete with the M25 and the Millennium Dome. Is that one Roman London? Oh yes, I see it is. Londinium. I didn't know the Thames was called the Flumen – Oh wait though, that's the Latin word for river, isn't it?'

'They're quite useful for finding places,' said Robert, pleased at Hilary's appreciation of his maps. 'But I like having them up: I like the orderliness of the progression from the original Roman settlement, all the way down to the present day. I shan't go to the meeting with Shona,' he said. 'I'll have to take the keys back before you close tonight and say I re-arranged my appointments and that the wine bar meeting won't be necessary.'

'She won't like that,' said Hilary, grinning. 'She'll be thwarted and rejected and we'll all have to put up with her sulking tomorrow. She hates to let one get away.'

'Well, this one is definitely getting away. It's a bit of a nuisance, though,' said Robert. 'I thought I'd hit on such a credible ploy for having the keys overnight.'

'You were going to look for clues to the ghost?'

'Yes. And I was going to take a closer look at the underground wall.' He stared at the keys she had put on his desk.

'Robert, you don't think . . .'

'What?'

'That we're becoming just the smallest bit paranoid? A bit – uh – infatuated with the Tarleton? I know I've been fascinated by it for ages, but . . .'

'Of course we're becoming paranoid *and* infatuated,' said Robert. 'But I'm beyond caring. I'm a sober – well, usually sober – practical and respectable surveyor. I don't go in for fantasies and I don't have "feelings" about buildings. I can't afford to; I see too many.'

'But?'

'But I'm beginning to agree with you that there's something very peculiar about that theatre. What did that old actor say in

139

those memoirs? That the Tarleton kept its secrets? Maybe there was a secret once – something relatively innocent, but something that started an eerie local legend about a man who wouldn't let his face be seen in daylight.'

'It's amazing how shivery that is when you say it aloud,' said Hilary.

'Yes. Has the owner really issued that instruction about the keys never being out overnight?'

'No idea. I still haven't been able to get into the filing cabinet in Shona's office. But I'm beginning to think the owner is a figment of everybody's imagination, Shona's included,' said Hilary. 'Or it'll turn out to be someone really off the wall: a defunct monarch or something. Maybe Charles II requisitioned it on the sly for one of his mistresses, or Jack the Ripper bought it to stuff victims behind the wall, or . . . That last one doesn't sound too wildly incredible, does it?'

'Yes, it does,' said Robert. 'For one thing it's the wrong era – that wall's later than Jack the Ripper by a good twenty years.' But he smiled, liking the way her eyes lit up with enthusiasm. 'Have you thought of requesting a search of land registry records? I think you can apply to HM Land Registry for copies of title information nowadays.'

'Can you really?'

'Yes, but don't get too carried away; there's no guarantee that it will be registered. Most property doesn't get registered until it changes hands. So if it's been in the same ownership for a long time, or been passed direct from father to son without a formal conveyance being drawn up, the land registry people probably won't be able to help. But it might be worth trying.'

'Let me write all that down,' said Hilary, diving into her handbag for pen and paper. Then, 'Are you really going to look at that cellar wall again?' she said.

'Yes, I am. But no, you can't come with me,' he said as Hilary started to speak. 'For one thing I don't know when I can do it, and for another thing you might be seen. It won't matter if I'm seen, because I'm supposed to be looking for the damp meter, but it'll matter if you are.' He hesitated, and then said, 'I could phone you this evening to let you know how I got on.'

'Yes, please. I'll be in all evening.'

She got up to go and Robert wondered if they had reached a stage where he could suggest meeting for a meal. But he still did not know if Hilary was linked up to anyone, and even if she was not, she might be seeing this as a semi-business relationship. It was clear that she loved her work and was deeply involved in the research side of it.

Caley Merrick had spent the afternoon at the Harlequin offices, addressing envelopes for a mailshot about a forthcoming exhibition. A two-day task, it was; Hilary Bryant had called him in, apologizing for what she called the dull nature of the work, but saying they hoped he would be available to help out. Caley had not said he would always be available for anything remotely connected to the Tarleton, or that he would have put up with far more than dullness to spend time in the Harlequin's offices. He had thanked her and gone along the next day.

He always worked at the little desk set aside for him in a corner of the main room, not intruding on anything, quietly getting on with whatever he was given, but listening to all that was said. The Tarleton was mentioned only occasionally. There had been an afternoon last month when some of the staff had got into a crazy discussion about it, vying with one another to make up fantastic stories about its history and reasons for its long closure. One of the freelance people, Judy Randall, had been there, and the two girls from publicity and the man from accounts had come in to see what the laughter was about. At six o'clock, with the office closing, they had all decided to go along to Linkman's to continue the discussion there. Hilary Bryant had asked Caley to go as well, but he had not done so, partly because he would have felt out of place and not known how to join in, but partly because he was afraid he might carelessly display too much knowledge about the Tarleton itself. It was important always to keep a guard, to be wary. But as he made his quiet way home, he thought about those people – Hilary and Judy and the others – who all had bright, interesting careers and bright interesting lives, and who would live in nice houses or apartments with families and friends round them. He did not quite hate them for all that, but he could not help remembering that he had only ever had a dull job and that he had always lived in the same narrow rather threadbare house, with not much money. What he did hate them for was the way they had made fun of the Tarleton.

But this afternoon, as he worked on the envelopes, the office was quiet. Miss Seymour was out at a meeting of the Southwark and Bankside Development Society, and Hilary Bryant was absorbed in some research; she was poring over a couple of old, foxed-looking books and some ancient copies of theatre magazines. From where he sat, Caley could see that one of the books was *Green Room Recollections*, and the other was *A History of London Music Halls*. The magazines were bound copies of the *Stage* and *Encore* between 1912 and 1916. Hilary was making a lot of notes, so Caley was careful not to interrupt her, except to ask if he should make a cup of tea for everyone at three o'clock.

When the street buzzer went Hilary jumped and looked annoyed at the interruption, but when it turned out to be Judy Randall she was pleased. Judy had brought in page proofs for a book – something about a television series on Edwardian dining tables it was, which the Harlequin had apparently helped with. She was a large colourful lady, very warm and friendly, and she drew Caley into the discussion, passing the proofs over for him to see, explaining that Hilary had done some of the background research for the TV programme.

'It's very interesting,' Caley said, studying the proofs. He added, 'It should sell very well,' and Judy beamed.

'And did you see they managed to reproduce the sheet music for that "Tipsy Cake" song?' she said to Hilary. 'The cover as well.' She flipped through the pages. 'Here it is. A sozzled-looking butler helping a cook to slosh sherry onto a jammy creamy sponge cake. You found the original for the song, d'you remember?'

'So I did. I came across it in that antiquarian place near St Martin's Lane,' said Hilary. 'It's reproduced well, hasn't it? The cover was a bit battered but it looks all right. I'm glad they didn't do one of those computer-repair jobs on it: it's old and it ought to *look* old. It was one of Toby Chance's songs. Chance wrote the lyrics and Douglas wrote the music.'

'Yes. It's way out of copyright, of course,' said Judy, 'but we've given them a credit anyway. The song's being used as a backing track for the episode on puddings next month – they're hoping to record it later this week, I think. The Harlequin will be listed in the acknowledgements, of course.'

'Toby Chance was part-owner of the Tarleton,' said Hilary, and Caley felt his heart skip a beat. 'I've been reading up on him a bit,' she said, still studying the proofs. 'I think he'd make a good subject for a radio programme sometime: one of those late-night mini-biographies. If I can find out enough to put a presentation together, I'm going to see if Shona will pitch it to Radio 4. Apparently Toby vanished around the start of the first world war which makes him a bit mysterious, so he could be quite an intriguing subject.'

'Oh God, not another mystery about that place,' said Judy, tucking her canvas trousers into the tops of her boots, preparatory to cycling through London's streets. She was wearing a woolly hat with a pom-pom today and a kind of Elizabethan tabard which looked as if it had been knitted out of magenta string. Caley could not help thinking Mary would have wondered how Judy could dress so peculiarly.

'I don't think there's really a mystery about Toby,' Hilary was saying. 'I expect he fought in the war and was killed. But when you think how the place has been closed for nearly a hundred years, you do wonder a bit. I know we all make jokes about the Tarleton, but it *is* a strange set-up.'

'Probably the lease ran out and nobody could afford to renew it,' said Judy and took herself off.

'What a disappointment if it really was just that,' said Hilary, half to herself. And then, to Caley, 'But they say life's full of disappointments, don't they?'

'Yes, they do.'

CHAPTER FOURTEEN

One of the disappointments of Caley's life was the knowledge that he had been grafted onto a stranger's family. It was how he had always seen it, all through the years from his earliest childhood memories. A nothing person with no roots, treated with false kindness, with a conscious air of you are no different to our own children. He was given the same things and opportunities as the others: schooling, outings, music lessons, swimming. He found swimming tiring, but he liked the music lessons which were at the house of a retired music teacher. The house smelt of biscuits and there were large pot plants obscuring the light from most of the windows, but Caley did not mind. He liked the patterns the music made and he was pleased when the teacher said he had a real talent.

'You should practise every day,' she said. 'One hour every day.' Caley did not say this would be difficult because there was no piano at home.

Sometimes, in those years when he was growing up and becoming aware of the world, he felt an actual physical pain from the longing to know his own family – to be able to listen to their memories and histories. But at that time it had not been very common for an adopted child to request the name of its natural mother – nor was it an automatic right – and it was not as easy to do so as it later became.

He was eighteen when he was given the few odds and ends that had apparently come from his own family's past. Here are some things we think belonged to your grandparents or great-uncles or -aunts, said his adoptive parents, smiling with delight at their own benevolence. Only a handful of things and they don't look very informative – a bit obscure, in fact – but now you're of age, we think you're old enough to have them. His adoptive mother had said, 'We haven't looked at them in any detail, and as you know we were never told your family's name – but you became a Merrick ever since you came to us as a small baby. It's how we've always thought of you. One of our own.'

'Some of the photographs are of this very area, so it does look as if your family might have come from these parts,' said his adoptive father, and added that he believed adoption agencies did try to keep a child in a similar background to its real family. 'Of course, we're your real family now,' he had said.

Caley had accepted the things without saying much, but nearly forty years later he could still remember how furious he had been not to have been given them sooner. Had the fools not understood that when you had never known your own family, you wanted every fragment of them you could get?

The obscure odds and ends were packed into an old shoe box. Caley carried it into the bathroom which was the only place to be sure of privacy in the house, and locked the door. The box contained a rag-bag miscellany, although at that stage of his life the dog-eared scraps of paper and the faded postcards sent to anonymous people – most of them faded to near-illegibility anyway – had not been especially important. The best prize was the photographs. Seated on the narrow windowsill, trying not to let the scent of lavatory cleaner permeate these precious scraps, Caley pored over the photographs, thinking that the faces might be his grandparents or great-grandparents or long-ago uncles or cousins. Meagre as they were, they were still fragments to be jealously guarded and on which to build dreams. From that day, he had begun to weave fantasies, doing so late at night when the family were all in bed, or at weekends when they went off somewhere in a noisy group.

When, shortly before his nineteenth birthday, the abrupt, frightening attacks of struggling for breath began and chronic asthma was eventually diagnosed, he had seized on it gratefully because it was a genuine reason not to go out with them. It was the middle of the Swinging Sixties, not that Caley ever swung anywhere or really wanted to. But the younger members of the family – the two boys and three girls – were always off to some disco or wine bar or club. Great fun, they said. He should come with them. Caley found it a relief to be able to say crowded places brought on an asthma attack, and that smoky pubs and cinemas were a nightmare. Best he stayed at home. They pretended to be sorry and concerned, but Caley knew they were secretly relieved. After a while he found he could almost will himself into an attack. This was useful, although he conscientiously avoided doing it too often, but it meant he was often left to his own devices; it meant he could lie on his bed, staring up at the ceiling, and think about the photographs and the people and places in them.

At those times he would take out the shoe box and pore over the faded ink and the smudgy faces and places in the photographs. He recognized most of the streets – his adoptive parents had been right that they had been taken in this part of London. People stood self-consciously in the small park where he himself had played as a child with his adoptive brothers and sisters, or posed against street backgrounds. One photo, clearly a professionally taken shot for a postcard, was of an ugly old facade with a playbill displayed in a case on the right of double doors, and the words, 'Benefit performance by Miss Marie Lloyd' just about readable. Caley recognized the facade at once: it was the old Tarleton Music Hall.

147

The Tarleton. He looked at the photographs again, and this time realized there were links to the Tarleton in several of them. A few blurry photographs, the half of a programme, some sheet music with the title missing, but with the words, 'First performed at the Tarleton Music Hall, in . . .' It was annoying not to have the date on that one, although there was another piece of music that had a faded date of February 1887 in one corner. One of the postcards said, 'Pleased to see you at the T last night – wasn't Bunstable a scream! We all had supper at the Linkman afterwards – pity you couldn't come. Fondest love, S.'

It was interesting, but at the time it did not strike Caley as particularly noteworthy. Someone in his family a couple of generations back had most likely been stage-struck. Some unknown great-aunt, perhaps, who in her giddy youth had dreamed of walking onto a stage lit by footlights or even by the flaring limes of the Victorian years, and singing or dancing in front of an adoring audience. Or someone might have been enamoured of one of the Tarleton's performers. Teenagers today collected photographs and articles about pop stars and fell in love with footballers from afar – this could be an Edwardian version of that.

But the more he thought about it, the more he began to wonder. Supposing it was something more than that? Supposing the Tarleton was in some way bound up with the family he had never known? He went through the box's contents again, this time looking for the Tarleton and finding several more links to it. In that moment his quest was born – he hit on the word 'quest' purely by chance, but he liked it for its romantic associations. A quest was a search, a hunt for something immensely precious. And the old Tarleton's the link, he thought, aware of a thump of excitement. It's a link to my real family. A secret link – something to be pursued without anyone knowing, without the risk of people spoiling it by making fun of it or asking senseless questions.

From that day he began to gather information about the Tarleton and its history, working quietly and unobtrusively, but with complete dedication. Nothing was too insignificant; he seized greedily on every sentence ever written about it, every shred of tattered gossip spun in green rooms, and every scandal and rumour whispered in taverns, recording everything in a thick notebook he kept in the shoe box. He pushed it to the very back of his wardrobe, folding an old jacket over it so it would not be noticed.

It was vaguely irritating that when he wanted to read his precious notes or look at the photographs and cards, he either had to wait for the others to go out or lock himself in the lavatory. After a time he waited for them to go out. It was impossible to lose yourself in private dreams when people kept rattling the door and demanding to know if you were all right, or whether you had eaten too much rhubarb pie at dinner and wanted a dose of bismuth.

Marriage to Mary when he was twenty-two interrupted the search, and the dreams receded for a while.

The noisy kindly adoptive family had moved away from the area by then. 'But we'll stay in touch,' they said firmly. 'You'll come to visit us and we'll come to visit you.'

'Oh yes,' said Caley, knowing he would not, knowing he would let the link gradually dwindle to an exchange of Christmas and birthday cards.

He did not tell Mary about his quest because she would not have understood it any more than his adoptive family. Why must he frowst over things that had happened years and years ago? she always said if he brought books home from the library, or made notes about local history. It could not be good for his eyes. Why not take up something practical? Gardening or even carpentry – carpentry was always useful in a house. Shelves and fitted cupboards and such like.

The marriage was not exactly a mistake, because Caley was fond of Mary and it took him away from the too loud family who had been kind but with whom he had not had much in common. It provided a degree of independence; he liked having his own small house which Mary had found for them, saying surely they could afford a mortgage on Caley's salary from the council. And hadn't he said something about having a small nest egg? You could not do better than invest a nest egg in property, said Mary.

'It's only a very small amount,' Caley said. 'Not really worth drawing on.' He had told Mary about the money in an unguarded moment and had since regretted it. It was somehow a deeply private thing, that money that had apparently been left to him by his real parents, and it was part of the dream. Secret. So he said they would have a mortgage for the house and they would afford it somehow.

The house was in Candle Street, which Mary said could not be better; it meant they would be near her sister and Caley's adoptive family were not far away – he would want to keep in touch with them, wouldn't he? The area was not exactly the best, but the house could be cleaned up really nicely and given a lick or two of paint, said Mary. Well, no, there was not really room for a piano – in any case, the neighbours would not care to hear piano music through the wall. And surely it was years since he had played anyway? Not since he was twelve or thirteen, wasn't it? So he would have lost the knack, said Mary comfortably. They could have a smart radiogram, though, which would be much better. Caley could play his music on that.

After the first shock of Mary's death was over, Caley was horrified to find that his main emotion was relief because he could return to his beloved quest. He still had his job at the council, but his evenings, weekends and lunch hours were now entirely his own. The wonderful thing about dreams was they did not fade or fray with the years. When, a week after the funeral, he opened up the old shoe box, the scent of the old papers rose up to him and the dreams were waiting, as bright and as alluring as when he was eighteen. But as he turned the contents lovingly over, a question came from nowhere that had never before occurred to him. *Why* did someone squirrel all these things away in the first place? Were they just a miscellaneous collection – things no one bothered to throw away in case they might one day be valuable? Or was there some meaning to them: something someone wanted Caley – or someone like him – to know and understand? Hard on the heels of this thought came the knowledge that the Tarleton itself had always been regarded as a bit of a mystery. Dark and silent and sealed up for all these years, yet maintained and kept watertight by somebody.

From that day Caley's quest became part of his life. He read and searched and researched. Living so near to Burbage Street meant there were secondhand bookshops and libraries containing old books on the area. Early on he found the privately printed memoirs of the old actor called Prospero Garrick. The book was tucked at the very back of a library shelf and when Caley thought of how he had so nearly missed it, he felt sick. According to the date stamp it had not been borrowed for over thirty years and it was remarkable that it had not been put on the 'For Sale' shelf (40p for fiction, 20p for non-fiction), or been sent for pulping, but somehow it been overlooked. Caley did not overlook it though; he had been scouring the shelves for anything to do with old theatres in the area generally, and when he skimmed down the index and saw the Tarleton's name, he had to prevent himself from stuffing the book greedily into his pocket there and then. The cover was faded and the paper was brown with age, but the minute he opened it, it was as if he had fallen backwards into the early years of the twentieth century.

He had not actually taken the book out on loan, because he never did anything connected with the Tarleton that might go on record and lead back to him. Even something as trivial as a library stamp might betray him sometime in the future, and he was constantly and almost obsessively afraid people would laugh at him. 'You, connected in some way with the Tarleton?' they would say. '*You?*' His adoptive family all those years ago would have seen it as a great joke; they would have taken to calling him Laurence

Olivier or Henry Irving, and asking when he was going up to the Old Vic to play Hamlet. Mary would have stared at him and said, dear goodness, whatever could he be thinking of, they weren't the kind of people who had anything to do with theatres.

So Caley was very secretive about Prospero Garrick's book. He took it over to one of the tables the library provided for students, and, acting as casually as possible, copied the relevant sections into a notebook.

The memoir was called: *An Actor Remembers*, and Prospero Garrick was not chary of talking about his appearances at the Tarleton, or, indeed, his appearances anywhere. As well as his monologues, he had, it seemed, also been part of a series of recruiting concerts in the early years of the first world war at various theatres. 'I generally gave them my Henry V St Crispin's Day speech,' he wrote. ' "Gentlemen in England, now a-bed, shall think themselves accurs'd they were not here/And hold their manhoods cheap whiles any speaks that fought with us upon St Crispin's Day." Ah, stirring stuff it was, and I fancy it was directly responsible for the volunteering of a number of brave young lads for the army! The ladies, too, were entranced with the rendering. It must be said I was not in my first youth by then, but the Voice was still as good as ever.'

The book had been published in 1929 by some small publishing house Caley had never heard of and was probably long since defunct. But finding it was an extraordinary experience. Caley spent the next few days preoccupied and wrapped in his own thoughts – Mary would have hated that: she would have tried to break in to his absorption, saying, someone's got the glumps today, and Caley would have had to repress his annoyance.

He made several subsequent visits to the library to make sure he had found all Prospero's references to the Tarleton. He was careful to allow himself just fifteen minutes each time, it was not very likely he was being watched, but he was taking no chances.

*

After she had taken the keys to Robert, Hilary went back to her office and spent the rest of the morning trying to work. She tried not to think too much about Robert, or to wonder whether he was actually in the theatre now, and if so, what he might have found.

She could hear the accounts people laughing about something upstairs, but her own office was quiet. Caley Merrick had finished his envelope addressing yesterday, and Shona, along with one of the freelancers, was sitting in on a presentation for a series of plays on Radio 4. The plays were set in an Edwardian spa town in 1900 and the commissioning editor had liked the writer's initial pitch but wanted an opinion on authenticity, which was why the Harlequin had been asked to provide a freelance. There would be a consultation fee, which was why Shona was accompanying the freelance.

All this meant Hilary had a free rein for an hour or so, and she was going to spend the time trying to trace the fruity old actor who had listened to the story of the Tarleton's ghost in a Bankside tavern called the Pickled Lobster Pot, and had set it down in his memoirs. She had not found out if the Lobster Pot still existed, or what it might these days be called, but if it was still a pub Hilary was going to suggest to Robert that they have a drink or a meal there. Purely for research purposes. She grinned at this last thought, because although she was calling it research, the truth was she was finding Robert, with his quiet, precise mind, very attractive. It was impossible to imagine him saying, as Gil had so often and so annoyingly said, that oh dear, it was too cold an evening to go out, or that he had been working so hard he was only fit for a hot bath and early bed on his own. Hilary was very glad indeed that the lukewarm relationship with Gil had petered out of its own accord.

Anyway, apart from Robert, the research was genuinely absorbing; Hilary would be doing it even if Robert looked like a bag of nails. The fact that he did not was just icing on the cake.

The actor's memoirs had been tentatively dated by somebody at

Durham University as being from the early 1930s so it might be worth travelling up there to talk to that somebody. This would not be a problem, it was a journey that could easily be made at a weekend. The problem might be that he or she could have left Durham and be living somewhere inaccessible like Tibet or the Cayman Islands.

In the meantime, there was the British Library which was supposed to have a copy of every book ever printed. Hilary thought this was a legal requirement dating back to about 1910 or 1911, but it might not cover privately printed memoirs and even if it did she had not got a title or the author's name.

She was perfectly prepared to scour the entire British Library for which she had a reader's ticket, but she thought some items were still housed within the British Museum and she did not have a ticket for that. She knew several people who had – Judy Randall was one of them because she was a voracious reader of odd subjects and quirky corners of history – but a reader's ticket was not something people would be inclined to lend. Also, the British Museum might be very diligent about checking identities against tickets; Hilary at once conjured up an image of herself being ignominiously frog-marched out of the august ivory tower for misappropriation of a ticket, and dumped unceremoniously in Russell Square.

She had got as far as discovering that the British Library was currently putting a large proportion of its out of copyright books on-line which, in the current situation, might be useful, when a letter arrived by special delivery. Hilary signed for it and opened the envelope without thinking very much about it. All kinds of peculiar missives turned up here, from tattered plays people had found in attics and thought might be valuable, to sepia photographs of great-uncles who had toured obscure provincial repertory theatres in the 1920s, or playbills for things like *Getting Gertie's Garter* or the original run of *Charley's Aunt*.

The special delivery contained none of these. It was a letter which looked as if it had been typed on an old-fashioned manual typewriter. Although the envelope had not been addressed to anyone specifically, the letter itself began 'Dear Miss Seymour'. It was dated the previous day.

Dear Miss Seymour

You will be aware that the restraint imposed on the Tarleton Music Hall by the terms of my father's will ended a year ago. I do apologize for not getting in touch with you before this: unfortunately, a period of ill-health precluded it.

However, I now feel strong enough to discuss plans for putting the theatre into use, and with that in mind, hope we can make arrangements to meet in order to discuss the possibilities.

I seldom travel far nowadays, so I wonder if you could visit me here as soon as possible? My house is some miles outside Glastonbury, but although the village is quite isolated I think the drive from London would not take much over three hours. If the journey is too far for you to make here and back in one day, I should be very happy for you to stay overnight. It is quite a large house, so it would not be a problem.

It is a strange feeling to know that the Tarleton is to be woken from its long sleep at last; I am unsure how much you know, but I expect you're aware that my father's will stipulated it should remain closed until fifty years after his death. He died in the mid-1950s, although the theatre has, of course, been closed for a total of almost a hundred years now.

By way of authorization, I enclose a letter from the bank with whom you have dealt all these years. The bank holds my father's will and the title deeds to the Tarleton, and I expect they could make these available for you if necessary.

I look forward to hearing from you and to meeting you.
     With kind regards
          Madeleine Ferrelyn

It was as if a hand – an elderly lady's hand, a little shaky but perfectly able to compose a clear, businesslike letter and add a firm signature on good-quality paper – had reached out of the past and clasped Hilary's own hand. For several moments the modern office with its computers and phones and faxes blurred and receded.

Madeleine Ferrelyn. The Tarleton's owner – its *owner*. The information for which Hilary had scoured filing cabinets and history books and back copies of stage magazines, to say nothing of contemplating an HM Land Registry search, had been presented to her out of the blue by the mundane medium of recorded post. The mysterious owner about whom she had spun so many fantasies was neither mysterious nor fantastic. She was alive and well and living just outside Glastonbury, and apparently planning to bring the theatre out of its long sleep because a restraint in her father's will had ended.

Hilary stared at the letter for a long time. It certainly answered part of the mystery because it provided the owner's name and address, but it also set up a whole new series of mysteries. Who had Madeleine Ferrelyn's father been and why had his will placed a restraint on the theatre for fifty years? Might it be some kind of entail? Hilary had only the vaguest knowledge of entails, but she did not think they included peculiar directives about keeping closed and sealed a valuable property which, handled correctly, might have earned the cost of its maintenance at the very least, and at best might have racked up some profit.

The address on the letter was Levels House, Fosse Leigh, Somerset, and there was a phone number. Hilary had never been to that part of England, but she associated it with Stonehenge, legends about King Arthur and pop festivals. It was disconcerting to discover that it might also hold the key to a mystery surrounding an old music hall.

According to Madeleine Ferrelyn (was she Miss or Mrs?), Levels House was just over three hours' drive from London. It was now twelve o'clock, which meant if Hilary left the office at once and borrowed or hired or stole a car she could be in Fosse Leigh, at Levels House, and talking to this link to the past by four or five o'clock. Or she could pick up the phone on her desk and dial a number and be speaking to Madeleine Ferrelyn in the next five minutes. This latter prospect was so remarkable she had to make a conscious effort not to reach for the phone there and then. Much as she wanted to know what lay at the heart of all this – much as she wanted to speak to this unknown lady – she could not bypass Shona, to whom the letter had been addressed.

The street door opening downstairs made her jump. It was only someone coming into the offices on the floor below, but it jerked Hilary back to the present. She took a photocopy of the letter, tucked it into her bag and placed the original on Shona's desk.

It was going to be very interesting indeed to see what Shona did about this, and it was going to be interesting in another way to talk to Robert about it. She resisted the temptation to phone him. But it was impossible to concentrate on anything serious, so Hilary abandoned the quest for the fruity actor and focussed instead on some overdue cataloguing that everyone had been putting off for weeks and would not require too much concentration. Shona phoned in at twelve thirty to say the Radio 4 presentation had gone very well and she and the freelance were going on to lunch. Hilary remembered that the freelance was a post-graduate student of twenty-four with soulful eyes, and supposed Shona would be carrying him back to her flat for most of the afternoon. If Robert brought the keys back, at least Shona would be out of the way when he did so, although that might depend on the freelance's willingness to be seduced and also his staying power.

She went out to the delicatessen on the corner to buy a

sandwich which she ate at her desk. Shona and the freelance were probably cosily ensconced in a Charlotte Street restaurant or a Soho bistro by this time, and Robert might be padding round the Tarleton.

It was rather a relief when a set of accounts which apparently refused to balance was brought down, and her help requested in untangling it. But as she worked, her mind was on this new piece of the puzzle she had just been handed, and she was wondering if Madeleine Ferrelyn in her isolated Glastonbury village was eyeing the telephone, wondering if her letter had reached London and how soon Miss Seymour from the Harlequin Society would phone.

CHAPTER·FIFTEEN

After Hilary left his office, Robert sat looking at the keys for several minutes. If he intended to behave correctly he had until about five o'clock to enter the place and investigate the underground room. If he intended to behave other than correctly he had a lot longer, in fact he had as long as he wanted.

He dropped the keys into his briefcase, and before he could change his mind went along to the nearest DIY place where there was a key-cutting service, surrendering the keys with reluctance, and arranging to call back at three o'clock. After this he went off to survey an empty warehouse near Waterloo station which was to be converted into trendy apartments for City types, working through it meticulously but finding it mind-numbingly boring because at the moment all properties that were not the Tarleton were mind-numbingly boring.

At two fifteen, planning ahead, he wrote a note to Shona Seymour, explaining that he need not, after all, trouble her to meet him that evening because he had found the damp meter in his car. He left the envelope unsealed so he could enclose the keys when he had collected them along with the newly cut copies. He was by now convinced that he was in the grip of some bizarre madness, because the list of his felonies was lengthening by the hour, and before much longer would include unlawful entering and wilful damage to property. The fact that he would make good the wilful damage before leaving the property was of no relevance. The fact that he would very much like to have Hilary with him while he was committing the wilful damage was of no relevance either. He was going to keep Hilary clear of the unlawful stuff as far as possible but he would phone her that evening, as they had arranged; if it was not too late and if she did not live too far out it might be possible to meet. He smiled at the prospect.

When he reached the Harlequin Hilary was in the main office, apparently absorbed in a discussion with two people over what looked like a set of accounts spread over the desk. Robert handed over the envelope with the keys and his note, winked at Hilary when the others were not looking, and went back down to the street. This was something else that was probably part of the current madness, because he was not at all the kind of person who winked at people. The girlfriends he had had to date had all been very conventional and quiet, and it would never have occurred to Robert to wink at any of them in such a rakish fashion.

For about the hundredth time he thought Hilary was having a very peculiar effect on him.

Shona's day, which had started out so promisingly, had ended disappointingly.

The presentation for the radio plays had gone very well – the Harlequin might not actually get a specific credit in the programme, but it would get generalized credit with several programme editors for providing such a good freelance. This was deeply gratifying. However, the freelance, who had been so constructive during the presentation, had not been at all constructive when it came to more intimate matters. Invited to lunch, he said he would be delighted to accept, but would have to be back at Muswell Hill by four o'clock, because his partner would be expecting him. His partner turned out to be called Igor and played in a rap band called Russian Revolution and Shona, by that time committed to buying an expensive lunch at a fashionable little trattoria, had to remind herself that you could not win them all and that some could not be won at all. There was still the pleasant prospect of Robert Fallon that evening.

But it seemed, when she got back to the office, that she could not win any of them today and there was no prospect of Robert Fallon on that evening and probably not on any other evening either. He had left her a note explaining that he had found the errant damp meter in his car. Therefore he need not trouble Miss Seymour after all and here were the keys, returned with his thanks.

Shona, reading this in the privacy of her own office, frowned at the neat writing and the infuriatingly courteous phrases. It was a pity he had got away, because she had found him attractive. She liked his eyes which were deep set and clear grey, set under strong brows, and she liked the dark brown hair which was cropped, but so thick it would feel like fur or velvet if you caressed it. He had put on glasses to discuss the report with her. They were modern with steel frames, but somehow gave him the appearance of a nineteenth-century scholar. She was just considering phoning him in case something could be salvaged for the evening, when she saw Madeleine Ferrelyn's letter.

As soon as Shona read it, all thoughts of Robert vanished. So after all these years, the Tarleton was going be brought back into the light by this unknown lady, and any secrets that might lie in its bowels would be dragged up into the light. The old nightmare stirred slightly.

In the outer office the phone rang, and she heard Hilary answer it, but the sounds were muted and faintly distorted, as if Shona was encased in thick glass. The two people from accounts came down the stairs with the PR consultant, grumbling about having to face the underground and how the Northern Line got more crowded every week.

After this, silence fell, although Hilary was still working; Shona could hear the soft tap of the computer keyboard. For the first time she realized it had probably been Hilary who had opened Madeleine Ferrelyn's letter, which meant she must have read it. Taking the letter with her, she went out to Hilary's desk.

Hilary looked up and smiled. 'Are you working late, boss?'

'Not very late. I'm going home in a minute.' Shona perched on the edge of the desk and said without preamble, 'You read Madeleine Ferrelyn's letter, I expect?'

Hilary hesitated slightly, then said, 'Yes, I did. It wasn't marked private or anything so I opened it without thinking—'

'I didn't mean that. I wondered what you made of it?'

'Very intriguing,' said Hilary promptly, 'and very mysterious.'

'Most people who've ever worked here have thought the Tarleton's mysterious and intriguing,' said Shona. 'I certainly have. We've never been told much about it: I probably don't know a great deal more than you.' She could almost feel Hilary's disbelief at this, but before Hilary could speak, she said, 'The instructions to the Harlequin Society about the Tarleton are very clear. We're managing agents and we have to keep it maintained, weatherproof and insured against all the usual risks. We also send in contract cleaners a couple of times a year – that isn't strictly necessary in an unused building, but we do it anyway. And we check that the pipes are sound and the electrical wiring isn't a fire risk. You know all that. The accounts go to a bank and they authorize all payments and settle everything on a quarterly basis. You probably know that as well. Over the years I've passed on any requests to buy the place or lease it, or put on the odd show or exhibition there, but the bank have always said the same thing: their client won't give permission. Their instructions are as specific as ours: the place has to stay sealed up and there's never been any hint as to why.'

'And it's been sealed up for more than ninety years,' said Hilary thoughtfully.

'Yes. My predecessor had to agree that we would only ever deal with the bank and that we would respect the request for secrecy until the restraint was lifted. I had to do the same.' She paused, then said, 'Strictly between us, Hilary, I do know that my former boss checked land registries and transfers of property to see if he could find out the owner's name, but he didn't find anything.' She did not normally talk to her staff quite so openly – she did not, in fact, talk to anyone so openly – but the Tarleton had always made her uncomfortable and it was rather a relief to be discussing it like this.

Hilary said, 'Isn't it a bit suspicious that there were no records?'

'No, not necessarily. The land was probably never registered. Nowadays there's a requirement to register any parcel of un-registered land if there's a change of ownership, but that didn't come into force until the late 1980s. And it doesn't sound as if the theatre has changed owner for a very long time. It sounds as if Madeleine Ferrelyn inherited direct from her father—'

'Who died in the late 1950s.'

'Yes. That means he could have owned it since the early part of the twentieth century.'

'Even as far back as 1914,' said Hilary. 'We've all speculated a bit about it, you know.'

'Of course I know. That's human nature.'

'But we didn't know there was a definite restriction in force.'

'I've never known the exact terms of it. I've always assumed it was some eccentric who owned it and that it never would reopen.'

'And now this,' said Hilary, glancing at the letter.

'As you say, now this. At least we know the owner's name at last, although not much more than that. But clearly I'll have to go down to Somerset to see her.' She paused. 'Would you like to come with me?'

It was obvious Hilary had not been expecting this. She looked startled, and then said, 'Oh. Yes, I would like to. Very much.'

'Good. Two heads are better than one for these things, and it sounds as if Madeleine Ferrelyn might want to involve us in the actual reopening which would be a plum for us. But if she intends it to be a living theatre again she'll want ideas and proposals. That's never been my strength, but it's one of yours. Could you draft a few ideas?'

'Yes, I could,' said Hilary with unmistakable enthusiasm. 'I'd love to.'

'Good.' Shona stood up. 'I'm a strong believer in striking while the iron's hot, so I'll phone her now and find out when she'd be free. We ought to be able to get there and back in a day if we set off early enough.'

She went into her office, closing the door, and Hilary, determined not to listen, opened a new blank screen on the computer, typed in the heading, 'The Tarleton', and enthusiastically began to make notes.

'It's more or less fixed,' said Shona, coming out fifteen minutes later. 'But she's asked if it can be tomorrow.'

'As soon as that?' Hilary was a bit taken aback.

'I hadn't expected it, either. I rather got the impression that having made up her mind to deal with this peculiar situation, she wants to get to grips with it before she can get cold feet. I don't see why we couldn't go out there tomorrow, though. I've got another meeting with the radio people at ten tomorrow—'

'The Edwardian spa plays,' said Hilary, remembering.

'Yes, and I can't cancel it because it's important to us. But we could set off about twelve, have lunch on the road, and be in Somerset about four.'

'That would mean an overnight stay.'

'Yes,' said Shona slowly. 'Mrs Ferrelyn has offered to put us up for the night, but I'm a bit hesitant to accept until we know more about her. Also, she mentioned not being in very good health. There's bound to be a local pub or a Travel Lodge or something. What about it, Hilary? Could you be available so quickly? Is there anything here you can't put on hold? Or anything at home?'

'I'd put anything on hold for the Tarleton, anyway,' said Hilary at once. 'I'd camp out in a field for it if I had to. Thank you very much for involving me.' Her eyes were shining and Shona could see she was already conjuring up ideas. Hilary said, 'What did Madeleine Ferrelyn sound like?'

'Elderly, certainly. But not noticeably frail or affected by any illness. Brisk and intelligent, in fact. She says she has a few ideas she'll put to us, but she's out of touch with modern theatre and modern marketing, so she'll leave most of it to us.'

'That'll be good,' said Hilary at once. 'Did she mention her father? The owner who created the restriction?'

'No, and I didn't ask. Can I use this phone to call her back to confirm? She says it's a three-hour journey, but I think we'd better allow a good four; it'll take us an hour to get clear of London. Oh – would you check availability at the nearest Travel Lodge or somewhere similar?'

'Yes, of course. And I'll get out some preliminary outlines to take with us. I'll have tonight and tomorrow morning to work on that.'

'I shouldn't think she'll expect anything elaborate at such short notice,' said Shona. 'This will be more a courtesy thing: an initial handshake. But we can get a sense of what she wants us to do, and we can tell her how far the Harlequin can actually take things.' She had been about to tap out the phone number, but she paused. 'Hilary, have you told the others about the letter?'

'No.'

'Ah. Then I think we'll keep this between the two of us for the moment. Everything about that place has always been so odd – I don't think this is a scam of any kind and the bank letter is certainly from the branch we've dealt with all these years, although I'll call them in the morning to check. But even if this Ferrelyn woman is the owner, it doesn't guarantee her sanity.'

She waited to see if Hilary would pick up her meaning and was pleased when Hilary said, 'Far from it. In fact you'd expect anyone owning a valuable London property like the Tarleton to try to find a way round that restriction.'

'Exactly. So the fewer people who know about this, the better, at least until we're sure of the ground.' She broke off, thinking. 'I don't normally like asking staff to lie, but could you possibly say you're taking a couple of days' holiday?'

'Yes, I could do that.'

'Good. It won't actually be counted as holiday, of course.'

'I wouldn't care if it was,' said Hilary.

'I can phone in to say those Radio 4 meetings have extended into the afternoon – no one's likely to question that. Good. I'll phone her back to confirm.'

Shona was businesslike but polite on the phone, saying she and her assistant, Hilary Bryant, would be with Mrs Ferrelyn the following day, around four o'clock, traffic permitting. No, they would not need to be put up for the night, they would book into an hotel somewhere – Well, if Mrs Ferrelyn was sure? They did not want to put her to any trouble . . .

When Shona put the phone down, she made a wry gesture to Hilary. 'She says there aren't any hotels for miles, and the local pubs and guest houses only do bed and breakfast in spring and summer. And it's absolutely no trouble if we stay at Levels House, because she has plenty of space, and a girl goes in a couple of times a week from the village to help with cleaning and so on: she'll ask her to make up a couple of beds.'

'I'm happy with that if you are,' said Hilary.

'I'll pick you up from your flat,' said Shona. 'I'll come straight there from the meeting – I'll phone to let you know when that finishes.'

'That would be great. I'll take all the Tarleton stuff home with me tonight – I'll leave a note on my desk saying I've got an unexpected family thing and I'm taking two days' holiday. I can put in a bit of work on the proposals at home tomorrow morning.'

'Thanks, Hilary.' Shona got up from the edge of the desk. 'Don't forget to lock up when you leave.'

'I won't. Goodnight, boss.'

CHAPTER SIXTEEN

Robert had decided to wait until half past seven before entering the Tarleton. He thought by this time Shona Seymour should have left her office and be on her way to wherever she lived.

He worked systematically through what remained of the afternoon, dictating the report of the warehouse survey, leaving the tape for the secretary he and his partner shared so it could be typed and despatched tomorrow. When possible they tried to post all surveys to clients within twenty-four hours of the actual work being completed. It could not be done every time because sometimes expert reports had to be obtained on drains, or samples of foundation soil had to be sent for analysis, but they were as prompt as they could be and their small company had become known as reliable and efficient. Robert thought that was why they had been appointed to the panel for the Theatres Preservation Trust.

At a quarter to seven he assembled the items he would need. These included a heavy-headed mallet and a small sledgehammer; carrying them from the car to the theatre would probably give him a hernia, but that could not be helped. He had bought a pack of plaster filler in the DIY centre – the kind sold in the thousands to people who were redecorating their houses and needed a very small quantity for areas of uneven plasterwork. He added a plastic bottle of water for mixing the filler and a triangular spatula, and finally enclosed the whole lot in a dustsheet.

He had no idea how easy it would be to knock out any of the bricks in the underground room: a properly mortared wall would not yield very easily to a few bashes from a sledgehammer wielded by one person, but the Tarleton's wall had not looked very well mortared. For safety's sake he was going to knock out bricks near the ceiling, and since the underground room had no electricity any holes he could not repair should go unnoticed.

He was not quite managing to ignore the memory of the intruder he and Hilary had encountered, but he had convinced himself that the man was a local eccentric or an oddball who had seen them go inside and followed them in to give them a fright. It would be a sick thing to do, but there were a lot of sick people around. There were also a lot of people who were perfectly normal who hummed snatches of song to themselves.

By this time he had given up trying to rationalize his emotions or his actions; what he did know was that this old theatre had got so deeply beneath his skin he did not think he would be able to concentrate properly on anything else until he had found out what was at the heart of the mystery. He didn't know how much of this feeling was due to Hilary, because she seemed to have got quite deeply beneath his skin as well. He was not yet sure what he was going to do about her, but he knew what he was going to do about the Tarleton, and that was get behind the wall.

When he unlocked the stage door and stepped into the well of darkness beyond, the scent and atmosphere of the old theatre enfolded him, and he smiled, thinking that any ghosts present tonight were friendly ones. He locked the door behind him, trying not to remember that the intruder had not been kept out by locks last time. As he went down the echoing passage, past the door-keeper's room where he and Hilary had hidden, he was annoyed to realize he was listening for the soft singing. He pushed the memory away and went down the second passageway that led below ground, the light of his torch slicing through the shadows.

Despite all the reassurances he had given himself, he was already starting to regret this mad expedition – and if he were to be found out he would be unceremoniously drummed out of the Royal Institution of Chartered Surveyors – but having got this far he would be furious with himself if he ducked out now. Also, Hilary would be disappointed if he told her he had chickened out halfway through; the thought of her disappointment spurred him on, and he pushed the heavy oak door and wedged it open. Everywhere was silent and wholly unthreatening, and he went determinedly down the steps, the torchlight picking out the worn treads and thick layers of dust and cobwebs clinging to the walls.

Once in the underground room he slung the haversack on the ground, and dragged one of the wicker skips out, positioning the torch on it so it would cast a reasonable working light. After this he turned to study the wall more closely, seeing that the mortar had been so roughly applied or so badly mixed that large sections of it had fallen out or crumbled to nothing. In places the wall was very nearly drystone, which should make it easier than he had hoped to knock out a small section. He placed the flat of both hands against its surface. It felt rough and cold, although he had expected that. What he had not expected was the sudden impression that someone was standing on the other side of the wall – barely a foot from him – and that this someone was also pressing his hands against the wall in an eerie mirror image of Robert's actions. For a truly dreadful moment he thought there was a whisper of sound from beyond the wall: as if the other person was saying, here I am, Robert ... I'm waiting for you ... I've been waiting a very long time ...

But this was nothing more than nerves and the sooner he satisfied his curiosity and got out of here, the better. It was now ten to eight, so in an hour's time he should be back in Platt's Alley, and with luck by quarter past nine – half past at the latest – he could be phoning Hilary from his car.

He unfolded the dustsheet and arranged it on the ground, because although it was disgustingly dirty down here he wanted to leave as little trace of his activities as possible. He would have liked to bring the extending ladder, but toting it along the street would have been dangerously conspicuous. Instead, he dragged a second, larger skip close to the wall, and laid the chisel, mallet and sledgehammer on top of it. After this, he checked his pocket for the spare torch, then climbed onto the skip, testing it cautiously first, relieved that it seemed to bear his weight. Cobwebs, disturbed by the movement, trailed ghostly fingers on his face and he brushed them away impatiently.

Even by stretching his arms to the utmost, he could not quite reach the cellar roof, which meant he would have to work on the bricks several layers down. It was unlikely that the removal of a small section of bricks would demolish the entire wall but Robert was taking no chances. It would be safer to work as near the ceiling as possible.

Focussing on a section of bricks four courses down from the ceiling, he swung the sledgehammer. It swished through the air and struck the bricks with a startlingly loud sound in the enclosed space. Robert winced as a cloud of dust showered down, gritty and dry and old-smelling, but when the dust cleared he saw that several of the bricks had cracked. So far so good. He swung the sledgehammer a second time, and then a third, and three bricks yielded, falling inwards and hitting the ground with a brittle splintering sound. A small breath of stale air gusted out from beyond the wall and Robert flinched, but was aware of a sudden surge of triumph. I'm going to do it. I'm really going to find out what this wall is concealing. He felt for the torch in his pocket and shone it through the small hole, but his line of vision was too restricted and he could see nothing but thick blackness. He would have to knock out several more bricks and he would also have to make sure they fell on this side because he wanted to replace as many as he could.

Moving with extreme caution, using the small chisel and trowel, he began to chip at the remaining mortar. It showered out in a pale powdery stream, but a few of the bricks loosened almost at once. Robert lifted out a couple, setting them on the dustsheet for remortaring in when he had finished.

After twenty minutes he had prised out six more bricks and laid them next to the first two. He shone the torch again, but although this time he thought there was a shadowy outline over to the left, the opening was still too small to see very much. He began to chisel at the mortar again, and this time the systematic tapping created a small echo from beyond the wall. Or was the echo on this side of the wall? Robert felt a thump of apprehension, but when he shone the torch round the cellar nothing moved and he returned to his task. Moments afterwards the echo came again and this time it sounded like footsteps in the passageway above. He froze, his heart pounding, his eyes fixed on the stairs, listening intently. What would he do if he heard that singing again? Or if a figure suddenly appeared on the steps, sharply black in the torchlight, but unmistakably dressed in a long overcoat and an old-fashioned hat with a deep brim hiding its face?

But even if there was someone up there, it was unlikely that person would have heard sounds all the way down here. Or was it? Robert himself had heard the noises down here, even through the layers of brick and timber. He stayed where he was, watching and listening for what felt like a long time, but when he glanced at his watch only about ten minutes had passed. There's no one there, he thought. It was just the timbers creaking or peculiar acoustics somewhere.

He turned back to the jagged opening in the wall. A foetid miasma came from it and Robert remembered how close the river was. He shone the torch inside again, and this time made out a tall oblong of something that might be wood or metal and that extended as far upwards as he could see, vanishing into the shadows overhead. The frame of the grave trap? It must be. It was more or less as he had thought: a rudimentary lift shaft, oblong in shape, and as far as he could see made of wood and metal strips. The sight of this monolith standing silently in the dark was slightly sinister. But why had such a large area of good storage space been made so completely inaccessible? To say nothing of losing the grave trap itself?

It was then that he heard what sounded like footsteps in the passageway upstairs and he turned sharply to look at the steps, then sprang off the skip and, holding the torch in one hand and the mallet in the other, went softly back up the steps and into the passage. He was aware of the absurdity of beating off a ghost with a mallet; he didn't believe in ghosts, anyway. What he did believe in were burglars and drug addicts – and poor sods of homeless people on the lookout for an unlocked door and an empty building in which to spend the night. But he had locked the stage door when he came in.

Nothing stirred in the stone passageways, but Robert went determinedly along to the stage door to make sure it really was locked. Yes, locked firmly. He glanced into the stage doorkeeper's room, but it was bland and unthreatening and he went back down to the cellar and renewed his assault on the wall. This time several more bricks tumbled out, and when he shone the torch he could see the complete outline of the grave trap. It was black and forbidding and even through the thick cobwebs and layers of dirt, the iron framework glinted in the torchlight. The curious thing was that as he moved the torch slowly round he had the impression that something in the atmosphere had shifted – it was almost as if something that had been crouching in the dark had looked up at the sudden intrusion and ingress of light. This would be sheer nerves, nothing more, and so far Robert could still see no reason for the amateurishly built wall or for the mystery that surrounded the theatre and its long closure. All that was beyond the wall was the other half of the cellar – the half that extended directly beneath the stage. When he shone the torch upwards he could see the joists supporting the stage itself, and there did not seem to be anything out of the ordinary. He was conscious of disappointment, because after the build-up – after the legends about ghosts and ninety-year twilight slumbers, and the secrecy surrounding the owner's identity – he had expected to find *something*. But there was nothing.

Or was there? He moved the torchlight over the grave trap mechanism again and this time was aware of a stir of apprehension. Something's not quite right, he thought. Something within the trap's mechanism, is it? He reached for the second torch, and shone both of them together, so that the light cast a wider, stronger circle. It showed up the trap more sharply: the inner platform – the floor – was at the very top of the shaft, as he and Hilary had already discovered. Robert could see it quite clearly, and he could see two thick L-shaped brackets holding it in place. Puzzlement stirred again: why had someone gone to so much trouble to seal this place up so very completely?

He brought the light down again and a face – a shrivelled, yellowed, sightless face, jumped into focus in the glare of the torches. Robert's heart leapt into his throat, and he heard himself say aloud, 'Oh God, oh no, oh no . . .' In the enclosed space his words whispered and trickled in the shadowy corners.

Lying directly under the iron platform, half twisted round one of the wood and metal struts, was an unmistakable outline. Human, thought Robert, trying not to shake. A human body. At least, I suppose it's a human body – I suppose it isn't some macabre old stage prop that's been left down here.

But he knew it was not a stage prop. He knew that what he was seeing was a very old dead body. It had been virtually mummified by some quirk of the airless atmosphere, and all that was left of some poor man or woman who had lain down here for so many years were bones and hair and dried skin. He sat down on the wicker skip, shaking and slightly sickened. Was this the secret? Was this what had been hidden all these years? But part of his mind was already saying: but why so very long? Why has the Tarleton been so fiercely guarded for almost a century?

He beat down a compulsion to run back up the stairs and into the safe normality of the streets, and forced himself to climb back onto the skip and shine the torch again. From this distance he could not tell if it was a man or a woman who lay there – he was not sure if he would be able to tell even if he was standing next to it. He could make out what must once have been clothes, but they were worn almost to threads by damp or nibbling creatures or simply by sheer age and it was impossible to know what they had originally been. He looked at the head again, trying not to wince at the way the lips had shrunk so that the teeth were exposed in a grinning snarl and at the sightless eyes. Strands of hair, faded and dried-out, adhered to the scalp, which Robert found almost unbearably pitiful. He moved the torch downwards. The feet had the remains of leather shoes or boots; they looked substantial and masculine, but they could as easily have been the high button-boots Victorian and Edwardian ladies wore.

You're absolutely anonymous, said Robert silently. Are you a murderer's victim? I suppose you must be. But were you killed somewhere else and your body hidden here and walled up? Or was it a macabre accident – did that thing crash down on you and kill you? He shone the torch onto the underside of the steel platform again. Was it mottled and stained? Were the marks old blood-stains or just mildew?

But whoever you were, he said, looking back at the body, someone – perhaps several someones – didn't want you found for nearly a hundred years.

At least half of him wanted to brick up the wall and forget what was behind it. This half pointed out, very persuasively, that no matter what he did, it would not make the smallest difference to the incumbent of the cellar. It might be possible to establish the cause of death – although that would depend on the cause – but it would not be very easy for anyone to track down the body's identity after so long. And even if that identity were eventually established, it was unlikely that the killer would ever be known. That being so, it would be the simplest thing in the world to repair the wall, tidy it all up and leave everything as it had been. And no one would be any the wiser.

Except that Robert would be the wiser. He would feel he had somehow let down that unknown man or woman. If he replaced the bricks neatly enough to conceal what he had done – as he had originally intended – and walked away from this, he would never be able to forget that vulnerable heap of bones. He would certainly not be able to forget how the face had seemed to be turned eagerly towards him as if waiting to be rescued and as if rescue had at last come. Were you dead when you were put there? thought Robert, packing away his tools. Or did you have to lie helplessly in that cellar and watch the wall being built, seeing the light gradually shut off, knowing you were going to die alone in the dark? He remembered that odd impression he had earlier of someone standing on the other side of the wall, listening and mirroring his own actions.

He left the wall exactly as it was, and went back up the stairs. By the time he stepped out through the stage door, locking it behind him, it was a quarter to ten. He would have to report what he had found to the police, although he would do his best to play down his own reprehensible behaviour. And if the Harlequin Society or the Tarleton's owner decided to make an official complaint, Robert would have to face the consequences. He had no idea what the consequences might be; he would make the point that he had been concerned as to what the wall might be hiding, but he was uncomfortably aware that he had secretly had a set of keys cut and that he had partly demolished a wall against the specific instructions of the Harlequin, who acted for the owner.

Once in Burbage Street, he paused, drawing in deep breaths of the cold night air, grateful for the noisy normality of the streets. It was raining: a fine drizzly rain like thin mist, but Robert would not have minded if it had been a blizzard. People were walking along in twos and threes, laughing and talking, and there were lights everywhere from cars and from the restaurants and bars. The lights were blurred by the rain and the people were a bit blurred as well, and there was a dreamlike quality to it all. He turned up his coat collar and walked down Burbage Street, but he had only gone a few yards when he glanced back and caught sight of a figure who had paused at the alley's entrance as if looking into the narrow cul-de-sac. Robert drew in a small sharp gasp. The figure was outlined against the rushing people and cars, but it seemed to be wearing a long coat and a slouch hat, pulled well forward . . . It was surely nothing more than a passer-by, muffled up against the cold rain, and yet . . .

He blinked and rubbed his eyes, and when he looked again the figure had gone. Tiredness, nothing more. Anyone would see phantoms after being down in that ghost-ridden old place with the remains of a body lying within a few feet. As he went towards the car park, above the hum of the night traffic he heard the distant chimes of some nearby clock striking the hour. He thought it might be from St Bride's church, and he thought he had never heard a sound as sweet and reassuring and blessedly *normal*.

By now he was feeling slightly better, although he was still a bit light-headed. He remembered he had not eaten since lunchtime and went into one of the late-night sandwich bars for cheese rolls and a can of Coke. At the all-night chemist farther along he bought a pack of moistened tissues because he probably looked as if he had been climbing half the Victorian chimneys in London. He had considered whether to wash in the old-fashioned lavatory in the Tarleton's foyer, but the water might not be turned on and in any case he wanted to get out as fast as possible. But the interview with the police was going to be a complicated one and Robert was damned if he was going to report finding a dead body in his present grubby state.

He sat in his car and drank the Coke almost at one go, grateful for the cold sharp taste, then wolfed down the rolls. Marvellous. The finest gourmet meal in the world could not compete with bread and cheese when you were really ravenous. After this he managed to wipe most of the brick dust from his face and hands with several of the tissues, then he drove out of the car park towards Canon Row police station.

The police were polite and efficient, but by the time Robert had explained the situation to three of them in turn, he was beginning to feel light-headed all over again, or as if he had fallen backwards into a dream belonging to someone he did not know. He knew, logically, that this was nervous reaction, but he found it difficult to push the feeling away and give a clear account.

At first he thought no one was going to believe him and he supposed they could not be blamed. They must have heard some weird stories over the years, but this midnight tale of a half-mummified body in the bowels of a deserted music hall must rank as particularly bizarre.

He told them he had surveyed the Tarleton in his professional capacity a couple of days earlier – at that point, by way of credentials, he handed them his business card – but explained that a second visit had been necessary to make sure of the underpinning to the main cellar. For this reason, he had removed a few bricks from an underground wall, to shine a torch through, said Robert. Well, no, he did not agree that it was late to be carrying out the work; he had deliberately saved this particular job for the very end of the day because he knew it would involve brick dust, and after he had done it he could go straight home and shower. He implied, without actually saying it, that he still had the official keys to get into the Tarleton and also that the owner's agents were aware of what he was doing. This was the kind of slick deceit he hated and it would rebound on him when Shona Seymour discovered what had happened, but Robert was going to worry about that tomorrow.

He described again what he had seen beyond the brick wall;

when questioned, he said yes, he was perfectly sure it was a real body, no, he did not think it was an old stage prop, he had thought of that for himself and he was absolutely sure.

In the end, they asked if he would mind coming along to the Tarleton there and then, so they could check all this out.

'Not in the least,' said Robert, who had already given up any thoughts of seeing his own flat and his bed until one a.m. at the earliest. 'I've left my car in an all-night multi-storey, so I'll have to collect it . . .'

But it seemed it would not be necessary for him to retrieve his car; the sergeant, along with someone from CID, would take a patrol car. 'Easier for parking, sir,' he said.

Being whisked through London in a police car shortly before midnight was not an experience Robert had ever expected to have, but it added to the surreal quality of the whole thing. This quality increased when he produced his keys and ushered the CID sergeant and his side-kick into the Tarleton, and down to the cellars.

The DS, whose name was Stuart Treadwell and who was about Robert's age, but casually dressed in denim jeans and a leather jacket, studied the broken wall for a few moments, then got onto the wicker skip and shone a torch through the gap.

'Oh yes,' he said at length. 'Yes, I see now what you mean. There's no question about it. Human remains for certain. It's very odd, isn't it?'

'Yes, very,' said Robert.

'It's half under that structure – what did you call it?'

'It's a grave trap. It works on the principle of a lift shaft, I think. But if you shine the torch all the way up, you can see where the platform – the floor – is bolted to the underside of the stage.'

Treadwell shone the torch and nodded, then glanced down at Robert. 'It must have been a bit of a shock to you, suddenly seeing a body in there.'

'It was.'

'You were intending to check – what did you say it was?'

'Underpinning and also evidence of river seepage into the foundations,' said Robert.

'I see. Well, I think,' said Treadwell, getting down off the skip, 'that we'll have to dismantle a lot more of this wall, although we're not going to do that tonight, of course. You're sure there's no other way of getting into that part of the cellar?'

'No. I went all over this place. That whole area is sealed off. You can't even get down from the stage through the trap opening.' Robert was glad to remember that he and Hilary had replaced the wooden section over the trap fairly neatly.

'Well, whoever our body is, or was,' said Treadwell, dusting down his jeans, 'it looks as if someone took a lot of trouble to make sure it wouldn't be found for a long time. I can't tell if it's male or female from here, but we've got a department who deals with this kind of cold case. They'll need to bring in spotlights and forensics and so on; I'll crank up the machinery for that as soon as we get back. It may be a natural death, although the circumstances are peculiar. Oh, we'll need you to supply an official statement, Mr Fallon.'

'Yes, of course.'

'But first off, we'll have to contact the owner.' He looked around him. 'Weird old building, isn't it?'

You don't know the half of it, thought Robert, but he said, 'I dealt with the Harlequin Society who act as agents for the owner. I can let you have the address and phone number.'

'If you would. We'll get in touch with them first thing tomorrow.' He led the way back upstairs. 'What we'd better do now, though, is make sure you get home all right. We'll hop you back to your car now – you're all right to drive home, are you? Where is home, by the way?'

Robert gave the address of his flat for about the fifth time that night, and said he was perfectly capable of driving home but would appreciate the hop back to his own car.

'No problem,' said Treadwell. 'How about if we get you to come back to the station tomorrow to make a proper statement? Say around two?'

Robert said two o'clock would be fine, and drove home with the car windows wound all the way down to dispel the musty claustrophobia of the cellar. As he unlocked his own front door, he thought he would ring Hilary as early as possible in the morning to explain what had happened. It would be better not to tell her all this while she was at her office, but presumably she would not leave her flat until around quarter past or twenty past eight, so he would phone just after eight.

He showered away the ancient dust that clung to him and thought soap and shampoo had never smelt so good in his whole life. Falling gratefully into bed, he hoped he would not dream about the unknown man or woman who had lain in the dark for all these years.

As he slid down into sleep, he wondered what on earth he was going to say to Hilary. He also wondered what he was going to say to Shona Seymour.

CHAPTER SEVENTEEN

Shona had reached home at half past six that evening which, given the average London rush hour, was almost a record.

Her flat was in a small wharf conversion near Allhallows Lane. The conversion had been done in the property conscious era of the yuppies about fifteen years ago; the flats were smart and sleek and Shona could not possibly have afforded to live here if her ex-boss had not given her the down-payment to buy the lease. She had initially refused it, but had managed to do so without any real conviction, intending him to renew the offer. He had done so, of course, and she had accepted because she was fed up with her cramped rooms in Tabard Square and anyway her boss could easily afford it. Once she moved in she made it a rule to invite him to dinner and bed at least once a month. She usually had the food sent in – there were several small restaurants in the area which would put together a meal and deliver it – but she always served everything on her own plates and left an apparently used saucepan or casserole dish in the kitchen, because her boss liked to think that as well as being an inventive and enthusiastic lover she was a good cook, and there was no point in spoiling the image.

She enjoyed living in the new flat. People said, 'Oh, what a nuisance for you to have to drive across the river to your office each day,' but Shona did not mind in the least. She liked driving in London; it confirmed that she now belonged to a world that had nothing to do with Grith House. The Shona who wore sharp modern clothes and zapped confidently along London streets had nothing to do with the Shona who had lived at Moil.

She had bought her first car with a small bank loan when she was twenty (Grandfather would have been shocked, and quoted the old line about neither a borrower nor a lender be), and her boss had paid for her driving lessons. He said it would be useful to the Harlequin if she could drive, so he would charge the lessons against his expense account and Shona need not feel guilty about accepting the money.

Shona had not felt guilty in the least, and after she passed her test she devised saucy little trips into the country for the two of them, and parked in remote areas so they could make love on the back seat. On these occasions she wore hold-up stockings under her skirt and nothing else. Her boss found it immensely arousing, and the danger of being seen added to the excitement for him. Shona did not much care if they were seen; what she did care about was paying her dues. It did not matter whether you paid your dues in cash, or whether you did so by stripping off in a secluded corner of Epping Forest: the important thing was never to owe anybody anything in life. Grandfather would have approved of this principle, although he certainly would not have approved of the form the payment took.

The Allhallows flat was on the second floor and had large windows with views over the Thames. This alone made it worth the hassle of negotiating Southwark Bridge each day. Shona liked to sit on the balcony on summer evenings, drinking a glass of wine and watching the river traffic; it was another of the things that distanced her from Grith House. She enjoyed thinking how dourly disapproving her grandfather would have been if he could see her enjoying what he would have called the fruits of sin. The sinning with her boss was not, in fact, particularly fruity, and as far as Shona was concerned it was money driven rather than passion driven. Even so, her grandfather would have called her a Jezebel and a painted whore of Babylon. He had been a humourless old martinet, and Shona was very glad to think he was safely dead and would never appear in her life again. She was glad that the boring pair, her mother and her cousin, would never appear in her life again, either.

The view from her flat's windows changed all the time. Tonight there was a faint mist rising from the river; it was not as thick as the mists that used to lie over Moil Moor when she was a child, but it was sufficient to stir the surface of her memory slightly. Shona could remember how she used to kneel on the windowseat in her bedroom watching the mists form, seeing ghost-figures inside them, frightened something was creeping towards the house ... *You were always frightened that it was me, weren't you?* whispered Anna's voice. *You thought I was stealing through the mists towards you ...*

It was extraordinary how clear Anna's voice still was at times, even after so many years. Shona frowned, closed the curtains on the Thames and its troublesome mistiness, and went into the bedroom to change out of her suit. It was an expensive suit, a sharp charcoal grey with a narrow skirt, and she had worn a fuchsia-coloured silk shirt under it. She had only left two buttons of the shirt unfastened for the office because at the moment there was no one there worth seducing, but she had unfastened an extra one for the doe-eyed researcher. It was a great pity the unfastening of this third button had been a waste of time and it was also a pity Shona had put on her new ivory silk underwear that morning. Grandfather, had he ever seen the ivory silk, would probably have condemned it as harlot's wear, and Mother and Cousin Elspeth, if told how much it had cost, would have been shocked to their toes and called it a wicked waste of money, quite apart from Shona catching her death of cold in such flimsy things. But they would have approved of it being put carefully away in the wardrobe, because they would not have thought it right to sit around the flat in office clothes. Shona did not think it right, either; it was one of the very few Grith House tenets that had stayed with her. She was not going out this evening so she pulled on jeans and a loose sweater.

Jeans had never been remotely considered as suitable garments at Grith House and would not have been tolerated. Edna and Mona Cheesewright on their twice weekly visits to Grith wore print overalls, and Mona sometimes wound a woollen scarf round her neck because Grith was a right old shocker for draughts and if she got a stiff neck it ran all down her arms. Shona, entering her teens, had pleaded to wear jeans and trainers like everyone else but was not allowed. She had to wear her school uniform during the week, jumpers and skirts at weekends and her afternoon dress on Sundays with her good coat over it for church. Looking back, she often thought it was as if Grith had got stuck around 1940, and never quite caught up with the modern age. Even in the relaxed late-1970s her mother still followed the practice of wearing second or third best in the mornings, with an afternoon dress for when lunch was over.

Mother had been wearing one of her afternoon dresses the day the water main burst somewhere in the valley, and men from the Water Board came out to Grith House because of it. Shona had not really understood what it was all about, but she had pretended to know because of being thirteen, which was practically grown up.

The Water Board men said the problem was caused by all the heavy rain after the long dry summer, and they would need to get to the mains water pipe. The man who had introduced himself as the foreman asked if there was a Mr Seymour and indicated he preferred to have a man to deal with. Mother said, with a tight-lipped expression, that there was no Mr Seymour; there had been a Mr Ross, who was her father, but he had died quite recently. Elspeth chimed in, saying they knew all about Grith House and could answer any questions about its structure perfectly well.

'What we need is to get to the mains pipe,' said the foreman again. 'They'll likely be in the cellar—'

Mother bleated something about the cellar always being locked on account of it being dangerous and no one ever going down there, and Shona saw her eyes go nervously to the screen halfway across the door in the corner of the hall. The foreman saw it as well and said, 'Is the cellar entrance over there? Yes, I see it is. Just behind the old screen. We can easily move that to one side. And if you'd kindly get the key, Mrs Seymour.'

Elspeth was saying something about a lot of upheaval, and Mother made ineffectual little darting movements at the men, trying to stop them moving the screen, making stupid excuses about not expecting this, no warning and everywhere in such a mess, oh dear me.

'We'll put everything to rights afterwards,' said the foreman firmly. 'But it won't do to let all that pumping water flood the whole of Moil. More than our jobs are worth.'

Shona thought he sounded a bit sarcastic when he said that about putting everything to rights, which was understandable; you could not say Grith was a palace, what with the sooty rooms and leaky gutters and the draughts whistling in under the rattly doors.

'I'm not at all sure I know where the key is after all these years,' said her mother, to which the foreman said that was unfortunate, because it meant they would have to smash the lock to get down there.

They were polite but unstoppable and in the end the key had to be fetched and the door had to be unlocked. Mother was quite a long time getting the key, when she came back there was a faint smell of whisky. Shona was sent into the dining room, because surely there was homework for her to be getting on with – or *something* for her to be getting on with? She went obediently, but she could smell the Moil Moor odour coming up from the cellar already. Like bad drains on a hot day. She left the dining-room door partly open so she could watch and hear everything. The Water Board officials clattered down the stone steps with Shona's mother following, while Cousin Elspeth went mutteringly away to get buckets and mops and cloths because you could not trust men not to make a mess.

Shona waited until Elspeth, carrying a pail of hot soapy water and hung about with brooms and cloths, had gone down the steps as well, then she came out of the dining room, hoping that if she was very quiet and careful no one would notice her. As she stepped warily through the cellar door the nightmare stirred faintly and there was the warning lurch of sickness at the pit of her stomach. But she went on because this might be the only chance she would ever get to find out what was behind that wall.

Silly! said Anna's voice in her head. *You already know what's behind the wall. You've known for four years. I told you I was getting nearer*, said Anna.

Shona hated the way Anna tried to grab her attention when something interesting was happening. She ignored her and edged down the first two steps, ready to scoot back into the dining room if anyone saw her. Her heart was thudding but she went down a third step and then a fourth until she could see all the way into the brick-lined cellar. There were the Water Board men rigging up lights; they had tried running an extension lead up to the hall, but Grith's wiring was so old that none of the plugs had fitted the extension, so Cousin Elspeth had looked out the storm lanterns they used in power cuts. The men had large torches as well, and they were setting out bags of tools and a dustsheet and they were exclaiming over little puddles of water on the ground. Shona could see the water that had seeped out from behind the wall: it gleamed slimily in the light and it looked like black blood.

But there was no blood that night. Don't you remember, Shona, that there was no blood?

Shona's mind began to fill with the familiar fear. For a moment she could hear the mortar being slapped into place, just as it was in the nightmare, and she could smell the wet cement and the old bricks that had been taken from the ruined wall in Grith's gardens . . . And then she thought: how do I know that about that old wall being used?

Because you saw it happen, said Anna's voice. *You saw them carry the bricks down here and build the wall. The bricks came from the old garden wall – they didn't dare draw attention to themselves by ordering anything from a builder's yard.*

The ruined garden wall had been all that was left of a much older house that had stood here a long time ago. When Shona was very small and guests still used to come to Grith, some of them had sketched the wall or painted it in watercolours. Ivy grew over parts of it and people said it was picturesque and Gothic, and how nice to see these fragments of the past. Shona realized she could remember the wall being there but not when or why it vanished.

In the underground room, the foreman was being stern about the trickling water. 'See that, Mrs Seymour? That'll be where the problem is. Straight on the other side of this wall. That's where your pipes are. Mains water, and sewage and waste alongside, very likely. Not a good arrangement, but I daresay it's been like that for a long while.'

'I suppose it must have been. You aren't going to knock out the wall, surely?'

The foreman said he was very sorry, but that was just what they were going to do.

'Oh no,' said Mother at once. 'No, I can't possibly give permission for that,' and Elspeth planted herself in front of the wall and said doughtily that it was a sad day if two unprotected females had to stand by and allow men to damage their home.

'I'm afraid this is an emergency situation,' said the foreman kindly but firmly. 'It gives us powers to go wherever necessary. We don't need anyone's permission. Maybe it'd be best if you went back upstairs, Mrs Seymour. And Miss Ross as well. No? Then stand aside now . . .'

They had sledgehammers and mallets, and the sledgehammers, plied with energy, fell bruisingly on the bricks. Showers of gritty-looking dust came down, but although the wall shivered it remained stubbornly in place. 'Again,' said the foreman, and the hammers struck the wall again. Old, bad-smelling brick dust began to cloud the cellar, and the pounding of the sledgehammers began to resonate inside Shona's head like a drumbeat. Or was it a frightened heart, beating in panic?

The bricks were falling away, breaking up as they hit the ground, and with them came the bad-drains smell again, but much more strongly. The lantern light flickered and as the workmen moved back and forth they cast misshapen shadows on the walls, exactly like the figures in the nightmare. The nightmare was coming closer . . .

Then one of the men said, 'Here we go – stand well clear everyone.' He swung the sledge-hammer one last time and, with a tumbling crash, a large section of the bricks fell away leaving a black jagged-edged hole.

Mother and Elspeth were gasping and coughing and backing away from the wall, and for a moment Shona was afraid they would come up the stone steps into the cleaner air and catch her, but they did not.

When the dust had cleared a bit the foreman picked up one of the lanterns, and Shona felt sick and dizzy because the night-mare was wide open and after all these years she was going to see straight down into its black core.

The hole they had knocked out was at waist height and beyond the wall was a tiny space, not much larger than a cupboard. It looked as if it had been part of the much earlier house that had stood here in days when a secret cubbyhole might be a necessity of life. People living here might secretly have been on the side of Lancaster in the Wars of the Roses which they had learned about in school – red roses for Lancaster and white for York – and they might have hidden soldiers. But Shona did not think you could have got more than a couple of people in there together and even then it would have been a squeeze.

The light showed a network of pipes, massive things, like the thick bodies of coiled serpents or giant black worms tangled together ... But there was something else in there that the lantern's light picked up: something that had been standing behind the wall and something that was still standing there, staring out at the occupants of the room, even though it must have been blind for a very long time ...

Shona began to tremble. The thing in the wall still had the remains of dry dusty hair and there was skin over the face, although the lips were pulled back from the teeth.

The foreman said in a strange voice, 'Oh Jesus,' and snatched up the nearest mallet, frenziedly knocking out more bricks, while the other two men scrabbled at the remaining ones with their bare hands. When the rest of the bricks finally came away, the thing toppled forward, and fell in a hunched-up heap on the dustsheet as if grateful to lie down after such a long time. The bones were held together by the shrivelled leathery skin and it was possible to see the remains of what looked like a suede jacket.

'Oh Jesus,' said the foreman again, staring down at the terrible thing. 'It's a— Oh God help us, it's a dead body. Years it must have been there – bloody years. What do we do? Get a doctor or the police? Somebody better phone them. For Christ's sake, who's that screaming?'

Shona could hear the screaming as well and it must be coming from someone standing very close to her, because it felt as if it was inside her head. She clapped her hands over her ears to try to shut it out but it went on and on. Inside it was a dreadful voice saying that this was the old nightmare, only this was real, it was *real* ... Mother and Grandfather really had walled up a woman that night and the woman had been there all these years ...

Elspeth, silly old Elspeth with her large face frowning, was clumping up the steps and grasping Shona by the arms, and Shona no longer cared about being caught because the nightmare had come true and nightmares were not supposed to do that, and she was more terrified than she could ever remember being in her whole life.

The workman said, 'For pity's sake get the lass out,' and Shona was aware of being half carried across the hall and up the stairs to her bed.

CHAPTER EIGHTEEN

The Moil police did not immediately take away the thing that had stood behind the wall in Grith House. They took photographs of it and scrapings of the bricks and the earth floor, and only when they had done all that did a police ambulance come to remove the body. The cellar was sealed up for several days so no one could go down there while all the tests were being made and the dead woman's identity was being established. Mother and Elspeth were asked lots of questions. No one asked Shona any questions, and her mother took two extra nips of whisky each night and said they would not discuss it; it was all too upsetting.

The policemen came back after a while, and said the body was that of Margaret Seymour's younger sister. There was no doubt whatsoever, said the inspector in charge of the case. They had checked dental records and they were very sure.

Mother said quickly, 'Oh, but it can't be. My sister left here a long time ago. Four years it would be. She went to London – she was always one for the bright lights and Moil was too quiet for her. She was a good deal younger than me, of course. Ten years, in fact. We never had much in common, and after she left we lost touch.' She dabbed her eyes, and Shona, listening unnoticed, thought: but you and Grandfather put her behind the wall. I saw you do it. I thought it was a bad dream, but it wasn't, it was real.

The two Cheesewrights, also questioned, confirmed that everyone believed Miss Ross had left Moil four years ago, or it might be nearer five. Edna had always thought her bound for a bad end, in fact. Swinging London, said Edna, as one referring to an incomprehensible and somewhat alien world. Hippies and discos and trying to see how many people could be crammed into a telephone box, put in Mona. They knew all about it; they read the newspaper articles. They were not in the least surprised that old Mr Ross's younger daughter had ended up behind a wall; there would be a man in it somewhere, they said, mark their words.

Questioned about this, Mother said, well, yes, her younger sister had had a lot of friends, but she and her father had not known many of them.

Men? Boyfriends?

'Oh yes, I'm sure she had boyfriends,' said Mother. 'Not here, though. Not in Moil. It's such a very small place, you see. But she had friends in York and in London. She spent a lot of time in London. There were several people she stayed with, but I don't think I'd have any names or phone numbers. Not after all this time. I'm not sure I ever had them, in fact; they were so much younger, you see.'

'Why do you think your sister went to London?' said the inspector. 'Was there a letter – a phone call?'

'There was a row,' said mother, speaking slowly, as if, thought Shona, she was testing each thing in her mind before saying it. 'A row with my father – he was a bit old-fashioned in outlook. He didn't always approve of the way my sister behaved and lived.'

'A row about anything specific? About a particular man?'

'I don't think so. Just over her staying out late or being extravagant. She'd treat Grith as an hotel, coming and going with no warning, no consideration for others. She had her own bit of money – our mother died in a car crash when we were quite young, and her money was invested in a trust fund for us. Not a fortune, but it meant my sister didn't need a regular salary in the conventional sense. She did a bit of modelling – clothes and underwear – for a few of the smaller magazines. And demonstrations for cosmetics in the big stores sometimes. That kind of thing.'

'Yes, I see,' said the inspector thoughtfully, and Shona saw he was forming a picture of a butterfly – a frivolous extravagant young woman who flitted between Moil and London, mingling with people on the fringes of modelling and magazines, and possibly encountering all kinds of odd characters as a result.

The cause of death had not yet been discovered, although, as the inspector said, it was a fairly safe assumption that the poor girl had been murdered – why else would the body be so carefully hidden? There were a few tests that could help establish how Anna Ross had died, he said, but there was only so far they could go with that: they were not magicians. There were no fractures to the skull or to any bones so they were testing for poison, but after four years there were only so many tests that could be made. The problem was that there was no 'overall' test they could make – you had to know which poison you were looking for. For instance, if you tested for strychnine, that would tell you if strychnine was present or not, but it would not tell you if any other poison was present. Arsenic, say, or morphine. And four years was a long time for most poisons to remain detectable anyway.

But as far as they could discover, no one had had any motive for killing Anna. No one had benefited financially by her death – her share in the trust fund left by the dead mother would go back into the pot. Mrs Seymour would benefit by that of course, but it was clear that the police did not really think Margaret Seymour had murdered her sister and walled up her body for the sake of an extra bit of money in a trust fund.

So they would see if they could trace any of her London friends, said the inspector, although after all this time it might be difficult and there were things in people's lives that they might not want dragging into the light of day.

'What kind of things?' said Mother, bewildered.

Well, jealous lovers or slighted wives, said the inspector apologetically. As for the macabre tomb itself – was Mrs Seymour absolutely sure there had been no kind of disturbance at Grith House around four years ago? Had the family been away during that year, perhaps? Or had any workmen been in? Builders, drainage people? Because you could not, said the inspector, apparently without irony, brick somebody up behind a wall in five minutes and you could not do it without a fair amount of disruption either.

Mother said, 'Yes, we did go away four years ago. We often did at my daughter's autumn half term. It's a nice time of year for a little holiday. No crowds. My father hardly ever came with us, but I think he did that year.'

'Ah. And where exactly . . .'

'We always stayed at a little bed and breakfast place in Whitby. I can let you have the address: I dare say they'd confirm it. We haven't been for about three years – certainly not since my father died – but if it's still the same people they'd remember.' She did not say that Grandfather had decided there was no need for these holidays and their own home was good enough for them.

'But you did go to this Whitby place four years ago? With your father and your daughter?'

'Yes. I could probably check the exact year but I'm sure it was four years ago.'

'That means the house would have been empty while you were away?'

'Yes.'

'Would anyone come in during that time? Had anyone a key?'

'One of the Cheesewright sisters would have come up one of the days, just to make sure everything was all right. They help with the cleaning and cooking. They have a key.'

'But no one else? No workmen?'

'Oh no.'

The inspector and his sergeant exchanged a look, and it was immediately clear to Shona – she supposed it was clear to her mother and Elspeth as well – that the police were deciding the killing and the walling up had been done while they were all at Whitby: perhaps that Anna had returned to Moil unknown to her family, and had had someone with her who had killed her and then hidden the body. It was a pretty far-fetched thing to have happened, but then the whole situation was far-fetched.

The Cheesewrights were surprised that Shona did not remember her mother's sister. 'Your aunt,' said Edna Cheesewright. 'You must remember her. Very lively, she was.'

'A pretty girl,' put in Mona.

'A bit artificial, of course. All that make-up she'd put on her face.'

'And slimming all the time so she'd have a good figure for all the modelling and photographing she got paid for. Cottage cheese, that was what she ate – sloppy tasteless muck. And she'd have that stuff like chopped-up straw for breakfast instead of a proper Christian plate of bacon and eggs. Muesli or some such she called it.'

'No one else ever touched it,' put in Edna.

'I should think not, it looked like bird food.'

'Your aunt was a one for the men as well, the little madam,' said Edna. 'But there, we won't speak ill of the dead.'

'Indeed we won't. But don't you remember her at all, Shona? She'd take you out many a time, and go to all your school concerts. You'd have been seven – maybe eight when she went away.'

'When we *thought* she went away,' corrected Edna.

But Shona had no memory of this pretty lively aunt who had apparently liked make-up and bright lights and men, and been careful of her figure for the modelling work. And whom everyone believed had gone to London, but had turned up behind a wall in

Grith's cellar twenty-four hours earlier and had been part of an old nightmare.

'Just imagine,' said Edna, 'we all thought she was in London all these years, but all the time Anna Ross never left Grith.'

Anna Ross. *Anna*. As soon as she heard the name, it seared through Shona's brain like a white-hot knife.

Anna was no longer a shadow in the mirror or a whispering voice in the dark, she was a real person – she had been Mother's sister – and she had been here all along, standing behind that wall. 'You must never go into the cellar,' her mother had always said, and her grandfather had locked the door and pulled the screen across it so people would forget the door was there.

Shona wanted to ask her mother about what she had seen that night four years ago, but she did not dare. Over the last couple of years Mother had developed a way of staring coldly at people if she did not like what they said: she quite often stared at Shona in this way and Shona hated it. But what would be far worse than Mother's frosty stare was if Mother confessed to being a murderess. Was that possible? Might she say, 'Yes, your grandfather and I killed Anna four years ago and bricked up her body in the cellar so no one would know. Your grandfather said she was wicked and immoral so we punished her.'

Shona thought she could just about cope with having an aunt who had been murdered, but she was not sure if she could cope with having a mother and a grandfather who had done the murdering. The plan she had always had to one day leave Grith House suddenly seemed more important than ever. She had thought Elspeth was stupid when she talked about locking bedroom doors, but now Shona took to locking her own bedroom door every night, and to be careful never to be on her own with her mother, unless Elspeth or one of the Cheesewrights was within shouting distance.

But the thing she found most puzzling of all – the thing she did not dare mention to anyone – was why, if Anna had died when Shona was eight years old, she had no memory of her.

But you do have a memory, said Anna's voice. *It's only that it's buried right down at the very deepest part of your mind. It's a bad memory, Shona, the worst memory of all . . .*

The worst memory of all. Something that must never be allowed to thrust its way into the light. *Never . . .* Shona did not dare look at this deep memory, but she knew it was there. Anna knew as well.

It was after this that Anna started to get into Shona's dreams. This was far worse than the shadowy shape in the mirror or the whispering voice, because in the dreams Anna screamed and writhed in agony behind a brick wall, begging to be let out. Several times Shona woke from these dreams crying and terrified, and her mother came to see what was wrong. The nightmare could not be told, of course, so Shona mumbled something about monsters and being chased. Mother said there was nothing to worry about; she would fetch a nice soothing hot drink from the kitchen. Everyone had nightmares at times, she said, and Shona would grow out of them.

But Shona did not grow out of them. At times they went away – for weeks and even months on end, and then, just as Shona was thinking they had finally stopped altogether, they would start again. Sometimes they came three or four times a night. When, years later, she came to London she thought the dreams would stay behind at Grith, but they followed her, like the spiteful ghosts they were.

Shona hated the nightmares, and now she was grown up with a proper life and a smart job with the Harlequin Society, she found them vaguely shameful. 'It's a child's thing to have nightmares,' she said to her GP, when a particularly bad bout finally drove her to seek help. 'Not something for an adult.'

'Not necessarily.'

'But to have them night after night,' said Shona, who was tired and jumpy and headachy, and fed up with not being able to concentrate properly on her work.

'Yes, that is perhaps more unusual. Have you thought about talking to someone – no, I don't mean a psychiatrist, I mean one of our counsellors, to see if there's anything at the root of them? Sleeping pills would just deal with the effect and I'd rather get at the cause if we could. I see from your notes you've only been in London a few months. And you're very young to be here on your own, as well. Just nineteen. I expect you're still finding your feet, making new friends, working hard. That'll mean a certain degree of stress, which won't help. I could make an appointment with one of our people – they're very helpful and discreet.'

'I don't think I will,' said Shona. 'Not at the moment, anyway.' Not ever, she thought. 'I'd really rather just have a sedative or some sort of sleeping pill for when they get out of hand.'

He was reluctant, but in the end agreed, emphasizing that she must only take the pills if absolutely necessary. 'They're apt to become habit-forming,' he said. 'That's why we tend to fight shy of them for patients.'

Shona said she understood and promised not to go over the top with them.

Nor had she. Three or four times a year she had to resort to the pills, but no more than that. A couple of times, returning to the surgery for a repeat of the prescription, the doctor talked again about an appointment with a counsellor, but Shona always declined. The second time he did this, she switched to a different surgery. Nearer her place of work, she said, when asked the reason for the change. It would be easier for her to get there. She did not say she disliked the searching way the doctor looked at her. The new set-up was a big impersonal health centre, where she hardly ever saw the same doctor twice and where no one talked about underlying causes or finding the root of the nightmares.

She continued to be strict about taking the pills because she did not want to draw attention to herself by repeating the prescription too often, but on the night before she and Hilary were to drive to Somerset to meet Madeleine Ferrelyn, she woke abruptly at three a.m., with her heart pounding and a feeling of dizziness.

It had been the familiar nightmare of screaming from behind the brick wall, of course, and Shona finally struggled out of sleep with the screams still echoing in her head. As she woke up to her familiar bedroom her heart was pounding and her head felt dislocated, as if something had wrenched it in two then put it back together, but had not quite lined up the two halves. She listened to see if Anna's hateful whispery voice was in her mind, but it was not. Anna liked to keep her guessing about that: she could be silent for weeks – even months – then just as Shona was starting to think she had gone for good, she returned.

Shona got up to make a cup of tea, which she drank looking out of the big window with the view of the old wharf. Even at this hour there were people about which she found comforting.

After she had finished the tea she got out road maps and spent fifteen minutes or so studying the route they would take to reach Fosse Leigh and Madeleine Ferrelyn. It did not look like a very long journey.

CHAPTER NINETEEN

June 1914

The journey to Bosnia and Sarajevo was going to be a very long one indeed, and from what Sonja Kaplen had said, it sounded as if it might be a rather uncomfortable one as well. Toby contemplated the prospect with mixed feelings.

He had mentioned casually to his mother that he was thinking of running over to Paris while the theatre was being spruced up during June. Just a week or two with Frank and old Bunstable, he said, hoping a week or two would be sufficient duration for Tranz's expedition. They wanted to get a bit of local colour for a musical comedy sketch Frank had in mind, said Toby, and when his mother expressed interest and enthusiasm, he felt like the lowest worm in creation. He felt even worse when he realized he would have to drag in Frank and Bunstable and ask them to keep out of circulation.

I'm hating this, thought Toby. I'm sprinkling enough lies round to make me feel like Ananias and I'm spinning enough deceptions to rival Judas, but I can probably tell them the truth when I get back. And part of him was starting to feel excited about what was ahead. He had never done anything like this before, and the farthest he had travelled was to France on a couple of occasions, and Italy on another.

Three days after he had attended Tranz's meeting with Alicia, Toby was summoned to a restaurant in Soho. He had expected this; he had thought Tranz's people would want to meet him properly before including him in the protest party, but he was rather pleased that it was Sonja who brought the message. She delivered it to the Tarleton where, as luck would have it, Toby was rehearsing. He broke off and persuaded her to come into the green room, routing out Bob Shilling to make tea for them.

Sonja seemed to like the theatre; she asked about the inscription over the stage door. 'Something about pleasing everyone, isn't it?'

'Please one and please all, be they great, be they small,' said Toby. 'It's attributed to Richard Tarleton – the man this place is named for. He was a sixteenth-century clown actor, and a genius at writing and performing what they called very long humorous songs. Not much different from what we do here today. It always delights me to have those words there, although I don't know who actually ordered the engraving. I'm only recently finding out how little I do know about the Tarleton. Do you like it?'

'Yes, very much.'

'I haven't shown you all of it – some of it's a bit dark and spooky.'

'I should think it would have to be. It's quite an old building, isn't it?'

'Yes, very. There's an underground room I used to think was haunted. I went down there when I was about five and frightened myself half to death. I was convinced someone was staring at me from dark corners.' Toby had no idea he had been going to say this and was rather annoyed with himself for having done so. She'll think you're the worst kind of idiot, he thought.

But Sonja looked at him thoughtfully, and said, 'All really old buildings hold some kind of atmosphere, don't they? Sometimes it's good and happy, but if something bad has happened in a building it can hold that badness. And some people are more sensitive to that kind of thing than others.'

Toby said, 'As an explanation for ghosts, that's masterly.'

'Have you actually got a ghost?'

'Certainly we have a ghost. No self-respecting theatre would be without one. But he was never especially frightening and he hasn't been seen for years, so we think he's probably moved on to more profitable haunting grounds. In here's the green room. I'm afraid it's dreadfully messy but no one ever has time to tidy it up.'

But Sonja clearly liked the green room's comfortable untidiness and the casual way in which performers and stage staff wandered around. Bunstable had brought in his evening's supply of kippers and had placed them on a cool section of windowsill to keep fresh. Encountering objections, he pointed out that they were well wrapped up, promised not to toast them over the gas fire again, and settled down tranquilly with a copy of the *Evening News*.

A Rose Romain dancer came in, searching for green cotton thread with which to darn Elise Le Brun's tights, because Elise could not be doing with holes in her tights when on stage and wanted them by six sharp. A double-act who tap-danced and sang banged the door crossly against the wall and demanded to know if Mr Chance had realized their names were spelt wrong on the poster outside, and more to the point did he or anybody else care, and really, dear, what was the sodding point of appearing in a theatre that couldn't even get your name right, excuse our French, miss.

Toby told Bunstable to take his kippers to Bob Shilling's room where the majority of the company would not have to endure the smell as well as the plaintive miaows of Codling the theatre cat who would trade his soul for a kipper, and suggested to the Rose Romain dancer that Le Brun be told to darn her own tights. He politely asked the tap-dance act how they were spelling their name that week, because as far as he could make out it changed according to the seasons or whether there was an R in the month.

'What nationality are they?' asked Sonja when the aggrieved tap dancers had taken themselves off. 'Mexican or something like that?'

'Golders Green, undiluted,' said Toby, straight-faced, and Sonja laughed.

'You're quite strict with them all, aren't you?'

'I have to be or they'd be like a rabble of badly behaved children. Fortunately they all have an immense respect for my mother, who was very successful at this theatre, so for most of them I've got a bit of her authority.'

'But you also hold them in considerable affection, I think.'

'That's rather astute of you,' said Toby. 'Yes, I do. Not many people outside the theatre see that. Most people only see what's on the surface.'

'What's under the surface?'

'A sort of fellowship, I suppose. We understand one other – there might be all kinds of feuds and bitching, with people stealing jokes or songs or lovers, but we all go through the same agonies and the same doubts and panics. It doesn't matter if you're a song and dance act or a juggler or if you train performing seals to jump through hoops. When you stand in the wings waiting for your call, the stage fright's the same for everyone and that creates a tremendous bond.'

'Yes, I see that.'

'Would you like to come to tomorrow night's show? I've got a new song and I'm quite pleased with it.' They were going to use the *Cinderella* scullery backcloth again, but Rinaldi had had the fireplace painted out and a few gargoyles and cobwebs painted in to create a haunted-house look. He was a marvel with paint and a brush. 'I'll get you a box all to yourself and take you to supper afterwards,' said Toby.

'Certainly not,' said Miss Kaplen at once. 'I haven't the time.'

'You have to eat, presumably?'

'Yes, but – what about Alicia Darke?'

'She can come as well if she likes, but I was thinking of just the two of us.'

'I didn't mean that.'

'I know you didn't. Alicia is just a friend, Sonja.'

'Ha!' said Miss Kaplen scornfully.

'Do come. You'll enjoy the performance – Bunstable's on the bill on Saturday.'

'The gentleman with the kippers?'

'Yes. He's a bit of a nuisance over his kippers – it's almost a superstition with him, I think – but he's a good comic. Very sharp, very witty. We've got a shocking old ham actor booked for next week – he's called Prospero Garrick, would you believe that?'

'Not for a minute,' said Sonja, laughing. When she laughed, her entire face lightened and she suddenly looked like a mischievous pixie.

'He does very florid monologues in a highly melodramatic Victorian style,' said Toby. 'My mother insists on booking him because she thinks it gives us a touch of class. We don't need class, of course – our audiences don't really want class.' He grinned. 'On a Saturday night, it's Bunstable and his ilk they want. The whole place wakes up then. I'd love it if you'd come.' He suddenly wanted her to experience the warmth and comradeship that filled the theatre on those nights, and he also wanted to see her wearing a silk evening gown in place of the rather shapeless, nothing-coloured coat and skirt she had worn both times they had met. So he said, 'And we could have supper at the Savoy Grill after the show and you can explain to me about the revolution.'

'I have no intention of going to the Savoy Grill with you or anybody else and I wish you'd stop calling it a revolution.'

'Isn't that what it is? What a pity. I was looking forward to shouting warlike slogans and singing revolutionary songs.'

Miss Kaplen said severely that she hoped Toby was taking the forthcoming protest seriously, because Tranz did not have time or energy to waste on people who were going to be flippant.

205

'I'm not flippant at all,' said Toby. 'I'm as serious as – as the Houses of Parliament or Magna Carta.'

'We're simply going to march through the streets and stage a protest rally outside the reception being held for the Archduke.'

'That's what everyone keeps telling me,' said Toby thoughtfully. 'But does it not occur to you that it's a very long way to travel to shout a few slogans?'

Toby had not been to the Soho restaurant referred to in the note Sonja had delivered, but when, as instructed, he asked for Mr Petrovnic, he was at once conducted to an upstairs private room.

Two of the patriarchal gentlemen were seated at a table, both drinking colourless liquid from small glasses, but when Toby bade them good morning they either did not understand English or considered him too far beneath their notice to acknowledge. Or perhaps anarchists, if they were anarchists, were apt to consider such trivial exchanges a mark of imperialistic decadence.

After a few moments, one of them pushed the bottle of colourless liquid over to him, indicating that he should pour himself a glass from it. It turned out to be vodka, which Toby disliked, but he took a sip for politeness' sake and set the glass down hoping no one would notice if he did not drink the rest. No mention was made of food.

Petrovnic arrived shortly afterwards, and although he did not shake Toby's hand, he sat opposite him and looked at him very intently indeed. Then he said, 'I am very glad to be meeting you, Mr Chance.'

'Thank you. I'm interested to meet you,' said Toby politely. 'I found your talk the other night very stirring.'

Petrovnic made a dismissive gesture as if this was of small importance, and embarked on a series of questions about Toby's allegiances and his political views, all of which Toby tried to answer as he thought Petrovnic would want and expect. He had been prepared for some mention of his father, but nothing was said: Toby could not decide if this meant they were treating him warily or if they had not connected him with Sir Harold Chance of the Foreign Office. Perhaps they simply did not think it mattered.

Petrovnic outlined the arrangements for the march, and the details of the main meeting point in Sarajevo itself. 'That will be the town hall of Sarajevo,' Petrovnic said, and the two other gentlemen nodded portentously.

'The Archduke is to direct army manoeuvres in the neighbouring mountains,' said one of them, and Toby heard that the man spoke with a stronger accent than Petrovnic's.

Petrovnic said, 'You can travel to Bosnia, Mr Chance? You have not family commitments that would prevent that? The journey will take perhaps four days.'

Toby was unsure if this was the reference to his father he had been expecting and thought there was an undercurrent in Petrovnic's tone he could not identify. But he took the question at face value. 'I have some commitments,' he said. 'But in the main I'm my own master and I can travel to Bosnia or the Isles of Gramayre or the Elysian Fields or anywhere I want at a moment's notice.'

This appeared to satisfy them. 'Before the start of our rally, we shall meet friends from Bosnia and Serbia in the Café Zlatna Moruna,' said the man who had talked about the army manoeuvres, 'which is a much more humble place than you will be used to.'

'Don't you believe it,' said Toby cheerfully. 'I've eaten and drunk in a lot of peculiar places in my time. The Sailor's Retreat on a Saturday night takes some beating.'

'Zlatna Moruna is nothing like your London pubs or this restaurant we are in today,' said the man, and Toby thought he sounded angrily proud.

'Then it will be a new experience,' he said politely.

'You will be given a map. Or,' said Petrovnic, 'we may be able to arrange for you to travel in company with some of our other friends. That might be better.'

'Thank you very much. I'll be there,' said Toby, although he was still not entirely sure if he would.

'Good. We are very pleased to have you with us,' said Petrovnic, and again there was the searching look making Toby remember all over again that these were the people who, according to Alicia, had been 'longing to meet him'. Unease stirred once more, because surely they were letting him into their organization very easily. Or were they simply grateful for any new recruits? Petrovnic said, 'Soon I shall inform you of the arrangements. Have we your address?'

'Care of the Tarleton Music Hall, Bankside,' said Toby, and saw Petrovnic's eyes flicker.

But he only said, 'Ah yes, the Tarleton. A theatre that has much history.'

'We like to think so,' said Toby, and this time there was no doubt about Petrovnic's reaction. But it was gone almost as quickly as it had come, and the man who had talked about the café in Sarajevo, said, 'He must take the oath to Tranz and to our leaders.'

'Certainly,' said Petrovnic. 'Mr Chance, you will take the oath?'

Toby had not expected this, but he said, 'Yes,' and when they handed him a sheet of paper, he read the words clearly and without flinching.

'Before God, on my honour and my life, I swear I will execute all missions and commands without question. I swear before God, on my honour and my life, that I will take all the secrets of this organization into my grave with me.'

As he made his way home the final few words of the oath were still with him. *I will take all the secrets of this organization into my grave with me.*

It was all a bit melodramatic and even slightly childish – a little like the secret societies Toby and some of his school friends had set up one long-ago autumn term. But as far as he could make out none of Tranz's intentions were actually criminal, although he supposed the protest itself might come under the heading of disturbing the peace, or causing a commotion. But neither of those were hanging offences and the very ease with which he had been able to join the group surely indicated its innocence.

Still, he thought, I'd better not tell the guv'nor or mother about any of it until it's all over.

'And you are certain young Chance will be loyal to Tranz?' demanded Petrovnic of Alicia that evening.

'Yes. He's not taking it entirely seriously,' said Alicia, 'because he never does take anything entirely seriously – at least, that's the impression he likes to give.'

'The flippancy is a pose?'

'I've never been able to decide. But I do think,' said Alicia, 'that you fired him with a genuine idealism, a kind of crusading spirit – as you do with everyone.'

'I am aware of that. I have a gift for it. And flippant or not, Toby Chance is a good addition to our group. You did well to get him for Tranz, Alicia.'

'You said you wanted him,' said Alicia, 'so I brought him to you.'

'Also Sonja Kaplen, I think. She is another good recruit.'

'Oh, Sonja thinks she wants to change the world. I don't understand her. I don't understand any of those young women. They aren't content to lead the lives their mothers led. They have too much energy, too much idealism.'

'Which is very good for Tranz. You will have a glass of wine?'

'Not if it's that vinegary stuff you serve at meetings,' said Alicia.

'From my own stock.'

'In that case I will have as many glasses as you care to give me.' She watched him pour the wine; his hands were slender and quick,

209

and when he leaned over her chair to hand her the glass, his fingers brushed her bare arm and Alicia felt a bolt of sexual longing. She willed him to sit next to her on the sofa, but he returned to his own chair. To conceal her emotion, she said, 'Sonja was an unwitting help with Toby: she accused him of being a decadent capitalist, then said he wouldn't volunteer for the Sarajevo trip because he did not care about oppressed nations. After that it was a foregone conclusion. Perhaps you should arrange for Toby to travel with her if you can. Also Ilena.'

'Ilena is a good idea. Chance is polite enough to respect her age and if he asks awkward questions, Ilena will give him that basilisk stare and he will be silenced.'

'He isn't easily silenced and he certainly isn't easily intimidated.'

'Whatever he is, he is the son of Sir Hal Chance and as such his presence will lend considerable force to the cause,' said Petrovnic. 'If we ever want to exert pressure on the British government, we would have a very good weapon in our hands with Toby.'

'A weapon?' Alicia had thought she was fairly unscrupulous, but she did not much like the sound of this. 'I'm not sure I care for the idea of using Toby – or anyone else – as a *weapon*.'

'It is for the individual conscience,' said Petrovnic. 'For myself I will use any means to further Tranz's work.'

'Have you ever met Hal Chance?' asked Alicia curiously.

'Briefly, many years ago.' The light flared in his eyes again and it was definitely not firelight; it was something harder and colder and something that was corrosive and dangerous. Hatred? Yes. Directed at Toby? No, thought Alicia, it's not Toby, I believe it's Hal Chance who's making him look like that.

For the first time ever Alicia was glad to leave Petrovnic. That sudden hard hatred in his expression had disturbed her, and the feeling remained with her as she made her way home.

Ever since she had met Tranz's leader she had wanted him with a violence that had surprised her. You could put whatever name you liked to the feeling – you could call it love or bewitchment, or you could call it plain unvarnished lust. On balance, Alicia, who possessed a strong streak of honesty, was inclined to opt for this last label. But whatever you called it, this emotion, for the moment, was rendering her helpless and enslaved, although so far it had not prevented her from enjoying sweet distractions with young men such as Toby Chance. But even Toby's seduction had been a part of her hunger for Petrovnic, because Petrovnic wanted Toby for Tranz. Have I simply been the acolyte, bringing the offering to the altar? she thought suddenly, and saw again the glare of hatred in Petrovnic's eyes. A shiver of dislike stirred in her mind.

It had once been said of Alicia Darke that she would go to bed with the devil if she thought the devil would give her a new thrill and when the remark was repeated to her she had been amused and rather pleased. Better to be known for your sins rather than not be known at all.

But tonight she thought that while she might certainly get into the devil's bed, she was no longer sure if she would get into the bed of a man whose eyes had shown that frightening glare when Sir Hal Chance's name was mentioned.

CHAPTER TWENTY

Toby was enough of a theatre man to recognize that to some extent Petrovnic was spinning an illusion, although that was not necessarily sinister: Petrovnic could be doing so for the best of reasons. But Toby's father had said that Tranz was suspected of being a breeding ground for saboteurs and spies: a machine to promote war between Serbia and Austria, and although Toby thought his father was clinging to an old-fashioned outlook, part of him was uneasy.

Petrovnic had said they would meet up with friends from other countries, which made Toby wonder if there might be a few fanatics who might try to stir things up, but as far as he could make out the planned protest was a matter of a march through the streets of Sarajevo, timed to coincide with the Archduke's arrival. And when he remembered some of the faces at the meeting he was reassured; it was impossible to think of the aristocratic old woman in black who had sat disdainfully in a corner, or any of the scholarly gentlemen who had been present, lending themselves to anything as vulgar as mob law. On the other hand, Toby was very easily able to visualize Sonja Kaplen leading a wild crowd of free-dom fighters through the streets, shouting death to the aristos and gleefully ordering offenders to be strung from lamp posts. He could not decide if this was worrying or exhilarating.

Sonja had eventually come to one of the Tarleton's performances as Toby had suggested and had appeared to enjoy it. She had not dined with him afterwards as he had suggested, but she had sat in the green room and drunk a mug of coffee which the inquisitive Bob Shilling had supplied, and talked to Bunstable and Frank Douglas.

'That'll be the one you're chasing half across Europe,' remarked Frank after Sonja left.

'I'm not chasing anyone anywhere.'

Several days later Sonja reappeared while Toby and Frank were on stage, polishing up 'The Ghost Walks'. She sat quietly in the auditorium until they had finished their rehearsal, then handed Toby a second note from Petrovnic.

This was to the effect that the journey to Sarajevo was to be made in a week's time, on 23 June. A train would leave Waterloo Station for Dieppe at ten o'clock on the morning of that day – Mr Chance would please make suitable arrangements to be on it. Unless anything unexpected or catastrophic occurred, they would arrive in Sarajevo on the evening of 26 June or, at the latest, the morning of 27 June.

The notepaper was thick and surprisingly expensive for a group that affected to disdain capitalism, and at the head, in defiant black type, were the words, 'Tranz is dedicated to promoting the crossing of boundaries and the creating of freedom for all.'

'The journey will actually take less time than I thought,' observed Toby to Sonja, having read the details.

'We might encounter delays – trains being late, or trains held up along the way. But Petrovnic has allowed a good margin for that.'

'Yes. I'd have to say, though, that he doesn't give people much warning for setting off halfway across Europe,' said Toby.

'That's because he believes people should be so dedicated to the cause, that anything else in their lives can be jettisoned at a moment's notice.'

'I don't know about jettisoning, it'll mean a lot of reorganizing of the Tarleton's programmes.'

'If you don't want to come, you can always back out,' said Sonja.

'I'm not backing out. Did you like my new song?'

'My God, you're an egotist,' said Sonja forcefully, and then, when Toby grinned, said, 'I did like it as a matter of fact.'

'Is that because under the comic surface it's about people struggling to make a living? Not always making the money last from pay day to pay day?'

Sonja said, 'Be careful, Mr Chance, or people might start to think you care about things like poverty and inequality. Real life.'

'I do care,' said Toby, stung to anger. 'I might live in Kensington but my mother grew up in the East End. Where, by the way, do you live?'

'Hampstead,' said Sonja furiously. 'That's got nothing to do with this.'

'No? When did you last have bread and dripping for your main meal of the day? Or visit Ikey Mo the Whitechapel pawnbroker? Or hide from the rent man? My mother did all of that in her time, and a lot of the people who work in this theatre still do it. I can't always help them, but sometimes I can.'

'I'm sorry,' said Sonja after a moment. 'I shouldn't have made that assumption. I really did like your song.'

Toby very much wanted to say, then come out to lunch and let's call a truce, but he did not. He said, 'I'm glad you liked it. It isn't quite as we want it yet, but it will be by tomorrow night. But now, if we're leaving on Friday I'll have to ask you to excuse me – there'll be quite a lot of arrangements here to make.'

'Yes, of course,' said Sonja and went without another word.

'You're getting mightily ruffled by someone you aren't chasing,' said a voice from the rear of the stage, and Toby looked up to see

Frank lounging against a piece of scenery, apparently studying a music score.

'Will you get it into your head that I'm not chasing her,' said Toby in exasperation.

'Well, whatever you're doing with her, I'd rather it was you than me. She'd frighten me to death. See now, will we make that second chorus of "The Ghost Walks" a bit snappier by putting in a repeat?'

In fact the Tarleton could be left almost entirely to its own devices while Toby was away. Rinaldi would make sure things ran smoothly, and if any of the acts failed to appear he would scramble something together to cover. Toby's mamma would help as well; she loved getting involved in the running of the theatre ('Madam never really retired,' Minnie Bean was wont to say indulgently), although she would probably disrupt all Rinaldi's arrangements. Rinaldi would not mind this in the least, however: Rinaldi had nurtured what Toby knew to be an entirely blameless passion for Flora for years.

Rinaldi and Minnie Bean both thought madam should return to the theatre. 'A benefit night,' Rinaldi said hopefully, and he and Minnie sometimes got together in the Sailor's Retreat to make elaborate plans, none of which had come to fruition so far. Toby could never decide if he was pleased or disappointed about that. On the one hand he had never seen his mamma on stage and would like to, but on the other hand, he had a secret, wholly irrational fear that she might be persuaded by Rinaldi and Minnie to reprise the infamous Flowered Fan dance. However much he loved his mother, she was nearly fifty years old and pleasantly plump, and Toby did not want to see her prancing in the spotlight clad only in a few flowers and sequinned tights, no matter how often Rinaldi said she had not altered in twenty-five years or Minnie's assertions that you could do wonders with a bit of whalebone.

Bunstable and Frank would have to lie low while Toby was away

215

because they were supposed to be accompanying him on a working trip to Paris. This did not bother Bunstable who said he was partial to a bit of intrigue pepping up your life, and that Toby would have to tell him what it was all about afterwards. It did not bother Frank either, who, being Irish, regarded intrigue of any kind as meat and drink.

The Rose Romain dancers were booked for two performances while Toby was away, which would please the audiences who enjoyed ogling Elise Le Brun's legs and speculating about her love affairs. It was unfortunate, however, that Flora had insisted on engaging Prospero Garrick to deliver some of his monologues next Thursday, because half the audience would boo and the other half would go off to the Sailor's Retreat after the first five minutes.

It was even more unfortunate that Prospero got the dates mixed up and turned up that same night by mistake. He presented himself grandly at the door of Toby's dressing room just as Toby was getting ready for his own performance, and was deeply hurt to discover he was not expected for another week. He said there were theatres in London who would have rearranged their entire evening's programme for him there and then. People queued up to hear his Richard II, said Prospero, and he could not see why Toby would not sweep a couple of acts off tonight's bill to accommodate him. Toby explained that it was impossible to do this and by way of a palliative listened to Prospero's entire Richard II speech, accepting a good many swigs from a silver flask along the way.

Prospero was mollified by Toby's interest and by the flask's contents. He told Toby that when he wrote his autobiography, which a great many people wanted him to do, he would make very favourable mention of Toby's theatre and of Toby himself. He then took himself off, and could be heard singing 'Come Where the Booze is Cheaper' as he wound an unsteady path to the green room.

Toby plunged his head into a bowl of cold water in an attempt to disperse the effects of Prospero's gin, and was just towelling his hair dry when there was a furious screech of anger from somewhere within the theatre's environs. It sounded like a soul in torment or Codling the theatre cat being skinned alive, but it turned out to be Elise Le Brun, beating off the lustful advances of Prospero who had wandered into her dressing room and embarked on a fruitily Edwardian seduction. Le Brun had shrieked to the heavens to be rescued, and was now demanding that her assailant was hailed off to justice.

When Toby pointed out that they could not have people making unsolicited pounces on Tarleton performers, Prospero beamed drunkenly, launched into a muddled version of the Shakespearean speech about making the two-backed beast, and said it was a tribute to the lady's charms, dear boy, and a mere bagatelle. Elise said bugger the charms, she was not being called a bagatelle, not by Prospero Garrick nor the king of England nor nobody. And, said Elise, growing shriller by the minute, they should all know that for all the speechifying, Mister Prospero bloody Garrick had been so soddenly drunk it had been obvious that he could not get his flagpole more than half mast anyway, which was no use to a girl at all, pardon the vulgarity, but it was enough to make a saint swear, it reely was.

'Ah, I fear I have been too merry with the fruitful grape,' said Prospero, not in the least discomposed. 'And there's the rub. The grape promotes the desire but takes away the perfor-formance – hic – beg pardon.'

'Whatever it does, you'd better go and do your fruitful grape-drinking somewhere else,' said Toby crossly. 'But you'll apologize to Miss Le Brun first. And Elise, if you don't stop screeching like a Billingsgate fishwife and get properly dressed, you'll miss your music and you'll be *off*.'

He left the green room on this note and returned to his own dressing room to prepare for the maiden performance of 'The Ghost Walks'. It had been planned for nine o'clock that evening, but between Prospero's gin and Le Brun's wrath, it was well after ten before Frank sat down to play the semi-spooky, semi-comic music he had devised.

As Toby waited in the wings, for a disconcerting moment he found himself remembering his mother's off-hand remark about the Tarleton's real ghost. 'I saw him once,' Flora had said. 'But it was one of those fog-ridden nights so afterwards I thought I might have been mistaken.'

You weren't mistaken, thought Toby. And I think you know you weren't mistaken. He's here, all right, that ghost, whoever and whatever he was. But I think he's benign. I think he's a friend.

When he walked out onto the stage he knew at once that the delay had not mattered. They don't mind, he thought, looking out into the dark smoky well of the auditorium, aware of the waves of warmth. They're so pleased at the prospect of a new Chance and Douglas song, they don't care we're running an hour late. The realization was both humbling and exhilarating.

> *On Friday nights the ghost walks*
> *Rattling its chains to itself;*
> *Because that's the night the ghost hands out the pelf.*
>
> *On Friday nights the ghosts walks,*
> *Glum and at times rather Gothic.*
> *In its chequered career, it had often appeared*
> *With Tarleton, Grimaldi and Garrick.*

When the audience cheered and when the gallery shouted for an encore and began a rendition of the chorus on their own account, Toby, nodding to Rinaldi to hold back the curtain, wondered how he could bear to leave his theatre for this mad jaunt across Europe in company with a group of people he hardly knew.

*

Two nights later was Tranz's final meeting before the Sarajevo venture, and Toby had persuaded Sonja to have supper with him beforehand.

She appeared to enjoy herself, although in the restaurant she told Toby that in a properly run country, people would not have to wait on other people.

'Quite right,' Toby had said promptly. 'And on that basis, I'll leave you to pour your own wine. Are you happy to eat the chicken you've ordered, or will it worry you that someone had to build the hen coop and farm the land and feed the chickens?'

'In an ideal world we would all share that kind of work.'

'Sonja, darling, the world isn't ideal and it never will be.'

'I know, but— Don't call me darling.'

'But you are a darling,' said Toby. 'Particularly when you're being serious. I love watching your expression when you're wanting to help the human race.'

'Well, you can make your contribution to that by helping me to some more salad.'

'The vinaigrette dressing is very sharp tonight,' said Toby, without expression, and she laughed, her face lighting up, and he wished they had not got to go to Tranz's meeting for ten o'clock, and that he could sit like this with her until at least midnight.

At the meeting Petrovnic made a speech that was essentially a final rallying call, about the voice of the people being heard and the freeing of all nations. Toby was still more than half hoping to be presented with a reason to honourably back out of this wild affair, but faced with Petrovnic again it was impossible not to be swept along by the magnetism and energy of the man.

'Our friends await us in Sarajevo,' Petrovnic said, his eyes glowing as he scanned the room. 'The Café Zlatna Moruna is their headquarters and will be ours also.'

'He makes it sound like Nirvana and the Promised Land all rolled into one,' murmured Toby to Sonja. 'Whereas I daresay in reality it's a scrubby little place with sawdust on the floor and in the food.'

'Be quiet, someone will hear.'

'I don't care if the entire room hears.'

Petrovnic was still describing their destination and the people they would meet. 'And perhaps even as we sit here tonight, they are gathered round a table, making their plans by flickering candle-light, drinking the wine of the country, painting word pictures for each other of how the world might one day be. Soon we will be with them, adding our voices to theirs, adding our faith to theirs.' His voice lifted, and took on the battle-cry note again. 'And when the Archduke Franz-Ferdinand reaches Sarajevo, a wild welcome will await him.'

He broke off, and a smile lifted his lips, and Toby stared at him and thought, my God, I wouldn't like to make an enemy of this one!

He had no idea if Petrovnic had sensed his hesitancy, but after the meeting he made his way quite purposefully to Toby's table and sat down, fixing Toby with his dark eyes. So far from framing an apologetic explanation that he could not travel to Bosnia, Toby found himself listening with absorption as Petrovnic talked quietly and earnestly, explaining about Tranz's aims and formation.

'Tranz was not born out of hatred for the Austro-Hungarian Empire,' he said, his eyes holding Toby's. 'It was born from the desire for independence and unity within a single nation. That is one of its main aims: to inspire and strengthen the sentiment of individual nationalities.'

'That's very admirable,' said Toby after a moment.

'We have literature – pamphlets about our formation – you would perhaps like to have one?'

'Yes, I should.'

'I will send it to your theatre for you to study before our journey,' said Petrovnic. 'And when we reach Sarajevo, I shall make you known to the people who are to lead our protest. Three of our most ardent workers have already been smuggled into the country and they await our arrival. One of them – a man called Gavrilo Princip – is a good friend and utterly devoted to the cause. He is extremely young – barely twenty – but he sees our work as a crusade, a torch to light his people on the path to their freedom.'

'Thank you very much,' said Toby, unable to think of a better rejoinder.

'All of us who work for Tranz have dreams of a better world, Mr Chance,' said Petrovnic. 'Strong dreams which we hope to realize.'

'Dreams of iron and blood?' Toby could not imagine what had prompted him to say this, but Petrovnic's eyes showed a brief spark of emotion.

He said, very sharply, 'That is war talk.'

'I know it is. Bismarck said it, about twenty years ago,' said Toby, meeting the other's regard unwaveringly.

'*Eisen und blut,*' said Petrovnic, half to himself. 'Well, it is true that sometimes it is not speeches and resolutions that decide the great questions of our time, but iron and blood.'

'War,' said Toby, trying out the word.

'We shall hope it does not come to that,' said Petrovnic, and stood up, nodded briefly to Toby, and went out.

Toby went home with his head spinning, realizing that so far from recanting, he was becoming drawn deeper in. Blood and iron, he thought. Petrovnic didn't like my saying that tonight. I don't like my saying it either. Bismarck, that defiant old aristocrat, one of the fiercest war-horses to come out of Prussia. What put him and his words into my mind? Was it because my father thinks a whole new war is coming out of Prussia before the year is out?

He would have liked to talk to his father about all this, and he might have done so if Sir Hal had been at home more and had he not worn a perpetually worried look.

'Foreign Office flaps,' said Toby's mother, when Toby remarked on this one evening. 'I try never to ask. He does get so furious with that sarcastic little man who quotes Napoleon and says we're a nation of shopkeepers.'

'Sarcastic little man?'

'Kaiser Wilhelm II,' said Flora drily.

Toby remembered how his father had said that one hell of a war was brewing and that most of Europe would be plunged into it before the year ended. One hell of a war . . . *Eisen und blut*. Perhaps it was better not to talk to his father at the moment. Perhaps it was better to let the fiction about a jaunt to Paris stand. It was at this point he knew that so far from pulling out of the journey, he was looking forward to it. Because wasn't Petrovnic right? Wasn't it vital that people stood up for justice and equality in the world? Listening to Petrovnic – confronted by the man's passionate beliefs and by the fervour of everyone associated with Tranz – he was swept along by the idea of righting the wrongs of the world and it was easy to be convinced of the sheer *rightness* of everything Petrovnic said.

CHAPTER TWENTY-ONE

Two days before Toby was due to leave for Bosnia, he and Frank Douglas spent the afternoon in a bare and rather dusty studio just off the Tottenham Court Road, making a gramophone recording of 'The Ghost Walks'. It was the first time they had done this and Toby was inclined to treat the whole experience with flippancy, because it was the sheet music of their songs that was important and that people bought.

Frank disagreed with him. 'Gramophone recordings are the way of the future,' he said. 'This will be a reproduction of our music performed by us – it'll be the way we want people to hear it. Sheet music's all very fine, but it can get torn or lost or thrown away. Gramophone records are more enduring. You never know who might one day be listening to this gramophone record we're making today.'

'Some descendant in the faraway future?' said Toby, grinning.

'Don't mock. And it'll be an interesting experience anyway.'

It was a very interesting experience, partly because neither of them had ever seen sound-recording machinery before, but also because they had not realized they would be expected to perform two songs.

'Didn't anyone *tell* you there were going to be two songs?' demanded the willowy young man who was supervising the procedure, whose temperament appeared to be mercurial and whose temper was unreliable. 'We *always* do two at a time, one on each side. You have to have one on each side.'

'Of course you do,' said Frank warmly. 'One on each side.'

'I daresay we could fudge up something for the – uh – the other side, couldn't we Frank?' said Toby, not daring to meet Frank's eye.

'Oh we could fudge up anything in the world,' said Frank, with such suppressed mirth in his voice Toby knew they were going to have difficulty in remaining serious for the length of 'The Ghost Walks'.

'We'll perform "Tipsy Cake" for the second one,' said Toby firmly, and thought that at least if the solemnity of either of them wavered on that one it would be in keeping with the song's mood.

'What a good idea. "Tipsy Cake" let it be,' agreed Frank cheerfully. 'See then, Mr – uh, Mr Willoughby, the full title is "All Because of Too Much Tipsy Cake". Will you have room for all that on the label?'

'Well, of *course* we'll have room for— Where is your accompanist?' demanded the willowy Willoughby suddenly looking round as if he suspected someone of hiding in the corner.

'It's me. I'm the accompanist,' said Frank. 'And I called in the fiddler from the Tarleton's orchestra as well, only I don't see him yet – Oh, wait though, is that him arriving now?'

The fiddler, clattering up the stairs and entering the studio noisily, was enthusiastic about the recording procedure, and inclined to study the machines with interest. 'I've never done a sound recording before, it's all very clever, isn't it?'

But after they had run through a few bars as a rehearsal, it seemed the combined sounds of violin and piano did not give sufficient resonance. They needed another instrument, said Willoughby crossly. No, he did not know precisely *what* instrument it ought to be, it did not bloody matter what instrument, but they needed another one.

'I'll see if I can get old Arthur,' offered the fiddler. 'I'll bet he'd love to do it. And it won't take long to fetch him, he only lives in Finsbury Park and he'll most likely be at home at this time of day—'

'Finsbury Park!' shrieked Willoughby. 'We haven't the *time* for you to go all the way to Finsbury Park and back again, for pity's sake! Vesta Tilley's coming at twelve o'clock for "Jolly Good Luck to the Girl Who Loves a Soldier", and we're doing "The Girl in the Pinafore Dress" and "I Do Like Pickled Onions" at two.'

'One on each side,' said Frank.

'Yes, and— Please *don't* touch that, it's the wax for the cutting of the record and if it isn't kept at the right degree of warmth you'll all come out horribly distorted.'

'Sorry,' said the fiddler, guiltily snatching his hand back.

'How about this for a solution,' said Toby hastily. 'If there's a second piano to hand, I could play at the same time as Frank.'

'So you could,' said Frank enthusiastically. 'And with a bit of luck we'll hit the notes at the same time, and even if one of us is a semi-quaver or two behind it'll sound like an echo. That'd be entirely in keeping with "The Ghost Walks".'

'Would it be sufficient – what did you call it? – resonance?' asked Toby, looking at Willoughby.

'Well, it might.' Willoughby chewed his lower lip and thought about it. 'We'll try,' he said at last. 'There's a piano next door; I'll see if there's anyone to trundle it in.'

'We'll all trundle it in,' said Toby, thankful to have got over this incomprehensible, but clearly important, difficulty.

The second piano, duly trundled in and tried out in chorus with the main piano and the violin, was pronounced to add more than enough resonance; in fact, said Willoughby, after they finished and the room was being reset for Vesta Tilley, he did not know when he had heard quite such good quality of sound.

'Did you not notice Toby playing all those wrong notes?' asked Frank innocently, and was hushed by Toby and the violinist, and carried off by them to the Pickled Lobster Pot for Dover sole washed down with copious draughts of beer. This light-hearted and entirely trustworthy friendship was something else Toby would miss for the next couple of weeks.

He arrived in good time at Waterloo station, although he was slightly daunted to discover that for this first leg of the expedition he would be sharing a compartment with one of the biblical-bearded patriarchs from the Bloomsbury house and the imperious, black-clad old lady with the grubby diamonds.

'I am Ilena Osapinsky,' said the lady, proffering her hand as Toby stowed his luggage on the rack. 'My title is baroness.'

'Is it? I'm so pleased, I love titles,' said Toby, who never normally gave them a thought.

'You are Mr Chance, I think?' pursued the baroness. 'The son of the former music-hall dancer. A lady who danced with a fan to aid the illusion.'

This was said with such icy disdain that Toby instantly said with great enthusiasm, 'Oh, you've heard of her! I'm so pleased. Yes, she did use a fan in her act – in fact we still have one of her fans, mounted in the drawing room in a glass case.' This was completely untrue: none of Flora's fans had survived, even though Minnie Bean had apparently tried washing one of them in warm water and soda crystals.

'You are probably more accustomed to first-class travel?' said the baroness rather sneeringly, as Toby looked round the carriage.

'Yes I am, but I believe the lunch they're serving in first-class is Brown Windsor Soup and roast mutton,' said Toby. 'So on that score alone I'm very glad not to be there today. I daresay the railway company didn't foresee the possibility of such overwhelming heat during an English June.'

The baroness appeared to lose interest. 'Is the woman, Alicia

Darke, not accompanying us on the journey?' she demanded of the patriarch,

'Apparently she is not.'

'I am glad of it,' said the baroness. 'For she would be a hindrance to the cause, ogling the men constantly and distracting them. She has long since wanted Petrovnic for a lover, you know that, I suppose?'

'I did not know it.' The patriarch looked interested. 'But if she wants him, she will have him.'

'Would you care to lay a wager on that, Ivor?'

'Such a liaison would not last a fortnight,' said Ivor. And then, 'I am told a fortnight is her usual time for wearing out a lover.'

'Indeed? Then today's young men have not the stamina that men possessed in my own youth.' She sent the startled Toby a look in which assessment and curiosity were equally blended.

'I will take your wager,' said Ivor, having thought it over. 'A sovereign?'

'You think small,' said Ilena. 'Ten sovereigns, or I do not trouble myself in the matter.'

'Ten sovereigns, then.' Ivor took out a pocketbook and made a note of it. 'But whoever claims to win must in some way provide proof.'

'The proof will be a mere bagatelle,' said the baroness, waving one bedizened hand. 'I shall provide for you the proof.'

Toby was so entranced by all this, he almost missed Sonja's arrival. But he saw her come pelting along the platform, pink-cheeked with excitement and exertion, and leapt out again to help her, pleased to discover she would be in the same compartment.

As the train began to chug its way out of the station, he leaned his head back against the seat and began to fit a tune to the rhythmic clatter of the wheels. He had brought a thick notebook and several sharp pencils with him; he might get a song or two out of this. But no songs came from the humming of the train's wheels, nor even from the overnight stop they made just outside

Paris – the second would be in Strasbourg. Toby had half thought there might have been some romance and some colour to be got from these places, but there was not.

The romance came when they crossed into the land that once had been a patchwork of petty dukedoms, ruled by palatines and margraves – the countries that clustered at the heart of central Europe: tiny sovereignties with rich threads of poetry woven through their histories. Forbidden amours in Bavaria and Bohemia – morganatic marriages and thrones renounced in the name of love. Mysterious suicide pacts in hunting lodges in Mayerling . . . Toby had not been alive in 1889, the year of the Mayerling scandal, but most children of his generation knew the story of the Crown Prince and his mistress and their mysterious deaths in the house deep in the forest. It was romantic and tragic and had all the elements of fairytale and it was a story that stuck in the mind.

As they left Germany and Austria behind, and began on the last leg of the journey into Budapest and Sarajevo, he remembered the sharp hard influence of Germany's Prussian overlords and that this was now a land ruled by a man who had spent the last few years strengthening his armies and building up his navy, and who regarded Britain with deep hostility and jealousy.

There were fitful glimpses of the Thames beyond the window of Sir Harold Chance's room in Westminster, and the room was cool and shady. After the heat of the streets, Alicia Darke was glad of this, even though she was wearing the thinnest of her silk gowns. She was also wearing silk beneath the gown, lace-trimmed and sheer because although she was not meeting anyone who might be counted as a potential lover this afternoon, it was as well to be always prepared.

Hal Chance could not be regarded in the category of a potential lover, not because he was a good twenty years older than Alicia, but because he was known to be too happily married to be seducible. But any man who had stirred up the disapproval of the entire Foreign Office by marrying a music-hall performer – and had then overcome the ensuing scandal with equanimity – would be intriguing. Alicia, meeting him for the first time, found him attractive and was instantly aware of the latent power under the urbane exterior.

But there was no point in wasting energy on the unattainable, so she took the chair offered, accepted the suggestion of a cup of tea, then embarked on her reason for the visit.

'Sir Hal, I am Alicia Darke and I am a friend of your son's. He is a remarkable young man and it's because of him that I'm here.'

'I think Toby is remarkable as well,' said Hal Chance. 'How can I help you, Mrs Darke?'

Alicia studied him, then said, 'I don't usually yield to the promptings of my better self, but I am doing so now. I believe Toby could be in considerable danger from a specific person. And I believe you could be in danger as well.'

She had expected him to be startled, but he merely looked wary. 'Mrs Darke, I am occasionally warned of a number of dangers, most of which prove to be false or imaginary. What kind of danger is yours?'

'I'm not a crank or a fanatic,' said Alicia, stung. 'And I don't know precisely what form the danger will take, but ... Have you heard of an organization called Tranz?'

She thought the wary look increased, but he said non-committally, 'I have heard of it. Are you a member of Tranz?'

'I was,' said Alicia. 'I wasn't especially sympathetic to its aims, although I will admit I was very sympathetic indeed to its leader. But initially it seemed a new diversion.' She gave a small shrug. 'Life can become tedious at times – one seeks for new excitements. But now I think there is something sinister about Tranz. Do you know any of its members, Sir Hal? Baroness Ilena Osapinsky for instance?'

'I know of her.'

'Is that the Foreign Office discreetly keeping watch on suspicious foreigners?'

He smiled, but only said, 'What nationality is she claiming at the moment? It's generally either Romanian or Russian.'

'Whatever it is, she currently conveys the impression of being more used to travelling in a troika across the Russian Steppes with outriders, than of rattling about London in hansom cabs,' said Alicia tartly, and he smiled again, this time with Toby's smile.

'She's an extraordinary old woman,' said Hal. 'I'm using the word "old" advisedly, because she could be any age between fifty and a hundred. The title varies between baroness and countess.' He looked at Alicia thoughtfully. 'My department would like to know about Tranz,' he said. 'And if there really is some kind of danger to my son, then *I* would like to know about it.'

'I might be exaggerating it or misinterpreting it,' said Alicia, 'but I don't think I am. If I'm right, your son, and possibly you also, stand in danger from Tranz's leader. A man called Petrovnic. Do you know of him?'

'I don't think so. The gentleman for whom you felt sympathy?'

'Did you know your son has recently become a member of Tranz?' said Alicia, choosing to ignore the last remark.

A snap of anger showed in his eyes, and his jaw tightened slightly. 'I didn't know that,' he said. 'Although I can see that it might attract him. Fighting the cause of downtrodden people, rebelling against the old order – But Toby should know better, damn him.'

'You'll have to direct your anger at me,' said Alicia. 'I was the one who enlisted Toby in Tranz. I did it because Petrovnic wanted him. At the time I thought it was simply that Petrovnic believed it would add to Tranz's standing to have the son of a Foreign Office official in the group. It seemed a reasonable assumption. And if Petrovnic wanted Toby, I wanted Petrovnic – I was prepared to do anything for him.' She paused. 'I'm being very frank with you, Sir Hal.'

230

'It will go no further. And now?'

'This will sound impossibly dramatic,' said Alicia, 'but it's perfectly true. A few nights ago Petrovnic talked to me about using Toby as a weapon.'

'A weapon? Against the government?'

'I thought at first he meant that,' said Alicia, 'but then I began to suspect – more than suspect – it was personal. I think he intends to use Toby against you in some specific fashion. Hatred is a strong word, but I think Petrovnic hates you. Could that be possible?'

'I know a little about Tranz,' said Hal slowly, 'but I don't know this Mr Petrovnic.'

'Petrovnic isn't his real name. That's something else I discovered recently.'

'It's not necessarily a crime to use a different name. Do you know his real name?'

'I do. It's Anton Reznik,' said Alicia.

The pronouncing of a name should not have produced such an extreme reaction, but Hal Chance turned white and made as if to clutch the edges of the desk to prevent himself falling forward. Alicia, remembering the tray of tea brought in earlier, poured a cup out, sugared it liberally, and thrust it into his hand. He drank it gratefully. As he set the cup down, his hand shook slightly, but when he finally spoke, his voice was perfectly steady.

'Anton Reznik,' he said, very softly. 'My God, so he's back ...' Then, meeting her eyes, he said. 'I'm very grateful to you for telling me this. For – for warning me. Reznik and I met – very briefly – many years ago. There was considerable bad feeling between us – a matter that was never really resolved. So he's leading that squalid group of political intriguers now, is he? And calling himself by another name.'

There was no need to describe to Hal Chance the means Alicia had employed to find out about Petrovnic: how she had talked to the self-styled elders of Tranz – to that bearded old gossip Ivor, who had known Petrovnic for so many years, to the flamboyant and haughty Ilena Osapinsky who would trade cupboard skeletons with the whole world. There was certainly no need to explain how Alicia herself had gone to Petrovnic's house when she knew he would be out, imperiously telling the manservant she would leave a note, then searching bureau and desk drawers while he was out of the room. She had not really known what she hoped to find that day, but she had wanted to find something that could be used against Petrovnic, because she could not bear Toby to be at the mercy of that burning hatred she had seen in his eyes. And perhaps a little because she wanted her own revenge against a man who had rejected her ... Yes, that had to be admitted as a motive, as well, if only in her private thoughts.

Hal was saying, 'Mrs Darke, whatever Reznik is planning, Toby's safe for the moment. He's in Paris for a few days with his music partner—' He stopped. 'Dear God,' he said softly, 'he's not in Paris, is he? He's with Tranz – with Reznik.'

'He's joined Anton's protest rally against the Archduke Franz-Ferdinand,' said Alicia. 'They left two days ago. By tomorrow night or the night after that your son will be in Sarajevo.'

When you have been married to someone for more than twenty-five years, you cannot help knowing if that person is troubled. Accordingly, after Flora and Hal had finished dinner that evening, Flora said, 'Hal, what's the matter?'

The direct question clearly took him slightly by surprise, but he said almost at once, 'Nothing's the matter.'

This was more or less the response Flora had expected. Hal was regarded by colleagues as remarkably modern in his outlook, but he still had a slightly old-fashioned belief that ladies should be protected. Flora had come up against this belief a number of times over the years and she found it by turns endearing, exasperating, or worrying, depending on the circumstances. Tonight was one of the occasions when she found it worrying, so she said, 'I know quite well there's something wrong, so you may as well tell me. Unless it's state secrets, in which case I'll understand.'

'It's not state secrets,' said Hal. He hesitated, then seemed to reach a decision. 'It's— Flora, it's Anton Reznik. He's come back.'

The name dropped into the room like a stone. Reznik. *Reznik*. The twins. That dark dual personality, that eerie impression of a single mind using two bodies ... But it was important not to give way to silly emotion or hysterics which would only give Hal something else to worry about, so Flora reminded herself that she had dealt with rowdy music-hall audiences with gusto and later faced cabinet ministers with aplomb. But when she spoke her voice betrayed her by its unsteadiness.

'Are you sure?'

'Fairly sure. He's apparently involved in some sort of shady-sounding political organization – I hadn't better tell you any more about that side of things.'

'We always knew it was possible that he might one day come back. Has he threatened you?'

'No.' He reached for her hand. 'But I think he's planning to harm Toby.'

A few minutes earlier Flora had successfully beaten down hysteria. This time she thought she would not be able to do so. Toby. If anything happens to Toby I'll die, she thought. Not even Hal could make up for losing Toby. She clenched her hands in her lap fighting for mastery, and presently was able to say, 'That's surely not very likely. Their paths wouldn't even cross. They wouldn't move in the same circles.' But there's the Tarleton, said her mind. That would be a link. If Reznik wanted to get at Toby it would be easy to do it through the Tarleton – to scrape up a meeting. She said, 'How do you know about this?'

'A friend of Toby's – a lady – who was worried about him, came to see me.'

'It would be bound to be a lady,' said Flora, trying for a lighter note. 'But Toby's in Paris at the moment, so he's surely out of

Reznik's reach—' She stopped, and looked at him. 'Hal, *is* Toby in Paris?'

'I don't think so,' said Hal reluctantly. 'I think he's become mixed up with – with Reznik's political group. They've gone on some wild journey into Eastern Europe.'

'But Toby wouldn't be fooled by Reznik or by some political organization,' said Flora, trying to ignore the growing panic by focussing on practicalities. 'He'd see through any attempt to – to lure him into a trap. Or would he?'

'If the trap was sufficiently attractive, he might not care,' said Hal. 'And if the lady herself was equally attractive . . .'

'Oh God yes, that's true. Hal, if that's brandy you're pouring, would you pour some for me as well? I know it's an unladylike drink, but—'

'But when did you worry about being ladylike.' He smiled as he handed her the glass, acknowledging the small private joke they had always had. 'Flora, I may have to find a way of dealing with Reznik. I mean an unorthodox way. If it was a question of Toby's safety or yours, then there's nothing I wouldn't do to safeguard you both.'

'And Toby? If he really has gone on some wild jaunt somewhere . . .'

'It depends on the somewhere,' said Hal. 'But I think he'll be all right.'

Flora sipped the brandy, grateful for the small core of warmth it set up inside her. 'Nearly thirty years ago Anton Reznik vowed to destroy you,' she said. 'I've never forgotten that.'

'Neither have I,' said Hal. 'I don't think either of us will ever forget what happened that night.'

234

CHAPTER TWENTY-TWO

1887

'I don't think either of us will ever forget what happened on
Monday night,' said Hal, three days after the Reznik twins' rape
attempt on Flora. 'But I do think we need to make sure those two
villains didn't cause any damage or any trouble. If I were to call
on Rinaldi this afternoon, would he let me into the Tarleton?
Better still, would you come with me? I'm not sure exactly where
he lives anyway.'

'I'm sure he'd let you in. But of course I'll come with you.'

It was a leaden November afternoon, and Burbage Street,
when they reached it, lay glumly beneath lowering skies. Rain fell
incessantly, splashing along the gutters and slopping into the
street drains.

'Dreadful weather,' said Hal, turning up the collar of his coat
as he sprang down from the cab and turned to help Flora. His
dark hair was misted from the rain; Flora suddenly wanted to
reach up to touch it. Instead she concentrated on avoiding the
puddles, and said the rain was apparently delaying the work on
the theatre.

'It's something to do with not being able to lay electric wires.

They can't risk touching live cables if they're wet – I think that's what they said, anyway.'

They turned right and then right again into Candle Square with the network of streets leading off it, and found the right house by the simple method of asking a passing postman where Mr Rinaldi lived.

'Number twenty-four,' said Flora, scanning the houses, which were small and narrow – almost identical to the street where she had spent her own childhood. 'There it is.'

'A polished brass door knocker and a window-box with late geraniums,' said Hal approvingly. 'Very nice. Is there a Mrs Rinaldi?'

'I don't think so.'

'Well, we'll hope he's at home.'

Rinaldi was at home and he opened the door to them as soon as they knocked. For a moment he stared at them without speaking. As if he thinks we're ghosts, thought Flora. But he wasn't expecting us, of course. Then Rinaldi seemed to recover himself. He said, 'You've heard, haven't you? That's why you're here.'

He was white-faced and Flora put out a hand to him. 'Heard what? Rinaldi, what on earth's wrong?'

'You don't know?' he said. 'No, I can see you don't. But I've only just known myself – they were talking in the Sailor's Retreat when I went in for my bit of dinner at twelve, and— I'm so sorry, please come inside.'

He showed them into a small parlour, and sat on the edge of a chair, twisting his hands together. 'It's Bob Shilling,' he said, and Flora felt a thump of apprehension.

'What about him?'

'He was knocked down by an omnibus,' said Rinaldi. 'They took him to All Saints' Hospital and he was unconscious for the best part of twelve hours. Concussion, they call it.' He seemed to be speaking more easily now he was launched on his tale. 'He'll be all

236

right, although he broke two ribs and an ankle. They say that can be put right.'

He paused and Flora said sharply, 'When did it happen?' She leaned forward, aware that Hal had done the same. 'Rinaldi, when was this?'

'On Monday night,' said Rinaldi. 'The night the Tarleton closed. The night we – the night those black-hearted villains were there. It was just before midnight – outside the Sailor's Retreat. Shilling was coming out after his supper and it must have been the last omnibus. Mostly they stop running at midnight. He was crossing the road to come back to the theatre to make the midnight round. Only he never did so because of the omnibus. No. And that means,' he said, speaking rapidly, 'that no one's been inside the place for two – almost three days. The workmen were to go in the very next morning, but they didn't because the weather meant they couldn't deal with the electric wiring.'

'I heard about that,' said Flora. She looked at Hal. 'It's bound to be all right,' she said. 'I mean – about the twins. Isn't it?'

'Sure to be,' said Hal, but Flora heard the uncertain note in his voice. 'But it was in my mind to make sure – that's why we're here now, Rinaldi, to see if you'll let us in.'

'It was in my mind as well, sir,' said Rinaldi. 'It was more than in my mind – I was just putting on my coat to go along to Platt's Alley when you knocked on the door. I'd be glad of your company.'

His eyes flickered to Flora and Hal at once said, 'My dear, you could perhaps stay here, if Rinaldi wouldn't mind. We shan't be very long.'

'No, indeed, I wouldn't mind you staying here—'

'I'm coming with you,' said Flora flatly. 'And you can argue until hell freezes, I shall still come with you, so we needn't waste any more time talking about it.'

Logically, there was no reason why Flora should feel this sense of urgency, and this choking fear, because even without Shilling's

237

midnight round, Anton and Stefan had only had to go back up the stone steps and out through the self-locking foyer door. They had known all that perfectly clearly. But supposing they had not been able to find the way, or Stefan had been more severely injured than they realized? What if the foyer door mechanism had not worked? Or supposing . . .

There aren't any supposings and what ifs, said Flora silently and firmly. It'll be all right. But as they turned into Platt's Alley she caught sight of Hal's expression and knew he was having the same nightmare images. When Rinaldi unlocked the stage door and they stepped inside, she could feel fear knocking in her mind.

They waited while Rinaldi collected the lantern from Bob Shilling's room, then followed him along the passage. There was not very much light from the lantern, but there was enough.

'Is the note still in Shilling's room? The one Hal left?'

'Yes. And the half-sovereign's in the envelope,' said Rinaldi.

Once in the inner passageway, Rinaldi held the lantern up so that its light fell on the oak door, and with his free hand he reached down to grasp the handle. Flora saw his expression change; she saw him look sharply over his shoulder at Hal. In the light from the lantern his face was a sickly yellow.

'What's wrong?'

In a voice that was suddenly dry and fearful, Rinaldi said, 'The door's locked.'

For a moment Flora did not take it in. Then she said, 'But we didn't lock it – there wasn't even a key.'

'There isn't one now,' said Hal grimly, bending down to inspect the door more closely. 'It might just be stuck – warped from the damp, perhaps.' He grasped the handle and tried it and Flora saw the door frame move. 'I think it *is* locked,' said Hal. 'The door itself is pliable within its frame – it's actually quite loose fitting. It's the lock that's stopping it from opening: you can feel it. Rinaldi, have you got the key?'

'I haven't, sir. I don't remember anyone ever locking this door, and I don't remember ever hearing tell of any key. That's the under-stage area beyond those steps: the grave trap shaft's down there, of course, and the rest's used for storage.'

'Then how can the door be locked now?'

'It's an old lock,' said Rinaldi, examining it again. 'Apt to be unreliable, maybe?'

'Apt to drop when the door's shut a bit too sharply? Is that what you mean?'

'It's the only explanation I can think of, sir. Unless someone came back in here and deliberately locked it. And there're only the two lots of keys to get into the theatre. I've got one set and Shilling's got the other.'

'And he's lying in a hospital bed, poor chap. I can believe six impossible things before breakfast,' said Hal, 'but I don't think I can believe in an unknown murderer somehow obtaining your keys without your knowledge, or stealing Shilling's keys from his hospital sickbed, and then sneaking in here to lock that door.'

'With a key that no one knew existed,' put in Rinaldi.

'Exactly.'

Flora glanced at Hal, wondering whether to mention again the shadowy figure she had seen – thought she had seen – slipping into Platt's Alley as they walked away on Monday night. At the time they had thought it was Shilling himself, but now it seemed it could not have been.

She said, 'In any case, there were only the three of us who knew what had happened. Oh, and that policeman – you were going to mention it all to him, Rinaldi. Did you do that in the end?'

'I did, but it wasn't the regular man,' said Rinaldi. 'It was someone standing in. He said he keep an eye out, though. Take a walk along Platt's Alley and so on.'

Flora instantly felt better. It'll have been the policeman I saw, she thought.

'I think we can acquit the policeman, regular or temporary, of anything questionable,' Hal was saying.

'So do I,' said Flora. 'But how do we get the door open?'

'Rinaldi, would you look in Shilling's room, just in case there is a key?'

'I will, sir, but I'm doubtful.' Rinaldi went off, and Hal stood closely against the door, pressing his ear to its surface.

'Can you hear anything?' asked Flora.

'Not a thing, but the door's very thick.'

'Try calling out.'

'Reznik?' called Hal loudly. 'Are you in there? Can you hear me? *Reznik?*'

The words bounced and spun round their heads in the narrow passage, and died forlornly away.

'Nothing,' said Hal, and looked up as Rinaldi came back, shaking his head.

'No key anywhere. Shilling himself would know if there was one, of course.'

'I daresay he would, but the fewer people we involve in this the better. Is there any other way of getting into the cellar? Any other door? Those two ruffians probably aren't there – they'll have got out through the foyer door as we told them. This lock probably clicked down when they came out, but . . .'

But you aren't sure, thought Flora. Neither am I. Neither is Rinaldi. She said suddenly, 'What about the stage trap? Does it still work? Could we operate it and get down that way?'

Rinaldi looked at her with respect. 'I should have thought of that,' he said. 'We don't use it very often, but it's kept oiled and in working order.' Taking up the lantern he led the way to the stage.

Flora was beginning to feel as if they were entering a nightmare. Nothing looked quite normal: the racks of clothes in the wardrobe, the familiar clutter of the green room, the odds and ends of discarded scenery . . . Everything's distorted, she thought.

Their footsteps echoed hollowly and several times it almost

seemed as if the echoes had a life of their own. As if there's someone following us, thought Flora uneasily, someone who's creeping along behind us, trying to match his steps to ours, but missing every so often. Is it someone who pads round the theatre, singing quietly to himself? No, I don't believe that. It really was just the building creaking I heard that night.

The pulley wheels that worked the grave trap were high up in the wings. Thick ropes looped round them and hung down; in the blue-grey dimness they were like slumbering snakes. Rinaldi lit several gas jets and there was an old-fashioned wall sconce in a miniature cage which burned up brightly when he fired it. The oozing shadows dissolved in the light, but the feeling of unseen eyes watching them remained. As Rinaldi opened the stage curtains, Flora moved to the side of the stage and looked out into the dark well of the auditorium and then up to the stage box. Nothing.

Hal was studying the pulley wheels. 'How does this thing work?'

'There's a hand winch. You turn it and it loosens the ropes and causes the pulley wheels to move.'

'Yes, I see,' said Hal, after a moment. 'What is it – a drum and shaft principle?'

'That's right. A simple invention but perfectly reliable.'

'The best inventions are usually very simple indeed. Shall you operate it since you know how it's done while I go down in the thing?'

'Begging pardon, sir, but it's my job to go down there, and I'm more familiar with it. The mechanism's easy enough to work – you just turn this handle.'

'Fair enough. Sing out when you're in position.'

As Rinaldi walked across the stage, the old wall sconce suddenly flared up more brightly and Flora had the feeling of distortion again. But what was it? Something about the theatre itself? Something about the trap mechanism? But Rinaldi would have seen if there was anything wrong. Then is it something on the stage? *The stage.* Yes, that's it, she thought. Something's wrong with the stage. But what? She scanned the stage intently but although there were still pools of deep shadow everywhere, nothing seemed out of place. But her heart was pounding and sweat slid down between her shoulder blades. Rinaldi stopped abruptly and looked back into the wings.

'Something wrong?' said Hal, and with the words Flora suddenly saw that one of the pools of shadow was too sharply outlined. That's where the trap is, she thought. That's what I've been seeing.

Rinaldi said, 'Someone's opened the grave trap.'

The words sent a cold thrill of horror through Flora, but she moved cautiously towards the yawning blackness near the centre, and Hal left his post by the winch and joined her. Seen closer, the open trap had an eerie resemblance to an open grave. It's just the name, she thought.

'It is open,' said Hal. 'Although I don't quite understand . . .'

'Well, sir, the trap's floor is always kept up here – to be flush with the stage. If an actor has to be lowered during a performance, he is. If it's the end of a scene we probably leave the platform down until the curtain's fallen, but mostly we bring it back up into place. That's the safe thing to do, you see. It's a quiet mechanism and the audience don't hear it being worked, or if they do, they don't know what it is. It was originally used for graveyard scenes – *Hamlet* and all of that,' said Rinaldi. 'We don't do much of that kind of thing now, but the trap's useful for panto sometimes. Demon kings and transformation scenes. But it's never *ever* left open like this – why, I made sure it was in place myself when we locked up on Monday night, I really did.'

He sounded genuinely upset, and Flora said, 'Then someone's opened it since then.'

Someone trapped down there in the dark, trying to get out?

They looked at one another. Hal said, 'Is that possible? If the twins really were trapped, could they operate that machine from down there?'

242

'It'd be difficult, sir. It's a heavy old thing, that platform – it's made of iron, in fact. But I suppose if you were desperate you might just about raise it from underneath.'

If you were desperate . . . If you were imprisoned in the dark, without food or water . . .

'Raise it to escape then lower it afterwards?' said Hal. 'That seems unlikely. But let's take a look.'

The lantern's light poured straight down into the open shaft. There were the wooden struts, stretching all the way down, with, almost at the bottom, the iron platform.

'If you tilt the lantern a bit more that way, sir, we can look all the way down—'

As Hal tilted the lantern, the light fell straight onto the platform at the bottom. Flora gasped and was aware of Rinaldi's soft cry in Italian. Something lay awkwardly on the platform: something whose sightless eyes were wide and staring, and whose face was the colour of clay.

Hal said, 'Dear God, it's one of the twins. And I'm afraid he's dead.'

'Are you sure, sir?'

'Not entirely, but – wind this thing up, Rinaldi. We'll have to get him back up here. Flora, you'd better wait at the side of the stage.'

Rinaldi was already at the winch mechanism, throwing his weight into raising the trap as quickly as possible. It seemed to move easily enough, but it was not, as he had said, entirely noiseless, and to Flora's ears the sounds were dreadfully like the moaning of a man dying slowly in the pitch dark.

As the floor of the trap came level with the stage, she tried to look away, but could not. The twin – they still did not know which of them it was – lay in that same grotesque huddle. Dried, darkened blood, spattered the edges of the iron floor, which Flora found grisly in the extreme.

Hal dragged the body clear, and bent over to examine it. 'I

think it's Stefan,' he said. 'Slightly longer hair than his brother.'

'Yes, that's Stefan,' said Flora, determined not to give way to emotion of any kind. 'Is he dead?' she said, as Hal felt for a heartbeat.

'I'm afraid he is, poor chap.'

'But where's Anton?' said Flora. 'Still down there?'

They looked at one another. 'We'll have to find out,' said Hal, at last. 'Rinaldi, if I stand on the platform, will you winch it down again?'

'Not alone, sir,' said Rinaldi, at once. 'Why, you don't know if that other one mightn't be lying in wait for you. I'll come with you.'

'But that means Flora would have to operate the mechanism,' said Hal.

'I could do that,' said Flora, eyeing the wheel and the pulleys.

'Could you?'

'I don't see why not. Let's try.'

'Rinaldi, you hold the lantern. And watch for Anton.'

'You'll feel it stop when it reaches the bottom,' said Rinaldi to Flora as the two men took up their places on the trap's floor. 'But we'll call up to tell you anyway.'

The winch was heavier than Flora had expected, but she managed to turn it reasonably easily. As the platform began to descend, the lantern flickered wildly, casting eerie shadows upwards onto the two men's faces, and Flora found it deeply disturbing to be lowering them into that sinister blackness, where Anton Reznik might be waiting for them, no longer entirely sane after being imprisoned in pitch darkness for three days. She glanced nervously at Stefan's prone body. Had it moved just then? Or let out a little pleading sigh? No, it was only the flickering and hissing of the gas jets.

She was thankful to feel the platform bump to a stop and to hear Hal's voice calling up that they were safely down, and she left the machinery and went back to the open trap, kneeling at the edge, peering down to see what was happening. She could not see either Hal or Rinaldi, but she could see movement and the lantern light, and after a moment Hal's voice came up to her again, echoing slightly.

'Flora? We've found Anton, and he's alive. But he's only just conscious, so we're putting him onto the platform to get him out. Can you wind it back up when I give the word?'

'Yes, of course.'

The return journey was a grim one. The old machinery creaked badly this time – to Flora's ears it sounded more than ever like the groans of a dying man – and with the three men on the iron floor it was heavier than before. But it reached the stage and Rinaldi sprang off the platform and came into the wings to lock the wheel into place.

Anton lay prone on the iron oblong, and at first Flora thought he was dead after all; his face was grey and his eyes were closed. But then she saw him blink and half open his eyes, and she realized that although his face was thin and sharp, he was alive. There were livid bruises on his hands and crusted blood where his nails had been torn away. Had he, then, tried to get through the cellar door?

Hal said, 'Flora, could you get some water for him? And some brandy as well if you can find any.'

'Yes, of course,' said Flora, glad to be able to do something. 'There might be some brandy in the dressing rooms, and if not, I'll run over to the Linkman.' When she got to her feet she found she was shaking so much she was afraid she would not be able to walk, but she forced her legs to obey her and once in the green room filled a tall jug with water. By a happy chance someone had left a half-full bottle of brandy in a dressing-room cupboard; Flora snatched this up along with a small cup.

'Only a few sips of water at a time,' Rinaldi said. 'Or he will get stomach cramps.'

The water, and then a small amount of brandy, revived Anton

245

slightly, and when Hal said, 'Reznik, are you hurt anywhere except your hands?' he said, 'Not much hurt.' The words came in a dry, difficult whisper. 'But Stefan—' He broke off. 'Stefan is dead,' he said.

'He is. I'm so sorry,' said Hal gently.

'Are you?' Even like this, Anton's eyes glittered with hatred as he looked at Hal.

'Anton, we're all desperately sorry about Stefan,' said Flora. The words came out awkwardly, because she was trying not to remember that embarrassing, frightening intimacy of three nights ago. 'You do understand it was an accident that you were trapped down there?' she said. 'We made an arrangement for you to be let out, but it went wrong.'

'No accident,' said Anton. 'This is your revenge.' He turned to look at Hal and Flora flinched at the expression in his eyes.

'It *was* an accident,' she said before Hal could speak. 'Of course it was. You must know we wouldn't have left you down there.'

'What I know is that my brother died and I nearly died also.'

Rinaldi was binding Anton's torn hands and fingers, using a ripped-off piece of curtain soaked in the water Flora had brought. Anton gasped in pain several times, but then seemed to relax a little.

'You've been remarkably lucky, sir,' said Rinaldi. 'Almost three days down here without food.'

'People have survived for three days without food,' said Flora.

'Not without water though,' said Hal. 'Reznik, we'll get a doctor to see to you.'

'Nothing is broken,' said Anton. 'Wounds heal.'

'What happened?'

'When we realized we could not open the door – that we could not make anyone hear us – we tried to operate the machine,' said Anton. His voice was noticeably stronger and a tinge of colour was returning to his cheeks, and he glanced across to the trap's

246

outline nearby. 'We thought to lower it halfway down so one of us could climb up and reach the stage.'

'But the platform's a sheet of iron,' said Rinaldi. 'And from below you'd be pushing against the mechanism.'

'It was heavy and difficult,' said Anton. 'The machine is clumsy and cumbersome, but we forced it far enough down to reach it, and I wedged the pulleys in place. Stefan stood on the platform and began climbing up. He used the sides of the shaft to lever his way upwards – it was difficult but not impossible. But the wedges were not strong enough. The machinery slipped, and because it had already been forced onto its downward journey, it completed that journey.'

'What happened?' said Flora, staring at him in horror.

'The machine came roaring down. Stefan was still on the platform. The force of the fall injured his legs – his ankles were broken, I think. And perhaps also the bones of his legs. He could not stand so he could not make the climb a second time. I could not raise the machine again, not on my own, not with Stefan on it. When I tried to pull him off the platform he screamed with the pain of his broken legs. I tried a second time and a third to move him, but it was too cruel, and I left him there, with my coat covering him. Then I tried to force the cellar door again but I could not.' He indicated his damaged hands angrily. 'So all we could do was lie helplessly down there in the dark, waiting to be rescued, or to die, we did not know which it would be.' The hatred showed again in his face. 'And it is all your fault, you bitch,' he said to Flora.

'We should have left you down there rot,' began Rinaldi hotly, but Hal waved him to silence.

'Accusations won't help anyone,' he said, 'but Reznik, if you use language like that again to Miss Jones, injured as you are, I shall knock you out.'

Anton hunched his shoulder angrily. 'Stefan was terrified,' he said. 'He was always terrified of the dark as a child – I always protected him. But this time I could not do so. When first we understood we were locked in that cellar, he crouched in a corner sobbing for hours, his arms over his head. He saw demons and spectres – he was afraid they were creeping towards him in the dark. After he was injured, he lay on the iron platform, screaming, on and on until his voice cracked. I had to listen. I listened to him die.'

'Of his injuries?' said Flora.

'Of madness from his thirst,' said Anton. 'It comes sooner than you think, the madness of thirst, and it is a terrible thing to hear someone die in that way—' He broke off, and sipped the brandy and water again.

Hal said, 'How did you survive yourself?'

'A small amount of rain water came in through a flaw in the brickwork,' said Anton. 'I managed to crawl over to drink a few drops. But I could not get Stefan to the trickles of water, or the water to Stefan.' He set down the brandy and suddenly grabbed Flora's wrist. His fingers were hot and dry against her skin and his eyes glittered. 'My brother is dead because of you. There will be a reckoning.'

'There will be no reckoning,' said Hal sharply. 'Your brother was the victim of a tragic accident. We all know quite well what happened that night.'

For the first time Flora saw Anton hesitate. Hal obviously saw it as well, because he said, 'There will be an inquest on your brother, of course, but the verdict will undoubtedly be misadventure.'

'I shall say you locked us down there. You will be guilty of murder.'

'Don't be ridiculous. No one locked you down there. It's an old lock. Unreliable. It simply jammed,' said Hal. 'But you were both drunk that night and you assaulted Miss Jones. I saw that for myself. Rinaldi saw it as well. In the fight Stefan fell downstairs and you both refused to come out. If you had done so, you wouldn't have been trapped. And,' he said, 'all of us would

248

testify to those facts if we had to.' He did not say, 'And since I'm a member of Her Majesty's Foreign Office, my word will be believed,' but Flora could see Anton thinking it. After a moment, Anton said, sneeringly, 'So that is your famous British justice.'

'That is our famous British truth,' said Hal coldly. 'Reznik, I will do what I can to help you with the practicalities of your brother's death if you wish it – perhaps there are papers that would be needed – papers you do not have ...' He let the sentence remain unfinished, and Flora saw at once that this, even more than Hal's Foreign Office standing, had struck some kind of chord in Anton. His eyes flickered, but he did not speak. After a moment, Hal said, 'And so you must accept what I have said.'

'I will accept it for the moment, for I do not waste my time fighting what cannot be defeated. I will deal with my brother's death by myself.' He broke off, then looked from Hal to Flora. 'But one day I will destroy you,' he said. 'One day I will destroy both of you for what happened to my brother.'

CHAPTER TWENTY-THREE

It was a matter of mild interest to those who moved in thespian circles or in the raffish world of the music halls, that the Tarleton was being refurbished and electrified that November. The management was looking towards the Christmas season, said people, and hoped there would be a lively panto this year. The Tarleton's rivals said sneeringly that if the place were to be plastered with silver and gilt and given electricity from roof to cellars, it would still be what it had always been: a gaff, a former blood-tub, fit only for the vulgarians.

Another section of the community was currently wondering whether there was any truth in the rumour that Sir Hal Chance had made moves to acquire the freehold of the theatre, and with an air of elbow-nudges and sly winks, asked if his deepening *friendship* with the infamous Flowered Fan could possibly have anything to do with this.

'I don't know how these things get out,' said Hal to Flora over lunch at Kettner's. 'There've even been a few comments in the newspapers.'

'I know. I'm sorry about that,' said Flora. 'It's the juxtaposition of our two names more than anything else. The sum is greater than the parts.'

'I don't mind it, you know. And that photo of us in the *Morning News* was rather a good one, I thought. Well, it was good of you, at any rate.'

Flora said the *Morning News* was a gossipy old rag and Hal grinned.

'In any case, it's perfectly true that I'm interested in buying the Tarleton,' he said. 'That's why I invited you out today to tell you about it properly. I've made an approach through my solicitors, to enquire if the present owners might negotiate a sale.'

'And will they?'

'They're being a bit guarded but the signs are very good indeed,' said Hal, eating partridge au choux with apparent enjoyment. 'They've already agreed to make last year's accounts available to my solicitor.'

As the main course plates were removed and the pudding brought, Flora found herself struggling against a feeling of inadequacy. Hal Chance had a title and a house in Kensington and an office in Westminster. He helped his masters deal with diplomats and people in foreign embassies, and he prepared reports for cabinet ministers about far-flung places with outlandish names which were part of the British Empire. He had solicitors who did his bidding and provided him with complicated-sounding balance sheets. I wouldn't know a balance sheet from a laundry list, thought Flora, and I wouldn't know how to go about buying so much as a potting shed.

I suppose I may as well go to bed with him if he asks me, she thought, dismally eating Kettner's exquisite charlotte russe; it's all I'm likely to get and at least I'd have it to remember when I'm old. Because Minnie will be proved right: when it comes down to it, all he'll want is four bare legs in a bed and no marriage lines on the mantelpiece.

Then Hal said, 'It's a massive undertaking, buying a place like that. If I think about it too much it rather daunts me. I've never actually bought any property before – I inherited the house I live

251

in at the moment, so things have been handed to me in a neat parcel so far.' He smiled at her and Flora instantly felt better. 'But I'd like to buy it if I can,' he said. 'Providing it isn't ridiculously expensive and the fabric's sound. Somehow, I always think of it as your theatre.'

So it wasn't entirely a question of a good investment after all. Flora said carefully, 'That's not because of what happened there that night, is it?'

'Stefan Reznik's death? No, certainly not.' He paused, and then said, 'That's all over, you know. The inquest brought in the verdict I expected.'

'Death by misadventure. Yes. I did think,' said Flora, speaking very carefully, 'that Anton would have made more trouble for you – for us. He was sick with grief that night, but those threats he made were very strong.'

'Anton didn't dare draw too much attention to himself at the inquest or anywhere else,' said Hal drily.

'Didn't he? That night you said something about him needing papers that he might not have. I didn't entirely understand that. Is he some kind of criminal? Were you telling him you knew something about him? Something discreditable? Illegal?'

'None of those things, really.' He thought for a moment, then said, 'Flora, Magna Carta, praise its ancient old parchments, grants Englishmen and women the freedom of movement and departure. In other words, we can come and go in this country and most other countries to our hearts' content. And thank God for it. But not all countries permit that. The Tzar, for instance, is a bit jealous of his subjects' movements. I believe it's quite difficult to leave Mother Russia – and one or two other countries besides – without very specific permission.'

'Is Anton Russian?'

'I don't know what he is, but if he isn't Russian he's probably from somewhere in Eastern Europe,' said Hal. 'Hungarian or Romanian, perhaps. In certain circumstances it can be very useful to be vague about nationality. And if Anton and Stefan left their native shores without permission – or because they were in some kind of trouble there … When I said that about papers, it was a bow drawn at a venture. Nothing more. But it struck home – we both saw that. And whatever the truth behind it all, it seems to have prevented him from making trouble. But, Flora, I wouldn't have said it if I hadn't known you and I were entirely innocent of Stefan's death. And neither of us bear any blame or any responsibility for what happened.'

'I know.'

'It doesn't alter the Tarleton for us, does it? When I said I thought of it as your theatre, I meant the successes you've had there,' said Hal. 'The pleasure you've given audiences.'

'Oh. Yes, I see.' Flora felt even better.

'I don't know the first thing about running a theatre,' he said, 'so I'd rely on people who did and just keep a – a controlling interest. I've been hoping you could give me your advice on that side of things.'

This was intensely pleasing and so interesting that Flora forgot about her pudding, and said she would try to provide some possible names. 'But the one person who comes instantly to my mind is Rinaldi. You really couldn't do better for a stage manager. He's quite young, but he's very good, very knowledgeable and reliable. He's been there ever since he was about twelve: he learned the work from his father, I think – he was the Tarleton's stage manager as well. It's a kind of backstage dynasty.'

'Yes, Rinaldi is a good idea.' He smiled at her. 'Shall we walk along Burbage Street and take a look at the old place with an acquisitive eye?'

'Now?'

'Well, finish your pudding first.'

As they went towards Burbage Street, Flora suddenly said, 'Hal, why are you doing this? Your work's with the Foreign Office.

Even with a management board, a theatre's a very long way from the things you're used to.'

He took a moment to reply, then said, 'Let's pose a theory. Let's say you and I thought of getting married. That's a purely theoretical assumption at the moment, you understand.'

'Yes?' said Flora. It came out quite calmly, but her heart had given a thump of delight.

'If that situation were to arise, I can't see how you could combine your stage career with being my wife. That's an old-fashioned outlook and it isn't mine, I'd like you to know. The world's changing, but I'm afraid it's not yet changed enough, and a lot of people would find it unacceptable for Lady Chance to dance on a stage.'

'I know that,' said Flora.

'And government circles – Foreign Office circles – are very hidebound indeed. For myself, I wouldn't care. I'd be proud of you. My God, Flora, if the prime minister himself challenged me, I'd tell him to— I'd say it was none of his business,' said Hal temperately. 'And I like theatre people – I've liked the ones I've met through you. But I can't, in all honesty, see that it would be accepted.'

'You mean me continuing to dance on a stage and consort with vagabonds and strumpets, while you spend your time with embassies and diplomats,' said Flora, hoping this did not sound catty.

'They'd all make you out to have been far more daring than you actually are,' he said, 'and it would end in ruining both of us. They'd strip you down to just sequins and ostrich feathers and precious little else.'

Flora thought, and is that what you really want to do to me, I wonder? Strip me? Is this just an elaborate ploy to get me into bed? How far can I trust what you're saying?

'It sounds as if I'd expect you to give up your career in favour of mine,' he said, apparently seeing nothing odd about having this discussion in the middle of a Southwark street in the Tarleton's shadow. 'I wouldn't expect it, but—'

'But the world – your world – would?'

'It has to be said that it would. And assuming this theory about marriage might be acceptable to you—'

'It would be,' said Flora at once.

'Would it? Good. I wasn't sure about that, you know. Well then, you'd have to be very generous about abandoning your stage life. And you'd have to be very sure indeed that you wouldn't resent that loss. That's what I'm grappling with,' he said. 'It's why I'm skirting round this with theories and unromantic plans because I'm worried you might resent it sometime in the future. I think you're one of these remarkable new women: after a time, marriage in itself wouldn't be enough for you. But for Lady Chance to have a – an interest in the managing of a theatre might go some way to . . .'

'Fill the gap?' Lady Chance, thought Flora. Oh God, I'd be Lady Chance. Is that terrifying or exhilarating?

'Yes, exactly that.'

He appeared to wait for a response, and Flora said carefully, 'Speaking purely theoretically, and always allowing for the unexpected, it sounds rather a good theory.'

'You think so?'

'I do,' said Flora. She saw his eyes narrow in the smile that was becoming familiar and beloved and she had to fight not to gaze besottedly at him or let him see that as far as she was concerned, heaven had just opened up in the middle of Burbage Street.

'Perhaps you could be part of some kind of governing board,' said Hal. 'Involved in the administration. It would be thought unusual – even a bit eccentric – but it would be acceptable. And it would still allow you a life within the theatre.'

'Respectable eccentricity,' said Flora. She thought, but I can't manage a theatre! I wouldn't know where to begin! And then, with the feeling that she was mentally squaring her shoulders, or could I? Couldn't I learn?

'There's another rather old-fashioned custom,' said Hal. 'Although it's a nicer one, I think. That's the tradition of a new wife being given a dowry by her husband.'

'I don't think . . .'

'Dowries can take all forms,' he said, speaking rather rapidly. 'Sometimes they can even take the form of a piece of property – such as the Tarleton.'

Flora felt as if she had experienced the extremes of several wildly differing emotions in the last ten minutes, but she tried to match his tone and the mood of this extraordinary conversation. 'Wouldn't that be a – rather an expensive dowry?' she said.

'Well, it will need quite a lot of money spending on it,' said Hal. 'In fact—' He broke off in what was clearly mid-sentence, and said, 'Oh hell— Flora come here,' and pulling her into his arms, began to kiss her so thoroughly and so passionately that Flora had to cling to him to prevent herself from falling down from sheer ecstasy.

When he finally released her, she managed to say, 'When you – um – cast off the correct civil servant, you do so with a vengeance.'

'Did you mind?' His arms were still round her.

'No!'

'Good.' He traced the outline of her face with the tip of a finger and shivers of delight ran all over Flora's body. 'How is that theory looking now, my love?'

'Very enticing.'

'It is, isn't it?'

They walked on, Hal keeping an arm around her waist. Flora thought it was probably as well the street was deserted, although she suspected neither of them would have cared if the entire House of Commons had stood on the kerb.

'Flora, if all this happens,' said Hal. 'If I buy the Tarleton and if you become part of it all—'

'Yes?'

'You won't ever be afraid that—'

'What?'

'That there are any ghosts there?'

The ghost of a young man who tried to rape me and who died in the dark, terrified and mad.

'I might,' said Flora. 'But it won't matter. There are ghosts everywhere. If you look, you find them in the most surprising places.'

The Present

Even after so many years, Caley Merrick thought if you looked, you still found ghosts in the most surprising places. They could walk next to you as you went along a street, your mind on the most mundane things – shopping or a bill to pay – and their presence could be so strong you knew if you turned your head you would see them walking alongside you.

Ghosts. In particular the Tarleton's ghosts. Every time he wrote envelopes in the Harlequin office and exchanged careful remarks with Hilary Bryant or any of the others, it seemed to him that the ghosts stirred.

It was barely a week after Mary's death when the longing to know more about his history – about his ancestors – above all about the links with the Tarleton – came surging back.

Caley was partly appalled at the strength of this feeling because he ought to be grieving – he *was* grieving, really, but beneath the grief was a slowly unfolding excitement at the thought of the old dream waking.

The council gave him compassionate leave. 'Take as long as you need,' the head of his department said, kindly.

As long you need . . . It meant that for as long as he needed, his days were entirely his own. No one would question what he did or where he went, there were no demands on him. The old dream began to take on a new shape in Caley's mind. At first he tried to ignore it, thinking it was wild and impractical. But gradually it gained a hold on his mind, and when he finally acknowledged it, he realized it had been there for a long time.

He must get inside the Tarleton. He must search the place for clues. There might be old posters, framed photographs; names, dates ... If there was an office of some kind, there might even be old account books stored away. The possibilities were exciting and limitless, but at first look, the prospects were not promising, particularly since he was resolved not to commit any kind of criminal act which might end in him being caught. But the idea would not go away, and Caley began to consider who might legitimately go inside the theatre. It was kept reasonably sound and clean; the windows that were visible from the street did not have the thick grime of neglect, and a firm had even put up scaffolding and blast-cleaned the stonework last year – he could remember how pedestrians had to sidestep the scaffolding for a couple of days. After thought, he telephoned local cleaning firms, working methodically through the phone book, pretending he was gathering general information about the services they could offer. He was not unappreciative of the fact that this was only possible because for the moment he was not shackled to that tedious council desk.

He kept his approach simple, asking each of the companies if they handled large buildings in the area, and at the eleventh attempt he got what he wanted. Whistle Clean handled contract cleaning for a number of the larger buildings; several names were mentioned by way of reference and the Tarleton was one of them. From there it was easy to probe a little deeper, and when Caley put down the phone he had the information he wanted. The Tarleton was looked after by a small company called the Harlequin Society who acted as managing agents. They commissioned a full cleaning service two or three times a year. Caley supposed the Harlequin employed other organizations to clean gutters and replace roof tiles, or ensure the roof joists were free of woodworm, and that squatters did not invade the dressing rooms or drug barons use the foyer.

He began to keep a detailed and methodical watch on the Tarleton, careful never to be seen too many times in the same place or to linger too long anywhere. He developed a little routine: on Mondays he bought provisions at one of the shops in Burbage Street: there were seven or eight of them, so it was simple to take them in turn. On Tuesdays he bought a newspaper or magazine at the newsagents. On Wednesdays he might have a cup of coffee in one of the coffee places or wine bars. On Thursdays he had a modest lunch out, going to the Linkman one week, the Kardomah Café the next, the busy self-service lunch place after that. Again, there were several places with a good view of the Tarleton, so he felt perfectly safe in not becoming too well known at any one of them. If anyone from his office happened to see him, they would think, poor Merrick. Trying to fill his days with futile little outings and shopping trips.

Caley knew his watch might be a long one, but he did not mind. In the event, it was not as long as it might have been. Three weeks after he began the vigil – just as he was beginning to think that even the most generous compassionate leave could not extend much beyond this – a van drew up outside the Tarleton and four ladies armed with mops and buckets and packs of cleaning fluids got out and went along Platt's Alley and through the stage door. Caley's heart jumped. He missed seeing the name on the van because a big lorry drove past, obscuring his view. It was probably Whistle Clean, but it was better not to make any assumptions. He walked unhurriedly along the street to buy a bag of apples at the greengrocer's, then took a long time choosing a newspaper. After this he sat down to do the crossword in the Kardomah's window. It was just on twelve; after fifteen minutes he ordered food. If need be, he would do more shopping afterwards, and then go into the self-service place for a cup of tea. No one would notice him, but he would be in sight of Platt's Alley for the next few hours.

The cleaners came out at four o'clock, the van drawing up again to collect them. This time Caley was able to see that it was indeed Whistle Clean. He finished his cup of tea in a leisurely fashion, folded his newspaper, and walked home.

The next day he went along to his old office, deliberately choosing a time when most of them would be at lunch. If he met any of his colleagues, he would say he was calling to see his boss, to discuss resuming work. But, as he had thought, the big open office was empty. His heart racing, his palms slippery with sweat, Caley went into the inner office which was his boss's. Leaving the door half open so that he would hear anyone coming back, he dialled the number of the Harlequin Society. The phone was picked up on the third ring.

'Harlequin Society, can I help?'

A cool, nicely spoken female voice.

Roughening his voice as much as he could, Caley said, 'It's Whistle Clean here. We did the Tarleton job yesterday.'

He paused, and, as he had hoped, she said, 'Yes,' with a slight question in her voice.

'One of the girls left her time-sheet in there,' said Caley. 'Can someone nip in to your office and have the key again, just for an hour? We need the time-sheet to raise your invoice, see.'

This was a bit of a gamble because he had no idea how the Harlequin or Whistle Clean operated when it came to invoicing, but the voice said, 'Yes, I should think so. Today, d'you mean?'

'Yes. I'll get someone along to you later. Sorry, what's your name?'

'Shona Seymour,' she said.

'OK, thanks Shona.' Caley would not, normally, have dreamed of being so familiar with a voice on the phone, but he thought it was in character.

Replacing the receiver, he was aware of the familiar constriction round his lungs, and although it was not really bad enough to need the nebulizer, as he walked out of the building, he used it in case anyone happened to see him. Merrick's in a bad way, they would say, if they saw him.

As he headed for the Harlequin office, he made a mental check of everything he had done, looking for flaws:

The phone call: if it were to be traced – unlikely, but it had to be considered – it would be traced to the big anonymous council department.

Whistle Clean themselves: it was possible that when he reached the Harlequin office, this Shona Seymour would have phoned them and been told no one there knew anything about the call or a forgotten time-sheet. But that could be dealt with. Caley could say it sounded as if the message had not been passed on, or there was a temp on phone duty today. He might even say he was the husband of the woman who had left the time-sheet behind, adding that his wife had not wanted to admit losing it to her boss. This last one was good, that was the one he would use if he had to.

It was the keys themselves that might be the problem. An hour was not very long, but he had not dared make it longer. Would it be long enough to get copies made? And supposing it was one of those special security keys where only named people could get copies cut? His stomach was churning as he mounted the stairs to the first-floor offices, and tapped politely on the door before going in.

Shona Seymour appeared to be on her own in the office. Again, Caley blessed the providence that had prompted him to make use of the lunch hour. She was quite young – perhaps twenty-one or twenty-two – but there was a gloss and a confidence about her that Caley found slightly intimidating. She collected the keys from a shallow wall cupboard and gave him a receipt to sign. He wrote 'C. Jones' in the careful rounded script of a man not overly comfortable with pen and paper, and added the name and address of Whistle Clean.

'I'll get them back well before you close,' he said.

'Oh yes, you must do that.'

Five minutes later Caley was back in the street, with the keys to the Tarleton in his pocket.

It was disconcerting to be told at the shoe-repair and key-cutting shop, that because of the keys' age, copies could not be made under the while you wait service; they would have to be sent out to Acton to a specialist locksmith. No, they would not be hand-cut precisely – a dying art, that! – but they would have to be done on a particular machine which the shop did not have on the premises. Caley was furious with himself for not foreseeing this.

'Can't you copy just one of them?' he said. 'We only need a spare just in case – any one of them would do. My boss will pay extra.'

There was some consultation, and the keys were carried into an unseen room. Caley heard mumbling voices, and the warning constriction caught at his chest. Oh no, not here. Not an attack, not something that will cause them to remember me . . .

But it was all right. One of the keys was for a slightly more recent lock – Caley had no idea which door this might be – and it could be done in the next half hour. Would that be all right? Caley said it would.

At half past three he had his own key, shiny and new, tucked inside his wallet, and by four o'clock he had returned the official bunch to Shona Seymour. He thanked her for her help, and as he went back down the stairs to the street, thought it was odd how a brief encounter with a complete stranger could change your life. Shona Seymour, in the few moments they had spent together, had been instrumental in changing Caley's life, in opening up something potentially very exciting indeed. She had taken his beloved quest to a new level. Thinking all this, he smiled. She would never know, of course. It was unlikely he would ever see her again.

CHAPTER TWENTY-FOUR

He chose the time for his first visit carefully, deciding on late afternoon. At this time of year – late November – daylight was almost gone by four o'clock and some of the street lights had come on. The rush hour was already under way so people walked quickly past the theatre without really seeing it.

Caley was pinning his hopes on the copied key fitting the stage door, which was not really visible from the main street. As he went down Platt's Alley a pulse of excitement was beating inside his head and his hands were trembling. Here was the door – there was an inscription carved into the lintel over it; it was weathered but still readable. 'Please one and please all, be they great, be they small.' This was clearly a quotation or part of a quotation; he would try to trace it when he got home.

He kept a sharp look-out for inquisitive passers-by, and was ready with his story about his wife having left her time-sheet here from yesterday's cleaning session. But no one challenged him, and he was not really surprised when the key turned sweetly in the lock. When you had right on your side, the mundane practicalities fell into place for you; he had noticed that before.

He pushed open the door and stepped inside and the past immediately folded round him like an embrace.

To most people it would be quite eerie to walk through the dark vastness of this old theatre, but Caley knew that despite the shadows and echoes there was nothing in the least frightening in here. He had known there would be ghosts, even before he read Prospero Garrick's book, but he knew they were friendly ghosts of all those people he had read about and longed to know. Bunstable, and Charlie the Clog Dancer. Prospero himself, of course. Was he here now, swirling his silk-lined cape, tipping his top hat as he went, the saucy old boy? And there would be Toby Chance and Frank Douglas, the composer; yes, they would surely be here. Caley had the sudden feeling that if he listened intently enough he would catch the faint strains of Frank Douglas's music, and the whispering echoes of Toby Chance singing the lyrics.

The clues he had hoped for were not there: whatever posters and photographs might once have hung on the walls had long since vanished, and although he found what was clearly a small office, there were no records or ledgers or stored correspondence. But curiously, this did not disappoint him as much as he would have thought. As he went cautiously through the dimness, peering into corners, looking into dressing rooms, into the old wardrobe, into a long bare room with battered chairs and collapsed sofas, he was completely unafraid and aware of a deep contentment. He thought: this is where I belong. I've never belonged anywhere before, but now I know why: this is my place in the world and I've only today found it.

It was those faint echoes of the music that drew him. The long-ago years seated at the old music teacher's piano in the room smelling of biscuits came back to him, and on his third or fourth visit he opened the dusty upright piano in the green room. At first he only placed his fingertips on the yellowed keys, but the next time he played a soft chord.

It was as if a light – a dazzling rainbow light – had been switched on inside his mind. The old instrument was badly out of tune and it was years since Caley had touched a piano anyway. But there was a moment – never to be forgotten, magical and wonderful – when the chord seemed to linger in the silence and he felt the music within his grasp once again.

At the next visit he tried a scale, and at the one after that he played, from memory, one of the simple early exercises he had learned in the biscuit-smelling room all those years ago. It was only then that it occurred to him that although the Tarleton did not seem to hold the clues to his past he had sought, it held something else. The music. He smiled, and had the sudden vivid impression that the people of the theatre had come to stand round the piano, and were nodding and smiling encouragement.

It was infuriating that now he could get in and out of the Tarleton reasonably easily, his time was so limited. Since Mary's death there was no one to question where he went or what he did, but he had to be at his desk in the council offices all day, which only left Saturdays and Sundays. How much better it would be if he did not have that dull, going-nowhere job – if his days were free. The notion of simply handing in his notice was out of the question; this quest and his dreams would sustain him on one level but they would not pay bills or buy food.

The asthma that had begun when he was eighteen still sometimes troubled him. It was not very bad, but it was there. Caley began to exaggerate it, at first just a little, but making sure it was noticeable. Climbing a flight of stairs he would pause halfway up and clutch his chest. If heavy files or boxes had to be carried, he would gasp and reach for the nebulizer. But if asked, he always said he was quite all right, never better, no cause for concern. He was careful to sound over-emphatic when he said this and to use the nebulizer a little more often than before.

The suggestion that he might work shorter hours came after a year. Not retirement of course, said his boss reassuringly, at least, not yet. Caley was still a relatively young man – early forties, wasn't it? But perhaps it would be easier for him to work less hours, and they could see how things went. Of course, once he reached fifty, if the council's medical officer agreed, early retirement with a small pension might be possible.

'Could I think about it, please?' asked Caley.

He pretended to think for a week, and then accepted the reduced hours, along with the reduced salary. It meant he would have to be careful with money for the next few years, but the new arrangement would allow more time to pursue his quest.

But the visits still had to be made with extreme care. Caley knew you could come to know people by sight, not necessarily speaking to them, but recognizing their faces in the street or on buses or the Tube. At first he tried to vary his appearance when he made the journey, which was not very easy because he did not have many clothes, but he tried wearing a scarf or a pair of spectacles, or even carrying a parcel. He thought no one gave him so much as a second glance.

But the resonances from Prospero Garrick's book were still with him, and it was this that gave him his real idea.

'He creeps through the darkness, still clothed in the long overcoat and muffler he always wore in life ... a wide-brimmed hat pulled well down to hide his face.' That was what Prospero had written, and although it was most likely an extravagant description of some perfectly ordinary local character coupled with Prospero's own taste for the melodramatic, remembering the words the spark of an idea flared deep in Caley's mind. He found his notes from Prospero's book; in the closing chapter which Prospero had called 'Curtain Call', there was another reference to the Tarleton ghost. Reading it again, the words seemed to leap off the page and seize him by the throat.

'In summary,' wrote Prospero, 'since all theatres have seen

comedies and tragedies, loves and deaths and murders, to my mind it is little wonder that they all also have their ghosts. They are the shades of the player kings and queens, the phantoms of pantomime, the wraiths of melodrama. They are the torch-bearers who hand down the traditions and the memories, from the early mummers, through the rowdy Elizabethans and the mannered Restoration players, down through the flamboyant Victorians re-writing the Bard to suit their own purposes . . . All the way down to the present time.'

It was so flowery that at the time Caley had very nearly skipped the whole section. But he had diligently written it all down, and now he was glad, because towards the end was that other mention.

'Even the dear old Tarleton's ghost,' wrote Prospero, 'that curious figure that seems to date from the start of the Great War and hid its face as it crept along Platt's Alley – even that was believed by some to hail from an older era. It had been seen before, say those greybeards whose memories are long and whose discourse is vivid and even loquacious, and who is to say they may not be right? Perhaps the Tarleton's ghost is a twice-born ghost. Who can tell? Not I.'

Caley closed the notebook thoughtfully. The impression was that Prospero had talked to one or two very elderly people who had contributed vagrant glimpses of their own pasts – although that might be as much due to a liberal hand with a whisky bottle as to a reliable memory. Originally Caley had not been very con-vinced about those earlier reports of the ghost, but rereading them now, it occurred to him that if the Tarleton's ghost had been seen twice, it might be seen a third time. It might, in short, cover Caley's own visits to the theatre.

The figure seemed to have been best known in 1914. How well known had the story been in those years? And how long-lived a tale had it been? There would not be anyone alive now who would have actually seen that figure prowling those fog-bound streets, but memories in this part of London went back a long way and

1914 was just about touchable at one or two removes, so that older people might have heard the stories. A person of seventy or seventy-five might remember parents talking about the mysterious figure. Someone of Caley's age might remember grandparents doing so.

To use the legend might draw attention to himself, which was exactly what he was trying to avoid. But even while he recognized the danger, he knew he was going to do it anyway: the prospect of identifying with the Tarleton's past in this way strongly attracted him. And he did not think there was much of a risk: if people saw a muffled figure walking into Platt's Alley most of them would not take any notice – you saw all kinds of oddly dressed figures nowadays and people were too busy to care anyway. One or two gullible souls might say, half-jokingly, half-nervously, that the Tarleton's ghost had been seen again, but they would be met with guffaws or jibes about one too many in the pub last night.

In his time away from the office he scoured musty-smelling secondhand clothes shops and theatrical costumiers, to find a long dark overcoat and the right kind of old-fashioned deep-brimmed hat, eventually tracking down both garments in a street market. They were exactly what he wanted – to the casual eye he looked like one of those old Viennese professors you saw in 1930s films. At worst he looked eccentric but not over the top. Most important of all, he did not look in the least like the Caley Merrick most people knew.

Putting the things on for the first time was an extraordinary experience. Whoever he had been, that dark-clad figure – whether he had been a real person or a ghost or simply a figment of somebody's imagination – wearing these things brought him and the past abruptly closer. I'm donning a mantle, he thought. I'm taking on the cloak of some long-ago actor or performer who perhaps died here, or did something here that left a strong imprint. A musician, perhaps? This last idea sent delight through him.

He liked to go along to the theatre in the early evenings. It pleased him to think he was walking along Burbage Street at the same hour as the Tarleton's audiences had done on their way to the theatre. He imagined them walking alongside him and hearing them discuss the evening ahead, saying, 'Toby Chance is performing a new song tonight,' or, 'Bunstable's on the bill this evening.' Perhaps arguing about whether they would have supper in the Oyster Bar or go along to the Sailor's Retreat for mutton and ale pie and a bottle of stout.

And once inside the theatre, the new trendiness of Bankside – in fact most of the twentieth and all of the twenty-first century – melted away. Caley loved that, and he loved the feeling that the ghosts welcomed him. He would never be able to speak of this to anyone, of course: no one could possibly understand how the ghosts liked to hear the old songs played and even quietly sung, or how Caley himself liked to play and sing them. He had scoured secondhand book shops in the area and had found several bundles of old sheet music, some of which were written by Toby Chance – Chance & Douglas it always said on the covers. Caley set himself to learn them – Mary had said all those years ago that he would surely have lost what she called the knack of playing the piano, but he had not. At first he had been unsure and hesitant, but he had persisted and gradually the old skill had returned. Not completely; his fingers were no longer as supple as they had been at ten and eleven years of age, but he was competent enough. He embarked cautiously on the music taught him all those years ago: simple versions of Chopin and Czerny nocturnes, old folk songs, and ballads.

But it was when he played the music and the songs from the early 1900s that the whole theatre seemed to come alight and alive, and the feeling of being at home, of belonging, was strong and sweet. Ghost song, that old doorman had called it. Caley liked this; he liked humming the ghost songs to himself as he went through the beloved rooms.

On his fiftieth birthday the retirement and the modest pension were finally arranged and, as he walked quietly away from his desk for the last time, he was conscious of an immense uplifting of his spirit. He would have to be very prudent and careful with his tiny income but he would have enough.

He never regretted the small deception he had practised on Shona Seymour all those years ago – the deception that had resulted in his copying the key.

Even when he had embarked on a new stage of his plan – that of becoming one of the Harlequin's casual workers – he had felt perfectly safe about meeting her again. It was unlikely in the extreme that she would recognize him: a workman seen all those years ago for about five minutes would not have made any real impression, and he knew he had changed a good deal since then. What was left of his hair was grey, and he had had to have most of his teeth removed six years earlier: the dentures he now wore had drastically changed the shape of his mouth. As for Miss Seymour herself, Caley thought her little changed, although the years seemed to have hardened her – given her several coats of enamel. He had wondered if she had someone in her life, and thought he would be very sorry for any man who became seriously entangled with her.

The possession of the Tarleton key had been – and still was – the most marvellous and precious thing in his life. He never walked along Platt's Alley without a lifting of his spirits and the feeling that the ghosts would be waiting for him, invisible but unquestionably near, waiting to hear the music he would play, waiting to see if he would wander into the stage box as he sometimes liked to do, humming one of the songs they knew.

When it rained heavily the alley was often semi-flooded and the long overcoat, so carefully searched for in the street markets, trailed in the puddles so that the hem became wet and bedraggled. For a few hours, while it was drying, it smelt of rain and age, but afterwards it smelt of the Tarleton itself. Over the years the other

270

things in his wardrobe came to smell of it, as if the theatre wanted to find its way into every corner and every fibre of Caley's life. Wherever you are, I'm there with you, it seemed to be saying.

After rainstorms the stage door was sometimes slightly swollen from the moisture and was difficult to open. This always caused a surge of panic. What if some officious busybody decided to fit a new lock or even a new door one day? But it had never happened and no one ever looked twice at the muffled figure walking quickly to the entrance to Platt's Alley.

And then had come the night when he stood in the stage box and watched Hilary Bryant and the unknown man levering up part of the stage. This had alarmed Caley, because it looked very much as if a detailed inspection was being made of the Tarleton – perhaps by a surveyor or builder. Hilary and the man hammered and crashed about on the stage, but Caley did not dare go too near the front of the box to see exactly what they were doing. At one point Hilary seemed aware of his presence, because she looked up at the stage box and said something, and the man shone the torch straight onto it. But neither of them could have seen Caley who stepped back at once and became hidden by the deep darkness within, and once warned it was easy to stay well out of sight and hearing. The Tarleton was full of nooks and crannies and hidey-holes and by this time he knew them all.

In the end they left the auditorium and went out through the stage door: there was the unmistakable sound of the old door opening and closing and Caley waited a few minutes to let them get clear. In case they might be lingering outside, he went out by the main street door. He did not have a key to that door, but it was one of the one-way exits that opened from inside, so all he had to do was lift and push on the bar that released the lock and slip out into the street, pulling the door firmly so the mechanism clicked back.

He walked home, a thin dark-clad figure, weaving its way through the crowded streets as quietly and as insubstantially as a

271

forgotten ghost. It was raining hard which meant people had their heads down and their faces shielded with umbrellas and no one noticed him.

His mind was in turmoil. He had come to know the pattern of the Tarleton's year very well indeed. He knew about the twice-yearly cleaning sessions and he knew Whistle Clean had been replaced by Happy Mops a while back, and also that there were annual fire regulation and electrical wiring checks and an inspection made for the insurance of the whole structure. None of that explained what Hilary Bryant and the man had been doing there this evening.

He lay awake for most of the night, reviewing everything he knew about the beloved building. Over the years, listening to people talk, reading everything that could be read, painstakingly piecing together fragments and shreds of information, one of the things he had learned was that there was something called a 'restraint' on the theatre: a very definite restriction – maybe even a legal one – that had held it in its dark silence all this long time. He had tried to find out more about this restraint, and he had hoped his recent association with the Harlequin might provide more information: he had imagined he would be able to find and read the file on the building itself, without anyone knowing. There would surely be such a file somewhere. But no matter how many files there might be on the old place, Caley had early on discovered that the main files were kept in Miss Seymour's office, which was always locked if she was not there.

But if you were going to open up an old theatre, one of the first things you might do would be to call in an architect or a builder to see what needed doing to the structure – specifically to see what needed doing to the stage.

Around five a grey light filtered through the bedroom curtains, and he heard the clatter of the milkman in the street below. He got up and as he washed and dressed he faced the possibility that the odd restraint might be nearing its end. The knowledge brought

272

a twisting fear, knotting his stomach with cramp, then moving upwards to his chest. It was a more severe attack than usual, but he groped for the nebulizer and inhaled for several minutes. After his breathing became easier, he made a pot of tea which he drank gratefully, then poured cereal into a bowl, trying to pretend nothing was wrong.

But everything might be wrong, Caley was already aware of that. If the restraint ended people would come storming into the Tarleton. They would fling open doors and windows so light came pouring in. They would tramp through the wonderful rooms and tear down walls or take up floors and rip out ceilings, planning how they would put on shows and plays again, never once giving a thought to the ghosts. And the ghosts would hate it! Caley knew that. The ghosts would shy away from the too bright light, and they would not understand the harsh modern music. And how would Caley himself bear it, knowing he could no longer come and go whenever he wanted? Knowing he could never sit in the green room with his hands on the long-familiar keys of the piano that might even have belonged to Toby Chance, pouring out the music that had become so much a part of him?

He looked rather despairingly round the little house; all those years ago Mary had said there was no room for a piano, and she had been right. In any case, Caley did not want to play his music here; he wanted to play it in the place where it belonged.

If the Tarleton really were to reopen, it would be the worst thing that had ever happened to him.

CHAPTER TWENTY-FIVE

At first Hilary enjoyed the journey to Fosse Leigh. Shona was an efficient driver, the car was comfortable and they had their work for the Harlequin Society in common: specifically, they had the Tarleton's future to talk about. Hilary had spent the evening in her flat and some of the morning, developing ideas for a really stunning reopening campaign. While she worked, she had tried not to look at the phone too often, or to will it to ring and for it to be Robert. It was silly to be disappointed that he had not phoned, because his foraging into the theatre's nether regions could have taken longer than he had expected. And when he got home (wherever his home was), it might have been so late he had not wanted to disturb her.

At the start of the journey she talked a bit about her preliminary ideas for the reopening, but she had the impression that Shona was not really listening. Probably she wanted to concentrate on driving: even when they were clear of the M25 and onto the M3 the traffic was heavy and they met a couple of hold-ups.

They turned off the motorway near Farnborough and had lunch at a prosperous-looking hotel, Shona remarking that since they were on Harlequin expenses, they might as well eat in civilized surroundings. Over the meal she seemed to relax a bit, but when they went into the hotel's plush washroom, Hilary thought she looked pale, although perhaps that was just the light which was rather self-consciously shaded.

But back in the car, Shona still looked pale and her eyes had an odd, unfocussed look. It was to be hoped she was all right to drive the rest of the way to Fosse Leigh and then back again tomorrow morning; Hilary could drive, but she did not actually own a car, mostly because cars in London were apt to be more of a liability than an asset. She was not very used to driving on motorways and Shona's car was a gleaming and patrician make, so the thought of giving it even the tiniest scrape was daunting. But perhaps it was just the fading light that made Shona look like that; even midway through the afternoon it was dark at this time of year.

If Robert phoned the Harlequin today he would get Hilary's voicemail. This was perfectly all right because she had recorded a new message on her office phone and also on her home phone, giving her mobile number. She had checked the mobile just before leaving London; Robert had not phoned, although Gil had. Hilary was by this time so deeply inside the world of the Tarleton, to say nothing of hoping for a call from Robert, that it had taken her a moment to think who Gil was. Oh yes, of course. Rather dreary evenings at the dismal restaurants Gil favoured and listening to earnest explanations about his health. Gil's message was fairly typical: something about sorry not to have been in touch, but the damp weather was affecting his sinuses. Hilary didn't phone back because she couldn't cope with Gil or his sinuses today.

She would switch her mobile off while they were at Levels House, but she would check discreetly for messages at intervals. At this point she had a mad image of herself sneaking off to the loo every quarter of an hour just to see if Robert had phoned, and this struck her as so exactly like the behaviour of a love-sick fourteen year old that she put Robert firmly from her mind and told Shona they only had about ten miles to go before they had to look for the Glastonbury signs.

Shona had felt slightly headachy ever since waking that morning. The night's bad dream – the screaming clawing thing trying to break out from behind the brick wall in the cellar – had dissolved, but it had left her with the usual feeling of disorientation. Before leaving London she had swallowed a couple of paracetamol, and thought she would have a more substantial lunch than usual; she and Hilary could drive off the motorway and find a reasonable pub or hotel somewhere. Cousin Elspeth had always believed in a good meal at midday: people needed a hot dinner she used to say, serving up stodgy meat and gravy concoctions and tutting if people did not leave clean plates or if Shona, then in her teens, asked for salad and cottage cheese in order to achieve a fashionable stick-like figure. Such nonsense, said Elspeth, who was four-square and dumpy and could not be doing with such vanity. When Elspeth clumped through Shona's nightmares, she always did so with a very heavy tread, and she always smelt of gluey gravy and cabbage boiled too long.

The journey took longer than they had expected, mostly because of a hold-up on the M3, and darkness had fallen as Shona drove the last few miles to Levels House. A drizzly rain was falling, blurring the view through the windscreen.

'It's quite lonely countryside out here, isn't it?' said Hilary, helping to wipe condensation from the windows.

'Whatever it is, this rain is a nuisance,' said Shona. 'It's difficult to see through it. It's a bit like the mists that used to roll in from the moors where I grew up,' she said, then thought: damn, I'm breaking one of my own rules about never referring to my childhood. To stop Hilary picking up on it, she said, 'Is that the sign for Fosse Leigh?'

'Yes. Turn right in about a hundred yards, then three miles along. I hope,' said Hilary suddenly, 'that Madeleine Ferrelyn

276

isn't some sad frail recluse with not much money and no family.'

'If she owns the Tarleton she can hardly be said to have no money,' rejoined Shona rather tartly. 'And she mentioned having plenty of space for overnight guests so the house must be quite substantial. This looks like the start of the village now.'

'Yes. It's quite small, isn't it?'

Fosse Leigh was very small indeed; Shona thought it was not much bigger than Moil. There was a straggle of houses along the road – some were pleasingly old, some were probably former tied cottages, recently tarted up, and there was a row of council houses. A church spire rose up at the far end, and there was a small square with a few shops, a post office, a village hall and a pub.

'There should be a manor house or the squire's residence looking down on all this,' murmured Hilary. 'The place where the village girls could always get domestic work and the squire's lady helped people in trouble. Rural paternalism. Early version of the welfare state.'

Levels House was about a mile beyond the village proper, and they almost drove past it because there were no street lights anywhere and the house itself was thickly screened by old trees. But Hilary spotted the sign on the gatepost in time, and Shona braked hard and reversed so they could turn in. Several times since leaving the motorway she had felt vaguely confused as to where they were going and had been grateful to Hilary who had said things like, 'That's the turning for Salisbury,' and talking briefly about the awesome cathedral there and the smaller one at Wells with its remarkable clock figures, and about Glastonbury and its Arthurian associations. It's all right, Shona had thought. I do know where we are, after all – it's only the remnants of the nightmare that's making me feel light-headed. I know quite well we're driving through Hampshire and Wiltshire, and this isn't Yorkshire with the mists coming in from the North Sea.

Even so, approaching Levels House brought a brief, shutter-flash impression of the old private roadway up to Grith. Thick rhododendrons fringed the drive: in summer they would be a riot of colour, but now they were dark gloomy shapes. The untrimmed laurel bushes at Grith had looked like that. They had blotted out most of the light, those laurel bushes, and they dripped moisture onto the ground so that when you walked along the drive you thought you could hear ghost footsteps creeping along behind you.

As the house came into view round the drive's curve, it was as if something made a vicious swiping blow at the centre of Shona's mind. It's Grith, she said to herself. You're going back to Grith. Anna's been pulling you back here, back to Grith, all this time. Would Anna be waiting for her?

But Anna was long since dead and this was not Grith, although it was probably the same age and was built in the design of that era for people of a certain income – people requiring spaciousness in an age when domestic labour was cheap.

But Grith was grey and black and lowering like a sombre and grainy old photograph, and it was set amidst the bleak Moil moors. Levels House looked exactly how Grith would look if it was treated to a wash of warm colour – twopence-coloured as they used to say of the old posters, against Grith's penny-plain. Instead of the moors of Moil, the backcloth here was gentler fields and hedgerows, but in essence everything was the same. The house had the same small, latticed windows and the same lowering eaves above them, like frowning eyebrows.

'Beautiful grounds,' Hilary was saying. 'How on earth does Madeleine Ferrelyn manage this all by herself, I wonder? That looks like an orchard beyond the gardens.'

Grith had never been called lovely or had its gardens admired; it had been dismal and far too large for Grandfather and Mother and Shona. Levels House had welcoming lights and an old-fashioned coach lamp over the porch, sending out a warm glow. No one ever hung lamps outside Grith, because no one ever came to Grith after dark.

For a few moments they thought no one was going to answer Hilary's ring at the bell, then there was the sound of rather slow footsteps and an elderly lady opened the door. She was tall and spare with short brown hair streaked with grey, and although she looked to be in her late seventies and leaned quite heavily on a stick, she had an energetic air about her and an apple-cheeked face as if she spent a good deal of her time out of doors. She wore a tweed skirt and pullover, with a bright red scarf knotted at the neck.

'Hello!' said this lady, looking and sounding pleased. 'You'll be Miss Seymour and Miss Bryant from London. I'm delighted to see you both. I'm Madeleine Ferrelyn – well, you'll have realized that. Come along inside. You'll be glad of a cup of tea or coffee after your journey, I expect. Rather you than me to go whizzing along those dreadful motorways. Wretched things, although I daresay they're a necessary evil.'

Immediately inside was a large hall like Grith's, easily big enough to use as a dining room as Grandfather had sometimes done. There was the same wide stairway leading up off it.

Madeleine Ferrelyn took them into a long, low-ceilinged sitting room with old-fashioned cretonne covers on the sofa and chairs, and a large fireplace with a thick oak mantel and copper brush and shovel in the hearth. Several framed prints and watercolours of the area hung on the walls and a bowl of bronze chrysanthemums stood on a gate-leg table. The scent of woodsmoke mingled pleasantly with the wet-rain scent of the chrysanthemums. It's all right, thought Shona. This is nothing like Grith. I'm back in the present. Safe.

Their hostess was saying she hoped the house would be warm enough for them, because the area was shockingly damp at times. 'We're a bit prone to the occasional winter flood here: there're what they call clay levels along the coast – effectively, sea walls – but there are peaty moors inland that are lower and the Severn estuary's got a high tidal range. Occasionally it gets past the defences and slops a bit further inland than it should. I'm used to it: I've lived here a very long time – it belonged to my husband's family but he's been dead a good many years now.'

'It's a lovely house,' said Hilary, looking about her. 'Oh, and we brought you this.' She handed over the small bag containing a whole Brie, a pottery dish of pâté and a bottle of Madeira. 'A contribution to your larder.'

'That's extremely kind of you. There was really no need, but – oh my, that Brie looks good. We'll have some of it to round off our supper. Now then, the cloakroom's off the hall if you want a wash and brush up after the journey, and your rooms are just at the head of the stairs,' said Madeleine Ferrelyn briskly. 'First right and second right off the landing. Bathroom's at the end of the passage. I won't take you up if you don't mind – the medics have banned me from climbing stairs more than once a day. A great nuisance, but there it is. But while you take your things up I'll be putting on the kettle, my dears.' The 'my dears' came out naturally in the country fashion.

'Thank you, Mrs Ferrelyn,' began Hilary.

'Make it Madeleine, do. Can't be bothered with fuss and formality. You're Hilary, that's right, isn't it?'

'And I'm Shona,' said Shona.

'That's a beautiful old Scottish name. How lucky you are to have been given it.'

Shona was glad she and Hilary did not have to share a bedroom: she disliked sharing a room with anyone unless it was a lover, and even then she tried to part company before falling asleep. Her room was comfortable, with the bed neatly made up, and fresh towels and soap on the little hand basin. There was a heavy old-fashioned wardrobe and dressing table with a lace runner, and a flowered carpet, slightly faded by the window where the sun would come in.

The curtains were open and Shona stood for a moment looking out over the gardens and the dark fields beyond. What had

Madeleine Ferrelyn said? The Severn slopes a bit further inland than it should ... *Moil Moor sometimes overflows*, Grandfather used to say. *After heavy rain the cellars occasionally get flooded ...*

But downstairs again, with the fire crackling in the hearth and a pot of tea set out on a low table, she began to feel better. Hilary produced her notes on the Tarleton and embarked on an explanation of the preliminary proposals, and Shona listened, content for the moment to let her take the lead. She had come up with some excellent outlines, especially when you remembered that this time yesterday the identity of the Tarleton's owner had still been a mystery.

'Whatever's staged on that first night has to be explosive,' Hilary was saying. 'Really memorable. I also think it should link to the Tarleton's past, even if modern stuff gets put on later.'

'Agreed.'

'An all-out Victorian evening would be quite good and make for lively publicity,' said Hilary. 'And we might end up having to settle for that. But I can't help feeling that would be a bit obvious, a bit predictable. What would be brilliant is if we could recreate the final show put on before the place closed. The closing night reclaimed.' She looked at them both.

Madeleine said, slowly, 'I like that idea very much, Hilary. But – would it be possible? Could you trace the details of that last performance? After so long?'

'I don't know yet. We might be lucky and turn up an actual programme or a poster. Or it might be a case of putting together fragments of information from old books and newspapers: one person might make mention of a single act in one place; another might make mention of another in a totally different place, and we'd join it all up. That would be long-winded, but not impossible. There are any amount of privately printed memoirs of old actors and all kinds of sources I could check. The internet's brilliant for a lot of research nowadays, of course – you often get drama students publishing theses on the net, and sometimes they give their primary sources – perhaps an odd playbill they've turned up or an old set of theatrical accounts. And what I had in mind,' said Hilary, 'was that we'd have replicas of those acts. Not mimicking the original singers or musicians or dancers – certainly not caricaturing them, either. Just performing them as they were written and as they were intended to be performed.'

'Reclaiming the past,' said Madeleine thoughtfully. 'I love the idea.'

'Do you?' Hilary's eyes shone. 'I'm so pleased. I love it as well. See, we could even set the acts against a huge backdrop of blown-up photos of the originals. We might have blown-up newspaper articles or advertisements of the time, as well: they'd be easy to find. The rest might take a lot of delving, but I'd love to do it,' she said. 'I'd organize everything for you. I mean – the Harlequin would organize it.'

'Would you? I've got a few old photographs from my father's time – you could see if they'd help as a starting point,' said Madeleine enthusiastically. 'And I think there are even some old programmes – it'd be too much to hope that the closing programme's there, but you might get some leads. Everything's stowed in the attic and I haven't been able to get up there for years, but we'll see about making a proper search.'

'I'd go up if you'd let me,' said Hilary eagerly.

'It's a bit of a climb. And you'd need to spend several days going through it all, although there is electricity up there.'

'Madeleine, I'd climb up Mount Everest for the Tarleton,' said Hilary, earnestly. 'I'd spend seven years in the attic – in any attic – if I had to. I'm so intrigued by that theatre that I can't bear the thought of – of anything second-rate for its reopening. I don't want us to short-change it.' She paused, a bit uncertainly as if she thought she might have gone too far, but Madeleine at once said, 'Hilary, you're a treat. Let's go all out for this.'

'The bar could serve the kind of food and drinks the audiences would have had in 1914,' said Hilary. 'We've got a very good freelance food expert on our register – her name's Judy Randall, and she'd fall on this project with absolute glee. We wouldn't charge 1914 prices, of course.'

She grinned, and Madeleine said promptly, 'I should hope not, indeed. Would you have the audience dressing up as well? Edwardian finery?'

'I considered that, but I think it's better not. It smacks a bit of *Old Time Music Hall*, and I think it might turn out a bit twee. Also,' said Hilary, 'I think the angle should be that this is a look at the Tarleton's past – a nod to the nineteenth century from the twenty-first. Taking a modern audience back ninety-odd years.'

'Yes, I see all that. I think you're right.' Madeleine glanced at Shona. 'Is this the right moment to bring up the sordid subject of coinage?'

'It has to be discussed at some point,' said Shona.

'Well, then, you'd better know right off that a small trust fund was left for maintenance of the place – it's administered by the bank, and it's what they use to pay your fee and the cleaning and insurance costs and so on. It really is quite small, though. I don't know the exact balance offhand, but I do know the bank were getting a bit worried as to whether it would last out until the restriction ended. There wouldn't be anything like the sum you'd need for all this, in fact I'm inclined to think the terms of the trust wouldn't allow the money to be used in this way at all.'

Shona registered that she and Hilary shared the same thought: *who* created the trust fund? But Hilary, hardly missing a beat, said, 'Finance is really Shona's area, but my idea was that we'd try to get backers or sponsors.'

She glanced at Shona with an over-to-you look, and Shona said, 'Yes, I think we could get backers.'

'Could you make that kind of approach on my behalf?'

'We wouldn't normally, but this is rather a special case,' said Shona. 'We'd like the Harlequin to be involved in the project as much as possible. It really is a piece of music-hall history. So

283

I think we could talk to finance people on your behalf, and also theatrical agents and designers. It would be good if a backer could take on the whole package, although we'd make sure that you – through the Harlequin – retained overall control.'

'I'm inclined to say I'll trust you with the whole works,' said Madeleine. 'My health isn't up to whizzing about talking to financiers and theatrical agents, even if I knew where to start, which I don't.'

'Well, we'll take it one step at a time,' said Shona. 'Hilary and I will draft out a more detailed plan on the lines we've talked about and I'll get costings. We can talk again in a week or so. Do you ever come to London, Madeleine?'

'Not for years and not very often even when I was in better health. Doctor's not so keen on my travelling anywhere now.' She tapped her chest. 'Heart's been unreliable for a few years – rather a bad attack last year which put the wind up the doctors, and then a stroke straight on top of it. That's why the date for the Tarleton over-ran. I knew the restriction had ended, but I wasn't in any condition to do anything about it.'

'I'm sorry to hear you were so ill,' said Shona conventionally.

'A wretched nuisance,' said Madeleine. 'But they keep me going with pills and pink stuff to spray onto my tongue if I get an attack.' She smiled. 'We won't discuss ailments. But you'll understand it makes it difficult for me to travel far.'

'It's not a problem,' said Shona. 'We can easily come down here again. And most things can be done over the phone or via email—' She broke off questioningly, and Madeleine said, 'I don't have a computer, but I'd be prepared to buy a laptop if it would help – I've been thinking it was time I put a toe into modern technology anyway.'

Shona said, 'On the money side, there are several grants we can certainly apply for and probably get – the government's keen on developing areas like Bankside. And once the place is up and running it should pay for itself – at least, that will be the aim. You could be as much or as little involved as you wanted to be. In any case, we'd report to you regularly.'

'The Harlequin's done a fair enough job all these years,' said Madeleine. 'And it's certainly respected the conditions in my father's will.'

My father ... We're both waiting for the right moment to ask who he was, thought Shona, glancing at Hilary.

Hilary had clearly registered the mention of Madeleine's father, but she only said, 'I'm assuming there was at least one of Toby Chance's songs that night – if not, I think we'd have to cheat a bit and put one into our own programme. I found one quite recently for a TV thing – it's called "All Because of Too Much Tipsy Cake" – and I don't think it would be difficult to unearth one or two more. I keep calling them Toby's songs, but correctly they were Chance and Douglas's songs, weren't they? That was the team: Toby wrote the lyrics and Douglas wrote the music.'

'We'd certainly have to use one of their songs for the reopening,' said Madeleine at once, 'because he was my father.'

Into the silence that suddenly fell, Hilary said, 'Toby Chance was your father?'

'What? No, my dear, I meant the other one. Toby's music partner. Frank Douglas. He was my father. He was the one who imposed that long dark silence on the Tarleton.'

CHAPTER TWENTY-SIX

'It's no use asking me why or how he ended up owning the Tarleton,' said Madeleine, 'because I don't know and he never said. The curious thing, though, is that he wasn't the kind of man you'd associate with owning property of any kind, in fact he was a bit of a rolling stone – even a touch irresponsible, although not where my mother and I were concerned. And I think my mother had a little money of her own.'

Hilary said softly, 'So all along, the mysterious owner was the man who wrote those songs with Toby Chance.'

'We've speculated a bit about who the owner might be,' said Shona. 'Of course, we have. But I don't think Frank Douglas was ever a contender, was he, Hilary?'

'No. I don't know that we knew much about him other than his name on some old song sheets. I thought it would turn out to be Toby who put that restriction on the theatre.'

'Toby Chance certainly owned the theatre for a number of years,' said Madeleine. 'And I always had the impression that my father acquired it from him after it was closed.'

'In 1914,' said Hilary.

'Yes. It was ceded to him by Deed of Gift in October of that year,' said Madeleine. 'That's one thing I do know, although I don't know much more than that. A Deed of Gift means no money is actually paid over, of course.'

'Yes, but it's a perfectly legal way of transferring a piece of property,' said Shona, 'although restrictive covenants can sometimes be written in, I think, and I'd guess that's what happened with the Tarleton.'

'It is. It's all wrapped up in legal jargon, but the burden of the gift is that it wasn't to be sold or used in any public way whatsoever until fifty years after my father's death.'

'That's a very long time,' said Shona. 'And it's extremely strange to leave such an inheritance to someone and then prevent it being beneficial.'

'It's almost as if he was handing you a – a task,' said Hilary. 'Trusting you to safeguard something.'

'Without giving me any idea of what that something was,' said Madeleine rather drily. 'I've done what the will requested, but I've never known why the request was made in the first place.'

'Didn't your father ever talk about the Tarleton?' asked Hilary. 'Didn't he say anything that might provide a clue?'

'He hardly ever mentioned it,' said Madeleine. 'I wasn't born until he was turned forty – 1933 that was, in case you were wondering.' She smiled. 'I think he'd always been a bit of a rover: he'd hear of something he'd like to do or be involved in – usually some theatrical venture – and off he'd go. While my mother was alive she usually went with him: they were a good pair. I was at school and they always came back for the holidays, and it all seemed perfectly normal to me. Sometimes he'd have friends from his music-hall days to the house – I liked that. They used to have evenings round the piano, singing and laughing. Impromptu stuff, but they enjoyed it. I was generally sent to bed, but when I was a bit older I was allowed to join in sometimes.' She suddenly looked very wistful, but then said, briskly, 'They're good memories I have of those years. But you see, my dears, it all meant I was never especially close to my father – not to either of my parents, really. And then when the war broke out my father was away a good deal, mostly with ENSA – they organized concert parties and plays for the troops and the allied forces.' She said this with a slightly questioning air, as if unsure whether they would know what ENSA was.

Shona knew quite well what ENSA was because of her years with the Harlequin, but she was grateful to Hilary for saying with unmistakable sincerity, 'I've always loved reading about ENSA.'

'There are some photos from those years along with the other stuff in the attic,' said Madeleine. 'My father toured a lot of the camps. But you do see,' she said, 'that I didn't really spend very much time with him and I certainly didn't know a great deal about his early life. I knew he was on the halls and I knew he wrote quite a lot of music – songs in the main, mostly in collaboration with Toby Chance. And he stayed in touch with some of the people from his earlier life – there was a disreputable old comic called Bunstable, I remember. He'd turn up from time to time. And Rinaldi who was stage manager at the Tarleton – I liked Rinaldi. Everyone did. And there were one or two dancers from the old days – my mother said they were probably no better than they should be. But she laughed when she said it, and she always gave them a meal or a bed for the night if they needed it.'

Shona glanced at Hilary and saw she was listening with absorption.

'My mother died at the end of the war,' said Madeleine. 'I was twelve. But it wasn't until my father died, ten years afterwards, that I discovered he was the actual owner of the Tarleton. It was quite a shock, although I'd have to say the discovery of the restraint was an even bigger shock.'

'It's a remarkable restriction,' said Shona.

'The will is very strongly worded,' said Madeleine. 'I remember asking the solicitor how legally binding the clause was and he said it couldn't actually be enforced, but that if I sold the theatre or opened it to the public he thought I might stand in danger of forfeiting the rest of the inheritance. The executors were the bank – the one you've dealt with – together with the solicitor's own firm. If I chose to ignore that clause, the bank were required to report to the probate authorities. The solicitor did admit he'd never come across anything quite like it – he had no idea which way a decision might go; he said it would be a test case.'

'Extraordinary,' said Hilary. 'So you decided to comply with it.'

'I sort of got swept along by various events,' she said. 'My father didn't leave me a lot of money, and I think what he did leave had originally been my mother's. I was rather badly off in those days – we all have difficult patches in our lives, don't we, and that was one of mine. So the money I did get was a bird in the hand as far as I was concerned. There wasn't anything like enough to start putting on performances, and I had no idea how to go about finding a backer or anything like that. I'd never lived in London and I wouldn't have known where to begin. And also—' She stopped and Shona waited.

'Also,' said Madeleine, and Shona had the impression she was choosing her words with care, 'the Tarleton was already regarded as a bit of a mystery – I knew that if I didn't know anything else. If I had contested the will, it could have caused quite a stir. And even ignoring the will and just opening the place up would have attracted some publicity. I didn't want that.' She broke off, one hand going to the left side of her chest, a white look appearing round her mouth.

Shona was aware of Hilary making an involuntary movement forward, and she thought: there's something Madeleine Ferrelyn isn't telling us. Whatever it is, it's distressed her to remember it. Her heart's clearly quite frail. Do we pretend nothing's happened, I wonder? Yes, I think we do. But why on earth didn't she fight that clause in her father's will all those years ago? Surely, given a choice, anyone would opt for the Tarleton? Its open-market value, even then, would have far outweighed whatever Frank

Douglas left – and it doesn't sound as if he left all that much.

Madeleine seemed to have recovered from that momentary spasm of pain or distress. She was saying television had put a lot of theatres out of business in the 1950s and early 1960s. 'And the Tarleton was already old-fashioned. Even I could see that a lot of money would have to be spent on it to make it even halfway viable.'

'So you decided to honour the requirement in the will?' said Hilary.

'Anything else seemed such a gamble, you see. So I thought I'd stay with the safe option for a few years at least – there was the small trust fund to keep the place maintained so it wouldn't become derelict. And then, as the years went by, I began to look on the place as a sort of investment. Almost as a pension fund.'

'People do that more and more with property these days,' said Hilary and Madeleine sent her a grateful look, 'specially since all those pension fund crashes.'

'Unexpected parts of London were coming back into fashion,' said Madeleine. 'Notting Hill and Docklands and so on. I thought Bankside might do the same.'

'As, indeed, it has.'

'Yes. I don't know why my father made that clause,' she said, 'but he was no fool for all his roving Irish blood, and he must have had good reason. After I married, the Tarleton, in cash terms, didn't seem so important. My husband wasn't a millionaire but he was quite comfortably off. My life was here – in Somerset – in this house. And as the years went along, when I thought about the Tarleton I found I rather liked the idea that I was doing what my father had wanted. It gave me a feeling of connection with him.' She studied them. 'Now you'll think I'm a hopeless romantic.'

'If you're a hopeless romantic, so am I,' said Hilary. 'Anyway, think of the fun we'd have missed. Think of the myths and legends that have grown up round that place, and how you've been at the heart of them. Adding to a little piece of theatre history.'

'What a nice way of seeing it. And you're quite right, Hilary.' She made another of the brisk determined movements, as if putting the past firmly in its place. 'Now, it's already getting on for seven o'clock and you'll be ready for some supper, I daresay? It's only very simple – a girl from the village comes in a couple of times a week to help with a bit of cleaning and gardening and shopping – that wretched stroke on top of the heart problems slowed me down a bit. But she's made a chicken casserole and there's an apple pie with my own apples from the orchard here. Oh, and we can make inroads on your delicious cheese as well. All right?'

'A feast,' said Shona. 'You're very kind.'

'Can we help with any of it?' asked Hilary.

'It's all set out, and the casserole only needs heating through. And I never think it's right to expect guests to help out,' said Madeleine.

'We aren't guests really, though,' said Hilary. 'At least – we're not the kind that need to be waited on.'

'In that case, I'd be grateful if one of you could carry the casserole to the table when it's ready. No need for anything more. But we'll be civilized and have a glass of that Madeira you brought before we eat, shall we?'

After the meal, Shona asked Madeleine if she would mind if they entered the substance of their talk onto the laptop right away.

'It would be quicker for us than writing sheaves of notes and then entering them,' she said. 'And I'd like to get it all down while it's fresh in my mind.'

'Of course you must,' said Madeleine at once. 'And if you're intending to do that, perhaps you won't think I'm discourteous if I leave you to it. I know it's only just on ten, but I'm used to early nights these days. The coffee pot's still half full and there're drinks and glasses in that cupboard. Help yourselves to whatever you want.'

'You've been very kind,' said Shona, smiling at her.

'I've enjoyed it immensely and I'm looking forward to the actual reopening. Goodnight to you both. Will breakfast around eight be all right?'

'Yes, but we can forage for ourselves perfectly well,' said Hilary.

'Not a bit of it. My girl from the village is coming in, and she'll do scrambled eggs and toast for you.'

'That would be lovely. Goodnight, Madeleine.'

Shona went upstairs with Madeleine to get the laptop from her case, and then she and Hilary spent another absorbed hour, pulling their discussion and all the ideas into a workable outline.

'It'll all be marvellous,' said Hilary, finally leaning back in the deep comfortable armchair. 'If we can bring this off, it'll be such a night.' She paused, then said, 'Did you think there was something – some memory – that upset Madeleine earlier on? When she was talking about not wanting publicity if the Tarleton were reopened? Just for a moment or two I thought she was going to have an attack of some kind – heart or something. Did you notice it?'

'There was something,' said Shona slowly. 'But whatever it was, it passed. Probably it was just remembering the past – her father and so on – that upset her. Whatever it was, I shouldn't think it's relevant to us.'

'No. What's relevant,' said Hilary, 'is that astonishing clause her father made in his will. It explains why the place has been closed all these years, but it doesn't explain what was behind it in the first place. We thought we were going to find out the truth about it all, but it sets up more questions than it answers, doesn't it?'

'It does rather. But I don't think we can pry into any of it very deeply.'

'No, of course not. And all families have secrets, anyway,' said Hilary. She stood up and stretched her arms. 'Shona, if you don't mind, I think I'm for bed. I know you did all the driving, but I'm absolutely zonked.'

'I sometimes think it's more tiring to be a passenger on a long car journey than it is to be the driver. You go on up, Hilary. Goodnight.'

'Are you coming up?'

'Not just yet. I'd like to get out a few draft costings for all this while it's still fresh in my mind.'

'OK. I'll take the coffee things out to the kitchen on my way. Don't burn too much midnight oil,' said Hilary, and went out.

All families have secrets. The words lingered after Hilary had gone, and the past stirred uneasily in Shona's mind again. Secrets . . . Secrets were dangerous things, they were better kept in dark places – walled up if necessary. But the Tarleton's secrets, whatever they might be, wherever they might be hidden, were nothing to do with Shona. That underground wall in the Tarleton was nothing to do with Grith's underground wall, or with what had stood behind it . . .

So there was no need for this faint sick uneasiness: the Tarleton could perfectly safely be reopened. It would be wonderful publicity for the Harlequin Society; it would not, in fact, do Shona any harm personally, either.

There was a faint clatter of crockery from the kitchen – it sounded as if Hilary was washing up the coffee cups. Shona listened, and after a few moments heard the soft creak of the stairs, and then the sound of taps running in the bathroom. The floor joists overhead creaked softly again and the bedroom door closed. The house sank into silence except for the occasional crackle of the logs burning in the grate.

What secrets might there be in Madeleine Ferrelyn's past? There had been that brief spasm of pain in her face earlier on – had that been caused by remembering her father, or had it been for some other reason?

Secrets . . . There had been so many secrets at Grith House.

*

Shona had not been looking for secrets on the day just before her eighteenth birthday, and if it had not been for Cousin Elspeth she would not have gone up to the attic that afternoon or any other afternoon. But the sentimental old fool, had thought it would be nice to take a few photographs to mark Shona's birthday, and had spent most of the morning fussing and flapping about, trying to find photograph albums. In the end, Shona had said exasperatedly, that the albums were probably in the attic and if it meant so much to Elspeth she would go and find them.

'Would you? I'd come up with you, but your mother hasn't been so well today.'

This was a euphemism for Mother being soddenly drunk yet again. Shona supposed they should be grateful that when her mother did become drunk (which was six days out of seven), she did it quietly and unobtrusively, falling asleep in her chair, occasionally crying over the harsh way life had treated her. The Cheesewrights probably knew about Mother's drinking because they knew most things, but they were reasonably discreet and loyal. Shona did not much care if they broadcast on national television that Margaret Seymour was getting through two bottles of vodka a day and three at weekends.

Occasionally her mother made determined assaults on the kitchen, declaring she would cook them all a meal – it was high time she pulled herself together; she had been feeling a little under the weather lately, but that was all over. A good strengthening stew, that was what she would make.

She normally got as far as cutting up the chicken or the beef before discovering Elspeth had moved everything round in the larder making it impossible to find so much as a stock cube. After this she declared they were all in league against her, hiding stock cubes and chopping boards, and then headed for wherever she had hidden the most recent of her bottles, leaving the kitchen in chaos. Several times Shona put the case to Elspeth for proper professional help for her mother, but Elspeth said they did not need folks poking into their private affairs; poor Margaret was just a bit low and there was nothing wrong in a little drink to cheer her up. Shona wondered what planet Elspeth was living on, because most days her mother was incoherent by lunchtime, although she was no trouble and could usually be safely left to sleep and brood in her chair by the fire.

It was anybody's guess if she would make any kind of effort for Shona's birthday or even remember it, but it did not much matter because the day would be much like all other days and all other birthdays. 'A small family celebration,' Elspeth had said, bustling about the kitchen, baking a lavish cake that nobody at Grith really wanted and would probably end in being given to the Cheesewrights.

Still, Shona supposed they might as well have a few photographs of the day if it would please silly old Elspeth who had found a camera from somewhere and bought a roll of film in the village. She went up to the attic just after lunch.

The photograph albums were not immediately visible, but then nothing was immediately visible because people seemed to have dumped all the household rubbish up here and forgotten it. Shona had brought a torch with her and began to sift through the larger packing cases, which were the likeliest places.

The albums – four of them – were finally found in a small suitcase which might once have accompanied some forgotten Seymour or Ross ancestor on weekend holidays. Shona lifted them out, flicking off most of the dust in the process, and then thought it was a shame to leave the suitcase up here; it was old, but it was a good leather case. She had not actually travelled beyond Moil since the long-ago half-term holidays at Whitby, but now she was eighteen she might soon be able to go off to live somewhere livelier, so a good suitcase would be very handy. She scooped out a few ancient magazines and some old sixties-type hair rollers that had unaccountably got inside, and as she did so a handful of clipped-together papers fell out of one of the pockets.

At first sight they did not look very important or interesting: they were most likely forgotten, semi-official notifications of something or other. Shona picked them up, intending to take them downstairs with the albums and burn them. It would be one less bit of useless rubbish up here.

At the head of the top sheet of paper were the printed words, *Thornacre Asylum for the Criminally Insane. County of Yorkshire.*

The address directly under this was vaguely familiar as being somewhere in North Yorkshire near the east coast, and the date was two years after Shona's own birth.

Shona stared at these words for quite a long time. She had been kneeling on the bare floor, but she suddenly felt as if she might topple forward, so she sat back, leaning against an old chair. *Thornacre Asylum for the Criminally Insane.* It was probably nothing to do with anyone now living at Grith. It was most likely an appeal for a donation or something of that kind. But odd words had already leapt up at her. Sudden death. Distress. Iain Seymour. *Iain Seymour. SEYMOUR.*

It was probably better not to read the letter. It was probably better not to know what it said. Or was it? Wouldn't she always wonder? Iain Seymour . . .

She took a deep breath and with the feeling of stepping neck deep into black swirling water, began to read the typed lines.

Dear Mrs Seymour

It is with deep regret that I have to inform you of the sudden death of your husband, Iain Alistair Seymour, yesterday (12th) at this institution.

I know this news will cause you considerable distress, and I am sorry that I must add to that distress by having to tell you that he died during a violent attack on one of our attendants here. The man is recovering, but is still gravely ill and I believe there are fears for the sight of one of his eyes.

There must, of course, be an inquest and also an official Home Office inquiry, so at this stage I am only able to give you the most basic details.

It seems that during the attack it was necessary to restrain Iain Seymour very forcibly. However, he broke away from the attendants holding him and threw himself down a flight of steel steps. His neck was broken in the fall and he died immediately.

As you know, it was unlikely that your husband would ever have been released from Thornacre, although during the eighteen months he was here I and my psychiatric team did all we could to reach him – sadly with no success. He was a sullen and withdrawn resident for all of his stay. In view of that, I feel your decision not to visit him was a wise one, and perhaps you will find some comfort in knowing it now seems unlikely that your small daughter can ever discover her father's identity. I cannot think any useful purpose would be served by her knowing and, as you are aware, I was always firmly in agreement with your decision not to tell her – a decision I believe was supported by your own father at the time.

I will let you know the arrangements for the funeral when they are made, and if you decide to travel up here to attend it, I could arrange accommodation at a nearby hotel, together with whatever transport you might need.

The interment will be carried out privately within the precincts of Thornacre itself and the press will not be told of the date. I cannot absolutely guarantee anonymity for you if you decide to come to the funeral, but I think you can be reasonably sure no one would connect you to Iain Seymour in any way.

Again, my sincerest condolences, and if there is any help

I can give at this most difficult time, I hope you will not
hesitate to let me know.

> Yours sincerely
> F. G. Hamilton
> Head of Psychiatric Medicine for HM Prisons
> Thornacre

Stapled to the letter was a newspaper cutting, yellowed and brittle
with age. The date was two days after the letter.

DEATH OF NOTORIOUS SERIAL KILLER

The famous 'Tantallon' murderer, Iain Seymour, yesterday
met his death in Thornacre Asylum, where he has been a
patient for the last eighteen months.

It is understood that Seymour (30), was involved in an
attack on two of the orderlies in the asylum, which, like
Broadmoor, caters solely for the criminally insane. Home
Office sources said a full statement would be released in the
course of the next 48 hours, but confirmed that Seymour
had died in a fall down some iron steps. An inquiry is to
be held.

Two years ago Iain Seymour was convicted of the killings
of four young girls, but was never sentenced due to his
mental condition. He is the son of Scottish wine merchants,
but other than that, little was ever disclosed about his background. At his trial he appeared to have no close relatives
and was accompanied only by his defence counsel.

His motives were, it was believed, wholly sexual – all the
girls had been raped before death and the police case was
that Seymour had killed them to prevent them reporting
the rapes.

During his reign of terror, Iain Seymour came to be known as the Tantallon Killer, due to his custom of burying the bodies of his victims near to the ruinous Tantallon castle in North Berwick.

Tantallon castle is steeped in Scottish and English history. It stands on a rocky headland surrounded by cliffs, and in its heyday, boasted one of the most spectacular mediaeval curtain walls – 12 feet in thickness – ever constructed. This curtain wall can still be clearly seen, even today, and one of the macabre aspects of Seymour's killings was that he would apparently take his victims to see this curtain wall by moonlight, before raping, then strangling them and burying their bodies on the lonely clifftop.

CHAPTER TWENTY-SEVEN

The dim attic was so quiet it might have been plucked out of the house – out of England – and set down on some silent dead world. Fragments of conversation – of questions and of evasive answers – whirled in Shona's head, like a child's kaleidoscope.

'Why haven't I got a father? Everyone at school has one?' 'Your father's long since dead. Don't keep talking about it.' That had been her mother, lips drawn tightly in, the shuttered look in her eyes. Shona had tried elsewhere to find out. 'Grandfather, it'd be nice if I had a father on sports days at school. For the fathers' races and things.' And her grandfather's reply, a little sharp: 'We can't always have the things we want in life, Shona. I hope you don't pester your mother with these questions.'

And all the time, her father had been this monster, this killer who had been so insane and so dangerous he had been shut away. Convicted of killing four young girls … Raped, then strangled them so they couldn't tell … STRANGLED THEM …

The half-open suitcase was still lying on the floor next to her and Shona suddenly saw how her mother must have packed this case with overnight things, tucked F. G. Hamilton's letter into it along with the newspaper cutting, and travelled to Thornacre to attend the funeral of the man who had murdered young girls in the shadow of Tantallon's curtain wall. It was curious how that term, curtain wall, imparted a theatrical flavour.

Had people at Moil known who her father was and who old Mr Ross's daughter had married all those years ago? Shona thought it unlikely: Seymour was not an uncommon name and it sounded as if the marriage had not been of very long duration. Her mother must have returned to Grith House, and probably she and Grandfather had spun some story about her being tragically widowed and no one had made the connection.

Shona had sometimes woven little daydreams about her father – about how he might have died a heroic death, rescuing someone from a burning building or a sinking ship. Later, seeing these images did not really square with Mother's tight-lipped secrecy or Grandfather's strict injunction not to pester her with questions, she had adjusted the vision. Perhaps her father had been one of the glamorous gentlemen spies in the Cold War – a James Bond character who had died for his country, but whose selfless contribution to it could never be acknowledged. This was a fairly satisfying image, although as Shona grew up, the daydreams blurred and then dissolved, and by the time she was thirteen or fourteen, divorce had become much more common – even in Moil – so that not having a father was no longer particularly unusual.

It was still just possible she had jumped to the wrong conclusion, but it was necessary to know for certain.

Forgetting about the photograph albums, Shona went back downstairs in a dream, the Thornacre letter and newspaper cutting in her hand. Elspeth was in the garden, but her mother was in the sitting room. It was early afternoon: a time when she would be about halfway to insensibility but able to understand and respond.

Shona did not bother with preambles or with working delicately round to the question. She thrust the letter into her mother's hand, and said, 'Is this true? Was my father a murderer? Was he shut away in an asylum?'

301

At first she thought her mother had not heard her, then she thought she had not understood. But at last, Margaret Seymour said, in a helpless defeated voice, 'You were never meant to know. You were to be always protected.'

Shona had to sit down very abruptly in case she fell down. She said, 'It's true?'

'Oh yes. We hushed it up, of course.' A vestige of the old Margaret Seymour showed briefly – the woman who had cared about respectability and who had valued her modest standing in the small community of Moil. 'No one was ever allowed to find out the truth,' she said. 'I came back to Grith as soon as – as soon as I knew what he was. We let it be thought I was a widow.'

It was more or less as Shona had guessed.

'Father was so good – you can have no idea how good he was to me, Shona. To both of us. Protecting you – that was all that seemed to matter.' The blurred eyes sharpened suddenly as if she had brought the world into focus for the first time for months. 'And we did protect you,' she said. 'Father and I and, later, Elspeth. We lied and pretended and we guarded you. We knew, you see, what you did that day.'

Shona said, 'I don't understand. Protecting me from what? From my father?'

Margaret Seymour said, 'From the consequences of your own actions, Shona.' She looked at her, then said, 'When you were eight years old, Shona – we all knew what you did, you see – we all knew you killed Anna.'

For a very long time neither of them spoke. Shona stared at the dishevelled figure in the chair, and as she did so, the sudden agonizing pain came in her head – the pain that split her head into two halves and opened up the deep chasm. From out of this chasm a hot scalding flood of emotion came spewing up, and within it were the memories and the knowledge of what had happened all those years ago. The terrible words lay on the air – *We all knew you killed Anna*. They had known – they had all known! – while Shona

302

herself had not known at all. But now there it lay, the clear memory of that night when she had been eight years old, and had decided to kill Anna.

Her bedtime in those days was eight o'clock because she was still only eight herself, although Edna Cheesewright said she was growing up faster than any of them could keep track of. When Shona reminded Edna that she was almost nine, and that next year she would be in double figures, Edna said, my goodness me, and supposed there would be a birthday party, and she and Mona baking a cake.

It was autumn; Grith smelt of woodsmoke from the open fire. Shona had gone to bed as usual, but had lain awake, staring up at the ceiling, wishing she had brought a drink or some biscuits with her. She was not supposed to eat anything after she had cleaned her teeth, but the more she thought about biscuits – some of Mona Cheesewright's fudgy biscuits baked that very day – the more she wanted them. She looked at the little bedside clock. It was a nice clock with a smiley face and hands in the shape of a curly moustache, and the moustache ends showed it was ten minutes past nine.

Mother and Grandfather would be watching the television news, and it ought to be possible to creep downstairs and do what Mona Cheesewright called *snaffle* a handful of the fudge biscuits, and be back upstairs without anyone knowing. She might take a glass of orange juice as well if she could manage it quietly. She would like Coke or Pepsi like other people had, but Grandfather said they were rubbishy teeth-rotting drinks. Still, she could have a pretty good private midnight feast with orange juice and biscuits. Shona often felt jealous when people at school stayed with each other overnight, perhaps after a birthday party or even for a whole weekend; they usually came back giggling about secret midnight feasts, and if there were brothers, the brothers had generally joined in and it had all got a bit rowdy. Rowdy or not, Shona wished she could have school friends to stay at Grith so they could have secret midnight feasts and giggle the next day at school. But her mother had not thought it a very good idea. Best with just the four of them, she said. Shona, her mother, Anna and Grandfather. A nice family party. In any case, Shona's grandfather did not like a lot of noisy children laughing and screeching all over the house.

No one would hear if Shona tiptoed down to the kitchen, although she would have to step round the floorboards in the hall that creaked so loudly. The Cheesewrights were always going to get their cousin who was a joiner to come along and do a little job on the floorboards, but Grandfather said there was no money for little jobs and in any case the Cheesewrights' cousin drank and chased women and he was not having him in the house.

Shona avoided the creaking floorboards and went along the hall. It did not sound as if the television was on after all, which was quite unusual at this time of the evening. When she stopped outside the door to listen, she heard Grandfather and Mother talking.

'She does behave so well,' mother was saying. 'Don't you think so? There's really no sign at all of—'

'I see signs,' Grandfather said. 'Margaret, I'm sorry, but I see them very clearly.'

'You watch her, I know.' Mother sounded as if she was going to cry.

'I'll always watch her. I'll always stay close. She doesn't realize it and I don't let her know, but I do. So do you. And I see that look occasionally.'

I see that look. A log must have fallen apart in the hearth just then, because the firelight in the room suddenly became red and Shona felt frightened.

'Ah, Margaret, don't cry,' her grandfather was saying, and there was the creak of his chair as if he had leaned forward to pat Mother's arm or take her hand. 'You know what I mean. We've both seen that look.'

Mother's voice came in a whisper. 'Yes,' she said. 'Oh yes. But she's all right, isn't she? We're making her all right.'

'We are now, but what's to do when I'm gone?' he said. 'I worry you won't manage to control her, and that's what I wanted to say to you tonight. We have to face facts, my dear: I'm well beyond the three score years and ten already, we both know that. So what I've thought is this. You'll remember Elspeth, your cousin John's eldest?'

'I think so. Yes, of course I remember her.'

'I've a mind to write to her, outlining the situation. Not making any definite arrangements, just saying there could be a time in the future when you'd be glad of her help here. You can offer her a good home – she's no place of her own – and there'd be a little money by way of a wage, I'd make sure of that.' There was a pause and Shona had the impression of her mother frowning as if thinking this over.

'She's a strong sense of family,' said Grandfather. 'We can trust her with the truth.'

'Yes,' said Mother. 'Yes, that would be an answer for – for later, wouldn't it? Yes, write the letter, would you?' She was crying properly now, and Shona heard her grandfather cross the room and then the chink of glasses.

'Thank you,' said her mother after a moment and Shona guessed he had given her some brandy or whisky. 'You're so good to me, Father. I'm sorry to be so emotional.'

'Natural you should get upset,' said Grandfather a bit gruffly. 'It's a bad business and it always has been, but it's not your fault – if it's anyone's fault, it's mine. I should have seen— I should have done something all those years ago. But the truth is that we were all fooled by a charming monster.'

A charming monster . . . Shona felt the hairs on her arms prickle all the way down to her hands.

'It seems so cruel,' her mother was saying. 'Not letting her lead a normal life. That's what upsets me most.'

'Her life's normal enough it seems to me,' said Grandfather and there was a sudden stern note in his voice that Shona did not quite understand. 'It's as normal as we dare let it be.' Then, sounding as if he was making an effort to throw off a heavy weight, he said, 'And now, shall we take a look at the television news?' and there was the sound of the TV being switched on, and the announcer's voice talking about some boring old war somewhere, and something called Watergate, which Grandfather listened to, and then said they might attach all the fanciful names they liked to this: to his mind this Watergate business was nothing but downright greed and deceit.

Shona had forgotten about the biscuits. She went quietly back to bed and lay awake for a long time, thinking about what she had heard. A charming monster, her grandfather had said. We were all fooled. And then he made that remark, in that peculiar voice, about a normal life.

Anna. It must be Anna they had been talking about. Yes, of course it was. Anna was the charming monster who had fooled them all – except that Anna had never fooled Shona, not for one minute. Shona knew exactly what Anna was – she was vain and selfish and evil. A charming monster, that was what her grandfather had called her, and Shona thought that described her Aunt Anna very well indeed.

It was not long after this that Anna told Shona to drop the 'aunt'.

'So *ageing*,' she said with her laugh people said was musical, but which Shona thought stupid. 'You make me feel about a hundred when you call me Aunt Anna. Or maybe I should get a lorgnette and an ear trumpet and talk like Edith Evans.' She put on a deep warbly voice when she said this, and looked about her, clearly waiting for everybody to fall about in admiration.

The really strange thing – the thing Shona could never understand – was that everybody did fall about in admiration. Even people you would expect to disapprove, liked Anna. They all said it must be wonderful for Shona to have this lively, pretty aunt who did modelling and such like – how exciting – and in a few years Shona would be able to go up to London with Anna. Even her grandfather, who had talked about Jezebels when Mona Cheesewright came to do the spring cleaning wearing a shocking-pink jumper one day, never seemed to mind the vivid clothes Anna wore, or the startling make-up. Mother said she did not know where Anna got the ideas for such things, but even Mother sometimes admired a lipstick or a new hairstyle. Neither of them seemed to mind, either, when Anna played loud music on the radio or the radiogram, or when she went to parties and came home in the middle of the night, and made plans to buy her own car – a bright red sports car, she said was what she wanted, and a man she knew in London was going to look one out for her. (Mona Cheesewright, hearing this, said, 'And where will she get the money for *that*, I wonder,' in a voice that made Shona think of the hard sour little apples that fell in the orchard.)

That summer there was a music competition in a nearby town; it was an important event and Shona's class sang 'Golden Slumbers' as their school's entry. Shona had not thought her grandfather would let her go to the competition – he thought if you went more than two miles beyond Moil you were going to places of sin – but he had seemed to think a twelve-mile journey in a coach, in company with twenty other girls and four teachers, was permissible. He even came along to watch, sitting in the front row with Mother and Anna. He wore his best suit and Mother had a neat navy two-piece with a nice silk scarf and Shona was pleased with them both; it was embarrassing if your family did not look right in front of your school friends. The trouble was that Anna did not look in the least right: when Shona saw what she was wearing she was horrified. Anna had on a trouser suit with extremely tight, calf-length trousers over high-heeled boots, a matching waistcoat, and a shirt cut like a man's. The trousers clung to her bottom which Shona thought very rude, and people stared which was annoying.

307

Shona's class won the competition which they agreed was brilliant, really great, especially since ten schools were competing and some had come all the way from York. Shona was the one chosen to go onto the platform to accept the cup for her school and everybody clapped. This practically made it Shona's own day. All the teachers would be very pleased and there might even be a piece in the newspaper with a photograph. She would ask her mother to lend her the little handbag mirror to tidy her hair just in case.

But there were no photographs and no pieces in the paper, and afterwards everyone crowded round Anna and admired her clothes, and hardly anybody talked about the competition or the cup or how nicely Shona had gone up onto the platform and shaken hands with the judges in a proper grown-up way. They were all more interested in that stupid show-off Anna in her rude trousers. Even the teachers said things like, 'How *wonderful* you managed to find time to come along, Miss Ross,' as if they thought the whole thing was really beneath Anna's notice. One of them said, 'My word, where on earth did you find such an outfit and those *boots*! You didn't buy any of those in this part of Yorkshire, I'll be bound.' Girls in Shona's class came up to her and instead of saying well done on collecting the cup, said what a smashing aunt she had; they had never seen anything like those fantastic clothes, and was it true she was going to be in *Cosmopolitan* modelling? Fathers and brothers stared at Anna's bottom. It was horribly embarrassing and it was the worst disappointment Shona had ever had and it was all because of Anna who was nothing but a monster – her grandfather had said so.

She lay awake for a long time that night thinking about it all, thinking how Anna had stolen the attention, just as she always did.

It was astonishing to Shona that Grandfather could be frightened of anything, but he had sounded frightened of Anna that night. He had seemed worried that he and Shona's mother might not always be able to control Anna – that one day Anna might do something really terrible and wicked. Grandfather was even making plans for after he died, telling Mother to send for someone called Elspeth to help her. Grandfather's idea of what was wicked covered a great many things – Shona knew that – but it still sounded as if Anna was really bad. A charming monster, Grandfather called her.

Shona was starting to feel sleepy by this time, but just before she tumbled over into sleep, she suddenly thought how extremely pleased her mother and her grandfather would be and how very good it would be for Shona herself if the charming monster – vain, selfish, hateful Anna – was no longer around.

If she was to die.

The trouble was Shona was not sure how hard it was to kill someone. People on television made it look easy, but probably it was not. If you wanted to kill spiders or beetles you just stamped on them, but you could not stamp on a whole person. Nor could you sneak up with a hammer or an axe to bash them over the head, because you would be seen and people like Mother and Grandfather would want to know why you were creeping round with hammers. Shona was not sure if she could actually bash Anna hard enough to kill her, and anyway there would be a lot of blood everywhere which would be horrid, as well as it going over Shona herself and being difficult to get rid of afterwards.

So how else could a person be killed? There were a lot of things Shona would not be able to do, mostly because Anna was bigger and stronger, but also because Anna was grown up. But there must be something.

Over the next few days she thought and thought. Whatever she decided on would have to be done without anyone knowing or seeing, which was another thing that was difficult because she was not often left on her own for very long spells. Mother took her to school and fetched her back each day, and she was almost always around, watching to be sure Shona did her homework, calling her to help with some dusting or a bit of gardening, or to help with the washing-up. If it was not Mother, it was Grandfather, wanting to know about her school work and asking if she would fetch a book from his study, or find his slippers or his reading glasses. It was difficult to make a plan to kill somebody when you were always being asked to fetch reading glasses or plant lobelia or help the Cheesewrights wash up.

Rather surprisingly, it was the Cheesewrights who gave Shona the solution. Edna had asked her cousin – the one who was always going to mend the creaking floorboards – to let them have something to get rid of the rats in the outhouses at Grith. A positive plague of them there were, said Edna, chopping parsley as fiercely as if it were the rats themselves. Mona said rats were nasty disease carrying vermin, and their cousin was bringing a tin of something called Rat-Banish to deal with the horrid things. What you did, said Mona, you put the stuff down and then went away, and the rats came out and ate up the Rat-Banish which they thought was food. But eating it made them very thirsty so they went off to find water. Once they drank the water, the poison started to work and they died. Very satisfactory, said Mona, and there would be no nasty rat bodies lying around for folks to clear away. Edna said they could not be doing with rat bodies, and told Mona to put on the broad beans, because Mr Ross was very particular about broad beans being correctly cooked.

The Rat-Banish, when the cousin brought it, was in a big round tin with a huge scarlet skull and crossbones on it, and POISON! in even bigger letters. That was so no one could eat it by mistake, said the cousin, although Shona thought you would have to be pretty stupid to eat something out of a tin with a scarlet skull and crossbones. Anyhow, said the cousin, tapping the tin, this would put paid to the evil little bu— Pardon, to the nasty little creatures. You did not need much: a good dessertspoonful on the floor of the potting shed and you would be rid of the rats for good.

Shona was not allowed to help put the Rat-Banish in the potting shed on account of it being dangerous, but she helped the

Cheesewrights find a pair of old gardening gloves for the cousin to wear. Edna said you could not be too careful and the gloves would be burned afterwards. The cousin said they would have a bit of a bonfire: it was romantic, was a nice bonfire. He dug Mona in the ribs and winked when he said this, and Mona said, 'Oh get off with you, our Ted.' Edna said they all knew what a one Ted was with the girls but they did not want vulgarity, thank you very much, and Ted went meekly back to his poison.

CHAPTER TWENTY-EIGHT

Shona thought for a long time about the rats who were going to eat poison without knowing. Would they die screeching and squirming? Or would they just fall down and lie stiff and lifeless?

Would something that killed rats kill a person and would that person screech and squirm? When she thought about Anna screeching and squirming – perhaps still wearing the rude trousers and the boots she had worn to the music competition – Shona was quite pleased.

She waited until Thursday afternoon. Once she got home from school she was supposed to do her homework. The Cheesewrights did not come to Grith on Thursdays, so this was the day her mother fussed about in the kitchen, cooking the evening meal. She spent hours on it. When Shona had her own house she would not spend hours cooking meals and then washing-up the dishes afterwards; she would pay someone to do it for her or she would go out to restaurants all the time.

Anna was off out somewhere – when Anna was at Grith she was almost always off out somewhere – and Grandfather was in his study, pretending to do a crossword from *The Sunday Times*.

All this meant Shona was on her own for at least an hour. She put on a pair of old woollen gloves that could be lost somewhere afterwards – no one would bother about a crummy pair of gloves – and went out to the potting shed, careful not to be seen from any of the windows. The potting shed was small and dark and secret-feeling. It smelt of compost and wood. The tin of Rat-Banish was on a high shelf so it could not be knocked over by mistake. The shelf was too high for Shona to reach, but there were some big old flower pots in the corner: she dragged one across the floor and climbed onto it. Then she reached up and, cupping her hands around the fat tin, lifted it down. Ted Cheesewright had used the edge of a screwdriver to lever up the lid and Shona did the same, being careful not to spill any of the contents. The lid stuck a bit then came up with a horrid sucking noise.

She had taken a plastic bag from the kitchen drawer and the metal scoop which Mona sometimes used for baking Grand-father's drop scones. The scoop could be lost along with the gloves and Grandfather would have to do without his drop scones until another was bought.

She had not known what the Rat-Banish would look like, and she had not known, until this minute, whether it would look like any of the food they ate at Grith – in particular any of the food Anna ate. If it looked grungy or if it was a sticky grey mess the plan would not work, because Anna was not going to eat any kind of grey grungy stuff and Shona would have to think of another way of killing her.

But as soon as the lid came off she knew it was all right. The poison was straw-coloured – little pellets and wisps and seeds – and it looked almost exactly the same as the muesli Anna ate for breakfast each morning – the muesli which no one else at Grith ever touched. Shona took four scoops of Rat-Banish and tipped them into the bag. Enough? Ted Cheesewright had said one dessertspoonful was plenty for the rats, so this much should be enough for one person. She sealed the bag with the plastic tie, stuffed the gloves and the scoop into a flower pot so she could

313

come back later to bury them in the garden, then went back to the house.

Her mother had stopped banging around in the kitchen and Shona could hear her upstairs. She went cautiously into the kitchen, which was empty, unless you counted the smell of stew. Listening for the sound of her mother coming back downstairs, Shona went across to the larder, which had marble shelves and floor. Here was the screw-top canister where the muesli was kept. The Cheesewrights were careful about storing things in jars and canisters on account of the paper and cardboard packets sometimes getting soggy at the corners because of the larder being a bit damp. Anna's muesli did not get soggy at the corners because of the canister, but it would get a lot worse than soggy after today. Shona tipped the bag so the contents poured out, replaced the lid, and shook the canister.

As she went back to the potting shed to get rid of the gloves, scoop and bag, she wondered how long it would take before Anna worked her way down to the poisoned bits of muesli.

Coming out of the potting shed she suddenly felt very odd as if something might have come tumbling down from a roof and smacked her very hard on the top of her head. For a moment there was a really bad pain, as if her skull had been wrenched into two separate pieces. She thought she was going to be sick because there was the same feeling of panic you got when you were going to be sick, but after a few moments this went away. By the time she got back to the kitchen door, the being sick feeling and the head split in two feeling had gone, although she thought one of the Moil fogs must have come rolling in without her noticing, because everything seemed misty and sounds were muffled.

Her hands were a bit dusty and the front of her jumper had dry earth on it as if she had been gardening. Shona looked at this in puzzlement for a long time, because she could not think how it had got there. She did not remember doing any gardening today: it was not something you did on dark November afternoons.

314

Perhaps she had been out to the potting shed and forgotten about it – yes, that must be it. Mother must have wanted one of the plant pots for her African violets; probably later she would say: Shona, did you fetch the plant pot, or the gardening apron, or the bundle of twine, or whatever it might be, and then Shona would remember.

She washed her hands and brushed the dry earth from her jumper, and went into the dining room to do her homework. While she was working out the sums which were tonight's task the misty feeling came back, making it quite difficult to do them properly. Mother did not say anything about sending her out to the potting shed, and Shona still could not remember why she had been outside, or how she had got earth on her jumper.

The next morning when she woke up the mist was still there, and it seemed to have got inside her head as well, because she felt as if it was stuffed with cotton wool. Perhaps she was going to get measles – two people at school were away with measles. But she ate her breakfast as normal, porridge and toast and a mug of milk. She and her mother always had breakfast together, then if it was a nice day they set out to walk to the school at half past eight; if it was raining or cold they did not need to leave until fifteen minutes to nine because they went in the car.

Today was Friday, so everyone at school was talking about the weekend. There was a birthday party on Saturday afternoon with a conjurer and everyone was to wear fancy dress. Shona had been invited to the party, but her mother had not thought it a good idea, so she was not going.

Mother collected her as usual at three thirty, bringing the car because it was raining. She looked a bit strange: her eyes were red as if she had been crying and she drove jerkily, as if she did not much care if they landed in a ditch. But when Shona said, 'Is anything the matter?' she at once said, 'No, nothing. Well – as a matter of fact, I have a bit of a headache. Nothing much – I'll take some aspirin when we get home.'

When they got home, her mother made toast in the kitchen – Shona usually had scrambled eggs or toast and honey when she got home from school. Mother toasted the bread and got out the jar of honey, and then she said, in a peculiar voice, 'Shona, your Aunt Anna won't be coming to Grith any longer.'

Aunt Anna. It took Shona a moment to think who Aunt Anna was. Oh yes, Anna. She said, 'Why not?'

'She's going to live in London. Some friends she has there—' Here, mother broke off, and Shona saw her face working as if trying not to cry. 'You know Anna,' said her mother with a dreadful attempt at sounding amused, 'a real little butterfly.'

There was something wrong with this – Shona knew there was and it was something to do with the peculiar feeling she had had for two whole days now. The misty feeling was hovering in front of her eyes now, making it difficult to see things clearly. She could not see this Anna person properly at all – there was just a vague outline of somebody who wore clothes people stared at, and who got in the way.

'But it will be better if you don't mention it to your grandfather,' Mother said, still intent on spreading honey on the toast. 'He's very upset indeed. Anna was the apple of his eye, you know.'

'No, all right. Can I have an extra piece of toast and honey, please, I'm absolutely starving because we had arithmetic today and it's really hard, arithmetic.'

While she was eating the toast and honey, her mother said, 'I think you should have an early night, tonight. You look very tired. And a bit flushed. You'd better have half an aspirin.'

Shona did not say she was not tired, it was just that the misty feeling was still all round her, like thick fog. Nor did she say that whatever had split her head in two yesterday was still making it ache. She had half an aspirin, which was quite an important grown-up thing to have, and then went to bed. Once there, she found she was actually very tired indeed and went straight to sleep. She woke up once, because of having a horrid nightmare – all about getting up in the middle of the night, and seeing her grandfather and her mother building a wall in the cellar and putting the body of somebody inside it. It was a really bad nightmare, but after a while she finally managed to go back to sleep and by morning she had practically forgotten it. It was not something to make a fuss about; everyone had nightmares.

A log broke apart in the fireplace, sending showers of sparks out, and Shona sat bolt upright, momentarily unsure where she was, her eyes refusing to focus on her surroundings.

Realization came back slowly. This was not Grith with its cold rooms and its black secrets that had to be covered up; this was Levels House in Somerset. Or was it? She put up a hand to her eyes, because the two halves of her mind were slipping out of alignment again – she could feel them pulling against each other. Waves of pain went through her head, then receded, leaving her perfectly calm. This was good; it was good to be calm when you had to do something that no one must know about.

She had been perfectly calm on that day over twenty years ago: the day before her eighteenth birthday when she had confronted her mother with the truth about Iain Seymour, and her mother had said those words that had lain on the air like thick slime.

We lied and pretended and we guarded you ... We knew, you see, what you did that day ... when you were eight ... We all knew you killed Anna.

In that moment, the glaring fury had swamped Shona: how *dared* her mother talk patronizingly of protecting her! Of lying and pretending and guarding!

With angry irrelevance she found herself noticing how her mother's hair had become untidy – pepper-and-salt, uncared for – seeing how her skin was dull and rough, the cheeks sunken and veined with tiny red lines. How old was she now? Late forties? Yes, that was all. But drink ruined people, it plunged them into strange twilight worlds where they no longer remembered the ordinary rules of life. Where they forgot to lie and pretend about things that mattered? Such as a man who had died a squalid death, branded as a strangler of young girls. (Against the curtain wall of Tantallon, that's where he did it.)

She should have been safe from the grim legacy of Iain Seymour because he was dead. There was a hammy old saying that dead men told no tales, and it was certain that Iain Seymour (she would *not* call him Father or even think of him as that!) would not be telling any tales.

Dead women told no tales either. And here was her mother, sunk in self-pity, drinking herself into an early death.

An early death.

Scarlet rage swamped Shona, and she reached for the bottle of vodka standing near her mother's chair. It was a quarter full and the top was loosely screwed on. Shona removed the top and flung the contents over her mother's chair. Ignoring her cry of protest and shock, she bent down and using the copper coal tongs, picked out a glowing red coal from the centre of the fire and dropped it onto the arm of the chair.

It caught fire at once, and the alcohol sent the flames shooting sky high. There was a scream of fear and pain and the brief impression of the figure in the chair struggling to get up. Clothes – hair – skin – flamed up, and Shona backed away and stood by the door, watching. Only when her mother stopped screaming did she run into the garden, shouting for Elspeth.

When it came down to it, no one in Moil was very shocked, although they were all greatly saddened. Poor Margaret Seymour, they said. A difficult life she'd had, what with being widowed so young, what with losing her sister in that macabre way some years ago. It was true there had been a few whispers about drinking and certainly she had not been seen much in the village over the last few years, but surely to goodness the poor woman could be allowed a few little nips now and then. Finding your sister's desiccated body behind a wall in your cellar could not be exactly good for your nerves.

Elspeth Ross, who had lived up at Grith for so many years, said Mrs Seymour was a martyr to crippling migraine attacks. Anyone who had ever suffered from migraine attacks – the real McCoy, not just your average milk and water headache – knew quite well that you could be laid low for forty-eight hours at times and couldn't even lift your head from the pillow. She had pills of course, but they were not always entirely effective.

There had to be an inquest, but everyone thought the verdict would be accidental death. A foregone conclusion, they said. She'd likely have been a bit fuzzy from taking the pills, and wouldn't have noticed a spark flying out from the fire and setting the chair alight. A very nasty, very tragic, death, but nothing in the least suspicious about it. They listened, with horrified but slightly guilty relish, to the tale of how poor Shona, poor child, had actually come running in to find the chair alight and her mother screaming, and how Shona had acted with remarkable promptness, shouting to Elspeth Ross for buckets of water to douse the flames, telephoning the fire brigade there and then. All too late, though.

The Cheesewrights, who were the main source of information, told everyone that the funeral would be held at Moil church, and Shona and Elspeth Ross had said mourners would be welcome at the house afterwards for a cup of a tea or a glass of sherry. Nothing elaborate, what with the sitting room still being in such a mess from the fire, and the insurance company not prepared to stump up the money until after the inquest. But people would likely make allowance for that.

Edna Cheesewright told Shona that she and Mona would see to the food after the funeral – no, it would be no trouble, they were pleased to think they could do something to help. Just sandwiches and rolls, they thought, although Mona would bake a few scones as well. All very plain, nothing frivolous. Shona thought the words

319

Grith House and frivolous were not ones that would occur to most people in the same sentence anyway, but she did not say so. She said she and her cousin would be very glad of Edna and Mona's help with the modest wake, and added that Elspeth had ordered a Cheshire cheese and a large ham for boiling.

The ham had to be boiled for a very long time, and the smell made Shona feel sick because it was dreadfully similar to the smell that lingered in the sitting room after her mother had gone up in flames. She suggested they might have been better to just order cooked ham for the sandwiches, but Elspeth said that was not how things should be done, and people would think it funny if they found themselves eating pre-packed, machine-sliced ham from a supermarket.

She was poking and prodding at the ham in the big saucepan, and looked up when Shona came in. Her face was flushed from the heat of the cooker and she had a tea towel over her shoulder.

She said, 'I'm glad you've come in, Shona. I wanted to say something to you.'

'Yes?' It would be something to do with the funeral which was tomorrow afternoon, or about what Elspeth herself was going to do now that Shona's mother was dead, or even a question as to whether the insurance people were likely to pay up so they could have the room put to rights. It had remained locked since the fire, although the assessors had had to go in.

Elspeth said, 'I wanted to tell you, Shona, that I know you found out about Iain – about your father.'

As if from a long way away, Shona heard her own voice say, 'I don't know what you mean.'

'You do know. You found the papers about him, didn't you? The letter and the newspaper cutting. You left them in the pocket of the skirt you had on that day – I found them afterwards. I'm sorry you had to find out like that. It must have been a dreadful shock. We never wanted you to know the truth.'

'Didn't you?' Shona looked at Elspeth, who should not be talking about this because no one must ever talk about it. But there she stood, her foolish sheeplike face mouthing something about having acted for the best.

'He was a very charming man, your father – I met him several times – but he wasn't sane. Even when it was proved, quite definitely, that he had killed those girls, he always said he had no memory of it. The doctors – psychiatrists and so on – said he had completely blanked out what he did. They used long words, medical terms, but that was the gist of it. It was as if his mind couldn't accept what he had done, so it buried everything.'

'But he was guilty?'

'Oh yes. Guilty but insane. He didn't remember. Just as you never remembered killing Anna all those years ago.' Then, as Shona made to speak, Elspeth said, 'We all tried to protect you. We all agreed you must be protected from the consequences.'

Memory stirred again, as it had done when she had been with her mother. Painful and raw, like the feeling when a fingernail is torn off below the quick.

'I don't know what you mean,' she said, but she did know. Anna. That was what Elspeth was talking about. That dark fear buried all those years ago. I killed Anna even though I didn't know about it afterwards. But they all knew, Mother and Grandfather. And Elspeth knew as well. Elspeth ... What am I going to do about this?

Elspeth was standing with her back to the oven, steam still rising from the boiling ham. The windows were blind and white with the hot dampness from the stove, and Elspeth's hair was frizzed from the steam: it would smell of the boiling meat. Horrid. Shona was aware of an odd feeling – a feeling she had not experienced when she killed Anna or her mother. It was a feeling of being huge and invincible. Nothing could touch her.

Her father had used his bare hands to strangle his victims, but for Elspeth it should be a more homely death.

She bounded across the kitchen, and before Elspeth realized what was happening, snatched up a heavy iron frying-pan and brought it smashing down on the silly creature's head. Elspeth gave a half-grunt and slumped sideways, half over the edge of the oven, not unconscious, but dazed. Before she could recover, Shona grabbed the long-handled tongs used for removing fish and chicken from the big fryer, and lifted the half-cooked ham from the saucepan, dropping it into the sink. Then she snatched the tea towel from around Elspeth's flabby neck and, hooking her hands under the stupid woman's arms, pulled her into a standing position. Using the tea towel to protect her own hands, she pushed Elspeth face down into the boiling pan of water, and held her there with the long-handled tongs.

The shock of the bubbling water brought Elspeth to her senses and she fought for all she was worth, clawing and kicking, and making dreadful wet bubbly screams through the water. Despite Shona's care some of the boiling water splashed onto her hands, raising little blisters. But she held on, and at last Elspeth's struggles stopped and she slumped forward over the cooker. Water cascaded everywhere in little hissing rivulets and Shona sprang back, then, using a dry tea towel, managed to switch off the heat.

The smell of Elspeth's boiled face was almost exactly the same as the smell of the boiled ham joint. It would take a long time to get the smell out of the kitchen.

CHAPTER TWENTY-NINE

———◆◆◆———

Shona scrubbed everywhere with bleach and cleaned the top of the cooker very thoroughly. She threw the ham joint away – she would tell the Cheesewrights it had turned out to be too tough for the sandwiches. The butcher, if he got to hear about it, would be upset, but Shona was not worried about the butcher's feelings. She was not worried about anyone's feelings. For the moment she was concerned over what should be done with Elspeth. She managed to check for a pulse and a heartbeat and was relieved when there was neither. Presumably Elspeth had died from shock, although Shona did not really mind what the stupid woman had died from. There she lay, her face the most repulsive mess Shona had ever seen. The skin was exactly the colour and texture of cooked meat and the boiling water had poached the eyes – Shona found this the worst part of all. She wrapped the tea towel round the head, knotting it firmly at the neck. This helped, but not much because the white tea towel gave Elspeth a hideous blank appearance. Shona kept imagining the dreadful boiled eyes swivelling this way and that, trying to see.

She knelt down to check the heartbeat again, and as she did so there was a brief shutter-flash of a picture: a man against the backcloth of an old ruined castle with a strange but somehow melodic name – Tantallon – and a curtain wall dramatically spanning the headland. Iain Seymour. Did you do this, Iain Seymour, when you killed? Did you bend over your victims to check for a pulse or a heartbeat before you buried them? Did they even find all your victims, I wonder? They aren't going to find any of mine.

Elspeth was dead, Shona was sure of it. She straightened up, her mind flying ahead. Tomorrow was her mother's funeral. That would have to go ahead – she did not think there was any way of avoiding either the service or the modest wake afterwards. She sat in the darkening kitchen and thought for a long time, and the first glimmerings of a plan began to form. The details were not there yet, but the more she thought, the more she was convinced it would work. The only trouble was that the body would have to be concealed for a little over twenty-four hours, until after the funeral. Could that be done?

The silly woman's own bedroom would have been the best place to hide her body, but Shona did not think she could get the heavy weight all the way up the stairs and even if she could, she would have to get it all the way down again. But the sitting room should be safe: it was still a sealed area because the insurance people needed to look at it again. But they would not do that tomorrow because of the funeral, and Shona would have dealt with everything by the following day.

It was horrid to have to handle the body, but it could not be helped. Shona half dragged, half carried it into the burned sitting room and put it behind the door. She threw one of the fire-damaged curtains over Elspeth and stood back to consider. Yes, it was all right. Even if anyone happened to look through a window from the garden (this was not very likely but you could never be sure), all they would see was the fire-damaged chimney breast, the charred remains of the chair, and what looked like a singed curtain lying on the ground. She locked the room and pocketed the key. So far so good.

Would the body be completely stiff by tomorrow night? People tended to think they knew about rigor mortis from reading whodunits and watching TV programmes, but Shona was not sure if she knew much at all. Grandfather's books were still in his old study though, and there would surely be something in one of them about rigor.

She found the entry in a set of slightly battered encyclopedias, although the information was a bit vague as medical information often was. You had to allow for warm rooms or cold rooms, it seemed, and also for the dead person's age and a few other things as well, but the gist was that rigor started to set in about six hours after death, stayed there for between twelve and eighteen hours, and then passed off again. Usually it had disappeared by thirty-six hours after death. This last bit surprised Shona; she had assumed that once a body had stiffened, it stayed that way. But it would probably make it easier to do what she intended tomorrow night.

The funeral was at midday and had to be got through without anyone realizing Elspeth was dead. Shona dressed carefully for it, in a black jacket. She tied her hair back and although she did not normally wear much make-up, today she put on quite a lot. People seeing this would assume it was to hide the traces of tears.

Everyone who came back to Grith House, which was most of the village, said how brave Shona was being in the face of such a shattering tragedy. It was all so dreadfully sad, wasn't it? And where was Miss Ross? Elspeth? Surely she was here?

'She couldn't face it,' said Shona. 'She hopes everyone will understand, but she simply couldn't cope. I know she seems to be one of those really strong people, but actually she's very sensitive. She just broke down this morning, and in fact she's in bed. I'm really worried about her.'

The local doctor, who happened to be one of the mourners, asked if he could help. Perhaps he should take a look at Miss Ross?

'Oh no, don't do that,' said Shona at once. 'She's taken a couple

325

of pills – Valium, is it? And she particularly asked that no one fussed over her. She hates fuss, you know. I expect she's fast asleep at the moment. But if she's no better tomorrow I'll phone you. Would that be all right? You'd come out to see her, I mean?'

The doctor said that of course it was all right and he would most certainly come out if wanted. He added that Shona seemed to have managed today's events very well, particularly since the main drawing room was closed up. He hoped that would soon be put to rights for her. Shona said she hoped so as well, and the doctor patted her shoulder in a fatherly fashion and wandered into the dining room to find a drink.

Every time anyone went past the drawing-room door Shona's whole body tightened with nervous tension and by the end of half an hour her neck ached and she felt as if she had been beaten with iron bars. Once she thought there was a sound from inside the room and her whole body leapt with panic. Had Elspeth not been dead after all? Had she fought her way out of the curtain shroud, and was she even now making her blind fumbling way to the door, beating on it to be let out? Nerves, said Shona firmly. She's dead as mutton. But she still found herself standing close to the locked door, as if barring the way of anyone who might try to go in – or anyone who might try to get out . . .

Out of consideration for Shona, people only stayed for an hour. The Cheesewrights stayed on, of course, stacking plates and carrying glasses out to the kitchen. Nonsense, they said, when Shona said there was no need and she would clear everything up herself; of course they would see to it all. They bustled about, reminding one another of choice little bits of the day, and remembering how nicely the vicar had spoken of Mrs Seymour, quite beautiful it had been to listen to him, and what a wonderful array of flowers there had been. Oh dear.

Edna said they would leave some supper out for Shona and for poor Miss Ross. She might feel like a bite to eat later, you could never tell.

'That's very kind of you,' said Shona, but inside she was screaming at them to go.

After what felt like a lifetime, they put on their coats and then Edna saw it had started to rain. They had not brought umbrellas and Mona did not want her best hat spoiled, so Shona hunted out an old one for them to borrow.

'If you make a dash for it now, you'll miss the worst of the storm,' she said, and the Cheesewrights, who did not like storms, went scurrying down the gloomy driveway with the thick laurel bushes on both sides.

The rain was coming down quite heavily: Shona could hear it dripping mournfully from the trees and splashing out of the leaking gutter outside the kitchen window. She waited to make sure neither of the Cheesewrights came back for something they had forgotten, then crossed the hall and unlocked the sitting-room door.

It was a gloomy room at the best of times, but with rain rippling down the window panes it was bathed in an eerie greenish light as if the whole house lay under water. Shona closed the door and looked down at what lay behind it. The thick curtain was just as she had left it. Or was it? Hadn't a fold slipped a bit? Exactly as if a hand had feebly tried to push it off? Nerves again, nothing more. Elspeth Ross had been dead since half past ten yesterday morning and it was now four o'clock so if the encyclopedia could be trusted, rigor should be almost gone. Shona changed into jeans and trainers, and found the cellar-door key. The rain had turned the hall into an underwater cave as well. She unlocked the cellar and the door swung open. There were the steps and the gaping darkness. She had resolved not to remember the nightmare of all those years ago, but she found that she was unable to ignore it.

Oil lamps flickering and Grandfather and Mother moving back and forth, building that wall, laying brick on brick, so a murdered woman could be hidden . . . So that no one would ever know . . .

No one would ever know about this murdered woman, either.

The wall built all those years ago was still more than half in place. The workmen had knocked out some of the bricks to get at the water pipes and the police had knocked out some more when Anna's body came tumbling out that day, but most of the wall was still there. And – this was the important thing – the bricks they had knocked out were still there as well.

Shona propped the door open, then went back to the drawing room. Elspeth's arm, when she lifted a corner of the curtain to feel it, was cold and very slightly stiff. Was that rigor wearing off? Presumably it was, which meant the next part ought to be relatively easy.

Once she had conquered her stupid revulsion at actually handling the thing that had been Elspeth Ross, it was very easy indeed. Shona was glad she had tied that tea towel over the face; even so, she kept imagining Elspeth's boiled eyes watching her reproachfully through the cotton. She left the curtain over the body, managing to make a kind of parcel by tying string round it at the ankles and wrists, then took hold of the ankles and dragged it out of the room. The parcelled-up body needed only a shove to send it falling down the steps.

Walling the body up took a long time, but not as long as Shona had feared. She had searched the outhouses beforehand and found a large bag of plaster filler – she thought it was the kind plasterers used when they were repairing walls in old houses. The bag had been opened, but it was still two-thirds full and some thrifty person had resealed it with a garden tie. Shona had been relieved to find it, because she had been thinking she would have to take the bus to the nearest DIY store or even a builders' merchant to buy something suitable. She had not wanted to do that partly because she had no idea what to ask for, and also because a young girl buying heavy-duty plaster mix and carrying it home on a bus might be remembered. But it was all right – there was the nearly full bag, and there were even instructions printed on it as to the amount and temperature of water needed to mix it. Carrying the sealed bag into the kitchen, she thought her grandfather and her mother must have bought several packs of this all those years ago: one packet would not have been enough to cement that wall in place. But there had been some left over, which Mother had stored in the outhouse because you never knew what you might want in the future.

Mixing the filler was not difficult. Shona carried two big plastic bottles of water down to the cellar and used an old plastic bucket which she stood on a couple of old towels. The towels could be burned afterwards and the bucket could be well washed and left outside to weather, which would get rid of any tell-tale traces.

She had brought torches and oil lamps and in the flickering light she again had the eerie feeling that she had gone back to that night just before her ninth birthday. Were the ghosts of Mother and Grandfather watching her, as she had watched them that night? Once she turned round sharply, thinking there had been a soft footfall on the steps, and once she was sure something blew cold sour breath on the back of her neck. But each time there was nothing and she turned back to her task.

Anna was here, of course, watching and jeering. *You're on your own now, aren't you?* said Anna. *You can't risk making any mistakes, because there's no one left who'll watch out for you ... So get it right, Shona, otherwise they'll catch you ... And you know what will happen if they catch you, don't you? Thornacre Asylum for the Criminally Insane ... That's what'll happen to you, Shona.*

I'm not insane, said Shona to Anna's spiteful ghost. I'm not.

They'll say you are, though, and they'll lock you away for the rest of your life. Thornacre Asylum, that's where they'll put you, Shona ... Perhaps they'll even lock you up in your father's old room ... And wouldn't that be a grisly way to sit out your life, said Anna.

Shona shivered and focussed on what had to be done. Elspeth's body was awkward and floppy and it was difficult to drag it through the opening of the partly demolished wall. When she finally managed to cram the flabby thing into the small space, it fell forwards, the shrouded arms dropping onto Shona's shoulders in a travesty of an embrace, the head lolling forward. Shona gasped and shuddered and pushed the disgusting thing back, wedging it more firmly. It sagged a bit, like a very round-shouldered person, but this time it stayed put. She was annoyed to find she was trembling so much she had to sit on the ground for several moments. Horrid dead thing with its scalded, boiled-meat face. The sooner it was bricked up and out of sight the better.

Don't make any mistakes, Shona ... You really can't afford to make any mistakes.

She began to spread the wet plaster filler onto the bricks, laying the discarded ones on top of each other in careful rows. The slap of wet mortar formed a rhythm in her mind. Tantallon, it said, like the old hunting cry, 'tantivy'. Tantallon, Tantallon, keep up, Shona, keep in step, or they'll find you out. They'll put you in Thornacre for the rest of your life. One brick on top of another, Shona, that's the thing. Tan-Tallon, Tan-Tallon ...

Iain Seymour would have known how it felt to cover up a victim's face. The newspaper said he had buried them on the headland – had he shuddered because they were staring sightlessly up at him? Had he been relieved when the earth finally hid their faces? But he had been mad and he had been caught. Shona was not mad and she was not going to get caught.

She managed to banish the nagging rhythm of the castle's name and to finish building the wall. It was surprisingly easy and as the jagged-edged hole began to fill up, it did not look at all bad. Probably a master bricklayer would not have passed it, but it was not very likely that any master bricklayers would come down here to make an inspection. If the house were to be sold, as Shona was already planning, builders would probably tramp round, but by that time the filler would have hardened and all anyone would see was an old cellar wall, uneven with age. The bricks themselves were genuinely old and she could smear them with dirt or soot as well. If she could drag something in front of it – something that looked as if it had been there for years – that would be even better. There was an old free-standing stove in the outhouse that might do if she could get it down here. It would take all night to dismantle and bring it down here piecemeal, then reassemble, but she had all night.

Anna whispered that no matter how much Shona covered her tracks, she would never be free of the memories. She would never forget what she had done, said Anna, it would be with her always. The wall and what was behind it ... Elspeth Ross, whom Shona had killed ...

But I will forget, said Shona silently. I *will*.

She had forgotten. The bustle of activity in her last few weeks in Moil had pushed the ghosts into the darkest, deepest places of her mind.

There had been the round of subdued farewells to people in the village – the Cheesewrights, the doctor, people at the school she had attended. She was sad to be leaving, Shona said to them all, but after Elspeth had decided to go back to her family in Lincolnshire the house had seemed too full of tragic memories. Oh yes, she would return for visits, she said, knowing she would never do so.

She placed Grith House with a big anonymous firm of estate agents in York – a company who specialized in renting country houses to people coming to work in the UK on two- or three-year contracts. She would have liked to sell the place outright, but she had finally decided she could not risk any kind of comprehensive renovation because of what was behind the cellar wall. The agents would let the house to people who wanted a reasonable family base during their stint in England, but who would not bother about more than surface redecoration. Short of leaving it standing empty, which would have been asking for all kinds of trouble, or continuing to live there herself with the ghosts, which she could not face, Shona thought this was the best solution. She would be able to check the house between tenancies and make sure the cellar wall was undisturbed. She instructed the agents to communicate with her through her bank, saying with perfect truth that she was moving to London, and was not yet sure where she would be living.

By the time she found the little Tabard Square flat and the job with the Harlequin Society, the deaths of her mother and Elspeth had become a dream – one of those uncomfortable dreams she had occasionally experienced as a child. Something unreal and something that dissolved when light shone directly onto it.

Until a mention of an old theatre, its name so very similar to Tantallon, touched a chord in Shona's mind. Until an old, hastily constructed wall beneath the Tarleton – a wall almost identical to the wall at Grith – brought the fears pouring back.

Anna's body had been found and her killer had remained a mystery. Shona had got away with that death. But if Elspeth's body were to be found, they would know it had been Shona herself who put the stupid creature there – there was no one else who could have done it. So the brick wall in the cellar must never be broken open, because Elspeth's body must never, *never* be found. It must always remain one of the secrets. Secrets . . .

This time when Shona came up out of the past, she was no longer so sure she was in Levels House. When she looked round her, the room with its soft comfortable chairs and pleasant oak mantel was blurry and indistinct, as if another image was trying to get through: the image of that darker, bleaker house where she had grown up. The fragments of memory – the terrible truth about her father, Anna, the deaths of her mother and Elspeth, the need to play a part to people at Moil – all whirled and spun in her head, but she forced them away, because this was not Grith: it was Levels House. She and Hilary had driven here earlier today.

Did you? said Anna's voice. *Are you sure about that, Shona? Are you sure this isn't Grith after all?*

Shona was no longer sure. It was difficult to keep things separate sometimes – the past and the present, Grith and the Tarleton, the Tarleton and Tantallon castle ... the Tarleton and Tantallon castle, both with its curtain, the one a swathe of velvet, the other a wall made of stone ... But the similarities did not mean they were both killing grounds. Tantallon had been Iain Seymour's killing ground, but it had no connection with the old theatre. She must be careful not to become confused. She got up, a little stiff from having been in one position for so long, and went out to the hall, closing the sitting-room door. The stairs had a delayed creak, just as Grith had, so you kept thinking someone was creeping up behind you.

She washed in the old-fashioned bathroom at the end of the corridor, then went into her bedroom and closed the door.

You don't think a closed door can keep me out, do you? said Anna. *I'm still here and I'll always be here. I'll always watch you. I didn't watch you that day you stole out to the potting shed because you hadn't murdered me then, but I watched you afterwards. I was there when you found out about Iain Seymour – a charming man, but a monster. Was he waiting for you that day when you read the newspaper cutting and the letter from Thornacre Asylum, Shona? Did the ghost of that charming monster reach out to you and did you take his hand?*

This was unbearable and it was unfair. Shona had had no idea what she was going to find that day in the attics at Grith.

Then that was very stupid of you, because you should have guessed there'd be secrets. All attics have secrets, said Anna.

All attics have secrets ... Shona felt the dull ache that had been hovering over her temples descend like an iron weight and press agonizingly down, splitting her head into two separate halves. She opened the bedroom door and stepped outside.

The main landing was wide and L-shaped; most of it was in deep shadow, although a thin light came in from an uncurtained window in the other half of the L, so it was possible to see the way fairly well. Anna came with Shona, of course; Anna would not have let Shona do this on her own: she did not alter much, the bitch, she was always there if there was anything furtive, always demanding attention.

The attic stairs were tucked behind a half wall at the very end of the landing and they were narrow and very steep. Shona went up them cautiously, wincing when a worn tread creaked loudly, but reaching the top apparently unheard. The door leading into the attic was not much more than a large hatch; it opened outwards onto the small landing but a black hook latch – the old-fashioned kind you saw on garden sheds and gates – had been fastened to it, presumably to keep the door in place. When Shona lifted the latch the door swung open quite easily and a little breath of dry warmth gusted outwards. So far so good. But when she ducked her head to go through, the door swung back into place, closing itself with a little soft click, and Shona jumped and turned sharply round. But it was only the sloping old floor that had caused the door to close and she relaxed and turned back to survey the attic. It was very dark, but after a moment she located a light switch near the door. It was probably safe to switch this on for a few moments; it was unlikely that a light would be seen up here and in any case she could not make a search in the pitch dark.

She paused, frowning. She could not remember why she had come up here, but her head still felt as if it was split in two separate pieces, so perhaps the reason was in the half she could not reach. She thought there were things in that half – things she had done earlier in case she had to carry out any kind of plan – but she could not get at the memory of them.

But attics were places where forgotten letters and newspaper cuttings lay undisturbed for years – letters that blew your whole world apart if you found them. Was there something about the Tarleton in these attics? Something that would bring its secrets boiling to the surface? The sick pain in her head increased. Secrets were dangerous, they had to be buried as deeply as possible. It did not even matter if they were not your own secrets . . .

Madeleine Ferrelyn had secrets. She had winced with sudden

pain at a memory earlier that evening. Or had it been fear? Was she afraid there was something deep in the Tarleton that might be uncovered? Something behind that wall?

And you mustn't let them break open the cellar wall, remember . . .

But that's the Tarleton wall, thought Shona. Not the wall at Grith. It wouldn't matter if they knocked the Tarleton wall down. Or would it? Oh God, I can't remember!

At first glance the attic did not seem to contain anything more sinister than discarded household junk, dust and cobwebs, but Shona began to explore, moving warily across the floor, remembering to test each section of the old boards before she trod on them. The attic looked as if extended across most of the house, which meant she might walk directly over Madeleine's or Hilary's bedroom without realizing it. They should both be fast asleep by now, but footsteps directly overhead might wake one of them.

Still with no real idea of what she was looking for and still moving through the blurred, head-aching confusion, Shona began to investigate the contents of three large cardboard cartons in a corner. The first two held things from the 1960s, and she moved on to the third, seeing that it contained gramophone records, all old 78s, some in battered sleeves with names so faded as to be almost unreadable, some lying loose. The record labels were all HMV. His Master's Voice. Was there anyone over a certain age for whom those words did not conjure up the famous image – the dog looking into the flaring horn, half puzzled, half curious about the sounds issuing from it? HMV as record-makers had long been absorbed into a conglomerate, but you still saw the signs over record shops.

There were six records in the box, and the top one had a date of 1917, so it was reasonable to assume the others would be of the same vintage. Shona began to turn them over, one by one, handling them with great care.

CHAPTER THIRTY

Hilary had been almost too tired to wash and undress before tumbling into the deep comfortable bed in the bedroom at the back of Levels House, although she was not too tired to check messages on her phone to see if Robert had called. He had done so – there was a brief message left at seven that evening, just asking her to call. She considered doing so right away, but it had only been a brief, casual-sounding message, and it was nearly half past ten which seemed a bit late to phone someone she did not really know very well. She amended this last part, because it felt as if she had known Robert for a long time; even so, half past ten was still a bit late and there was also the fact that she was having to struggle to stay awake. It had been nice to hear his voice; she smiled as she got into bed, thinking she would call tomorrow morning.

It annoyed her to be so extremely tired, because she wanted to lie awake going over everything that had happened. That strange clause in Frank Douglas's will – that was a peculiar thing. Madeleine had said it could not legally be enforced, but legal or not she had complied with it. Was there anything strange about her having done so? Hilary was only half inclined to accept what

Madeleine had said about not wanting to risk the rest of the inheritance; the market value of the Tarleton, even then, would surely have far outweighed her modest-sounding inheritance.

Hilary wanted to think about the actual reopening of the Tarleton, as well. Reclaiming the past ... She would try to track down that old actor's autobiography – he had appeared on Toby's stage so he would have known Toby. Hilary would quite like to have known Toby, as well: she was hoping they would be able to find some more of his music for the reopening. There was the idea she had had for a radio biography programme as well; she would still like to try that and might be able to work on it in tandem with the opening ...

Toby seemed to have strayed into her dreams, because she thought she could hear him singing. The sounds seemed to be coming from a long way off, but there was a faint background hum, so it was impossible to hear any actual words. That would be the hum of all the people in the Tarleton's audience, of course. The song was not one she had ever heard before – or was it? She listened intently; it was a distinctive melody and sounded as if it was mostly backed by a piano.

Hilary came up out of sleep as abruptly as if something had shaken her, and discovered she was sitting bolt upright in bed. Moonlight was coming in through the partly opened curtains and her heart was bumping. For several moments she felt dizzy and strange and it was difficult to push back the waves of sleep. The surroundings confused her, because the furniture was all in the wrong place and the scents were not the scents of her bedroom ...

Then she recalled she was at Levels House. Her watch, which she had put on the bedside table, showed it to be a quarter to midnight which surprised her because she felt as if she had been deeply asleep for much longer. She remembered thinking about Toby as she fell asleep, wondering about the radio programme, and she remembered hearing him singing ...

It was then that Hilary realized two things. One was that the music in her dream was not unknown after all. She had heard it before – only once, but it was an occasion she was not likely to forget. She had heard it in the darkened Tarleton, on the night she and Robert had glimpsed the ghost.

The other thing was that she could still hear it.

Hilary sat very still. The likeliest explanation was that she was asleep, and dreaming about Toby. The next likeliest explanation was that somewhere in the house someone was playing an old record. This was a bit far-fetched, but the evening's discussions might have revived old memories for Madeleine, and she might have some of her father's old recordings and be playing one of them quietly in her room. But would anyone do that at midnight, with two guests in the house? And it's the Tarleton's ghost song, thought Hilary. It really is the song Robert and I heard that night, I'm sure of it. Even if I am still dreaming, I'll have to find out where it's coming from.

She swung her legs out of bed, and this time felt so dizzy she had to grab the bedside table to stop herself toppling over. What on earth had Madeleine's 'girl from the village' put in that casserole? Or had it been the coffee – it had been a bit too strong and quite bitter and Hilary had surreptitiously poured most of her second cup down the sink.

She waited for the dizziness to recede and after a moment was able to make her way to the door. She had not bothered to bring a dressing gown, but her pyjamas were fairly substantial and she had brought soft moccasins as house shoes. She slid her feet into these and, trying to be as quiet as possible, inched the door open and peered out.

The music was coming from overhead. The attic? Surely no one would be playing music in an attic at this time of night? Hilary advanced a cautious step or two out of the bedroom and trod on a sagging floorboard that creaked like a gunshot. At once the music stopped. Damn, thought Hilary, glancing to the front of the house

338

and Madeleine's bedroom. But nothing happened, and she went on down the landing, past Shona's bedroom door which was closed. She paused, wondering if she should knock. No, better not. She would just go quietly along to the attic stairs and see if she could hear anything from there.

As she reached the foot of the stairs, she began to doubt she had heard the music at all. It could have been coming from outside the house – a car radio in the lane, perhaps. Yes, but it was the music you heard that night inside the Tarleton, she said to herself. Or was it? She was suddenly not quite so sure.

She glanced behind her to the shadowy landing, uneasily aware of how isolated this part of the house was, wondering whether, if she called for help, she would be heard but she went all the way up the stairs to the small door at the top. There was an old-fashioned latch fixed to the edge of the door, but the hook hung loose. Did that mean someone was in there? There was only one way to find out. Hilary was not particularly tall, but the door was very low and narrow and she had to bend down to get through. It closed behind her almost at once, which was slightly sinister; Hilary reached back to make sure it would open again. Yes, it was all right.

There was a dry powdery scent in the attic – Robert would have said, caustically, that it was probably dry rot and remembering Robert's dry irony was so heartening that Hilary instantly felt better. She thought the scent was simply age and stored-away memories.

It was not pitch black in the attic, but shadows clustered thickly and cobwebs dripped from the roof rafters, stirring slightly. She felt along the wall hoping to encounter a light switch, but there were only the rough bricks and timbers of the house itself. Damn. Would she have to find her way back to the door and prop it open to get some light? She tried a bit lower and her hand brushed against something that seemed to move slightly, then closed on thick rough fabric – oh God, it was the sleeve of a coat, someone was standing inside the attic – someone wearing a long concealing coat . . . Without warning the words of the old autobiography slid into her mind. 'He creeps through the darkness, still clothed in the long overcoat and muffler he always wore in life . . . a wide-brimmed hat pulled well down to hide his face . . .'

Hilary snatched her hand away at once, her heart pounding, her mind spinning with the macabre image. Ghost or not there was certainly someone here – someone was in the attic; she could hear the faint sound of breathing.

She began to feel her way back to the door, and as she did so there was a scrape of sound from deeper in the attic, and the music began again. It filled the dark attic and sent ice-cold shivers down Hilary's spine. She had not imagined it: it really was the tune she and Robert had heard that night, and if ever there was ghost music, this was it – this scratchy old music drifting through the darkness. And then, from out of the confused fear, she picked out that one word. Scratchy. The music was *scratchy*. It's a gramophone, she thought. Someone's playing an old record up here in the dark.

This time her hand found the light switch and she flipped it down. An uncertain glow flooded the attic, casting a pool of light over the piles of household junk, partly intriguing, partly sad, partly eerie. Outside the light, crouching in the corners, were what looked like bundles of newspapers and magazines, and boxes of anonymous cloth – curtains and bedspreads and old clothes.

The music was still playing, the piano making little trills and runs rather like the hammy music written for spooky old silent horror films, easily conjuring up images of cartoon ghosts in white sheets. And now Hilary could hear the lyrics.

> On Friday nights the ghost walks
> Rattling its chains to itself;
> Because that's the night the ghost hands out the pelf.

> But on Friday night the ghost walks,
> Always as white as a sheet
> Cheerless as sin, so they buy it some gin,
> And some bedsocks for its feet.

The words were perfectly clear, and the scratches and the sheer age of the recording were clear as well. Hilary looked across to where the music came from and saw the outline of an old gramophone with the famous flaring horn. Standing behind it was a dark shape and Hilary's heart began to pound, because surely it was wearing a long cloak.

The ghost walks, THE GHOST WALKS . . .

The figure moved into the light and Hilary saw it was not a long cloak at all, it was simply that the shadows had twisted themselves into the semblance of one. Nor was there any deep-brimmed hat to hide the face which was perfectly identifiable. It was Shona Seymour – or was it? As the figure moved towards her, Hilary had a sudden hideous doubt. It looked like Shona and the clothes were the ones Shona had worn today, but the eyes were all wrong – they were wide and staring and the lips were wider as if their owner was smiling a dreadful mad smile.

And then this nightmare figure stopped and let out a cry of fury. 'Hilary. No! *No!* It's not meant to be you! It's meant to be Madeleine. You bitch, you'll spoil everything coming up here – Where's Madeleine? I switched off the light so she would have to feel her way through the darkness.'

Hilary was already backing to the door. Her mind was in a whirl of confusion and fear, but it was appallingly clear that something had happened to Shona's mind – a breakdown – a brainstorm if there was such a thing.

She said, 'What am I spoiling? What do you mean about Madeleine? Shona, what is this?'

'You're supposed to be asleep,' said this person with Shona's features. 'I gave you sleeping stuff – why aren't you asleep?'

'I don't understand—' began Hilary, then stopped, remembering the coffee that had been too strong.

'I put sleeping pills in your coffee,' said Shona, as if she had heard Hilary's thought. 'I've only just remembered I did that – it was in the other half of my mind, the half I can't always reach. But I remember it now. I crushed them in a tissue while I was fetching the laptop and tipped them in your coffee. You never noticed, did you?' Her voice took on a curious childlike glee that made the hairs prickle on the back of Hilary's neck

'I didn't notice,' she said, 'but I didn't drink all the coffee because it was too strong.'

'I expect I was thinking I might need to get you out of the way,' said Shona. 'I expect I was covering all the options. It's always as well to do that.'

I'd better humour her, thought Hilary, but I'll have to get out of here – back downstairs and raise the alarm. But do I call the police simply because Shona's played an old record in an attic at midnight and is acting a bit weirdly? She remembered the only other person in this remote old house was an elderly lady with a frail heart and she also remembered that no one knew they were here – Shona had specifically said they would not let anyone at the office know in case the meeting with Madeleine fell flat. And she put sleeping stuff in my coffee, thought Hilary, shuddering because the thought of Shona doing this, but not remembering until now, was very creepy indeed. But she managed to say, in quite an ordinary voice, 'That was very clever. I didn't realize you'd done that.'

'I'm a lot cleverer than people give me credit for.' Again it was a boastful child. 'And when I do a murder I'm cleverest of all.'

Murder ... The ugly, powerful word shivered on the dusty old floorboards and stirred the thick cobwebs that dripped from the roof joists.

'But you see, Hilary,' said Shona, 'tonight it's got to be Madeleine who's murdered. She's got to hear the music.' A lock of her usually immaculate hair fell forward over her face, but she seemed not to notice which added to the strangeness; the Shona Hilary knew was always perfectly groomed. 'She's got to be frightened, you see. That's the plan. She's got to be frightened enough to have another heart attack. I found one of her father's songs up here – I've been playing it – I found the gramophone over there – it's one of the old wind-up machines and at first I didn't think it would work, but it does.'

'An old acoustic gramophone,' said Hilary slowly. 'Yes, I see. She'd hear music coming out of the past. Her own father's music – ghost music. Yes, if she recognized that, it would come as a massive shock. But why do you want to frighten Madeleine into a heart attack?'

'Oh, don't be so stupid!' said Shona, and now it was the demeanour of a spoilt child, stamping its foot. 'If Madeleine dies, or even if she's ill for any length of time, the Tarleton won't reopen.'

'Why don't you want it to reopen?' Her hands are curved like talons, thought Hilary, trying to beat down rising panic.

'You're such a silly bitch,' said Shona. 'It's because I must never let anyone find out what's behind the cellar wall.'

This isn't a breakdown, thought Hilary, staring at her. She's mad – Oh God, she really is. As gently and as soothingly as she could, she said, 'Do you know, Shona, you sound quite different tonight. Not a bit like the boss I've known for the past four years.'

Shona did not appear to have heard. She said, 'No one must ever – *ever* – know what's behind that wall. I don't always remember about it – sometimes it's years and years before I remember. The trouble is that it's in the other half of my head. And sometimes it's the wall in the Tarleton's cellar and sometimes it's the wall in Grith's cellar, and I don't always know which is which.' A look of puzzlement crossed her face.

Trying to keep her voice gentle, Hilary said, 'What's behind the wall? What's so bad it must stay hidden?'

343

'Anna was there at the beginning,' said Shona at once. 'For a long time I didn't know about that – I used to hear her calling to be let out, though. Then some workmen found her – she was ugly and shrivelled up, but it served her right. Sometimes I still hear her calling to be let out – she screams all night sometimes. That's when my head splits into two halves.' She stopped, and Hilary wondered if this was the moment to make a dash for the stairs.

'But no one's ever found Elspeth,' Shona went on. 'And it's important no one does. They'd know who killed her, you see. They'd know it was me – no one else could have done it. It took me all night to wall her up down there and it was very hard work, but I managed it. I don't know if she screams to get out, but I've never heard her. And I like thinking of her down there in the pitch dark all by herself. But if anyone knocks the wall down they'll find her – that's why it's important that the wall stays intact.'

'Do you mean the Tarleton wall?' said Hilary, groping for facts.

'I don't know! I told you, I don't know which one it is!' cried Shona. 'I knew once, but I don't know now! I can't always get at the other half of my mind!'

'It doesn't matter,' said Hilary quickly. 'Who was Elspeth?'

'I boiled her face,' said Shona, and incredibly and dreadfully, a mad giggle bubbled out of her mouth. 'That's a bit like the thing children say, isn't it? "Go and boil your head," they say. That's what I did to Elspeth. But you do see that I've got to stop people knocking down the wall, don't you? I daren't let them find Elspeth.'

Hilary still had no idea if Shona was talking about the wall under the Tarleton or not, but she thought if she was going to make a dash for it, she had better do so now. She began to move backwards towards the door, half a step at a time, praying she did not stumble over anything and draw Shona's attention to her. But as she felt for the door her hand brushed against an old great-coat hanging near it, and at the soft stirring of the folds Shona's eyes snapped back to awareness, and she looked at Hilary with a frightening glare. Hilary's heart gave a leap of panic, then her fingers closed on the light switch. She pushed it and darkness, thick and stifling, rushed down.

If facing Shona had been bad before, in the dark it was a thousand times worse. Shona gave a cry of fury and the madness that had been already apparent seemed to fill the whole attic. Hilary fumbled for the door, but for several nightmare seconds her hand met only bricks and timber. Her eyes began to adjust to the dark, which meant Shona's eyes must be adjusting as well. Icy sweat broke out on her spine, because if she did not find the door immediately . . .

It was here! She pushed it open and scrambled through. Shona's furious cry followed her, but she banged the door into place, and fastened the hook into its slot on the frame. As she did so Shona pushed hard against the door causing it to shudder. The flimsy latch held, but Hilary had no idea if it would hold for long enough for her to get to the phone and call for help.

There was no sound from Madeleine's part of the house which was good: for an elderly lady with a bad heart to be woken abruptly and told there was a potentially dangerous woman in the house might be fatal. It might have the very result Shona had been aiming for when she played that creepy music.

She could almost feel Shona's mind working behind the door, planning, calculating. She'll guess I'm intending to get to a phone and call out the cavalry, thought Hilary, and she'll try to talk her way out of it when they get here. Will she say she caught me in the attic, instead of the other way round? Whatever she says, there's still that person she talked about – Elspeth, she said. She bricked her up in a cellar. I can't believe any of this is happening.

The sitting-room landline would be quicker than finding her mobile and switching it on, and she was about to make a sprint for the ground floor when Shona renewed her assault on the door. The old timbers creaked ominously and it was obvious that Shona would only have to make a couple more attempts and the door would burst open. Hilary took a deep breath and ran down the twisty stairs. Above her, Shona had redoubled her efforts – at any minute she would escape from the attic – and at any moment Madeleine would surely be woken by the noise. Hilary had no idea what Shona would do, but it was clear she had to get the police here as fast as possible.

She reached the ground floor and dived into the sitting room, scanning the darkness for the phone. There it was near the French windows: one of the old black sit up and beg kind, with a receiver and old-fashioned dial. Hilary lifted the receiver, her hand going to the 9, and stopped, frowning. There was no dial tone, just a flat blankness. She jiggled the receiver rest, but nothing happened. Trying to beat down panic, but aware that Shona could erupt out of the attic at any minute, she dialled anyway. Her hands were wound so tightly around the receiver her knuckles hurt.

Ten precious seconds ticked away before she acknowledged that the phone was dead. Had it been unplugged? Could Shona have planned so far ahead? Hilary picked up the phone cable and felt along it, more than half expecting to find it had been pulled from its socket.

Somebody had cut the cable, very neatly and sharply, just where it came out from the socket. The socket itself was low down near the skirting board, and the cut cable would only be discovered if someone tried to make a phone call – and people who had guests for the evening did not normally make phone calls. Shona did it, thought Hilary. She either did it early in the evening when Madeleine and I were putting the supper together, or later, when we went up to bed and left her down here. She said there were things she couldn't remember – something about things being in the half of her mind she couldn't reach.

The horror of the situation broke upon her in an almost overwhelming flood, but she forced herself to think. Could she get back upstairs without running into Shona and barricade herself into her bedroom? No, of course she could not, she needed to get help – a phone in a neighbouring house or the village. What about the car – was there any chance that Shona had left the keys in the ignition? But memory showed her Shona locking the car when they arrived and dropping the keys in her handbag. And there was Madeleine to consider. Hilary could not leave Madeleine on her own in the house with Shona.

She heard the attic door smack hard against the wall overhead and footsteps coming down the narrow stair to the landing. She's got out, thought Hilary, every muscle tensed, expecting Shona to come straight downstairs. But she did not. There was the sound of sharp knocking upstairs – hands rapping peremptorily against wood.

'Madeleine?' said Shona's voice, friendly and polite. 'Madeleine, it's Shona. Can you open the door? Something dreadful's happening – it's Hilary. She's had some kind of brainstorm. We need to get help.' There was silence, and Hilary heard Shona knock again. In the same soft friendly voice, she said, 'Please open the door, Madeleine. Please let me in.'

Hilary instantly forgot about her own safety and was halfway back up the stairs, shouting as loudly as she could.

'Madeleine – it's a trick! Whatever you do don't open the door to her. Lock it or barricade yourself in! The phone wire's cut – I'm going for help!'

She had no idea if Madeleine could hear, but as Shona knocked again, she heard, faintly but clearly, Madeleine calling back. 'I don't know what's going on but I'm staying here until I know it's safe to come out.'

This was a relief, because it sounded as if there was a lock on Madeleine's door. But Shona was coming along the landing and at any minute she would be on the stairs. The main front door had a bewildering array of locks and bolts which would take several minutes to open – minutes Hilary did not have. The stairs creaked and a shadow appeared on the wall. She's coming! thought Hilary in panic, and grabbing one of the raincoats from the old-fashioned coat-stand, ran through the house, slamming all the doors behind her, because if Shona had to open doors it would give her a few extra seconds to get outside. She pulled the raincoat round her as she went, making for the kitchen because all houses of this age and size had at least two doors, and surely she had seen a garden door?

There it was, the traditional half-glass, half-wood door. There was a lock, the key was in the lock, and there was a bolt at the top. Hilary's hands were shaking so badly she could hardly turn the key, but she managed it and reached up to slide the bolt back. The door swung open and cold, rainy night air met her.

Uncaring of the fact she was only wearing a raincoat over pyjamas and thin-soled moccasins, Hilary went out into the night. The prospect of playing hide and seek with a self-confessed murderess in the dark garden was a nightmarish one, but if she kept to the shadows she should get down the drive and onto the road. From there she would have to run until she came to a house, then hammer on the door and hope they would phone the police. She took a deep breath and sprinted across the lawn in the direction of the drive. Rain lashed her face and the thick bushes fringing the drive were squat black shapes like crouching monsters ready to pounce on her. Twice she flinched, throwing up her hands defensively, because it seemed as if one of the shadows was lurching towards her, but she reached the gate without mishap and went out onto the narrow country road. On a bright night she would probably have been able to see the outlines of nearby properties clearly, but with rain and clouds blotting out the moon, she could only see hedges and fields. Left or right? Devil or deep blue sea? They had driven through Fosse Leigh village, and about a mile beyond it, then they had turned right into Levels House. Had there been houses on the stretch of road between the village and this house? Hilary thought there had been two or three. In any event, she would feel safer heading towards a place where there were buildings – where there would surely be a pub with people living on the premises. Even so, as she turned left, she had the feeling that she was flipping a mental coin.

She had got no more than fifteen yards when something happened that sent a chill through her whole body. The soft sound of footsteps coming towards her – coming from the direction of Levels House. Someone was creeping along the dark road after her.

CHAPTER THIRTY-ONE

Robert woke at quarter past ten, and realized he had either forgotten to set the alarm, or had slept through it.

This was terrible because almost certainly the police would have been in touch with the Harlequin office, which meant Hilary would already know the full extent of the melodrama and was probably wondering why he had not called her. The thought of Hilary thinking he had not bothered to tell her about the body behind the underground wall was so dreadful that Robert pulled on a dressing gown, tipped some orange juice into a glass from the fridge, which he swallowed at one go, and headed for the phone at once. Even if the police were already crawling over the Harlequin and the Tarleton, surely Hilary would understand when he explained everything, including how it had been well after three a.m. when he finally got home.

It was infuriating to find that her direct number was on voicemail. Robert tried the mobile number, but that too went straight to voicemail and he hung up without leaving a message. Describing the discovery of a partly desiccated body could not really be done in a two-minute recorded message; also, he had no way of knowing where Hilary might be, or who she might be with, when she listened to it. He would try again later.

After he had showered, dressed and drunk some coffee, he telephoned his office to give an edited version of what had happened and explain that because of it he did not think he would be able to get in today. His partner was at first inclined to be sceptical, but Robert was not given to spinning wild stories about finding mummified human remains, in fact he was not given to spinning stories of any kind, so the partner fetched Robert's diary and they spent the next half hour sorting out the two appointments Robert had for that day, and discussing the report for the yuppie apartments near Waterloo Station. Robert's notes about that were in a file on his desk, which meant the client could at least be given the gist of his findings.

'Very precise and methodical,' said the partner, reading them. 'All the way from the wood rot in the floor joists down to stress fatigue in the metal underpinning.'

'Only battleships and surveyors get stress fatigue,' said Robert, and rang off.

DS Treadwell phoned almost immediately after this to say he was in the Harlequin offices and trying to trace the Tarleton's owner.

'Shona Seymour's out at meetings with some radio programmers apparently,' he said. 'She left a note on the receptionist's desk late last night to say she'll be tied up all day and not to expect her back in the office until late tomorrow. Her mobile's switched off, but I've left a message asking her to call me. No one's sure which radio studios she was going to, and her assistant's taken a couple of days' leave – sorry, did you say something?'

'No.'

'Anyway, the assistant's mobile is on voicemail as well. I didn't leave a message – if she's on holiday she might be anywhere – she might be out of the country. It's annoying they're both away at the same time, but these things happen. I'll see you later, Mr Fallon. You're coming into the station at two aren't you?'

'Yes,' said Robert, and rang off, wondering why Hilary had not mentioned that she would be on holiday today. Perhaps there had been a crisis of some kind: some family thing. He reminded himself that he did not really know much about her. After a moment he tried her flat, but this phone, too, was on answerphone. Robert did leave a message this time, not mentioning the body or the Tarleton, just saying he had been trying to reach her, and asking her to call back.

At one o'clock he ate a couple of sandwiches, and set off for Canon Row to make his statement. This turned out to be a bureaucratic labyrinth, made worse by a tedious wait for people who, as far as Robert could tell, had left the building, could not be found, or could not be bothered. He had expected the statement-making to take about forty-five minutes; in the event, it took nearer two hours. DS Treadwell looked in to say they had not yet heard from Shona Seymour.

'We've left another message on her voicemail, but she still hasn't replied,' he said. 'A bit odd for someone who's supposed to be such a sharp businesswoman, but she might be out of range of a signal or in some long-winded meeting and not wanting interruptions. We'll have to open the cellar up reasonably soon and get forensics in and the body out, of course, but that body's not going anywhere on its own, so we'll wait another few hours. I'd rather have the owner's authority before we start tearing walls down – or at worst let him know what's going on.'

'Isn't there anyone in overall command of the Harlequin set-up?' asked Robert.

'There's some kind of governing trust, but it doesn't sound as if any of its members have much to do with the actual running of things so we're not bothering with them unless we have to,' said Treadwell. 'What we're doing today is taking a brief look in the Harlequin's files for the owner's name and address. The receptionist has found some keys to Seymour's office, and everyone's being very cooperative. There's a part-time worker who's helping out as well.'

'I wish you luck tracking down the owner's identity,' said Robert. 'As far as I can make out, it's been shrouded in mystery for the best part of a century.'

'We'll keep you posted,' said Treadwell.

Robert left them to it and fought his way back through the traffic, reaching his flat at twenty to five. He had not realized how strongly he had been hoping to see his own answerphone blinking cheerfully, and to hear Hilary's voice on it. But it was silent and no one had phoned.

Caley Merrick hoped the police had not seen the shock that had gone through him when they turned up at the Harlequin offices that morning.

He had gone in at ten to finish the mailing he had been doing that week. Just an hour's work it would be – the flyers to be stamped and posted – but it would mean a few extra pounds at the end of the month which was always welcome, and it also meant an hour spent in the place which he felt was a link to the Tarleton.

The receptionist told him Miss Seymour was not in today – Caley remembered hearing about some radio meetings – and that Hilary had taken a day's holiday. He was not sorry to hear Miss Seymour would be out, because she always made him feel nervous, but he had hoped he might be able to get Hilary to talk about the Tarleton and find out what she had been doing there that night.

But here were the police, headed by a rather brash young detective sergeant called Stuart Treadwell, saying that a body – actually a dead body dating back to goodness knew when! – had been found behind a wall in the Tarleton's cellar. Yes, it was certainly an extraordinary thing, said DS Treadwell; they were looking into it, of course, and one of the first things they needed to do was contact the owner so they could open up that part of the old cellars. That was why he and two of his team were here now.

Caley thought, afterwards, that it was a good thing he was so used to hiding his emotions, but even so, he stared at DS Treadwell in utter amazement before he managed to ask who had actually found the body.

'A surveyor found it,' said Treadwell. 'He was investigating the foundations for sewage leakage or something,' he added, and Caley remembered the unknown young man he had seen with Hilary Bryant.

'We've left messages for Miss Seymour and we'll most likely wait for her to contact us, but she's proving a bit elusive so we're taking a quick look through files here to see if we can find the owner's address.' He indicated the spare desk in Shona's office where his men were already flipping through manila folders; Caley thought they were not doing so very thoroughly, just riffling the top pages of each one. He glanced across at the two large filing cabinets in the corner – the cabinets he had so often wanted to open.

'Yes, I see,' he said. 'Thank you for explaining,' and got himself out of the office and into the little kitchen on the landing because he was afraid he was going to be sick.

In the event he was not sick but had to sit on the stool in the kitchen for quite a long time, struggling for breath, dizzy and shaking. Even with the inhaler it took quite a long time for the attack to subside, and he was aware of a dull ache round his ribs and up into his throat, but he was able to consider what this might mean to him.

A body had been found in the Tarleton – a very old body from the sound of it – and the police would have to go in to investigate. That was unavoidable. DS Treadwell had mentioned opening up one of the old cellars, which probably meant the under-stage cellars. Wherever it was, though, it would mean massive disruption – you only had to watch a TV crime series to know about forensic tests and people tramping in and out. Caley felt sick again, thinking about that. He had often worried about what would happen if the theatre were to reopen and he had even played over horrid little scenarios in his mind as to how it might come about. But he had never imagined it happening like this. He was aware, as well, of fierce jealousy at that unknown man, that surveyor, who had caused this disturbance.

But the thing to remember was that the police investigation would only be temporary: it would only go on for a week or two, then everything would be as it had been before. He could live through that; he could watch and wait for the time when the Tarleton was his once more.

Despite these reassurances, when he stood up, his legs were trembling and although the sick feeling had passed he still felt unwell. Catching sight of himself in the little square of mirror over the sink he was shocked to see a grey-faced old man looking back at him. This would not do at all; even if the police did not notice anything wrong, the office staff, who knew him fairly well by now, would do so. He turned the cold tap full on and splashed water over his face, then he put the kettle on to make coffee for everyone.

By the time he carried the tray with the mugs of coffee into the main office, an idea was taking root in his mind. At first he dismissed it, but it thrust itself into the forefront of his mind, pointing out this was an opportunity he might never have again. It was a day when everything was upside down: filing cabinets that were normally locked were open; files were being carried back and forth; people were wandering round, ignoring their usual routines. If ever there was a time when Caley might get his hands on the Tarleton file, this was surely that time. He was aware of a sudden throb of excitement.

He distributed the mugs, deliberately ending with the two police detectives working in Miss Seymour's room. Speaking off-handedly but politely, he asked if there was anything he could do to help – everyone else was quite busy today. Perhaps he could take the files out of the drawers or something?

At first he thought DS Treadwell would dismiss the offer, but then he said, 'Well, if you've nothing else to do, that might be useful.'

'I could bring them across to the desk in batches for you to check through,' said Caley, chewing his lower lip as if working this out. 'And replace them in the right order after you've looked at them. It would keep them in place and it would mean less mess for the office.' This sounded as if he was more a part of the office than was actually the case, and it also sounded as if he was quite knowledgeable about the filing system. It seemed he had struck the right note, because the DS said that would be useful, thanks very much. So Caley, hoping his asthma did not betray him, began to carry stacks of files back and forth, eight or ten at a time, scanning their labels as he did so, praying he would see one labelled the Tarleton and that if he did, he would be able to remove it without being noticed. It was the longest shot in the world, but it might just come off.

It did come off. There were two files labelled 'Tarleton Music Hall'. Caley had not expected two separate files, but he found the first one in the main office – it was a large document wallet, and he was able to slide it beneath the envelopes on his own little corner desk. The ease with which he did it surprised him. The receptionist was in the room at the time, but she was on the phone, making notes as she talked.

The second file was unexpected – Caley was not really looking for a second one – but there it was, near the back of Miss Seymour's own filing cabinet. It looked to be more of a correspondence file with a metal clip for holding papers and letters in place. Caley's heart was racing and sweat prickled between his shoulder blades, because Treadwell's men were in the room with him, but in the end it was easy to subtract it from the drawer and drop it on top of a pile already checked. He gave the two men a new batch to work through then, moving casually, slid the Tarleton file inside his jacket and walked into the kitchen, collecting the other from his desk on the way. He could not hide two files under his jacket, but surely it was perfectly ordinary for someone to walk across an office with a file? He did so openly, picking up the used coffee mugs as he went as if going to wash them up. Once on the little landing outside, he pushed both files inside the folds of his overcoat which was hanging on the rack inside the door.

Then he went back to the office and continued helping the police with their search. Unobtrusive, helpful Mr Merrick. That nice little man who occasionally comes in to address envelopes and run errands. A pity he had to go home at lunchtime, but he would have his own life and commitments. The Harlequin would not represent his entire life. Caley knew that five minutes after he left they would have forgotten about him.

When he reached his house he locked all the doors and went into the little back room which Mary had designated as their dining room and which still had the gate-leg table by the fireplace. Caley put the two files onto the table and sat down, looking at them. His heart was racing as fast as it had done earlier, but now it was racing with excitement and anticipation. I've stolen two files, he thought. I've obstructed a police investigation. He did not care. This is going to be it, he thought. This is going to be the moment when I find the link I've wanted since I was eighteen. The mysterious owner. The person who might hold the key to my real family.

He opened the document wallet first, sliding the sheaf of papers out, seeing almost at once that they were unlikely to hold any secrets. In the main they were bank statements showing payments made in and out, and accounts from cleaning companies. There were also current insurance cover notes, certificates from the electricity board and fire authorities. All of this was information he already knew.

At first look the second file was no more promising. There were a few letters to and from the bank, and some correspondence with a builder who had renewed some guttering two years ago – Caley remembered that being done because he had had to dodge the builder. The letters were all clipped together, and he began to turn them over, conscious of deep disappointment, thinking he need not have gone to so much trouble to get the files out.

And quite suddenly, there it was. A single sheet of paper, loose in the file as if someone who was careless or in a hurry had just slipped it inside, not realizing it had slid between earlier letters. It was rather unevenly typed, with a printed address at the top and a signature at the bottom, and it looked like a photocopy. Caley sat very still, staring down at it, seeing the printed words dance back and forth across the page, forming crazy, unreadable shapes.

It was from the Tarleton's owner. Its *owner*. She was a lady living in Somerset, a lady called Madeleine Ferrelyn, and she had written this letter as recently as three days ago. And whatever the police might do to the theatre was a mere fleabite, because Madeleine Ferrelyn had already started the process that really would spoil Caley's life. He read the letter again, this time not feeling sick, but feeling as if he was being drawn down into a black and lonely well.

'. . . the Tarleton is to be woken from its long sleep at last,' the letter said. '. . . my father's will stipulated it should remain closed until fifty years after his death.'

A brief anger welled up inside Caley – how *dare* she write those words. How dare this Ferrelyn woman talk so lightly of bringing back to life the one place where he belonged: the place that had become his life, the place where he could make music flow from the battered old piano, and where he felt he was among friends who understood him. It did not matter that the music was old and most of it virtually forgotten, and it did not matter that the friends were the ghosts of people long since dead and also forgotten:

the music was wonderful to Caley and the people were not dead to him. He could not lose those marvellous hours he spent there, it would be like ripping out most of his life.

He left the letter in its folder – he had no idea yet what he was going to do with it or whether he could risk destroying it – and sat very still for a long time. At last, moving jerkily as if something was forcing him to unwillingly do its bidding, he reached for the phone to dial the number for National Rail Enquiries. Connected to an anonymous operator, he asked about trains from London to Glastonbury. Fairly early in the morning, and a direct train if possible. It was disconcerting to be told there was no railway station in Glastonbury itself, but Caley asked if they could advise him of the nearest one to a place called Fosse Leigh. He thought it was quite near Glastonbury. Could they help him with this? He made himself sound older than he really was and a bit shaky, because it was remarkable how sympathetic people were if you did that.

National Rail could indeed help him. In ten minutes Caley had the information that the nearest railway station to Fosse Leigh was Castle Cary and there were some through trains from Paddington. The journey would take about an hour and a half. Yes, there was a train at 8.34 a.m. Would he like to book a ticket now and collect it from the station?

But it was automatic to Caley not to do anything that could ever be traced back to him, so he said he would think about it, and rang off. Then he found one of the old map books from his cupboard – he and Mary had occasionally taken a little holiday at Herne Bay or Hastings and the maps had been useful – and saw that Fosse Leigh was only about ten miles from Castle Cary. It was not ideal, but it was better than he had hoped. There might be a bus service, but it was more likely that he would have to get a taxi from the station. It would all be a bit expensive, but he would draw out some of his savings.

As he folded the maps away, he wondered if DS Treadwell or

his men would find any other way of tracing Madeleine Ferrelyn. He did not think it was very likely.

It was six o'clock when Robert's phone rang. He snatched it up, willing it to be Hilary, and was aware of a stab of disappointment when he heard Treadwell's voice.

'I thought you'd like to know we've finally got a name and address for the Tarleton's owner,' he said. 'We had to go through the Harlequin's bank and they weren't very keen about releasing the information, but we pointed out that this was a police investigation, no matter how far back the crime, and that we had a body to move. At that they saw the argument and supplied the information. It's owned by a lady living in Somerset. A Mrs Ferrelyn – Madeleine Ferrelyn, in a village near Glastonbury. We've tried ringing her, but there's no reply, so we'll get the local man to go along in the morning. It can wait until then – from what the bank said she's an elderly lady, so we don't want to alarm her unnecessarily.'

'You haven't heard from Shona Seymour yet?' asked Robert.

'No. We've tried her flat as well, but she's not there.' He paused, and Robert said, 'Is something wrong?'

'Probably not.' But there was the definite impression of hesitancy. Robert waited, and Treadwell said, 'It's just that Shona Seymour's meeting – it was with Radio 4, by the way – seems to have ended at half past ten this morning. The people at that meeting thought she was going back to her office right away.'

'Is that particularly odd?' said Robert. 'Couldn't she have just sneaked a day off for some private thing of her own?' But he remembered that Hilary seemed to have sneaked a day off as well.

'Well, yes, but when we went out to her flat we had a word with the doorman,' said Treadwell. 'It's one of those rather plush quayside conversions and they have a kind of janitor-cum-security guy. He said Shona Seymour went in shortly after eleven this morning, then went straight out again with a small suitcase. He remembers

360

particularly, because he made some remark about her going away, and she said yes, she would be away for the night, and would he go up later to push the evening newspaper all the way through her letter box so as not to advertise that the flat was empty.'

'It's still not really very odd,' said Robert, but he was aware of a vague uneasiness. 'In any case, it can't be connected to that body in the Tarleton's cellars.'

'No, but what is odd is that we didn't find any files on the place while we were at the Harlequin offices,' said Treadwell.

'You didn't?' Robert managed not to say that Hilary had referred to a file with bank statements.

'Not so much as a Post-it note,' said Treadwell. 'And the fact that Shona Seymour seems to have taken off without telling anyone where she's gone – and that she did so immediately after you found that body is a curious coincidence. Still, there's probably a very ordinary explanation.'

Robert hung up, frowning as he considered this new development. He realized he had not eaten since the scrappy meal he had made for himself at midday, and disinterred some lasagne from the fridge. After he had eaten it, he tried Hilary's flat and mobile again; both were still on voicemail, but this time he left a message on the mobile, just saying he hoped she was all right and asking her to call him, deliberately making his voice sound offhand.

But the feeling of unease was mounting. The thing he could not put out of his mind was the memory of that shadowy watcher in the Tarleton's box that night, and of the soft-footed figure who had stolen through the darkness, humming quietly as it went. Robert had tried to brush it aside at the time, but he had known, deep down, that someone had been standing in the box at the side of the stage, watching himself and Hilary. And now Hilary and Shona seem to have disappeared and were not responding to phone messages, and the Tarleton file, which Robert definitely knew existed, had also disappeared.

How easy would it be to get this Madeleine Ferrelyn's phone

number? Robert did not have a complete address, but it was an unusual name and he could probably get it from one of the directory enquiry services. Could he phone an unknown lady though, just on the off-chance that Hilary was there?

By nine o'clock he faced the fact that he was not going to sleep that night unless he was sure Hilary was all right. He dialled directory enquiries, and asked for the number of a Mrs Madeleine Ferrelyn. The address was near Glastonbury, he said, hoping this would be enough.

The voice at the other end sounded a bit bored. It said, 'Would that be Ferrelyn of Levels House, Fosse Leigh, county of Somerset?'

'Yes,' said Robert, never having heard of Fosse Leigh, and was given the number.

He sat staring at it for a long time. Mrs M. Ferrelyn, Levels House, Fosse Leigh, Somerset. It was not so very late to make a phone call; he could simply say he was trying to trace a friend – that there had been a mix up over a message somewhere – but that he thought she might be there, and then apologize if she was not there after all. Or could he? But the memory of that shadowy figure in the theatre's box kept presenting itself to him, and he snatched up the phone and dialled the number before he could change his mind. There was a series of clicks and then a high-pitched continuous whine. Robert swore, and tried again. The result was the same on the second attempt and also on the third. Fault on the line? He fought his way through the labyrinth of the telephone fault-reporting system, and was eventually told that yes, there was a fault on this line and it would be passed to the engineers to deal with.

'How soon . . .?' began Robert, but the voice could not give any information on this point. It would be for the engineers to make tests, it said. It might be a local fault – this was a call centre in Glasgow and they had no knowledge of local conditions.

'I'd be grateful if it could be treated as urgent,' said Robert, and rang off.

He spent ten minutes telling himself he had no idea what he was going to do next, but of course he did know. He was going to get out his maps and see how long it would take him to drive to this place, this Fosse Leigh, where the mysterious owner of the even more mysterious Tarleton apparently lived. When he looked at the map Fosse Leigh seemed to be a very small village indeed. It ought to be easy enough to find Levels House and if everything seemed all right, he would simply turn round and drive home. He did not know, yet, how he would establish if things were all right but he would think of a plan as he drove.

A part of him still did not believe he was going to go haring off into the unknown in quest of a female. He was sensible and cautious and never yielded to mad impulses. He amended this: he had been sensible and cautious and not given to impulse until he met Hilary Bryant.

He marked the route on the clearest of his maps, picked up his jacket, collected his wallet and car keys, and went out of his flat and down to his car.

There were times when you had to cast sense and caution to the winds. In any case, he would probably find it was not a very difficult journey at all.

CHAPTER THIRTY-TWO

June 1914

It had not been as difficult a journey as Toby had feared.

They reached Sarajevo around midnight on 26 June which was not late for Toby who was used to theatre hours, although Sonja's face was white with tiredness. Even so, as they got down from the train and stood on the small platform in Sarajevo her eyes glowed with fervour. Ilena Osapinsky appeared hardly to have flagged at all: Toby thought she somehow gave the impression that having partaken in so many rebellions and revolutions in her life, this was just another in a long line. He could not decide if this was a calculated impression or if it was genuine. The bearded Ivor, who looked slightly crumpled from the hours on the train, took her arm and helped with her luggage.

The accommodation turned out to be in the house of someone Toby supposed was a Tranz member, but the language spoken was beyond him and he had no idea what was being said. They were shown to two bare but clean rooms at the top of the rather ramshackle house: Toby was to share with Ivor and there were two other beds in the room, both with a few belongings already set out on them. Toby wondered if Petrovnic would be sleeping in one of the other beds and hoped he would not.

A supper was served on a scrubbed-top table in what appeared to be a kitchen. There was a large pot of stew, with coarse-fibred bread, rice and fruit. Ilena refused to eat anything except a small portion of the fruit, but Toby, who was hungry, accepted a large helping. The meat could have been goat or rabbit or even human flesh for all he could tell, but he found it excellent and attempted to convey his appreciation to their hosts by gestures.

Afterwards coffee was offered; it was so thick and strong Toby only managed a few sips, but Ilena drank two cups with relish and informed the company that on her father's estate in the old days, they had always had coffee of this flavour.

'Does that mean she really is a baroness?' murmured Sonja to Toby.

'Either that, or her father was the estate handyman,' said Toby, and Sonja laughed, then remembered about being earnest and purposeful and told him to be quiet.

He woke next morning to bright sunshine streaming through the windows, to find himself alone. If Ivor or anyone else had occupied the other beds, they had made them neatly and left the bedroom quietly. There was a polite tap at the door, and the house's owner put his head into the room, to say, in slow difficult English, that Mr Chance was please to join them for coffee and discourse with the master.

'Is the revolution about to start?' asked Toby, who was feeling considerably better after a night's sleep.

'Excuse?'

'I'm sorry, I was being flippant. I'll be downstairs in five minutes.'

Sonja was already seated at the kitchen table, and Petrovnic was talking in a low voice with Ilena and Ivor. He looked up as Toby came in, favoured him with a brief nod, then, raising his voice, said they were to assemble at the Café Zlatna Moruna in one hour's time.

'Battle orders?' murmured Toby to Sonja as Petrovnic went out.

'It's one way of putting it. Coffee?'

'Not if it's that syrupy stuff we had last night.'

He was glad, however, to find that the host's 'coffee' translated as a plain but perfectly acceptable breakfast of some kind of porridge sweetened with honey, together with more of the coarse-fibred bread and fruit. He ate everything and drank plain milk.

'I don't know what animal the milk's from,' said Sonja, peeling an apple.

'I don't care if it's from a herd of elephants. Let's walk through the town before the meeting at the café, shall we?'

There were flags and flowers decorating the streets, together with several large posters depicting the Archduke who had the distinctive heavy Habsburg jawline and a luxuriant moustache. Toby and Sonja found Sarajevo attractive. As they walked through the streets there were glimpses of a river glinting as it ran under old stone bridges. A rather imposing cathedral shared part of the view with what Toby thought was a mosque. 'All beliefs catered for,' he said to Sonja.

'Don't be so flippant.'

'If I can't be flippant when I'm hundreds of miles from my home and its responsibilities—'

'This looks like Zlatna Moruna,' said Sonja. 'We'd better go in.'

'Petrovnic was right when he said it was humble.' Toby surveyed the exterior of the café dubiously. 'I can't wait to see how our Ilena behaves in here.'

The café was much as Toby had expected: a bare-floored place with small tables, and flagons of wine served at the tables. A modest choice of food appeared to be available. The windows looked directly onto the street, but they were so small the café was perpetually dark, and gas jets flickered and popped even at eleven o'clock in the morning. There was a smell of oil and cigarette smoke on the air.

The café was filled with people – most of whom were men – talking in earnest little clusters round the tables. Toby had the feeling of stepping deeper into a den of secrecy and he paused in the doorway, exchanging a look with Sonja before sitting down and accepting a glass of wine from the earthenware jug ordered by Petrovnic.

Also at the table were three young men whom Petrovnic introduced to the English party. Their leader was clearly a boy of about twenty called Gavrilo Princip: Toby remembered Petrovnic mentioning Princip before they left London – 'He sees our work as a crusade,' Petrovnic had said – and Toby studied him with interest. So far from looking like someone about to embark on a crusade, Gavrilo Princip looked as if he should be in bed with wintergreen on his narrow chest and a camphor kettle steaming in a corner. He coughed frequently, several times touching a handkerchief to his lips.

Their English was virtually non-existent, but nods of greeting were exchanged. Toby, by this time wondering what he had got himself entangled in, watched their faces as they talked, trying to glean meanings from gestures or expressions, but not really doing so. Eventually, Petrovnic spoke in English, stating that the Archduke Franz-Ferdinand would leave the army camp where he had reviewed the troops at ten o'clock the next morning. The fleet of motor cars bearing him and his attendants would travel down a wide avenue called the Appel Quay to Sarajevo town hall for a formal reception, and Toby thought Petrovnic just managed to refrain from spitting at the prospect of something so traditional and formal.

'There will be much security?' asked Ilena.

'There will be some,' said Petrovnic, and broke off for another of the incomprehensible exchanges with the hollow-eyed Princip.

'It seems His Imperial Highness does not regard Sarajevo as hostile territory,' he said. 'He expects a warm welcome from the people of Bosnia.' He said this with what Toby could only think of as a sneer, and saw Ilena and Ivor exchange smiles with the three young men who had joined them.

'Here are your places for the procession,' said Petrovnic, producing a rather dog-eared sketch map. 'Mr Chance, you and Miss Kaplen will be at the Appel Quay. There are several stone bridges spanning the river and your places are near the Cumurja Bridge.' He indicated the place on the map then, glancing at the others, said, 'The main body of the protest march will set out from the museum which is here. We shall converge on the Archduke's car when it reaches the intersection and surround it with our people.' He looked at them. 'You understand?'

'Oh yes,' said Toby, and as Petrovnic struck a match and burned the map he stood up. 'If you don't mind, Miss Kaplen and I will take a walk to the Appel Quay now and find the exact spot.' He stood up. 'Sonja, will you come with me?'

Once outside, Toby said, 'This isn't a protest march – you do know that, don't you? Petrovnic wouldn't dot people round at different places for a march.'

'He'd group them together,' said Sonja, nodding in agreement. 'There'd be banners and placards, and we'd be told what to shout as we went along.'

'There speaks a veteran of protests,' said Toby. 'I suppose you're a member of the suffrage movement, are you?'

'As a matter of fact I am and I've marched with them several times, but I don't see—'

'Good for you,' said Toby, 'I'm all in favour of the vote for the ladies. My mother is as well – I believe she's thinking of joining the movement.'

Sonja stared at him. 'Really?'

'Yes, really.'

'Wouldn't that go a bit against the grain with Sir Hal?'

'I shouldn't think so. If it did she wouldn't pay any attention.' Despite the severity of the occasion, he smiled. 'You really do have an extraordinary image of my family, don't you?'

'I'm adjusting it by the hour,' said Sonja. They had reached the end of the street, and were within sight of a small park.

'Shall we go in there?' said Toby.

'Yes, let's.' They walked along a narrow path to a small wrought-iron seat overlooking a copse, and sat down.

Toby said, 'I've listened to my father talking about the situation here – about the resentment that's felt towards Austria. It's not just the Bosnians themselves who resent what Austria did: it's most of Europe.'

'Also Russia,' said Sonja, nodding. 'And now Germany is Austro-Hungary's staunchest ally—'

'And the Kaiser will make a friend of any country who will help him. It's all a tangled spider's web of hatred and jealousy and greed,' said Toby. He broke off and looked at Sonja. 'You have no idea how refreshing it is to talk to someone who understands what's going on in the world.'

'Of course I understand. But you know, Toby,' said Sonja, 'I don't often admit to fear, but I'm beginning to be very frightened of what's happening here today.'

'So am I. Because I think,' said Toby, 'that what we're seeing is a plot to attack Franz-Ferdinand. Even to kill him.'

She turned to look at him. 'Twenty-four hours ago I would have strongly disagreed,' she said, 'but now I'm dreadfully afraid you could be right. But I can't see why they would do something so appalling.'

'As a message,' said Toby, grimly. 'A message to Austria – no, not a message, something much stronger. A warning. Narodna Odbrana and the Black Hand and all their satellite groups telling Austria to get out of this country.'

'Yes,' said Sonja slowly. 'Oh God, yes, I hadn't seen it like that.'

'Austria has occupied Bosnia for over twenty years; five or six

369

years ago, she actually took the country over and made it part of Austria.'

'Yes, I know all that,' said Sonja rather impatiently. 'That's why I thought Tranz came here. To protest at Austria's imperialist greed.' She hesitated, then said, 'Toby, I might not approve of imperialist archdukes, but I do draw the line at outright murdering them.'

'I'm very glad to hear it,' he said, smiling at her. 'I've never entirely trusted Petrovnic for all his extravagant rhetoric and dubious charm, and I certainly don't trust that shady baroness, or those three ruffians we've just met. And if bullets really are fired at the Archduke tomorrow – or if knives are used . . .' He made an impatient gesture. 'I can't believe I'm even saying this,' he said. 'It's like something out of fiction. It's like the *Prisoner of Zenda*. But if I'm right – I pray to God I'm not – but if I am, and if the Archduke dies or is injured tomorrow,' said Toby, 'then it could be the final act that will push Europe into war.'

'And we'd be part of it. We'd appear to have condoned it.'

'Worse than that,' said Toby, 'we'd appear to have contributed to it. If there really is a plot to assassinate the heir to the imperial throne, we're already part of it.'

'Will you be all right on your own?' said Toby, as they went up to the sparse bedrooms that night.

'Yes, I will, and if that was a suggestion that we might share the same bed – or even the same room – the answer's no.'

'Sonja, the last thing on my mind at the moment is seduction,' said Toby. 'In any case, I don't think you're someone I'd want to simply seduce.'

'Oh,' she said, a bit blankly, and Toby reached out to trace the line of her face.

'I think this is going a bit deeper for me than seduction,' he said, very seriously. 'But I think we'd better get plots and archdukes out of the way before we talk about that.'

'Quite right,' said Sonja briskly, and went into her own bed-room.

The previous evening Toby had been so tired from the long journey that he had slept very well, but tonight he did not. Just as he was dropping off to sleep, a church clock in the square outside sonorously chimed midnight. After this, it chimed determinedly every hour for the entire night and marked the half hours with a sequence of notes that sounded like a cat being strangled.

Or, thought Toby, trying to get comfortable in the narrow bed, like a man screaming not to be murdered.

By the time Toby and Sonja reached the Appel Quay next morning, the day was already uncomfortably hot and the streets were packed with sightseers, eager to cheer the imperial couple as they drove through the streets.

'Except that they aren't all eager,' observed Toby to Sonja. 'There are quite a lot of resentful faces.'

Before breakfast, Toby had told Sonja that if they had the least shred of proof as to Tranz's intentions, he would find the British Embassy and ask for their help.

'But it's all so vague – nothing would stand up. So I think all we can do is watch Petrovnic and the others as closely as possible, and draw everyone's attention to them if they look like doing anything suspicious.'

'Such as drawing a gun,' said Sonja, thoughtfully. 'We'd have to be very loud about it all though; if we just say politely, "Oh dear me, that man's got a gun," no one will understand us. Especially since we do not speak their language.'

'That's true. But if we yell and point and indicate that some-thing's wrong, it should alert people and halt Petrovnic and his gang in their tracks.'

They were in place shortly after ten, fairly far apart, but within sight of each other. A nearby church clock chimed several times – half past ten, then a quarter to eleven – and Toby began to feel extremely nervous. Shortly before eleven a cheer went up, and his heart performed a somersault. This is it, he thought. If anything's going to happen, it'll be in the next few minutes. He edged his way to the front of the crowd, who were leaning forward, eagerly trying to see the first approach of the cars, lifting children onto their shoulders for a better view. Nothing's going to happen, thought Toby, looking at the happy anticipation on the faces of the people. Nothing so violent as murder could possibly happen in this old, sun-drenched city, with the mellow stone buildings and bridges, and the sunlight glinting on the river. This is the civilized twentieth century for goodness' sake; assassinations don't happen.

A military band struck up nearby, and a delighted cheer went up. Toby saw the first of the imperial motor cars coming slowly along the wide avenue, a faint heat haze in its wake from the exhaust fumes. The crowd surged forward, waving flags, some of the young girls throwing flowers onto the road, the children shouting excitedly. The car crossed the Cumurja Bridge, the second one close behind it, and Toby saw it was open-topped and the imposing figure of the man on all the posters was seated in the back, a lady next to him. That's the infamous Countess Sophie, he thought. The one the other Habsburgs said wasn't good enough for the imperial line, but who Franz-Ferdinand married anyway. He studied the lady with interest.

Franz-Ferdinand and his wife were nodding regally to the crowds, occasionally raising their hands in a majestic salute. And then, as the open car came over the bridge, the Habsburg pennant on its bonnet fluttering in the breeze, something came spinning out of the crowds – something that was squat and black against the bright sunshine. As it hurtled through the air Toby heard several people shout in sudden fear, and his heart lurched with terror. It was happening after all – someone had thrown a bomb, and he had missed seeing it.

The bomb was still spinning across the street when the Archduke's car suddenly shot forward, as if the driver had realized what was happening and was trying to get clear of the bomb before it went off. Instead of landing inside the car, which had obviously been the intention, the bomb skidded across the bonnet and fell into the road immediately behind. There was a split-second when everything froze and Toby was aware that he had thrown both his arms up to cover his head. A fierce explosion tore through the air and scarlet flames shot upwards. Splinters of glass and metal rained down over the crowds and spirals of black smoke billowed up into the sky, tainting the air with an acrid stench. People screamed and clawed at their neighbours in an attempt to get clear of the mess, shouting for their children, wringing their hands and crying. With deep relief, he saw Sonja about thirty yards away; she looked stunned and there were smears of grime on her face, but she was clearly unhurt, and after a moment, she plunged into the screaming tangle of humanity where the bomb had exploded.

About a dozen people were lying on the ground, most of them bleeding and bewildered-looking. There was no sign of Petrovnic or any Tranz people, but as Toby scanned the crowds, he saw a man whom he recognized as one of the students from Zlatna Moruna running away. That's the bomb-thrower, thought Toby, and in the same moment several people started after the student. The boy ran towards the parapet of the bridge, and leapt onto it. For a moment he was outlined against the smoke-smeared sky, then one hand went to his mouth and he threw his head back. Five seconds later he jumped from the bridge into the river.

Toby glanced back at the line of cars and saw to his relief that they were moving away, and the figure of the Archduke had turned to look back. Then he's all right, thought Toby. They've failed. And it doesn't look as if anyone's very much hurt. Oh, thank God.

The man who had jumped into the river was already surrounded by several men who had gone in after him. Toby took them to be police of some kind; they were trying to handcuff the man. Toby saw with a slight shudder of disgust that he was retching and bending over to be sick.

'He must have swallowed something,' said a voice at his side, and he turned to see Sonja. 'He meant to kill himself – either by poison or by drowning.'

'He miscalculated on both counts from the look of it,' said Toby, 'because the poison's only made him sick and the river's barely two feet deep at that point – he was lucky not to break both his legs.' He took her hand and hooked it firmly under his arm. 'But it's all right,' he said, 'they failed. It's all over and they've caught that boy.'

'What about the injured ones? Can we do anything to help them?' said Sonja, looking towards the bridge.

'I think they're all being tended,' said Toby. 'Let's walk along to that park again, shall we? I think we should keep out of the way if at all possible. We could try to buy some ham and rolls or something and have lunch there.'

By dint of pointing to the food on the shelves, they managed to buy not ham, but a kind of liver sausage which the obliging shop owner sliced and put into crisp rolls for them. They ate them sitting on the same seat as yesterday, neither of them saying much, both of them still deeply shocked. Toby saw Sonja shiver, and he at once put his arm round her and drew her against him.

'It's just that I'm cold,' she said, leaning against him.

'That's the shock. It'll go off after a while. No, there's no need to move – you aren't heavy and it feels comfortable like this.'

'It is comfortable like this,' said Sonja in a subdued voice.

The smoke from the Appel Quay seemed to be clearing, and Toby was about to suggest they walk back to the house where they were staying, when they heard shouts from the centre of the town, and cries that were clearly cries of panic.

'What on earth—?' began Sonja, standing up and looking towards the park gates.

'Oh God, did we relax too soon?' Toby grabbed her hand and they ran back towards the streets.'

'Appel Quay again?' said Sonja, as they went.

374

'I don't know. No – the Archduke was going to the town hall, wasn't he? If anything's happened to him, that's where he'll be now.'

But they did not need to go as far as the town hall. The Archduke's unmistakable motor car was skewed across the road just off the Appel Quay, in Franz Joseph Street. It was surrounded by people, but Toby and Sonja could see the two figures in the back. Franz-Ferdinand had blood streaming from his mouth; at his side, his wife was slumped forward, blood staining the front of her gown.

Within an hour it was known throughout the city that both the Archduke and his wife were dead. It was also known that the man who had fired the shots that killed them was Gavrilo Princip, and that he, like the bomb-thrower, had swallowed poison which was so old it had done nothing more than make him sick.

Toby managed to talk briefly with a Reuter's man who was French but who had reasonable English to match Toby's smattering of French. He told Toby that as Princip was led away, he had shouted defiance, telling the military that he was dying anyway so they might as well nail him to a cross and burn him alive, and his flaming body would be a torch to light his people on their path to freedom.

'He has, I believe, the tuberculosis,' said the French journalist, tapping his chest descriptively. 'A wild and misguided young man, one feels.'

'We'll have to get out,' said Toby to Sonja afterwards. 'If we stay here we'll be dragged into this. The minute they know who my father is . . .' He looked at her. 'How far will you trust me?'

'Infinitely. But what are we going to do?'

'I think,' said Toby slowly, 'we're going to disappear.'

CHAPTER THIRTY-THREE

July 1914

The small, hastily assembled group of men sat round the table in the Westminster room, and looked towards the man seated at the head.

'Thank you for attending this meeting,' he said. 'We'll waste no time, we all know what's happened in Sarajevo, and we all know what the consequence will be for this country and several other countries. But this afternoon we need to address a more personal part of the situation. Hal, you still haven't heard from your son?'

'No.'

'He told you he was bound for Paris?'

'He did, but I was later told it was Sarajevo,' said Hal. 'I made what enquiries I could, but you know how impossible communications are with that part of the world. The information I was given seemed reliable enough, but I wasn't entirely sure of it. People frequently have personal vendettas, axes to grind.'

'I'm afraid it seems Toby really did travel to Sarajevo though,' said the chairman. Then, clearly uncomfortable with what he had to say, 'Hal, I'm afraid I have to tell you – and all of you – that our embassy in Bosnia has telegraphed to tell us that two official police statements have been received, both saying Toby Chance was present at the two incidents on the twenty-eighth: the bomb-throwing near the railway station which missed the Archduke, although it killed and injured a number of people. And then, shortly afterwards, he was part of the shooting, which killed Franz-Ferdinand and his wife.'

There was a brief silence, then Hal said, 'Yes. I see. Thank you for being so frank. Who made the statements? Or could I hazard a guess as to one of them?'

'Well . . .'

'Anton Reznik – probably styling himself Anton Petrovnic,' said Hal.

'Yes. The other was a lady calling herself the Baroness Ilena Osapinsky,' said the chairman. 'We haven't got transcripts of the actual statements, of course, although we'll try to get them. But it seems their content is fairly clear and also very damning. Petrovnic says your son was standing next to the gunman – his name is Gavrilo Princip – and helping him line up the Archduke's car in his sights. He also says Toby was with the other man who threw the bomb. Osapinsky says much the same.'

'Both statements might be discredited,' said Sir Hal after a moment. 'Those two are Tranz members – I believe Reznik is its leader. As for Osapinsky, her title and her background are both questionable and I wouldn't trust her from here to that door. While Anton Reznik himself—' He made an impatient gesture with one hand. 'I spoke a moment ago of personal vendettas. Reznik harbours a deep hatred for me and my family.'

'Ah?' The chairman looked up from making his own notes. 'Indeed?'

Hal said in a remote voice, 'Many years ago he was considerably enamoured of my wife. There was great ill-feeling when she rejected him.'

'Oh. Yes, I see. I don't think we need to go into old feuds, gentlemen,' said the chairman and there was a mumble of agreement all round the table.

'But,' said Hal, 'Anton Reznik will have half a dozen sycophants at his beck and call: people prepared to commit perjury if he tells them it will further Tranz's cause.' He frowned, then said, 'I should like to say this before anyone else does. I'm very well aware of the possible consequences of all this. If it became known – however mistakenly – that the son of a permanent secretary in His Majesty's Foreign Office was part of the assassination conspiracy, the integrity of this government could be seriously compromised. At the first suggestion of that, I should, of course, resign.'

'My dear chap, we'll hope it doesn't come to that,' said the chairman rather uncomfortably.

'Forgive me, but I think it might.'

'If so, the work you have done over the years would not be disregarded,' said the chairman at last.

'I'm delighted to hear that,' said Hal politely.

'It may be that some other position could be arranged for you.'

'I can't imagine what. This country has been poised on the brink of war for a long time. Despite diplomatic efforts, we all know it can't be much longer before a state of war exists between ourselves and Germany, and we know Franz-Ferdinand's murder will probably be the final trigger. My son appears to have been involved in releasing that trigger. Moreover, he now seems to be at large somewhere in Europe. What this committee needs to decide now is whether we can hope Toby's actions will remain unknown, whether we can keep them quiet.'

'Providing he isn't found, I think we could be optimistic about that,' ventured one of the men. 'Is there any kind of hue and cry out for him?'

'No,' said a thin man who presented a severely legal appearance and had been making copious notes. 'Our communications with other countries are a touch unreliable in the current situation, but we don't think the Bosnian authorities are especially worried about one minor conspirator getting away.'

The man who had asked about a hue and cry observed that the Bosnians probably had too much on their plates anyway.

'None of the newspapers mentions Toby's name,' volunteered one of the younger ones.

'Yes, but that's probably because they're all focussing on the assassination itself and the man who actually fired the shots.'

'Narodna Odbrana is referred to in most papers,' said the same man, 'but Tranz doesn't seem to be mentioned anywhere.'

'I shouldn't expect it to be,' said Hal. 'Tranz is one of about half a dozen splinter groups of Narodna Odbrana. Not very important in the eyes of the newspapers, and it doesn't sound as if Gavrilo Princip was actually a member of Tranz.'

'Taking all the facts into account,' said one of the older men slowly, 'I'm inclined to think we could adopt the good old British masterly policy of inactivity here.'

'Sit tight, do nothing, and hope for the best?'

'Yes. No charges have actually been made against Hal's boy, although . . .'

'Yes?'

'I'm sorry to tell you this,' said the man, 'but two days ago our embassy in Bosnia telegraphed saying the Sarajevo authorities have requested that if Toby surfaces in this country, we hold him on a charge of conspiracy and intent to commit murder. They want us to watch ports and ferries.'

There was a sudden silence.

'What about Anton Reznik himself?' asked the younger man who had talked about the newspapers. 'Isn't there also a danger from that quarter?'

'Yes, there might be,' said the chairman thoughtfully. 'Even if we find Toby and somehow protect him, if Reznik is as . . . vengeful as Hal indicates, he could make the whole thing public.'

'Hal, is that likely? You know more about Tranz than the rest of us.'

'Which isn't a great deal,' said Hal drily. 'But I believe Reznik is a man in the grip of an obsession. His prime goal now will be to ruin me.'

'By ruining Toby?'

'Yes. But,' said Hal, thoughtfully, 'at the moment, as a member of Tranz, Anton will have to lie very low. Life will be quite difficult for him. We could make it even more difficult by having Tranz declared a threat to national security. That would send Reznik even more deeply into hiding and spike his guns. Matthew, can that be done fairly quickly?'

The legal-looking gentleman nodded. 'It can,' he said. 'It won't be difficult after the Sarajevo affair, and when the war comes we'll have all manner of extra powers anyway. We should be able to have Reznik himself listed individually as a traitor or a dissident or an agent provocateur. We can make it all three in fact.' He scribbled several notes.

'Make sure the newspapers know about him, as well,' said the chairman. 'In case Reznik approaches them to spread the story that way. We need to discredit him before he tries to discredit Toby Chance – and in the process discredits Hal and the rest of us.'

'Very well, sir.'

'What about your informant, Hal?' asked the chairman. 'The person who told you Toby was mixed up in this? You said you thought it was reasonably reliable information.'

'From what we've just learned today it seems it was very reliable indeed,' said Hal. 'It's a lady, by the way; someone who was a member of Tranz for a while, although I'm inclined to think it was only in a superficial way – I think she saw it as simply a new diversion. She seems to be having what I should think is a very uncharacteristic attack of conscience. She didn't go to Sarajevo, by the way, and we haven't got anything against her.'

The chairman leaned forward. 'Hal, forgive me, but – you haven't heard from Toby, have you? Or formed any view as to where he might be?'

'I haven't heard from him and I have no idea where he could be,' said Hal. 'And it pains me to say this, but for everyone's sake – my son, my wife, the British government – I'm starting to believe it might be better if Toby never turned up at all. It would keep the whole thing secret for ever.'

'That's an extreme point of view,' said the chairman.

'It's an extreme case,' said Hal.

Flora had discovered that the place she felt nearest to Toby at the moment was in the Tarleton itself. It was deeply comforting to sit in the stage box – the box always regarded as Toby's own – and know this was his place. The warm friendliness of the audiences was both soothing and strengthening. When she watched the lighted stage it was easy, as well, to pretend that Toby would suddenly stroll onto the stage, looking like an aristocratic ragamuffin with his black hair slightly dishevelled.

The Tarleton audiences missed him; Flora heard a number of them asking where he was and when they would see him, and wasn't it high time for a new Chance and Douglas song? Occasionally this almost reduced her to tears, but at other times she drew strength from it.

But there was more than Toby's absence to occupy the audiences at the moment. People were talking about the imminence of war – of the shooting of the Archduke which the newspapers all said would plunge most of Europe into conflict. There were not many people who had previously heard of Sarajevo, in fact there were not many people who had heard of Bosnia, but everyone who could read knew about the murder of the Archduke Franz-Ferdinand. People who could not read it for themselves had it read aloud to them by their friends. Dreadful. What was the world coming to when a royal personage could not ride through a few streets in a motor car without a bunch of madmen taking pot shots and hurling bombs? Even people who were apt to denounce royalty in general and the Habsburg house in particular, said the culprits should be strung up and made an example of.

Flora listened to all this, and she also listened to the rumours about the Tarleton's future. If there were to be a war, might it close? people asked. Somebody said it was what happened in times of war, but this was shouted down, because wars were just the time you wanted a bit of light-heartedness here and there.

'I suppose,' said Flora to Hal that evening, 'your colleagues at the Foreign Office – that grisly little committee they put together to discuss Toby – all expect me to creep into a corner and hide away for the rest of my life.'

'Toby wouldn't expect you to do that. I don't expect it, either,' said Hal.

'Well, I shan't do it. I'm not ashamed of Toby and I never will be. So I'll help with running the Tarleton until he comes back.' She broke off, then said, 'Hal, he didn't do it. He wasn't part of the plot to kill Franz-Ferdinand.'

'My dearest love, I know that as well as you do.'

'We're being watched, aren't we?' said Flora miserably. 'I mean, this house is being watched to see if Toby turns up.'

'To almost any other woman in the world, I would say, no, of course we aren't being watched. But as it's you – yes, I think you're right.'

'Is it Anton Reznik's Tranz people or the Foreign Office who are doing the watching?'

'I don't know. It could be both. Reznik might be anywhere in the world by now, and he won't dare show his face openly in London, but he'll have people here.'

'I suppose I always knew he would come back one day. You knew it as well.'

'Yes.' He came to sit beside her. 'Flora, I'm a government

official and I'm not supposed to be fanciful or imaginative. Dammit, I don't think I'm even supposed to have an imagination! But the night Stefan Reznik died seemed to draw down a – a darkness. Ever since, I've had the feeling that the darkness was still there, somewhere inside the Tarleton, lying dormant, but waiting.'

'It was,' said Flora. 'It still is. Toby knew it was there. Do you remember how he went down to the cellar one day when he was five, and was absolutely terrified. He said there was something there – something that watched him. I don't believe in ghosts, not in the conventional sense, but I've never been able to go into that underground room on my own.' She reached for his hand. 'Hal – he will come back, won't he? It'll be all right, won't it?'

'Yes,' said Hal. 'Yes, of course it will.'

But would it? wondered Flora.

CHAPTER THIRTY-FOUR

The Present

Hilary was beginning to believe that the world had shrunk to this dark rain-swept night, and to this eerie country lane with trees reaching down to claw at her face, and someone stealing along after her.

She had no means of knowing how far she would have to go before reaching another house and there was no way of knowing if she was going in the right direction to find one. The hedges were high on each side, but as she went on they thinned a little and she caught sight of what looked like a main road, quite a long way off, but with the occasional sweep of car headlights. Was it the road they had travelled down on their way to Levels House? Hilary stopped and listened to see if she was still being followed, but could not be sure. The wind was dragging at the trees and there was the pattering of the rain on leaves, and for all she could tell, an entire army could be marching along after her.

It was still difficult to believe all this was happening – that Shona – of all people, the svelte and efficient Shona Seymour – had crouched in the attic and played that music to lure Madeleine up there. Had she actually meant to kill Madeleine? Hilary still found it incredible that Shona had talked about killing – about murdering someone called Elspeth and hiding her body behind a wall. Had she really been working for a murderess for the last four years? It was bizarre and unbelievable. She'd had meals with Shona, helped her give presentations – she had admired and *liked* her ... She could hardly believe Shona was behaving like this – or that she might be creeping along through the dark after Hilary now.

It was a main road up ahead after all. Hilary rounded a curve in the lane and saw, with deep thankfulness, the outline of a fairly large house on her left. There were no lights in any of the windows, but there was a small lamp over the porch. She looked over her shoulder again. Had something darted out of sight into the cover of the hedge? She was not sure, but she began to run towards the house. If Shona came hurtling out of the night and attacked her, Hilary would scream as loudly as possible and hope she was near enough for someone to hear and come to the rescue.

She was level with the gate when two things happened.

The darting shadow she had glimpsed a moment earlier reared up and ran straight at her.

And the headlights of a car coming towards her sliced through the blackness.

Robert had driven for almost three hours with only the briefest of stops at a garage just outside Salisbury where he had topped up with petrol.

The journey had been easier than he had dared hope, and once clear of London the traffic had been fairly light. He put on the car radio for company and to keep him focussed, and also because it might provide a degree of normality in a world that was starting to become very far from normal. As he drove, he tried to think what he would do when he finally reached Levels House. It would be well after midnight when he got there, and he could hardly hammer on the door of a strange house and request admittance. This was the trouble with impulses; they almost always landed you in a peculiar and potentially difficult situation, which was why Robert always avoided them. Yes, but this is about Hilary, he said to himself. I don't care how peculiar and difficult the situation will be when I get there.

He turned off the main road and headed towards the village signposted Fosse Leigh, and he was just slowing down to look at the names on the gates of houses, when a white blur swam into his headlights – a blur that incredibly had Hilary's face. Robert stamped on the brakes and skidded to a halt. He was half out of the car when Hilary fell into his arms.

Shona Seymour, barely recognizable, her hair plastered to her head with rain, came running out of the darkness towards them.

The thing Hilary was to remember afterwards was the way that Shona, confronted with Robert, stopped in mid-flight and suddenly regained something of her former poise. To see the tousled figure stop dead in the middle of the road and struggle for a semblance of sanity, then greet Robert as coolly as if this was no more than a chance encounter, was grotesque, but also pitiful. She appeared to find nothing odd in encountering him in the middle of a rain-sodden lane at midnight; she merely said, 'How nice to see you, Mr Fallon. I think you've met my assistant, Hilary Bryant, haven't you?'

'I have,' said Robert. 'Hello, Hilary. You're drenched. You'd better have my jacket.' He had put it round her shoulders before she realized what he was doing, and although his abrupt appearance was wildly puzzling Hilary thought explanations about that could come later. Trying not to sound too panic-stricken, she said, 'Robert – uh – there's been a development – rather – alarming—'

Was he sharp enough to pick up that she was trying to warn him against Shona? She was immeasurably grateful when he said, in a completely ordinary voice, 'I realize that but we can have the

386

explanations later. Miss Seymour, would you like to get into the car? It's raining quite hard, isn't it?'

Shona did not move. She said, 'We've been chasing an intruder. Hilary got it into her head that someone had broken into the house where we're staying. Absurd, of course, there was no intruder, it was all Hilary's imagination.' She smiled at him. She was still standing in the road and Hilary willed her to get into the car but she did not.

Robert said, in the same mild, unthreatening voice, 'That must have been quite an upset. Why don't we go back to the house anyway? Is it far?'

He looked at Hilary, who said, 'It's just along there on the right.'

'Good. Miss Seymour while you get into the car, Hilary can go into the house to let your friends know what's happening.'

He's keeping us apart, though Hilary. He's seen that dreadful mad look in Shona's eyes.

'Do be careful of my jacket, Hilary,' said Robert. 'There's a mobile phone in the left-hand pocket – I think it might be switched on.'

His meaning could not be much clearer. Hilary, seeing Shona was at last getting into the passenger seat, began to walk back to Levels House as quickly as possible, feeling in the pocket for Robert's mobile as she did so. It was still raining and she was icy cold and shaking so violently she thought she might not be able to tap out 999. She managed it at the second attempt, hesitated between asking for police or ambulance, but thought the police would be better at this juncture. 'Ten minutes,' said the impersonal voice at the other end. 'They'll be coming from Upper Leigh, see. Will that be all right?'

'Yes, thank you,' said Hilary gratefully and, as she turned into the drive, saw with relief that there were lights in one of the upstairs windows, and that the curtains moved slightly as if Madeleine was looking out. She remembered she had unbolted the kitchen door earlier, and used it now to get back inside. She sped upstairs to call out to Madeleine that everything was being dealt with, the police were on their way, but it might be as well if Madeleine stayed where she was until they actually arrived.

'I understand, Hilary. Are you all right?'

'Yes, I think so. Are you?'

'Quite all right,' said Madeleine in so firm a voice, that Hilary was reassured. She went back downstairs to unbolt the front door for Robert, and found that in his company it was quite easy to behave almost normally; to watch Shona resume her chair by the fire and to suggest to her that they had a cup of tea.

'I'd like some tea,' said Shona, sounding so entirely sane that Hilary wondered if she had dreamed the events of the last hour. She switched on the electric kettle, then went up to her own bedroom and pulled on the clothes she had worn for the journey, towelling her damp hair.

The police arrived as she was going back downstairs. A stolid-looking constable sat rather awkwardly in the sitting room, but the young alert-looking sergeant followed Hilary into the kitchen and listened carefully as she gave him a hasty version of the night's events.

'I don't know how much of what Shona said is fact and how much is fantasy,' said Hilary. 'And I don't know quite what you do in this kind of situation – whether it's medical or criminal or what it is. But you'll have to do something because I think she's dangerous.'

'And she talked about having killed someone called Elspeth?' said the sergeant.

'Yes. She said it took all night to wall Elspeth up after she killed her and it was very hard work. She said if anyone knocked down the wall they'd find the body.'

'Well, that'd be easy enough to check, I daresay.'

'She said she'd drugged my coffee as well – sleeping pills. Then she tried to attack me – only I managed to get outside.'

'What I think we'd best do,' said the sergeant, 'is ask Miss

Seymour to come with us to the police station. It's the next village – only a matter of eight miles. We'll say we want a statement from her about what's been going on – about the intruder she mentioned to Mr Fallon. We'll get the on-call doctor and we'll make a decision from there as to what happens next.'

'That sounds fine,' said Hilary thankfully.

Shona looked surprised at the request to accompany the sergeant and his sidekick to a police station, and for a moment Hilary thought she would argue.

'All just routine, miss,' said the sergeant off-handedly, but Hilary noticed his barely perceptible nod to the constable who at once moved to Shona's side. She had no idea what would happen if the dreadful madness flared in Shona's eyes again, but Shona merely shrugged and asked Hilary to fetch her coat and handbag from her bedroom.

'And now,' said Robert at last, when Shona had been ushered into the waiting police car and Madeleine had come downstairs and been introduced, 'would you please explain to me what on earth's been going on?'

He was polite and quiet with Madeleine, and was efficient and courteous about pouring brandy for Hilary and also Madeleine, and switching up the heating. He used his mobile to contact the telephone fault service, explaining that there had been a serious case of vandalism at the house and there was an elderly lady here in frail health.

'So if her phone could be repaired as quickly as possible, I would be extremely grateful,' said Robert. 'First thing tomorrow morning? Yes, that would be very acceptable. In the meantime, is there any way you can switch any incoming calls to a mobile? That's excellent. Here's the number ... And thank you very much for your help.'

He set his mobile on a table where it would be easily accessible, and Hilary, watching and listening from the reassuring warmth of an armchair, thought there was probably no situation in which he would not remember to be polite. She curled her hands round the brandy glass, and saw how he occasionally looked across at her and how his eyes narrowed when he smiled. But when he sat down and looked first at Madeleine and then at Hilary, and asked for an explanation, she thought she would not be able to give one.

Then Robert said, 'Would I be right in thinking it began with the bricked-up cellar wall in the Tarleton?' and Hilary said, gratefully, 'Oh yes, it would.'

She embarked on the tale of everything that had happened in the past twenty-four hours.

Shona knew she was being extremely clever with these oafish policemen. She had gone along to their absurd police station because she had been brought up not to make a scene, to behave with dignity and restraint. She also knew they did not really believe she had done anything wrong, but she supposed they had to investigate the story she had given to Robert Fallon about an intruder.

She could deal with policemen: the only slight concern was what she might have said to Hilary earlier on. She could not remember much of that and groped in the unreachable part of her mind for the knowledge. Could she possibly have mentioned Anna or Elspeth? Surely she would not have done that; she had become so used to guarding her words that it was by now second nature. But there was always the small possibility that it had come out of that other unpredictable half of her mind, and that this half had gained the ascendancy for a short while. So just in case that had happened she would be very careful.

The police station was at a place called Upper Leigh and it was a poky little building with a couple of plodding constables, one of whom looked about fifteen. They locked her in a dreadful room, explaining they would like a doctor to see her. Shona looked at them in surprise because she was here to make a statement about an intruder and could not imagine why she would need a doctor. Unless that sly bitch Hilary had made up some distorted story about her? This suddenly seemed entirely possible. Shona would not have thought Hilary would behave so spitefully; it went to show you could not trust anyone.

To shut them up she said she would see their doctor if they insisted. But she knew her rights, she said: they were not dealing with a run-of-the-mill petty thief or teenage lout and if they were locking her up, she wanted her solicitor here. She was perfectly polite, and they were perfectly polite back. They said they would arrange for her solicitor to come in, although they were afraid it might not be until the morning. In the meantime, she might as well try to get some sleep. There was a bed in the room – yes, they understood it was not the kind of thing she was used to, but until all this was sorted out . . .

Shona took off her shoes and lay down on the narrow bed, making herself as comfortable as she could. It was not entirely dark; a faint glow came from a low light in the corridor outside. It showed up the ugly bleakness of the room and the squalid half screen with the lavatory and washbasin behind it. It showed up the grubby paintwork and floor.

She did not sleep, and the hands of her watch had moved round to three o'clock when she gradually became aware that the faint light was showing up other things in the room: people standing in the corners – three people in particular. Anna, with the flesh rotted away from her bones, dried and shrivelled, and weary from standing behind the wall in the cellar all those years; Cousin Elspeth, stupid, sheep-faced Elspeth, her head still tied up in the tea towel that Shona had wrapped round it, but able to see Shona all the same, able to shake her horrid raw head in disapproval of everything Shona had done. Mother was there too; Shona supposed she should have expected that. Mother, her mouth awry from the vodka, her hair messy and uncombed.

They were here to gloat over her downfall – Anna was very gloating indeed – and to disapprove. 'Oh my goodness me,' said the thing that was Cousin Elspeth. 'My word, what bad behaviour. Well, madam, you deserve everything you get.'

Shona scrambled back to the corner of the bed, and huddled there, wrapping the blanket round her, not daring to take her eyes off these dreadful things who had somehow found her and got into this sleazy room. It did not much matter how they had done so; what was clear was that despite all she had done, Elspeth had somehow got out from behind the cellar wall.

Presently she realized there was a fourth person with them. She had not seen him at first, but now she saw him very clearly. He was not gloating or disapproving. He was standing next to her mother, holding her tightly as if he owned her, as if he had rights over her, and her mother was hating it, Shona could see she was absolutely hating being so close to this man.

He had frightening eyes – *knowing* eyes – and terrifying hands. Shona had never seen him in her life before, but he smiled at her and said wasn't this nice, a real family reunion, and very soon now Shona might be living in the place where he had lived himself. Iain Seymour. The man who had raped and strangled girls, the Tantallon Killer, Shona's own father.

Shona pressed back against the cell wall, her hands clenched, ready to strike them if they tried to come any nearer, and began to scream.

Shortly after three a.m. Madeleine suggested they all try to get a few hours' sleep.

'We'll have to be giving statements and filling in all kinds of official forms in the morning,' she said. 'So we may as well get some rest. You can stay down here on the settee, Robert, or you can have the room Shona Seymour had.'

'You have the bedroom, Robert,' said Hilary. 'If no one minds, I think I'd like to stay down here. Would that be all right,

Madeleine? I'll just curl up on the settee – it's beautifully warm here.' She did not say that the thought of returning to the bedroom where she had been so abruptly woken by that eerie music was more than she could face tonight, but she thought Madeleine understood.

'Of course,' she said. 'My girl who helps in the house will be here around eight. Robert, I'm sorry I can't offer you pyjamas or shaving things, but I think there might be a spare toothbrush somewhere.'

Robert said, 'I think I could sleep on a length of clothes line tonight. You're being very kind and I'm very sorry you've had all this disturbance.'

'I seem to have survived it,' said Madeleine. 'I daresay most of it's my own fault for keeping that Gothic pile in London closed up all these years. Any sensible person would have ignored that absurd will of my father's and sold it or hired it out long since.' But she frowned slightly, and Hilary saw the brief twist of pain she had seen last night. There's still something she's not telling us, she thought.

'There's a bit more disturbance you'll have to deal with, I'm afraid,' said Robert. 'It's actually in the Gothic pile, and it's my fault.' He glanced at Hilary, and then said, 'Last night I knocked down part of an underground wall in your theatre.'

'You did it!' said Hilary. 'I didn't think you would when it came to it.'

Madeleine was looking at them both, clearly puzzled. 'Robert, how do you mean, you knocked down a wall? In a car accident or something?'

'No. I borrowed the keys from the Harlequin and had a copy made without anyone knowing,' said Robert. 'Entirely unprofessional and also criminal.'

'Dear me, how very enterprising of you. Why did you do that?' She did not sound angry, she sounded faintly amused and intrigued.

'Because,' said Robert, 'I was absolutely convinced there was

393

something odd in that place – and that it was behind a cellar wall. At some time someone had sealed that area up very thoroughly indeed. I don't know when the sealing was done, but I couldn't account for it. I'm a surveyor,' he said, 'so if I find a mystery in a property, I want to know what it hides.'

'It was that wall that kept disconcerting Shona,' said Hilary. 'She kept identifying it with a wall at her childhood home – Grith House. And behind the wall at Grith House was the cousin she had murdered – Elspeth. At least, that's what she said. She was terrified Elspeth might one day be discovered.'

'If it's true she was probably driven mad from living with that fear for years,' said Madeleine thoughtfully. 'How dreadful and tragic.'

'I didn't know about Shona's cousin when I looked at the Tarleton's wall, of course,' said Robert. 'But Shona *was* defensive about the place, and that, together with the ban on any reopening – well, I decided to find out for myself what was behind the wall and under the stage.'

'So you knocked down the wall.'

'Only a small part of it,' said Robert, then, speaking very seriously, he said, 'I will give you the appropriate name and address of the Royal Institution of Chartered Surveyors if you want to make an official complaint about what I did. You're perfectly entitled to do that.'

'I've never bothered over much about royal institutions and officialdom,' said Madeleine. 'Let's hear the rest of the tale.'

'I got enough bricks out to see through to the under-stage area,' said Robert. 'And – this part's a bit distressing, so—'

'Robert, in the last few hours I've dealt with a mad killer prowling through my house!' said Madeleine. 'I shan't jib at an ancient mystery behind a wall.'

'At some time in the distant past,' said Robert, 'someone had put a – a dead body in the Tarleton's cellar and bricked it up.'

'Good God,' said Madeleine, staring at him. 'How appalling.'

'Are you all right?' said Hilary anxiously.

'I'll let you know when I've heard the end of the story. But I'm an old lady, Hilary, and we get fairly used to the idea of death. Other people's deaths, at least. Robert, I know we've only just met but I wouldn't have thought you were at all the kind of person to get tangled up with dead bodies, never mind smashing down walls in other people's properties.'

'I'm not,' said Robert. 'But on this occasion ... Anyway, I found the body. It wasn't particularly grisly, by the way, just rather sad, and I reported it to the police.'

'Did you really? I suspect a great many people in that situation would have put the bricks back as neatly as possible, got out fast, and hoped no one would ever find out what had been done.'

'Throwing the illicit key in the Thames,' added Hilary.

'I nearly did,' confessed Robert. 'But – this will sound ridiculously sentimental – it was the body itself that stopped me. I don't mean physically – sorry, Hilary, it didn't suddenly sit perkily up like a horror film – I mean mentally. Emotionally. I simply couldn't brick it up again and leave it lying down there in the dark.' He looked back at Madeleine. 'I did wonder if it might have something to do with the reason for the theatre being closed all these years.'

'I'm wondering the same thing,' said Madeleine. 'But my father's request was that it stayed closed for fifty years after his death. So it would have had to be a very important dead body.'

'True. I don't know if it can ever be identified,' said Robert.

'I expect they'll try, however. What an extraordinary thing. My father really did leave a legacy and a half to me, didn't he? But thank you for explaining all that, Robert, and for being so honest.' She smiled at him. 'I'm sorry about the poor soul who was shut away down there all this time, but I can't say I'm particularly upset over a few bricks being knocked out in a cellar. I daresay it can be rebuilt if necessary.' She stood up. 'I really am going to bed now, my dears,' she said. 'Sleep well.'

It was a good feeling to lie on the deep soft settee with the fire dying down, and to know that Robert was upstairs. It was astonishing that he really had broken through that intriguing old wall and found a body after all. But it had to be a body, thought Hilary, smiling as she drifted into sleep. Anything less would have been a let-down.

Who had the body been? Could it even be Toby? But Hilary did not want it to be Toby: she did not want to discover he had lain down there in the dusty darkness all these years. Stupid, because it could not matter to him where his body lay. But she would still rather it was not Toby.

A thin sunlight trickled into the big kitchen next morning. Madeleine's 'girl who helps' turned out to be a cheerful soul who clattered round, scrambling eggs, grilling bacon and brewing coffee. It was surprisingly comfortable to sit at the kitchen table with Robert and eat vast quantities of food. Robert looked slightly raffish because he had not been able to shave; Hilary found this deeply attractive, but she was starting to feel too anxious about Shona to give much attention to this.

'You're too nice about her,' said Robert when Hilary expressed this concern.

'She's my boss.'

'From what you told me last night, she's a psychotic murderess,' he said.

Madeleine, who was sitting composedly drinking her own coffee, said, 'She's certainly a very disturbed lady.'

'You saw that?'

'Well, I thought as soon as I met her that she wasn't entirely calm,' said Madeleine. 'I think that's why I trusted you rather than Shona last night, Hilary. When you told me to lock myself in my bedroom, I mean.'

Shortly after eleven Hilary went upstairs to collect her coat and handbag before Robert drove them to Upper Leigh, to the police station. The hall was on the west side of the house and the morning sun had not worked its way round here so the hall, which only had narrow windows by the door, was rather dim and shadowy. Hilary paused at the foot of the stairs to study a framed photograph of a group of people, hoping they might be from Madeleine's family – specifically hoping her father might be one of the group. She had got as far as identifying the clothes as probably belonging to the mid-1920s, and was enjoying looking at the faces and speculating about them when there was the sound of a car stopping in the lane outside the house, its door being opened and closed, then the sound of it driving off. Footsteps came slowly down the gravel path. Hilary glanced towards the door, assuming it was a chance caller for Madeleine, hoping it would not delay their departure, and then felt the quiet hall with its scents of age and polish, blur and shiver all round her.

Whoever was walking along the gravel path towards the house was singing softly, in the way a man might whistle to keep up his spirits or to keep himself company.

But the song the unknown caller was singing was the song Hilary had heard in the dark old Tarleton Music Hall with Robert. It was the song Shona had played on the old gramophone last night. Toby Chance's 'The Ghost Walks'.

CHAPTER THIRTY-FIVE

Caley was extremely nervous by the time the taxi drew up outside Levels House. It had been a worrisome journey; he had spent most of it in trying to work out exactly what he would say when he reached his destination and he was still very unsure about that. He also hoped very fervently that it would not be what he thought of as a grand house.

It was not until the train drew into Castle Cary station that it suddenly occurred to him he might not be Madeleine Ferrelyn's only visitor. Shona Seymour would have received that letter two – no, three – days ago. Supposing that was the reason for her slightly puzzling absence from the Harlequin office? This possibility sent a wave of panic through him. What would he do if Miss Seymour was already at Levels House? But he had not come this far to back out now, so he got a taxi from the small taxi rank outside the station, and gave the address.

The house, when they reached it, was not grand, but it was quite large and you could see at once that it had been lived in by people who were not wildly wealthy, but who did not have to worry over-much about money. Caley had not really expected anything less, but he still had to fight against a feeling of panic all over again, because people like himself did not knock at the doors of houses such as this one, and coolly request admittance. He paid the taxi driver, careful to add a modest tip, and it was not until the man had driven off that he noticed the two cars parked in the drive. Might Shona Seymour really be here, then? He stood very still, trying to decide what to do.

If it had not been for the ten-mile journey to the railway station, at this point he really would have fled back to London. But he reminded himself that he had no real reason to be afraid of Miss Seymour and he had a perfect right to be here if he chose. He straightened his collar and brushed down his jacket, but as he walked towards the house he realized he was humming a snatch of one of the Tarleton's songs. It was a nervous habit, but it was something that always gave him confidence, almost as if the Tarleton people – Caley's own people – were with him and as if they were saying: it's all right; we're around you, we're helping you along. Today they said: you've come here to protect us, remember that. And you have as much right as anyone to be here, remember that, as well.

His heart was pounding and he had to pause to pat his pocket to make sure the asthma spray was safely there. He had thought out what he would say and do when the door was opened, but he knew this pre-arranging of a scene hardly ever worked, because the other person did not know his or her part in the play.

It did not work now, because the person who opened the door was someone he had not expected to see: Hilary Bryant. Caley had been partly prepared for Shona, but he was thrown completely by Hilary's appearance and for a moment he could not think what to say.

Hilary was looking startled, but she said, 'Mr Merrick? Caley? What on earth are you doing here?'

Caley managed to pull himself together sufficiently to say,

'I wanted to see – is Mrs Ferrelyn in? Mrs Madeleine Ferrelyn?'

'Well, she is, but—' Hilary broke off and Caley saw a door open beyond the hall and a fairly tall lady come out.

'Hilary, was that someone at the door? I thought I heard—' She saw Caley and looked at him questioningly.

'Mrs Ferrelyn?' said Caley.

'Yes.'

Caley had known who she was without asking, and he went straight into the little script he had compiled for himself. He said, 'You don't know me, but my name is Merrick and I would like to talk to you about your – about the Tarleton Music Hall.' He had intended to say 'about your theatre' but when it came to it, he could not. My theatre, he thought. In everything but name, it's my theatre. It always was, ever since the first time I stepped inside.

Madeleine said, perfectly politely, 'Unfortunately, we have to go out very shortly and it's an appointment we can't easily change, but I have a few moments to spare.'

She clearly thought he was some kind of salesman, although the mention of the Tarleton had caught her attention. At least she had not slammed the door in his face. Hilary said, 'Madeleine, Mr Merrick – Caley – helps us at the Harlequin office sometimes.'

This at least established a kind of credential and Madeleine Ferrelyn led Caley into the sort of room he would have liked in his own house: large and low-ceilinged, with deep soft chairs, good curtains and carpet, French windows looking out over a big garden with a small orchard . . .

'This is Robert Fallon,' said Madeleine Ferrelyn, and Caley saw that Robert Fallon was the man who had been on the Tarleton's stage with Hilary that night. Of Shona Seymour there was no sign.

'Please sit down, Mr Merrick.'

Caley sat facing her, plaiting the fingers of both hands together, then unplaiting them because that was an outward sign of nervousness.

'You said this was about the Tarleton?'

'Yes. You own it, Mrs Ferrelyn.' It came out awkwardly and in a rush.

'I do own it, although I don't understand how you know that. Unless the Harlequin office—' She glanced at Hilary, who said, 'It's unlikely. Even I didn't know it until two days ago.'

Madeleine looked questioningly at Caley. She did not quite say, what has my ownership of the Tarleton got to do with you, but he knew she must be thinking it.

He said, 'I've studied that theatre since I was a young man. More than thirty years now. I know so much about it. All its history – I've read about the people who performed there and worked there.' He hoped this was not coming out too humbly; he was trying to keep firmly in mind all those long-ago remarks about being too humble, not pushy enough. But his next words came out with a desperation that even he could not miss.

'Is it true that the restraint has ended at last and that you're going to reopen it?'

'Perhaps. A bit more than perhaps.' It came out kindly enough, but it came out firmly.

'I see.' Caley sat back in his chair. Throughout the journey here he had planned how he would ask that question and that she would look at him kindly and say that since he felt strongly about this they could perhaps discuss it. That would have given him the opening he wanted. But he had not bargained for the presence of Hilary Bryant or Robert Fallon, and with them in the room his courage failed him. I can't do it after all, he thought.

Madeleine said, 'Mr Merrick, I don't understand. You've sought me out without in the least knowing me, and you've presumably made a journey to find this house—'

'I've come from London,' he said.

'Which is quite a long way. You've come all that way, out of the blue, just to ask that question about whether I'm going to reopen a theatre? I'm sorry,' said Madeleine briskly, 'but none of that is credible. What's this really about?'

Caley summoned up a remaining shred of resolve, and said, 'It's about the man I think was my grandfather.'

'Yes?' said Madeleine, but Caley thought a wariness had entered her voice.

He said, 'I never knew my grandfather – I never knew any of my real family, because I was adopted as a baby. But when I was eighteen I was given a box of papers that had belonged to my family – miscellaneous stuff, but interesting. Among the papers was this.' He reached into an inside pocket, and from a wallet, took out an old sepia photograph. Handling it with extreme care he gave it to Madeleine.

She took the photograph and absolute silence closed over the room, and then Madeleine, who had not had any physical reaction to the astonishing events earlier on, looked at the photograph and, giving a cry of unmistakable pain, hunched over, clutching at her heart.

'She's all right,' said the paramedic, straightening up from Madeleine's chair, 'and fortunately she had the GTN spray. You said that seemed to stop the pain?'

'After about ten minutes,' said Robert. 'Not long before you arrived.'

'That's very good. You were right to call us, though. But the ECG is clear, and if the GTN halted the pain so quickly it was almost definitely angina and not another infarct.'

'What . . .?'

'Heart attack,' he said. 'Has there been anything to trigger an attack – unusual exertion or stress of some kind?'

'I'm afraid there has,' said Hilary.

'Ah. Well, then, I think she'd better come in to hospital, just to be completely sure. Sorry, Mrs Ferrelyn, but you know how it goes.'

'Will you take her now, or could I do that?' asked Robert.

'I'd like Robert to do it, if that's all right,' said Madeleine.

'Anyway, you're one of the motorbike paramedics, aren't you? I'm feeling considerably better, but not quite up to riding pillion.'

'Can you drive her in?' said the paramedic to Robert. 'I can get an ambulance if not.'

'Of course I will,' said Robert.

'There's no need to break the speed limit, but within a couple of hours. Ask for emergency assessment. They'll do bloods and so on, Mrs Ferrelyn, and probably another ECG.'

'I know the routine by now,' said Madeleine drily.

'I know you do.' He patted her arm. 'I'm fairly sure it's a false alarm this time,' he said, 'but let's make sure.'

After he went there was a rather awkward silence. Then Hilary said, 'Madeleine, I'll pack an overnight bag for you, shall I? If you tell me where things are.'

'That would be kind. But there's no rush for a moment, Hilary dear. First, I'd like you to see the photograph.'

She turned to Caley, who said, 'Are you sure? The paramedic said to go to the hospital fairly soon.'

'I'm perfectly all right,' said Madeleine, and Caley looked at her for a moment, then passed the photo to Hilary.

Hilary took it with interest, and Robert leaned forward to see it as well. It was a shot of a young man of around twenty, standing outside a building Hilary recognized as the Tarleton, and it was possible to make out a poster on the theatre's wall advertising a Marie Lloyd benefit night.

'This would be 1910 or thereabouts?' said Hilary to Caley.

'I think so,' he said. 'I told you I was eighteen when I first saw this. I looked a lot different then, of course – more hair for one thing.' For the first time a glint of humour showed. 'But allowing for the different clothes, I might have been the young man in that photo.' He paused, then said, 'The name is written on the back.'

As Robert took the photograph and turned it over, Madeleine said, 'You don't need to look on the back. I didn't need to, either. I know who it is.'

And Robert said, 'Frank Douglas.'

'I'd better tell you the truth before Robert carts me off to be stuck with needles and photographed from all angles,' said Madeleine.

'You don't have to,' began Hilary. 'You've just had an angina spasm.'

'I do have to,' said Madeleine, her eyes still on the quiet figure of Caley Merrick seated opposite her. 'Don't I?'

'Yes,' he said. 'Only if you're well enough, though. But if you can – it would mean so much to me.'

'To me, also.' She paused, and when she spoke again her voice was subtly different, almost as if it was a much younger woman's. 'I was seventeen,' said Madeleine, 'and I was unbelievably naive – today's seventeen year olds would never believe how naive I was. I was in my last term at school. A place in Dorset it was – I was very happy there.' Hilary saw with relief that there was no longer the frightening bluish look round her lips, but thought they must make sure she really did get to the hospital within the hour.

'My parents were abroad,' said Madeleine. 'But I was used to that – I'd grown up during the war years, remember, and my father was touring with ENSA. My mother usually went with him. She died right at the end of the war, and from then on my father travelled even more – but he always came back to England for school holidays, or I joined him wherever he was. That year he was in Italy, working with some theatre company. I was going to spend the summer with him – he said I'd learn some Italian and enjoy the sunshine.' She paused, but Hilary thought it was not a pause of pain or weakness; it was more that she was trying to arrange the memories in order.

'Before the term ended, I had an affair,' she said. 'An older man – his name isn't important, he was a temporary member of staff at the school, giving us a series of talks on music. That was the starting point, of course. I told him about my father, and he was interested.'

'Music,' said Caley softly, and she looked at him and smiled.

'Yes,' she said. 'He was a musician. I should like to tell you it was all deeply romantic, but it wasn't really. It was hasty and furtive – he was torn with guilt afterwards and I was embarrassed.' She made a dismissive gesture with one hand. 'We don't need any sentiment about that. But after he had gone – and I never knew where he went – there was the consequence. I was to have a child. Well, today that wouldn't have mattered much, no one gives it a second thought, do they? They have the child and carry on with whatever they were doing, somehow weaving the child into the pattern of their life and adjusting where necessary. Or they have an abortion. But this was 1950: an illegitimate child was a deeply shameful thing and abortion was illegal. I was horrified and I had no idea what to do. In retrospect, I know I could have told my father – he wouldn't have given a hoot for any scandal and would have supported me to the hilt. But I didn't realize that at the time. You don't always think very logically at seventeen. So I wrote to one of the dancers who had sometimes stayed with my parents: her name was Elise Le Brun – it wasn't her real name, of course, but it was what she was always called. She was getting on for seventy by then, but she was one of those indestructible Cockneys. She always said she could tell a few tales about her youth, although she never told them to me – but my father said she had been quite a girl in the old Tarleton days. Whatever she had been, she was kindness itself to me,' said Madeleine. 'I stayed with her – my father thought I had cancelled the Italian trip because I wanted to spend that summer with a school friend – and Elise got me into a nursing home for the birth.' She looked at Caley. 'Forgive me for what I did afterwards,' she said, 'but I was half bullied, half coaxed into it.'

'You gave the child away for adoption,' said Hilary. She could not quite associate this unknown child from that long-ago hasty love affair with the quietly spoken man she had known slightly at the Harlequin offices, but the facts were gradually becoming clear.

'Yes. Elise helped with that as well; she came from Southwark

405

herself – she'd lived around the Tarleton since she was small, I think. She knew of two families who loved children and would like an extra one. She swore to me that they were kind and good, and that although they weren't very well off they were reasonably comfortable.'

'They were,' said Caley. 'They were kind and warm and no one in the family ever wanted for anything.'

'I was distraught at the prospect of giving you away,' said Madeleine, her eyes on him. 'But I couldn't see what else to do. And I trusted Elise – I even had a romantic idea that it would be nice for you to be near to the Tarleton – that you'd hear some of the tales about it, even that you might meet people my father had worked with.' She gave a half smile. 'It's teenage girls' magazine stuff, isn't it? But I told you I was naive and it was how I saw it. I managed to make over a little money to you – some that my mother had left me and that I inherited when I turned twenty-one – so you would have a little money of your own.'

'They never told me where that came from,' he said. 'It was just a bank account – money on deposit in my name. But I thought it could only be from – from you and I was grateful. It felt like a link.' He paused, and then said, 'I had the other link, though.'

'Yes,' she said. 'The box of things that had been my father's. The day before they took you, I remember I snatched up photographs and old playbills and things more or less at random, and stuffed them into an old shoe box. I think I wanted you to know there was a link to that theatre.'

'I did know,' said Caley. 'I knew from when I was eighteen. I've spent most of my life tracing the links and finding out about the people.' He hesitated, then said, 'I used to go into the Tarleton quite often. I managed to get a key . . .'

He stopped uncertainly, and Madeleine at once said, 'If you got hold of a key I don't care how you did it.'

'I liked going in there,' he said, 'I liked the feeling that I was encased in the past, that all the memories and the history were there. It ought to have been eerie, but somehow it never was. I found it friendly. Welcoming. There's an old piano in the green room – out of tune, but playable. I'd learned the piano as a child, but there'd been no piano in my life for years. I began to play again.'

And, thought Hilary, as well as that, you used to sing very softly when you walked through the theatre. Robert and I heard you that night. And I heard you again when you walked up the drive to this house earlier on. But I don't think I'll ever mention it and I don't think Robert will, either. How immensely sad this is.

'I never wanted you to reopen the place,' said Caley. 'I loved it so much as it was, with its memories and its history. I know that sounds mad, but it's how I always felt. I never minded the piano being out of tune or the building being dark and empty.'

'I remember Rinaldi – the Tarleton's stage manager – once telling me it was a place that had its own magic,' said Madeleine, and he looked at her gratefully.

'It has, hasn't it?' he said. 'And as the years went along and nothing ever happened, I thought it would never be opened. I thought I was safe.'

'With your piano and the ghosts,' said Madeleine softly. And then, 'But don't you understand that you were the main reason I didn't open it.' She leaned forward and took his hand. 'I knew its history: I grew up knowing it. How people in that part of London had speculated about why it suddenly closed down in 1914; how Toby Chance – the owner at the time – vanished around then. No one ever knew what happened to Toby,' she said. 'I suspect my father knew, although he never said. But Toby's disappearance set up a little legend of its own. In his day he was the darling of the gallery, the hero of the shop girls and maidservants. My father once said no one else ever got a look in with the women when Toby was around. But you see, it all meant people liked to wonder about the Tarleton and make up tales about it – it almost became a sort of local haunted house for some of them. If I had reopened it when my father died – well, it was still only the 1950s and there were people alive who could remember those old stories. There would have been a flurry of local interest and publicity. And that was what I was so afraid of.'

This time she looked at Hilary, as if saying, help me with this part, and Hilary said, 'You couldn't risk the truth becoming known. About – about what had happened to you – that you had an illegitimate child.'

'I didn't much mind for myself, but I minded for you,' said Madeleine to Caley. 'I visualized you growing up in some nice conventional home. Being happy and secure and settled. I never knew the name of your family, but Elise said they lived quite near to the Tarleton, so I was afraid it would all come out and would harm you.'

Robert, who had been listening with absorption said, 'And that's why you honoured your father's request.'

'To begin with, yes. And then, as the years went by, it somehow seemed a good thing to keep the place closed. I met my husband, and we were happy and moderately well off. I told you last night that I came to see the theatre as an investment, didn't I? That was true. Then, later – when it would certainly have been safe to open it up – my husband became ill. It was a long illness – multiple sclerosis – and my whole life was taken up with it. He had quite long periods of remission, and during those periods we travelled a good bit. He wanted to make sure of seeing all the places in the world he had never seen. I wanted to make sure of seeing them with him. I didn't give the Tarleton much thought all those years.'

'I'm glad you never opened it,' said Caley. 'But to do so now . . .'

Madeleine said, 'We'll talk about that some more. I promise I won't do anything you'd dislike. But I hope you'll come to stay with me here if you can.'

'Could I?' It was almost painful to see the eagerness in his expression.

'Only if you want to,' she said. 'But I hope you will want to.' She

408

hesitated, and then said, 'You mentioned playing a piano in the old green room.'

'Yes?'

Madeleine said, 'I have a piano here. Quite an old one. It's in the dining room on the other side of the hall. I never use that room nowadays. I used to play the piano a little as a child – my father hoped I might have inherited some of his talent so I had music lessons. But I wasn't very good, I'm afraid.'

Caley said, 'An old piano . . . How old?'

'It belonged to my father,' she said very gently. 'I had it brought here after his death – it was a link to him. I had so many memories of him playing it – writing music on it. It'll be shockingly out of tune, but it could be properly tuned, if—'

'Yes?' This time it was not just eagerness in his face, it was as if a light had come on behind his eyes.

'If there was someone who wanted to play it again.'

CHAPTER THIRTY-SIX

In the middle of the afternoon, the attic at Levels House was no longer the eerie place it had been the previous night. Hilary switched on the light and contemplated with deep pleasure the task ahead of her.

'Ferreting into the past?' Robert had said earlier.

'Yes, but I've got the owner's permission to ferret,' said Hilary promptly, and he smiled in the way that narrowed his eyes.

Caley had returned to London – Robert had driven him to the station for his train after delivering Madeleine to the hospital. Caley had been grateful and a bit awkward. Hilary rather liked him and when she thought how he had wandered in and out of the Tarleton by himself for all those years, and how he must have schemed to get the few hours working for the Harlequin Society, she felt deeply sorry for him. She was not sure if he might need a bit of skilled help to deal with his fixation on the place, and then she remembered that she was nearly as fixated on it as he was. She also remembered that Robert had been so fixated he had smashed open the cellar wall, which she did not think he would normally have dreamed of doing. Perhaps, as Rinaldi had said to Madeleine, the Tarleton had its own particular magic.

A police inspector dealing with Shona Seymour had telephoned just after lunch. The phone was still not repaired, but the call had been transferred to Robert's mobile, as arranged. The inspector sounded rather fatherly; he said he thought Miss Bryant and Mr Fallon would like to know that Miss Seymour was not in a very good mental state; in the early hours of this morning they had called in a doctor as a matter of emergency, and she had been taken to the psychiatric unit nearby. As things stood, there was no question of her answering any charges, in fact for the moment there was no question of actually charging her. Yes, of course they would let Miss Bryant know of all developments, said the inspector. Well, yes, if she could arrange for a small suitcase to be brought in with a few clothes and night things, it would be very helpful. Very kind.

'I'll do that as soon as I can,' said Hilary, remembering that Shona's overnight things were still at Levels House.

'We'll need to contact a next of kin,' said the inspector. 'Would you know who that might be?'

Hilary had a wild desire to say, well, there's a cousin walled up somewhere in Yorkshire, but just said she did not know. 'But the Harlequin Society might stand as some kind of proxy or take on power of attorney. Sorry I don't know the right term, but you'll get the meaning. She's worked for them for twenty years. There's a governing board – they're a bit inaccessible, and I think it's just half a dozen people scattered all over the country. I could find out about that for you.'

'Would you do that?'

'Yes, certainly. Um – would I be allowed to visit her?' Hilary had not wanted to ask this, but she had not been able to bear the thought of Shona alone and perhaps bewildered. A friendly face – even the face of someone Shona had tried to kill twenty-four hours earlier – might be helpful.

'Best not,' said the inspector. 'But it's nice of you to offer. We'll keep in touch.'

The hospital had also telephoned, to report that Mrs Ferrelyn had checked out as absolutely fine, but they would keep her with them overnight, and repeat the tests in the morning just to make sure. All being well she would be discharged tomorrow.

Robert was going back to London that evening, but Hilary would remain at Levels House for another day or so. And this afternoon, she was going to take up Madeleine's suggestion that she explore the attic.

As she switched on the light and surveyed the attic, she was dimly aware of sounds from downstairs. Robert was staying to have supper with her before setting off – he said the roads might be less congested late at night – and they were going to have the remains of the chicken casserole. It was nice to know he was in the house and even nicer to think of sitting over a meal with him later on. Hilary smiled at this prospect.

But for the moment, the past was folding itself round her – a very particular fragment of the past: 1914, with the world on the brink of the war that was to end all wars – that 'frozen instant before the cataclysm'. Had the Tarleton's ghost legend started then? It seemed to be grounded in 1914, and 1914 was when the theatre had closed. Might the ghost be something to do with the Great War? Because whoever you were, Mister Ghost, said Hilary to herself, you do seem to originally hail from then. 'And what did you do in the war, Daddy?' 'Oh, I was mutilated by mustard bombs in the trenches, so I wrapped up my face and took to prowling up and down an old alleyway by a deserted music hall, frightening the locals and setting up a really good ghost story by way of cover ...' Was the solution to the ghost as simple – as tragic – as that?

She discovered the box with the old records which Shona must have found last night. There were six of them in all; the dates were mostly the early 1900s and the names on the labels were names that had become woven into the fabric of music-hall history. Marie Lloyd, Dan Leno, Charles Coburn ... All curios in their way, and from the look of it all original recordings. They might sell for a good deal of money; Hilary would make sure to tell Madeleine about that.

And there it was, the record Shona had played last night. It looked as if she had removed it from the old gramophone and returned it to its box. Destroying the evidence? Hilary suddenly wondered how mad Shona had really been last night.

The label on the record was badly faded, but it was readable. 'The Ghost Walks. Chance & Douglas © 1914. Lyrics by Toby Chance, music by Frank Douglas.'

Under that, in smaller lettering, were the words, 'Sung by Toby Chance. Recorded 1914, London.'

Hilary sat back on her heels, staring at the record. This was something Toby had written over ninety years ago – something Madeleine's father had set to music and that had been captured inside this thin circle of black vinyl. The song Caley Merrick knew about, perhaps because the music had been in the box of memories handed down to him, or perhaps because he had sought it out for himself. Whichever it was, it was the song he had sung to himself when he walked through the theatre.

Hilary had never heard of 'The Ghost Walks', but that did not matter; Toby and Frank Douglas had probably written a great many songs that had not survived. She turned the disc over and saw that 'All Because of Too Much Tipsy Cake' was on the other side. Hilary smiled, because this was like meeting an old friend.

The gramophone itself was nearby. It was an old wind-up machine, as she already knew, with a tone chamber and the characteristic trumpet-shaped horn. On one side was the handle for winding. It looked as if Shona had wiped it clean with a length of old curtain or screwed-up newspaper from one of the boxes. With infinite care Hilary pulled the machine into the centre of the floor, then laid the record on the turntable.

And then she stopped. She knew how Toby's lyrics read on a sheet of music, because she had found the sheet music of 'Tipsy Cake' in the St Martin's Lane bookshop. They were light and witty and mischievous. But reading them was a whole world away from hearing Toby's own voice.

Last night she had only heard a few scratchy lines of this record, and she had been so frightened of Shona that she had not been in any condition to judge either the song itself or the singer. She did not mind that the sound quality would not be good; what she did mind was that hearing it properly might be a massive disappointment. Toby might have a terrible voice, hitting wrong notes all over the place, or the record might have been made when he was no longer very young – Hilary had no idea when he had been born – and it might be the cracked voice of old age. And even if he hit the right notes with the precision of a newly tuned violin, he might sound stilted and formal – in fact he probably would, because most music-hall performers were so used to an audience, they could not strike the spark without one.

This was crazy. Toby was interesting because of the Tarleton and all the mystery, and it did not matter if he sounded like an elderly tin can or a stuffed dummy. She turned the handle and the turntable moved, jerkily at first, and then with more assurance. In the quiet attic with its scents of age and memories, a forgotten old song – a song written almost a hundred years ago by two men who had been part of the lost world of music hall – began slowly and scratchily to live again.

And Toby Chance's voice was as true as any Hilary had ever heard. There were no false notes, and it was not the cracked voice of a failing or ageing performer. It was a voice that was alive and alight with life, and the singer sounded as if he was on the verge of laughing, because he was loving every minute of performing and because he loved his theatre.

It was only then it occurred to her to look in the rest of the boxes in case there were other records to be found. She spent an absorbed hour, finding photographs and old programmes from Frank Douglas's ENSA days. It looked as if there had been some connection with concert parties for first world war troops as well;

there were a couple of envelopes with sepia photos marked 1916. Several had a slightly plump lady with beautiful eyes, clearly wearing a stage costume, standing in front of heart-breakingly young soldiers.

There was sheet music in the same box – some of it Chance and Douglas songs. 'Tipsy Cake' was there again, and also 'The Ghost Walks'. Riches, thought Hilary gloatingly, seeing with delight that both were hand-written on musical score paper. Both bore a squiggle of initials in the bottom right-hand corner – T.C.

At the bottom of the box was a single sheet of paper, and as Hilary lifted it out she saw it was not music, but a brief letter, written in slightly untidy handwriting, as if the writer had been impatient to get the information down on the paper, or perhaps had been in a hurry when writing it. The paper was brittle with age and the ink had faded, but not badly, probably because the paper had been protected by being beneath the rest. It was undated and there was no address. With her heart beating faster, she read it.

Dear Frank,

Here's the new song lyrics. If you can put one of your incomparable melodies to it, that would be wonderful. I visualized it as something like 'The Man Who Broke the Bank at Monte Carlo', but you'll be sure to compose something better, I know.

Put it somewhere safe for the moment, will you, because we obviously can't do anything with it yet. But perhaps one day it *will* be performed, and people hearing it might understand the clues and know the truth about my part in that wretched ill-starred business in Sarajevo, and about Tranz and all the rest of it. I hope so – I'd hate future generations to believe I was one of the plotters who assassinated Franz-Ferdinand.

The letter ended with no signature, but there were the same squiggled initials as on the sheet music. T.C.

August 1914

'At first I liked being in the Tarleton because it was where I felt nearest to Toby,' said Flora to Hal, 'but it's becoming unbearable now. We've got the new concert on, though: Rinaldi and Frank and I did it between us. Could you come with me to that, Hal? It's meant to lift people's spirits in the midst of all the war gloom in the newspapers. Ever since the formal declaration last week, people are frightened. Suspicious of each other. They don't quite know how to behave yet.'

'I know.' Hal, who had been staring out of the window, said, 'And the show must go on?'

'Yes. Without Toby if necessary.' A spasm of pain twisted her face, then she said, 'Theatres are important at times like this.'

'I understand that. Of course I'll come with you.'

The Tarleton's boxes were not often used, but Flora asked Rinaldi to open one of them for the concert. The stage-right box, she said. It had a good view of the stage, which meant she and Hal would be able to see everything – also the audience would see them, and that might help quell the speculation about Toby's continuing absence.

'That's assuming there is an audience at all,' she said to Hal as they went inside.

'You said it was a full house.'

'Rinaldi said it was. Every seat sold and standing at the back for twopence. He wanted to open up the old stage box as well, but I told him not to bother,' said Flora. 'I always think of it as Toby's place. It's where he went to watch a performance.'

As the house lights went down and the footlights came up, Flora was aware of the warm affection of the audience. They love this place, she thought gratefully. It's part of their lives – it's part of my life, as well. She was managing to keep a tight hold on her emotions, although she felt as if the smallest wrong word would cause her to collapse in a sobbing heap on the floor for Toby whom she might never see again and who might, in any case, be dead.

Here came the acts, one following another with seamless professionalism. The Rose Romain dancers opened the evening, which the audience enjoyed, all the way down to Elise Le Brun's astonishing costume. 'Far more daring than anything I ever wore,' murmured Flora to Hal.

Then came a sketch which Bunstable had written about a confused traveller at a railway station getting his tickets and his destinations mixed up. It set the house rocking with laughter, because everyone loved Bunstable.

Prospero Garrick closed the evening with a Shakespearean speech.

'He wanted to do something rousing,' said Flora to Hal. 'Something appropriate for a war. So he's giving them his Richard II; he says it will rally them.

'Will he be sober?'

'Rinaldi and Bob Shilling were going to lock him in the wardrobe and hide the gin. But I suspect he'll dry and end in making half of it up as he goes along.'

'Iambic knitting,' said Hal.

'Yes, but he does it so well that no one will know. In any case, most of the Victorian actor-managers rewrote Shakespeare to suit their own purposes. Prospero's only harking back to an old tradition.'

But when Prospero came onto the stage they both saw he was perfectly sober; Flora thought that for all the portliness of his build, he cut an imposing figure on a stage. He was not wearing costume but had flung a cloak round his shoulders, and put on high leather boots into which he had tucked the tops of his trousers.

He came right up to the footlights, and said, 'My dear friends, you all know we are now engaged in a massive conflict which may rage across an entire continent. Let us remember that we go into that conflict as Englishmen and heroes.' He looked round the theatre, as if listening, then lowering his voice, said, 'And let us also remember that we shall be *victorious*!'

He stepped back, and Hal murmured to Flora, 'Not at all bad. For once he kept it nicely simple.'

'I hope he finds remembering Richard II simple.'

But Prospero did remember. And really, thought Flora, for all we make a bit of a laughing-stock of him for his drinking and his mannerisms and his florid way of dressing, he's a dear amiable old boy and has the most remarkably beautiful voice.

Prospero's remarkable voice was easily reaching every corner of the theatre tonight, and the words written by Shakespeare were as relevant in this August of 1914 as they had been three hundred years ago.

> This royal throne of kings, this sceptred isle,
> This earth of majesty, this seat of Mars,
> This other Eden, demi-paradise,
> This fortress built by Nature for herself
> Against infection and the hand of war,
> This happy breed of men, this little world,
> This precious stone set in the silver sea,
> Which serves it in the office of a wall,
> Or as a moat defensive to a house,
> Against the envy of less happier lands,
> This blessèd plot, this earth, this realm, this England . . .'

Tears were starting to Flora's eyes, and she reached for Hal's hand in the dimness. Damn Prospero and his beautiful voice and damn William Shakespeare and his genius for plucking at people's emotions as if they were violin strings, she thought. This blessèd plot . . . this England . . . Yes, that matters so much, she thought.

But if I've lost Toby nothing in the world will really matter, not ever again.

Hal suddenly leaned forward and said, 'Flora. There's someone standing in the stage box.'

And then Flora saw, half concealed by the curtain, the shadowy figure in the long concealing cloak watching them.

It was difficult to make their way from the box because there were so many people who were pleased to see Flora, and who must be listened and talked to. They're Toby's people, thought Flora. And once they were my people. I can't ignore them. Yes, but there's someone in the stage box, Toby's box . . .

Somehow she smiled and accepted the congratulations on the evening, agreeing it had been one of the best, lively and colourful, a real Tarleton night, the music wonderful, Prospero Garrick's performance stirring . . . Yes, a shame Toby had not been part of things, but he would be here next time, oh yes, of course he would . . .

At last they were across the foyer and going up the stairs leading to the stage box. As they approached, a beat of apprehension pulsed inside Flora's head. It would not be him, of course it would not . . . It was ridiculous to think it, even for a moment. And yet it would be so like Toby to make such an absurd, dramatic, *dangerous* gesture – to return in the face of the danger.

Hal opened the door of the box and Flora went in. The figure turned to face her. Even though he was standing well back from the spilling light of the auditorium, and even though a dark beard framed his face, Flora knew him at once. She gasped and flung herself into her son's arms.

CHAPTER THIRTY-SEVEN

Toby sat on the battered couch in the green room and looked about him with deep affection.

'In the last few weeks,' he said, 'there were times when I thought I should never see any of this again. Or any of you. You have no idea how it feels to be home.'

'You have no idea how it feels to have you home,' said Flora, who was seated on the old couch with the broken springs. Sonja Kaplen had curled up on a pile of curtains; she had appeared after the performance with Frank Douglas, and had been introduced. Toby had noticed that both his parents looked at her with interest. Frank was in the far corner with Hal.

'Having acknowledged all the emotions,' said Hal, 'we have to decide what on earth we're going to do with you.' He regarded his son with a mixture of affection and exasperation. 'If you had to plunge us all into this mess, did you have to do it quite so dramatically?'

'I'm sorry,' said Toby. 'I really am. If I'd known the truth about Anton Petrovnic – I mean Reznik – I wouldn't have had anything to do with him. And if I'd had the least suspicion he was using me to settle an old score with you, I'd have run a mile in the opposite direction. Although I'd have to say if we're talking about being dramatic, this business of a thirty-year-old vengeance is more than dramatic, it's pure melodrama.' He looked from one to the other of them. 'And even now I don't think you've told me everything about that,' he said.

'I don't think so, either. But I've told you the gist. Enough for you to understand the background.'

'Fair enough. Anton is clearly a vain egotist with an obsession,' said Toby. 'And I don't think he's entirely sane.'

'Probably not,' said Hal non-committally.

Toby did not question further. He said, 'As for Tranz itself – in case you think I've been gullible or naive about that, in my defence I'd have to say that they were persuasive and credible. And so far from than seeming to be the gang of cut-throats and murderers they were, in the main they were intelligent and articulate.'

'You look a bit like a cut-throat yourself at the moment,' said Hal. 'The beard . . .'

'At first that couldn't be helped,' said Toby. 'But then I thought it might serve as a partial disguise, so I let it grow a bit more.'

'I quite like it,' said Flora. 'It's rather dashing and romantic.'

'I like it as well,' said Sonja, who had accepted a bottle of the beer which Frank had produced and was drinking it with perfect composure. 'Toby's right about Tranz being persuasive,' she said. 'They fooled all of us – they certainly fooled me. They made their aims sound so admirable – worth fighting for. The liberation of a country under the iron sway of a greedy empire . . . And we really thought it was nothing more sinister than protest marches and public demonstrations.'

'And "The workers have nothing to lose but their chains . . . and only a world to gain"?' said Hal, rather drily.

'Of course. Don't forget the chaining to the railings, either.'

'I wasn't forgetting it.'

'You think it's misplaced romanticism, don't you?' said Sonja.

'No,' said Hal. 'I'm not surprised you were both taken in. Anton

421

Reznik can be extremely attractive when he puts his mind to it.'

'Oh, Toby never had any judgement of people,' said Frank. 'Shocking thing, isn't it, after the excellent company he's kept all these years.'

'Did you really only reach London today?' asked Flora.

'We did,' said Toby. 'It took longer than it should have because we didn't know if Reznik's people were watching for us or if the police were, or even if we were marked as enemies of the state and being hunted by the government. Any government. When we finally reached London we didn't dare come to Kensington or go to Sonja's people, because we didn't know who might be around. For the same reason we didn't dare send a message either. The only person I could think of who might not be watched – and who I could trust – was Frank.'

'And I was about to eat a blameless lunch in my rooms, with no more thought in my mind beyond tonight's performance,' said Frank. 'When Toby told me what had happened – I mean, what had really happened – I sent out for more food, and then smuggled them into the theatre.'

Toby looked at his father. 'Anton and Baroness Ilena made statements saying I helped with the shooting, didn't they?'

'Yes.'

'That's what we heard in Sarajevo. There was a Reuters man there we got to know slightly – a Frenchman – and he said one of the conspirators was believed to be a Mr Toby Chance. Mercifully,' said Toby, 'he didn't know my name and he didn't seem to have made the connection with Sir Hal Chance of the British Foreign Office, so he didn't see that there was anything worth reporting. But it meant we knew the statements had been made. It was a safe bet that they would charge me if they found me.'

'I wish,' said Sonja savagely, 'that I had managed to make a statement refuting that. But we didn't dare draw attention to ourselves.'

'Miss Kaplen, even if you had made a statement, Anton Reznik would only have brought in more witnesses to back up his version,' said Hal. 'No, Flora, I'm not being gloomy, I'm being realistic. If we break this thing open and Toby is brought to trial, no matter how hard we fight to prove his innocence we might fail.'

'And if that happened?' said Flora.

'Toby would hang,' said Hal. And then, 'My dear love – don't look like that.'

'I'm perfectly all right,' said Flora determinedly.

'There's also the point,' put in Toby, 'that in that situation, that old business about the Reznik twins and Mother might come out.'

'I wouldn't care,' said Flora at once. 'Not if it meant you were cleared.'

'I'd care,' said Toby. 'One of them died that night, didn't he?'

'Stefan. Yes.'

'But Toby, if it came to a choice between proving your innocence and reviving an unpleasant incident from the past, there'd be no question as to which we'd choose. Your life and your liberty are worth far more to us than a few weeks of embarrassment.' Hal made an impatient gesture. 'Dammit, don't you know we'd do anything in the world – that we'd suffer anything necessary . . .'

'Thank you,' said Toby, after a moment. He frowned, then said, 'I wasn't part of the conspiracy, you know. I had absolutely no idea what was going to happen until that morning.'

'We all know that.' This was Flora again.

'And once Toby did realize what Anton was doing, he tried to think of a way of preventing it,' put in Sonja eagerly.

'We both tried. But we didn't manage it,' said Toby angrily. 'I wasn't there when they actually shot the Archduke, although only Sonja can swear to that. But I was there when the bomb was thrown – I was within yards of the man who did it. I'd even met him the previous night – dozens of people had seen us at the

423

same table. I'd met Gavrilo Princip as well – the man who eventually fired the fatal shots.'

'We all sat round a table in a disgusting little café while they talked,' said Sonja. 'Neither of us could understand what was being said, although I don't suppose that would count for much. Ignorance isn't a defence in the eyes of the law, is it?'

'I'm afraid not,' said Hal. 'How intelligent of you to know about that, Miss Kaplen.'

'I wish you'd stop being so formal,' said Sonja. 'I find it very difficult to discuss murder and mayhem with people who call me Miss Kaplen.'

Hal smiled, then said, 'Toby, it's been quietly agreed by my masters that this entire business – your involvement, those statements, even the fact you were in Sarajevo at all – must be kept very secret indeed. That being so, I can't see how you can stay in England for the foreseeable future.'

'I'd already seen that for myself.'

'The Bosnian authorities have already put a request through our own embassy that we hold you on a charge of conspiracy if we find you,' said Hal. 'The minute Anton Reznik – or his people – knew you were here, they'd have made the whole thing public. They may still do so.'

'If I thought I could prove my innocence against Reznik's statement I'd stay and fight,' said Toby.

'The cards are too heavily stacked; you'd be damned from the outset. Later on it might be possible to bring everything out into the open and clear you. But in the meantime we have to think what we're going to do with you.'

'And Sonja?' said Flora. 'Have you family who would help you?'

'None to speak of,' said Sonja rather curtly. 'Just guardians.'

'Ah. No parents?'

'They died when I was small.' Her voice had a hard, frozen sound, and Hal said, 'I see. I'm very sorry.'

'Toby, how did you get out of Sarajevo?' said Flora.

'For about a week we didn't,' said Toby, grinning at her. 'We reasoned that if we were being looked for, they wouldn't expect to find us still on their doorstep. So we found an hotel on the outskirts and booked ourselves in as Mr and Mrs Kaplen.'

'It was perfectly proper,' said Sonja quickly. 'A large room with two beds. Not that I actually approve of observing those outmoded conventions.'

'Good. Nor do I,' said Flora, promptly. 'It's Toby who's unexpectedly traditional under the flippancy.'

'No, I am not,' said Toby. 'Show me a convention and I'll instantly flout it. But as a matter of fact we were too worried about what might happen to us to be anything other than extremely proper. We spent most of the time at the windows, watching to see if a detachment of the military came marching up the street to arrest me. Sarajevo was still seething with all kinds of authorities.'

'What then?' asked Hal.

'Very simple. After about a week, we managed to hire a motor car from a little place near the railway station. We drove west until we reached the coast – the Adriatic. Then we went north and into Italy.'

'But you can't drive a motor car,' said Flora.

'I can now,' said Toby, grinning. 'So can Sonja. You should have seen us bouncing all the way up the coast until we reached Trieste. It's great fun, driving. People come out to cheer you on. And we hired one of those new ones with a windscreen – it shields you from insects and stones and you can go at the most amazing speeds. The motor gave out at Trieste, unfortunately, and from there we simply got on trains. Once we reached Calais, we got the ferry and trusted to the gods of travel that no one would realize who we were.'

'What we think now,' said Frank, 'is that Toby will have to hide out in the theatre until we can decide what to do with him.'

'You'll stay in here, Toby?'

'Yes.'

'What about Sonja?' said Flora. 'She could stay with us, couldn't she, Hal?'

'Indeed she could.'

'No, I couldn't,' said Sonja. 'It's too much of a risk for you. I'm going to book into some quiet and anonymous hotel, and lie low until we've made a plan.'

'My dear girl—'

'Sir Hal, you know it's too dangerous for me to be seen at your house,' she said. 'And it's only likely to be for a few days – a week at most. I'll be a whole lot more comfortable than Toby will in here.'

'I'll be in luxury,' said Toby.

'Not next Thursday night you won't,' said Flora. 'There's an evening of music booked.'

'Oh Lord, is there? But I can hide somewhere while that's on,' said Toby.

'We'd have to bring Rinaldi in on that,' said Flora slowly. 'But I think that would be all right. It wouldn't be the first time he's shared a secret about this place, and he's utterly loyal.'

'We thought Rinaldi could probably be recruited as an ally,' agreed Frank.

'But there's Bob Shilling as well,' said Hal, suddenly. 'Did you allow for him? Does he still make his midnight round?'

'He does, but that's about all he does these days,' said Toby. 'He lives quite nearby – just off Candle Square – and when there isn't a performance, he just walks along to the stage door around midnight, takes a look everywhere to make sure it's all in order, and goes back home. All I'd have to do would be to keep out of his way for that short time.'

'What about food?' asked Flora.

'We brought milk and bread with us,' said Sonja. 'Oh, and some tins of sardines.'

'Toby can't live on bread and sardines.'

'I could. It wouldn't be for long.'

426

'And milk goes off very quickly in this heat,' said Flora. 'We'll have to bring food in to him. And some sort of bedding. Would that be noticed, though? People coming and going when the theatre's more or less closed?'

Toby, Sonja and Frank looked at one another, and despite the severity of the situation, an expression of mischief lit their faces.

'Once upon a time,' began Toby, 'strange tales were told about this theatre.'

'I don't quite . . .'

'Once upon a time,' said Frank, 'a strange figure was seen around Platt's Alley.'

'A figure no one ever quite identified,' put in Sonja.

Flora and Hal stared at them. Then Flora said, 'Dear God, you're going to revive the ghost legend!'

'Will any of that work?' asked Flora as she and Hal entered their house sometime later.

'It's the kind of mad scheme that might. As for the ghost – well, as those three irresponsible creatures said, we only need to mention here and there that it's been seen again. A couple of references in the Sailors' Retreat and the Linkman. You could tell Minnie Bean – that ought to get the gossip going. And Rinaldi, of course. I'll go to see him first thing in the morning, to explain what's happened.' He looked at her. 'What did you think of Sonja Kaplen?'

'As a future daughter-in-law, you mean?'

'Ah, you saw that as well, did you?'

'Oh yes. Her whole expression changes when she looks at him. As if a light were shining behind her eyes. What was that you said to her about the chains of the workers?'

'Karl Marx,' he said. 'She recognized it at once, of course. That's a highly intelligent girl. I foresee some interesting discussions ahead. I've often thought Marx had some very sound doctrines.'

'Do you know,' said Flora, 'you're a constant delight and surprise to me.' She saw him smile, and said, 'Hal, Sonja will be all right in that hotel, won't she?'

'Yes, of course. You saw for yourself when we went in with her. They gave her a very nice room.'

'I always thought I should hate the girl Toby finally decided to marry,' said Flora, 'but now I've met her, I don't. I like her very much indeed.'

'She's a bit of a firebrand,' said Hal. 'But I rather like that. You realize they may not get round to the actual ceremony? They may not even be able to – it could draw attention to Toby.'

'As long as Toby's safe and well, I don't care if he lives in sin with twenty women in five different continents,' said Flora. And then, quite suddenly, 'Oh, damn, I vowed I wouldn't cry, I *promised* myself I wouldn't . . .'

'Cry all night if you want to,' he said, and his arms came around her. 'Because he's back with us, and he's safe.'

'Will he remain safe though?'

'Yes,' said Hal very firmly indeed. 'Toby will survive.'

CHAPTER THIRTY-EIGHT

There had been times over the last weeks when Toby had not been sure if he was going to survive. He thought no one had realized this, except Sonja. He felt better now they were in London, but he still felt strung up with apprehension.

He had expected to find the dark empty Tarleton slightly eerie, jumping at every creak and sigh of the old building, but he did not. This is my place, he thought after his parents left with Sonja and Frank. This is the place I know and that knows me. He made up a makeshift bed on the green room couch and fell into a deep sleep from which he did not wake until seven the next morning.

The days blurred and unless he went out to the foyer where there was a narrow window alongside the main entrance, he had no way of telling if it was night or day. For this reason he was careful to keep his watch wound up because of Shilling's midnight round; but when it came to it, he always heard Shilling coming in and it was easy to slip out of the green room and stand in the deep shadow of the stage box, or in the wardrobe room. Shilling made his round faithfully and efficiently, although on the second night of his stay, Toby heard him uncork a bottle of something and caught the faint aroma of whisky or brandy. He smiled as he stood in the darkness of the stage box; he did not in the least blame Shilling for having a few swigs from a bottle on his lonely vigil.

Sonja and the others came in fairly frequently, usually bringing food – cooked chicken and ham which his mother packed in greaseproof paper, veal and ham pies, and thick wedges of cheese. Toby made tea on the green room gas stove, throwing the tea leaves down the lavatory near the dressing rooms, but he did not dare cook anything in case the smell made Shilling suspicious. Rinaldi came several times, shocked at the situation in which Toby found himself. 'Oh, Mr Toby, what a pickle it all is. That I should live to see the day when you're locked inside your own theatre.'

Toby's father came only once. Toby guessed he was not very comfortable with the secrecy or with the concept of the ghost figure, which everyone else was rather guiltily enjoying, although Rinaldi said he could not bring himself to entirely approve, because it was tempting Providence to call up ghosts.

But Hal was able to tell Toby about events in the outside world, which Toby greatly appreciated. 'When this is over, the map of Europe will have changed for ever,' he said. 'In any case, our lives will all be vastly different until the war ends.'

'Over by Christmas?'

'Not for a minute,' said Hal. Then, 'Did your mother tell you she's already making plans to take a touring group of performers to the army bases – wherever the army bases eventually are.'

'She did tell me.' Toby had found his mother's ideas rather good; he had contributed several suggestions of his own which Flora had seized on enthusiastically.

'I'm hoping she won't actually be going into any danger,' said Hal. 'I don't think she'll be close to any battlefields. But I'm not trying to dissuade her.'

'She wouldn't let you anyway,' said Toby. 'Not if her mind's made up.'

'Exactly.'

When Toby asked if any of them had yet thought of a way of getting him out of the country, Hal said they had not. 'There's this new passport system now – much stricter than before. It may even come to a question of arranging a false one for you.'

'Might it? Could you get that done?'

'I think so. My God, I never thought I'd hear myself say that. But there's still the problem of where you would go.' In a rare gesture of physical affection, he laid a hand on Toby's arm. 'Somehow, though, I will get you safely through this.'

Frank came in most days. He generally stayed for an hour or so, drinking beer, discussing future work. Toby wanted to write some lyrics about the assassination, and Frank was trying out a few bits of music that would fit them. Toby knew they could probably not perform the song for a very long time, but perhaps one day they could. Or perhaps one day somebody else could.

Frank was also working with Flora on the idea of staging entertainments at army and even naval bases. A small touring company, he said – perhaps even more than just one. Songs and musical sketches and a few comic acts, of course. People needed to laugh when there was a war rampaging all across Europe. They would use men who were a bit too old for actual fighting.

'But you'll be fighting?' said Toby, and Frank grinned and said, God yes, was there ever an Irishman who passed up the chance of a scrap. Things were still a bit disorganized, but he would be signing up for the army when they had Toby sorted out. In the meantime, he was enjoying helping Toby's mamma with her plans.

Toby found all these discussions deeply reassuring because they helped him believe there would one day be a return to normality.

Sonja brought books to help pass the time. Toby's mother had arranged for her to have a key – and she came each afternoon, looking waif-like and defenceless in the long cloak.

The Tarleton's musical concert was going ahead. 'We can't avoid it,' Flora said, sitting in the green room, sharing Toby's picnic lunch. 'It's been planned and there've been posters in a lot of places, and to cancel it would draw attention to the theatre which is what we're trying to avoid. I'm sorry, Toby, but you really will have to remain out of sight for a few hours that night.'

'In the cellar?' said Toby.

'It would be the best place.'

'With the door locked,' he said, expressionlessly.

'Yes. We can't risk anyone coming in by chance and finding you.' They looked at one another and Toby knew there were two quite separate memories in their minds: one was his own child-hood terror of the cellar; the other was his mother's own, very private, memory of something that had happened before he was born. He had not pressed for details of Stefan Reznik's death or the thirty-year-old quarrel; his father had simply said the twins had attacked Toby's mother; there had been some violence and Anton's brother had died as the result of a tragic accident.

'Rinaldi's taking lanterns and plenty of candles down there,' Flora said. 'And it really won't be very long.'

'I know,' said Toby. 'It's all right.'

It was not really all right, of course, but it was still the best arrangement. But despite his resolve, as soon as Toby stepped inside the cellar, the childhood fears came rushing back, and when Rinaldi turned the key in the heavy old door at the head of the stairs, he had to beat down an impulse to rush up the stone steps and shout to be let out. He walked determinedly to where Rinaldi had set up a slightly battered chair. There were two lanterns in a corner, together with a box of thick candles and matches, and there was milk, bottled beer, and a cold chicken and fruit. To pass the hours, Toby had a copy of a fairly new play by Bernard Shaw, whose work he admired. The play was called *Pygmalion* and was described as an anti-romantic comedy; Toby thought if anything was designed to drive back the sinister atmosphere of this place, it was Shaw's witty intelligent dialogue.

But as he read, he found himself constantly looking up from the page, sure that something had moved in one of the corners or that he had heard a stealthy footstep at the head of the stairs. Towards seven o'clock he had the sensation of the theatre filling up. He glanced towards the far end of the cellar, to the grave trap. When its floor was winched up to the stage as it was now, it sealed the cellar off from the stage fairly effectively, but several times he heard faint strains of music. He hoped the evening was going well, and he laid *Pygmalion* down for a moment, imagining the audience listening and enjoying themselves. I wish I was up there, thought Toby. If I have to leave England because of all this, how will I manage to leave the Tarleton? And then, with a lifting of his heart, he thought, but Sonja will be with me.

An hour later, he replaced the burned-down candles with new ones, ate part of his supper, and returned to Shaw. Eliza Doolittle was starting to acquire a veneer of polish and gentility, although Toby liked her better as the urchin in the opening scenes. He took a drink of the beer and he was just embarking on the second act, when he heard a sound at the head of the cellar stairs, then soft footsteps coming down towards him.

For a wild moment he thought his nightmares were materializing, but the footsteps were too light to be sinister. A shadow fell on the wall of the stairs, and then Sonja Kaplen appeared.

Toby put down Shaw and the beer, and said, 'What are you doing here? I thought we'd all agreed that everyone would stay clear of the cellar until the theatre was empty.'

'That's exactly why I'm here,' she said. 'Because everyone is staying clear until the theatre is empty. I borrowed Rinaldi's cellar key – I promised to let him have it back by eleven, though.' She came over to him and sat down, and although she had spoken quite coolly and normally, her eyes were wide and fearful as if she was unsure of her reception.

Toby took her face between his hands, and began to kiss her.

It was like the igniting of a forest fire, or the undamming of a vast river. The emotion that had simmered between them for the past weeks – the emotion neither of them had dared acknowledge in

433

the face of the other dangers – blazed up, fierce and overpowering, sweeping everything else away.

She was wearing plain cotton underclothes – Toby, more accustomed to ladies such as Alicia Darke who calculatedly wore silk against their skins, found this so unexpectedly endearing that he had to blink back tears.

'What have I done wrong?' she said, seeing this.

'My darling girl, you haven't done anything wrong – you've done everything right, but this ought to be happening in some silken bedroom with moonlight and starlight or a rose garden or something ... And I'm not sure it ought to be happening at all, because if I don't stop now, we'll end up doing something you might regret.'

'I shan't regret it,' she said. 'I'd like it to be you and I don't care about moonlight and rose gardens.' She looked up at him, suddenly hesitant. 'Only I'm not exactly sure what I should do ...'

'Oh, Sonja,' said Toby helplessly and, as he pushed her back onto the rumpled pile of old stage curtains, he realized that neither of them would have noticed if the entire world had become suffused with moonlight or if the scent of all the rose gardens in Isfahan had been in the room with them.

When he entered her she gave a gasp of surprised pain and stared up at him in sudden fear. 'It's all right,' said Toby, very gently. 'From now it gets better.'

'Oh,' she said, a few moments later. 'Oh God – yes, I see what you mean ...'

She lay against him when it was over, her hair tumbling round her shoulders. She was soft and sweet, and Toby could not imagine what he would do if he had to lose her. He told her this, and saw the delight in her eyes.

'They tell you about the hurting part,' she said a few moments later. 'I think that's to put you off behaving – um – immodestly. But no one ever tells you what's after that bit of hurt.' She turned on her side so that she could look at him. 'Does it get even better than that?'

Toby looked at her. Her eyes, seen so close, had tiny flecks of gold in them. 'Let's find out, shall we?' he said, and began to kiss her all over again.

Sonja eventually left him shortly before ten o'clock.

'If I stay any later I might be seen,' she said. 'They'll be coming out of the theatre quite soon. I'll just mingle with the crowds and seem to be part of the audience.'

'Come back tomorrow? Please, Sonja.'

'Yes, please.' She stood up, pinning her hair back into place. 'I'll have to lock the cellar door again. I'll hate doing it, but I'll give the key back to Rinaldi and he'll come down to let you out.'

'You do know you've chased away all the nightmares of this place, don't you?'

'Have I? I think you've chased a few away for me as well,' she said. 'I told you I didn't believe in outmoded conventions, but—'

'But you did believe in some of them?'

'Just the one that nice girls don't do this before marriage,' she said, and again there was the fearful look in her eyes.

'Marriage might redress the balance, though,' said Toby. 'But I'm damned if I'm proposing in this place. I shall insist on the moonlight and all the other things for that.' He saw the light return to her eyes, and said, 'Let's just think about the present. How will you get back to the hotel? Will you be all right?'

'Rinaldi will get me a cab in Burbage Street. In any case it's quite early by the standards of London streets. I'll be perfectly all right.'

Toby listened to her go up the steps, and heard the lock turning in the door. He disliked the prospect of another hour down here by himself, but it would soon pass. He tried to return to *Pygmalion*, but could not. Instead he lay back on the chair and watched the shadows made by the flickering candles, and thought about Sonja, and wondered if they really would get out of all this and how, and where they would go. The thought of spending the rest of his life with her was so deeply satisfying he refused to contemplate the alarming obstacles that reared up to gibber at him. There would be a way.

When he looked at his watch again it was a little after eleven. Rinaldi would appear at any moment. Toby listened, hoping to hear the cellar door being unlocked, but nothing happened. It was completely silent overhead; everyone would have gone home by now, or along to the Linkman or the Pickled Lobster Pot. Something must have delayed Rinaldi; it was not like the old boy to be late for anything; he was very particular about punctuality. It was the politeness of kings, he sometimes said. And it was now twenty minutes past eleven. Toby put down Shaw and went up the stone steps to make sure the door at the top really was locked. It was just possible Rinaldi had unlocked it without him hearing, assuming he would go out of his own accord. But the door was firmly locked. Toby considered shouting, but then it occurred to him that despite the apparent silence, there might still be people around and that was the reason for Rinaldi's absence. He would give it a little longer.

His watch was showing ten minutes after midnight and he was becoming concerned, when he finally heard the door being opened. Toby was about to call out, asking where on earth Rinaldi had been, when there was a second sound. The cellar door was being locked again, this time from the inside. Whoever had come into the cellar had locked himself in with Toby. A beat of apprehension started up in his mind, but before he could think what might be going on, there was the sound of someone descending the steps. Someone whose footsteps were nothing like Rinaldi's quick brisk steps.

There was no time to turn down the wick of the lantern, but acting on instinct Toby snuffed out the two remaining candles. As quickly as possible, he snatched up the empty beer bottle as a weapon, and darted across the cellar to stand behind the grave trap's frame.

The cellar was almost completely dark except for the dull glow from the lantern, and in this sullen light a shadow appeared on the stair wall, red-tinged and menacing. It came down the last few steps and was in the cellar with him.

Anton Reznik. And in his hand was a gun.

He stood at the foot of the steps, looking round, and Toby knew that despite the dimness Anton had seen him. In the smeary light Anton smiled and Toby flinched because it was a smile so utterly devoid of sanity and of any kind of humanity, it was as if something sharp and cold had skewered between his ribs. But he remained where he was, hoping that if Anton did fire at him, the grave trap's frame might provide a form of shield. He entertained a fleeting hope that the gun might not be real, but he was too familiar with stage props to believe for more than a couple of seconds that this was a prop. This was small, black and wicked, and unquestionably genuine.

'Well, Toby,' said Anton softly, 'so I was right when I thought you would run for home and your safe little nest.'

'What do you want?'

'To kill you. To execute you in your own theatre. You should have been executed by the British government as a spy – a conspirator in the assassination of Franz-Ferdinand. That was what I planned for. A public shaming. In this country you would have been hanged; in Bosnia or Germany they would have shot you, which is what I shall do tonight. And when Sir Hal and your mother find your body, they will understand.'

Toby said furiously, 'You know damn well I had nothing to do with the assassination. Those statements you and Ilena made were flat-out lies. It was your stupid melodramatic revenge for something that happened thirty years ago, wasn't it? What happened that night, Anton? I know your brother died that night and I'm sorry for it. But did my mother reject you? Did my father fight you

437

and dent your dignity? Or humiliate you? Have you brooded over it all these years?' I'll keep him talking, he thought. Because surely Rinaldi will come in soon. Or will he? Anton must have got the key from him and he's locked the door.

'Your mother – also your father – were responsible for my brother's death,' Anton Reznik said, moving nearer. 'Did your father tell you how we were imprisoned in this place without light or water?' said Anton. 'How we were shut in the pitch darkness for nearly three days? Stefan could not bear it – he was always afraid of the dark, from a small child. He died in agony and terror.' He took a step nearer. 'And on that night I told your father that although your justice system would not punish him, one day I would do so. That I would destroy him for Stefan's death. And that is what I am doing now – I am destroying Hal Chance through you. It is not as good as the punishment I originally planned, but it is nearly so.'

'Did you set up Tranz just to destroy my father?' said Toby, trying to assess whether he could dive forward and wrest the gun from Anton before he fired it. 'Was that all Tranz was?'

'Tranz was perfectly genuine and its aim was the death of one more of that imperialistic blood-sucking Habsburg line,' said Anton. 'We always intended the Archduke to die that morning. But I also intended that you would die, Toby – that you would be caught and charged and found guilty of a political murder.' A spasm of fury twisted his features. 'You should be in prison now, awaiting trial,' he said. 'You would have been found guilty and executed – I would have made sure of it. There would have been other statements, other eye-witness accounts.'

'But I gave you the slip,' said Toby. 'How infuriating for you. Purely out of curiosity, Anton, how did you get in here?'

'By attending tonight's performance, of course. There was a slight risk that if your father or mother were present they would recognize me, but it's thirty years since we met and in the event, they weren't here. When everyone was leaving, I slipped into the gentlemen's lavatory in the foyer and hid there. When I was sure the audience had all gone – and that your doorkeeper had done his rounds – I came out.'

'How did you know I was here in the first place?'

'Oh Toby,' said Anton, 'I watched your family, of course. Your parents and your closest friends. I watched this theatre as well. I had done that before you even came to Tranz, of course, so I knew what you did and where you went and who your friends were. Did you never sense you were being watched all those weeks ago?'

'Yes,' said Toby after a moment, remembering the night he had first attended Tranz's meeting with Alicia. He had been sure someone had been watching him that night – first in the theatre itself, then later in Platt's Alley. 'Yes, I did.'

'For the past week I have again watched this theatre, and I saw how, at certain times of the evening, occasionally the afternoon, a furtive figure in a dark cloak stole along Platt's Alley and let itself in through the stage door.'

'The ghost legend,' said Toby, half to himself. 'So it didn't work.'

'Probably most people were fooled, but I was watching too closely. Ghosts don't sometimes appear tall and broad-shouldered, and sometimes small and slender. Nor do ghosts need keys to unlock doors.'

'How did you unlock the cellar door?' He's relaxing his guard a bit, thought Toby. He's liking telling me all this, showing me how clever he's been. Dare I make a move now?

'I got the key from Rinaldi,' said Anton. 'I had to knock him out, of course. He's not dead, only unconscious. I shut him in the doorkeeper's room.'

'That was a bit risky,' said Toby at once. 'It's not like you to leave potentially damning evidence. Rinaldi will certainly inform the police what you did, and if he doesn't, I will.'

'By the time it comes to that, I will be on the other side of an ocean,' said Anton. 'Canada. I have good friends who will help

439

me leave this country. But you won't be able to inform anyone of anything, because you will shortly be dead. If your police and your government won't execute you, then I will. And I will do it now.'

He moved forward, and Toby knew he had left it too late. Anton was going to shoot him. But even as this thought formed, something over his head stirred, and there was a faint creaking. Both Toby and Anton looked involuntarily upwards, and Anton let out a cry of horror.

The floor of the grave trap – the floor that had been flush with the stage above them – was being slowly winched down.

Toby saw at once that the sound and the sight of the moving mechanism was reviving some deep and terrible memory for Anton, and he saw as well that there might never be a better moment. He bounded forward, knocking Anton to the ground, managing to pinion the hand that held the gun. Anton fought like a wildcat, and although Toby raised the beer bottle to bring it smashing down on the other man's head, Anton managed to reach up and knock it away. It rolled out of reach and broke in a corner of the cellar.

As the two men grappled, the trap came lower, the pulley wheels, stiff with disuse, screeched protestingly. Toby managed to knock the gun from Anton's hand and grab his wrists and hold them tightly together. He risked glancing behind him and saw there was someone on the floor of the trap, although he could not see who.

'Who's there?' he shouted, but before there was any response Anton had seized his opportunity. He pushed Toby aside and sprang to his feet, snatching up the gun. As he levelled it, Toby instinctively threw himself flat on the ground, expecting a shot to go zinging through the cellar. But Anton did not fire. The mechanism of the trap had come to rest on the ground, and a figure leapt from it and hurled itself at Anton. A figure that was tousled, bruised and had blood seeping from one cheek.

Rinaldi. His eyes blazed with fury and Toby leapt to his feet and shouted, 'Be careful – he's got a gun!' but Rinaldi did not hesitate. He knocked Anton to the ground, beating at his face with angry clenched fists.

'You evil bastard!' screamed Rinaldi. 'You devil!' The Italian accent, normally hardly noticeable, was strongly apparent.

'You think you have a score to settle with this family!' shouted Rinaldi. 'I know what you have done to Mr Toby these last weeks! I know the evil plans you make! But we know about scores and reckonings in my country, and I shall settle all the scores tonight! Tonight you will not get away, you rapist! You will die now, as you should have died thirty years ago! I shall kill you and lock your body away down here. And this time, Signor Anton, this time when I turn the key in the cellar door, no one will rescue you as they did thirty years ago!'

The two men rolled over on the brick floor. Toby, frantically trying to see his chance to dive in and overpower Anton, was wary of the gun, but as he was about to dive forward and trust to luck, it went off, the shot echoing over and over in the enclosed cellar.

Both Anton and Rinaldi seemed to jerk and then lie still, and Toby thought, oh God, oh dear God, which of them is it! Not Rinaldi – please not Rinaldi, dear faithful old boy.

A figure got up from the ground, and he saw with horror it was Anton who had fired the shot and Rinaldi lay on the ground, bleeding from the heart.

Anton turned the gun on Toby – there was now surely no way of escaping. Toby dived back behind the grave trap again, and it was then that there was a movement from overhead, from the opening in the stage where the trap's floor had been. A cool voice said, 'Don't fire again, Anton. If you do, I will certainly shoot you, and from this range I won't miss.'

It was Alicia Darke.

She was kneeling on the edge of the grave trap's opening, pointing a small pistol down into the cellar. Even from here, Toby could see the cold anger in her eyes.

Anton said sharply, 'Shooting from there will not kill me, Alicia. Even if you hit me, I can still shoot Toby.'

He began to back to the foot of the steps, keeping the gun levelled at Toby. Toby glanced at Alicia and saw that for all her earlier threat she was uncertain. She's not going to risk it, he thought. Anton's going to get away. He looked across at Rinaldi again. Rinaldi's chest was sticky with dark blood, and his head had fallen back, the eyes open and sightless. Toby knew he was dead, and for a moment the pain of this was so fierce he could not concentrate on what was happening. When he looked back Anton was already at the foot of the steps, still facing the cellar, still levelling the gun at Toby's heart.

'And now Alicia, I am out of your range,' he said.

'Not really,' said Alicia. 'I can be through the foyer and in the stone passage at the cellar door before you get it unlocked. So if you were still considering shooting Toby, I advise against it, because you would have me to contend with in about three minutes' time.'

'My dear, you wouldn't really shoot me, would you?'

'Without a moment's hesitation,' said Alicia, at once.

'Alicia, let him go,' said Toby urgently. 'Or he will certainly kill you as well as me.'

'Certainly I would kill that faithless bitch if I had to.' Anton was out of sight on the curve of the steps, and seconds later came the sound of the door being unlocked and then locked again.

CHAPTER THIRTY-NINE

Toby was starting to feel as if he had been scooped up out of one nightmare and dropped neck-deep into another. There was a strong feeling of déjà vu as he sat in the green room again with his parents, although Alicia was in Sonja's usual chair, discussing what must be done.

After he had established that Rinaldi was dead, Alicia had winched the grave trap back up to the stage with Toby on the platform. He had scribbled a brief note to his father and, wrapped in one of the long dark cloaks from the wardrobe room, had risked going out into Burbage Street to find a cab driver who would deliver it. Alicia had objected to this in case Anton was still lurking, but Toby argued that if anyone had to face Anton, it had better be him. Just in case, he had borrowed Alicia's pistol.

As he went out, she said, 'Remember – not the first cab in the rank, nor the second, but the third,' and Toby's sense of unreality increased and he heard himself saying, 'I didn't know you read Conan Doyle.'

'My dear boy, he's my constant bedside companion.'

The note merely said there was a development that Sir Hal would wish to know, but all was well with the main parties. Toby did not really think the note would be intercepted, but he had deliberately made it as uninformative as possible.

'It won't be intercepted,' said Alicia when he came back. 'I shouldn't think any of Anton's followers are within fifty miles of London. They'll all be too scared to show their faces.'

'Anton wasn't.'

'Anton came back to this country for the sole purpose of killing you,' said Alicia. 'He reached London ten days ago and came to my house. Really, he was so arrogant. He believes all females are wildly in love with him. Unfortunately, most of them are, but this time he misjudged.'

'Did you take him in?'

'I did, but only so I'd know what he was doing,' she said. 'I told him I was going to Canada to escape the war and he assumed he would come with me.'

'Are you going to Canada to escape the war?'

'I might,' she said, 'or I might remain here and become earnest and selfless and help with the war effort. I daresay there would be things I could do, although not anything in uniform, I don't think. Rather unbecoming those uniforms for nurses or canteen workers. I should organize and supervise. I would be rather good at that, and one can wear those rather fetching tailor-mades to supervise.' And then with an abrupt change of mood and with unusual seriousness she said, 'Toby, there are times in life when you have to make a choice. I made a choice ten days ago when I opened the door and saw Anton. Perhaps I made the choice even before that, when— But we should concentrate on the immediate. Is it very difficult to brew tea? I see there's a gas stove and a kettle . . .'

She reverted to her normal slightly flippant, slightly bored manner, and while they waited for the kettle to boil, Toby went back to the stage and lowered the grave trap again, staring down at Rinaldi's body. 'I'm so sorry,' said Toby. 'You died in my place, and I'm thankful to be alive and I'll never forget you or what you did.'

Hal Chance arrived shortly after one a.m., Flora with him. Toby took them straight to the green room, but before he could make introductions, Alicia said, 'Lady Chance. I am Alicia Darke. I daresay you might prefer not to know me, since I have a certain reputation in some circles, but this is a situation where the ordinary conventions have to be put aside.'

'How do you do,' said Flora. 'I'm very glad to meet you. I've never bothered overmuch about conventions. You know my husband already, I believe.'

'I do.'

'Mrs Darke turned king's evidence a few weeks ago,' said Hal, looking at Toby. 'She came to warn me you were about to go mad-rabbiting across Europe with that blaggardly killer Anton Reznik.'

'Unfortunately,' said Alicia coolly, 'I was a little too late to prevent what happened.'

'You were halfway to Bosnia by then, Toby,' said Hal. 'Out of reach.' He sat down and accepted the tin mug of tea Alicia handed him. 'May we know what's happened here tonight?'

'Anton Petrovnic – whom you know as Reznik – was here and tried to kill Toby,' said Alicia. 'However he has now scuttled back into hiding and Toby is safe. You do not need the details of the attack.'

'You do need to know that Rinaldi is dead, though,' said Toby, and saw his mother's eyes darken with pain. 'He was trying to get me away from Reznik and Reznik shot him,' he said.

'Oh Toby, no—'

'And he made an extraordinary statement just before he was shot,' said Toby. 'I haven't quite made sense of it yet, but Rinaldi went for Anton very violently indeed. As he did so, he shouted something about having meant to kill them thirty years ago—'

'He did *what*?'

'He said,' repeated Toby carefully, 'that Anton would die tonight as he should have died thirty years ago. And that this time,

445

when he turned the key in the cellar door, no one would rescue him.'

Flora and Hal looked at one another. 'The locked door,' said Flora. 'Oh God, we thought the latch had dropped of its own accord, but – Hal, could Rinaldi have deliberately locked those two in that night?'

'I think he could,' said Hal slowly. 'Yes, I do think it. Rinaldi would have done anything for you. Apparently he would even have committed murder.'

'So,' said Flora slowly, 'if we hadn't gone to his house that day, would he have left them to die?'

'Let's think he wouldn't. Let's think he just meant it as a punishment and that he intended to let them out.'

Flora said suddenly, 'Do you remember how I saw someone dodging through the mist? We were walking away from the theatre and I looked back and thought I saw a figure going into Platt's Alley. Only everywhere was shrouded in that thick river fog and I was never sure.'

'We thought it was the local constable doing his rounds,' said Hal, remembering.

'Yes, but in view of what Toby's told us, isn't it more likely to have been Rinaldi going back to lock the door? And,' said Flora, 'there had been someone in the theatre earlier. While Anton and Stefan were on the stage with me. Soft footsteps and someone singing very quietly. I told you about that. Could that have been Rinaldi as well?'

Hal said, 'My dear, if Rinaldi really had been in the theatre that night, and if he had seen those two attacking you, do you honestly think he would have walked round singing? Done nothing to help you? He'd have been on the stage in two seconds, tearing their hearts out. Whatever you heard that night, I don't think it was Rinaldi.'

'But – it was so clear,' said Flora. 'The twins heard it as well. They looked up – it startled them. I can remember it so clearly.'

446

She looked first at Hal and then at Toby. 'If it wasn't Rinaldi, then *who was it?*'

For a moment, no one spoke, then Hal said, 'Flora, you told me once that the Tarleton has its secrets, and that it likes to keep them.'

Toby looked round. Perhaps there really is a ghost here, he thought, and almost at once came the awareness of a faint creaking somewhere beyond the cosiness of the green room: a measured, almost rhythmic sound, as if someone was walking softly through the theatre. Mingling with it, just for a moment, was a thin, barely audible sound. It might have been the wind stirring in the old timbers – it probably was – but it might also be someone singing very softly.

The Tarleton has its secrets and it likes to keep them . . .

The Present

'It was dreadful seeing Shona like that,' said Hilary to Robert as she got off the train at King's Cross. 'She just sat in a chair and – sort of hugged her secrets the whole time I was there. The pitiful thing is that she doesn't realize her secrets are all pretty much known.'

'What sort of a place was it?'

'Something between a prison and a hospital,' said Hilary, as they crossed the small square outside and headed for the car park where Robert had left his car. 'Perhaps a bit more hospital than prison. Quite well run, as far as I could tell. They think she did kill that woman she talked about – Elspeth. She was some sort of cousin, apparently. One of the doctors told me the local police searched Shona's old childhood home – it's a great gloomy place somewhere in the Yorkshire moors. They found the body of a woman walled up in the cellar, exactly as Shona kept saying that night at Levels House.'

'How did she react when she saw you?'

'I don't think she really knew who I was,' said Hilary. 'She kept talking about Elspeth and Anna – she seemed to think they were in the room with her and to be listening to them.' She shivered. 'I'm glad I went and I might try to go again, but I can't tell you how good it was to step off the train and see you waiting for me.'

'I can't tell you how good it was to see you step off the train and come racing down the platform towards me,' he said, putting his arm round her waist and holding her against him for a moment.

'Where are we going?' said Hilary presently, as they reached the car park.

'I'll drive you back to your flat. Would you be too tired to have dinner later? We could go out somewhere nearby.'

'Or,' said Hilary, 'we could stay in.'

Robert looked down at her. 'Could we?'

'Would you like that?'

'I'd love it.'

'I can cook a reasonable meal,' began Hilary.

'I wasn't thinking about the food,' he said.

Shona was being very clever about keeping her secrets in this new place. They kept sending people into the room to talk to her, to try to get the secrets out of her, but she could outwit them all.

The latest one they had sent was a youngish female – Shona thought she had seemed familiar and had relaxed a bit and been getting ready to talk in a friendly way to this person. But just in time she realized this was another of their tricks to make her talk about what she had done to Elspeth, Anna and Mother. She was not falling for that one!

Elspeth and Anna – Mother too – were actually becoming a bit of a nuisance these days. They planted themselves at the foot of her bed every night, or they stood against the wall – Mother was still messy and unkempt from the vodka, which was disgusting. Shona could not make them go away, even though she screamed and sometimes flew at them, scratching and clawing at their faces with her fingernails. They did not like the clawing at all; Anna absolutely hated it, because it disarranged her hair and spoiled her make-up. She was still a vain little cat.

At times Shona thought the people in this place guessed about Elspeth and Anna and Mother coming into the room; she thought they tried to get her to open up about what was happening. They were soft and insinuating with their questions, but she was not falling for that, either! She was perfectly polite, as she had been brought up to be, but she did not give anything away.

The worst thing of all, though, the thing that really terrified Shona, was Iain Seymour with his frightening eyes and hands. He was nearly always in the room now.

Of course I'm here, Shona, he said. *I always told you I would be. Both of us inside Thornacre together.*

Shona did not scream at Iain Seymour or try to scratch his face. She huddled in a corner of the room, trying to make herself as small as possible, and folded her hands over her head.

'There are three pieces of news,' said Hilary, as she and Robert sat in the comfortable sitting room at Levels House two days later. 'And we've saved them up so we can tell you properly, with as many of the facts as possible. Robert's going first, though.'

'Only because my side is more mundane,' said Robert, 'and Hilary wants the drama of being the finale. Mine's about the body from under the Tarleton's stage. It's being formally buried on Friday. There's still no identification and I don't think there ever will be, but there is one rather intriguing thing the police have told me.'

'Yes?'

'It's apparently the body of a man in his late fifties or early sixties. There was a bullet in his ribs, so they're assuming he died of gunshot wounds.'

'Poor man.' Madeleine waited, and Robert said, 'But they found something among the remnants of his clothes, and this is the interesting part. It doesn't tell us his identity, but—'

'But it sort of gives him an identity,' put in Hilary.

'It was a small photograph,' said Robert. 'They let me see it. It's very old and very faded, but it was possible to make out the features. It was inside a leather case – probably a wallet, which had helped preserve it.'

'Who . . .?'

'A lady of about twenty-five,' said Robert. 'Not pretty in any conventional sense, but very striking. It was sepia, of course, so it was impossible to know the colouring, but she had dark eyes, and those marvellous slanting cheekbones.'

'Is there any clue as to who she was?' said Madeleine.

'Only a first name,' said Robert. '*Flora* was written on the back. That's all. No date, nothing else, although when I described the hairstyle to Hilary she thinks it might be around the late 1890s. I'm trying to get permission to have one of those computerized copies made of it: I don't think the police will mind – there's a bit of red tape to get through, but I think it will be all right. So you can both see it, and have a copy if you like.'

'I'd like a copy,' said Madeleine at once, and considered for a moment. 'Flora.'

'Yes. It could have been anyone.'

'Toby's mother was called Flora,' said Madeleine.

'Was she? Are you sure?'

'I think so. Yes, I am sure. My father mentioned her a few times. He said she was very attractive, very unusual, but not pretty in the fashion of her day. Could the body be Toby's after all? Or Toby's father?'

Robert and Hilary exchanged glances, then Hilary said, 'Madeleine, while you were in the hospital I spent some time in the attic, as you know. I wasn't sure what I was hoping to find, but I thought there might be more about Toby and your father.'

'And was there?'

'Well, some,' said Hilary. 'I've unearthed a lot of photographs and old programmes – some from Frank Douglas's ENSA days.

Some sheet music as well, and some Chance and Douglas songs. "Tipsy Cakes" is there and "The Ghost Walks" – they're actually hand-written, and they're initialled. T.C.'

'Toby Chance,' said Madeleine.

'Well, it's a reasonable assumption. They're in this envelope for you. I'd love to get them framed and made part of the Tarleton's reopening,' said Hilary. 'Although a collector would probably pay a fair sum for them if you wanted to sell.'

'I don't want to sell,' said Madeleine, taking the envelope. 'They're part of the Tarleton's history. Let's have them on display, as you suggest, Hilary.'

'Good,' said Hilary. 'But in the box beneath them was this letter, and that's the second thing we want to tell you.' She took the letter she had found from its careful wrapping and laid it on the low table in front of Madeleine.

'Toby again?' said Madeleine, staring at it.

'I think so. Read it.'

'Remarkable,' said Madeleine, having done so. 'Extremely suggestive. Did you find the song itself? The one he refers to?'

'No. I spent ages searching for it before I had to go back to London,' said Hilary, 'but I didn't find it. That doesn't mean it mightn't still be up there, though.'

'Or,' said Robert, 'that it mightn't simply have been destroyed.'

'Lost for ever? Don't be such a pessimist, Robert.'

'He's right though,' said Hilary, smiling at Madeleine.

'How significant is it?' said Madeleine, reaching for the letter to study it more closely. 'I mean – how far could it go in solving the Tarleton mystery? I'm no historian, but that Sarajevo assassination was the start of the first world war, wasn't it?'

'It was indeed,' said Hilary. 'The assassination of the Archduke Franz-Ferdinand sent shock waves through most of Europe and finally plunged it into the Great War. I've never heard of Tranz, though and neither has Robert.'

'I was on shaky ground with the assassination as well,' said Robert rather wryly.

'Your forte is knocking down walls,' said Madeleine briskly. 'Hilary, I've never heard of Tranz, either. But Toby – if it was Toby who wrote that letter – talks about having played a part in that.'

'And not wanting to be thought of as one of the plotters,' said Hilary eagerly.

'But look here,' said Robert, 'how likely is it that Toby – or the writer of that letter – would have written a song with clues in it? Would anyone have put something so important – something that meant so much to him – inside a song?'

'It's very likely,' said Hilary. 'Some of those old songs were a whole lot deeper than people realize now. Have you ever heard Albert Chevalier's "My Old Dutch"? "We've been together now for forty years, and it don't seem a day too much . . ." People still use that line – parodying it, of course, but it's still remembered. But the song itself was written about an elderly couple forced to go into the workhouse and being separated for the first time ever. It's the husband's lament – it's his farewell to his wife as they take the last walk together up the hill to a grim old Victorian workhouse. I want to howl whenever I think about that,' she said.

'And I thought you were such a cynic,' said Robert, smiling at her.

'I do my best to be.'

'OK, I accept that a song with hints in it could have been written,' said Robert. 'But who was actually behind that murder in 1914? Do we know that? I mean – was it a single person or country, or some sort of underground political organization?'

'I don't know, but it should be easy enough to find out.' Hilary reached out to touch the letter with the tips of her fingers, as if by doing so she could touch the past and its secrets. 'Could this be the clue to Toby's disappearance at last, d'you think? Was he mixed up in that political killing in Sarajevo?'

'Or made to appear as if he was?' put in Madeleine. 'Framed? He says he'd like people to know the truth one day, and for people to understand.'

'But why couldn't he tell them the truth at the time?'

'I can't imagine,' said Hilary. 'And I shouldn't think we'd ever be able to find that out. But if there was some involvement – if he was there that day, say – that could have provided a good reason for him to vanish.'

'Unless—' began Madeleine, and stopped.

'Yes?'

'Unless the body you found in the Tarleton's cellar *is* Toby.'

Hilary and Robert looked at one another. Then Hilary said, 'Madeleine, can I get that photograph of your family from the hall? The one of the group with the 1920s clothes and hairstyles? It's just near the front door.'

'Yes, of course. Why . . .' But Hilary had already gone into the hall and was back holding the large framed photo which she had been studying the morning Caley Merrick arrived.

'This is the third thing to tell you,' she said, placing the photo on the table, then taking from her bag an extremely battered book.

'Prospero Garrick,' said Madeleine, leaning forward to read the title. 'My goodness, it's the old boy's autobiography,'

'You wouldn't have actually known him, would you?' said Hilary. 'I mean – he was way before you were born.'

'I didn't know him, but I knew of him. Elise Le Brun used to tell a very good story of how he'd get happily drunk on performance nights, and make rather fuddled attempts to seduce the females. All perfectly amiable, apparently and no one was ever really offended.'

'He wrote his autobiography in the late 1920s,' said Hilary. 'I found a small extract from it on the internet and managed to track down a copy – there are so many good secondhand book-finding set-ups these days. I've read it and it's unashamedly egocentric, but I think he sounds rather a nice old boy. And he mentions quite a number of the people he performed with. Toby Chance is one, of course.'

'Yes, I think Prospero quite often appeared at the Tarleton.'

'Prospero – or his publishers – included quite a lot of photographs,' said Hilary. 'Most of them are pre-first world war – that's probably because they show Prospero himself when he was a fairly young man. There are quite a number of him – bewhiskered or wearing natty waistcoats, or dressed as Richard II or Hamlet, always in the most incredible make-up. But there's also this one.' She turned the pages, being careful of their fragility, and then placed the book alongside the photograph of Madeleine's family. 'The book's photo is dated 1912,' she said. 'But look at it side by side with your family group. Do you see it?'

Madeleine looked at the two photographs: the one in the old actor's book, the other in the narrow oak frame.

'But, Hilary – this surely isn't right? Are the names wrong, or something?'

'I don't think so,' said Hilary. 'Neither does Robert.'

Madeleine said, 'But the caption under the photo in the book says it's Toby Chance.'

'Yes.'

'But that's the man I knew as Rinaldi,' said Madeleine.

'If Toby really was mixed up in the assassination at Sarajevo,' said Robert, 'afterwards he'd have been a hunted man – whether he was guilty or innocent. Certainly in this country and possibly abroad as well.'

'For Toby to take Rinaldi's identity would have been perfectly possible,' said Hilary. 'They had passports in those days, but there weren't National Insurance numbers or bank cards or driving licences, or any of the things we have now.'

'And during that war there was a lot of confusion about people missing and turning up again, or being wrongly identified on battlefields,' said Robert. 'Toby could have got away with it.'

'But,' said Madeleine, frowning, 'if Toby took Rinaldi's identity, what happened to the real Rinaldi?'

'I think the real Rinaldi is who Robert found in the cellar,' said Hilary. 'We can't know what happened or who shot him, but it would all fit.'

'I wonder if that's the answer,' said Madeleine slowly. 'If we take this letter at face value, it means Toby would have had to hide from – well, from people who believed he'd taken part in a political murder, I suppose. Police or governments or both. And where better to hide than in someone else's identity. Hilary, my dear, you shouldn't be researching theatrical history, you should be writing historical mystery thrillers.'

Hilary grinned. 'If we're right about this, it means you knew Toby Chance quite well. You realize that?'

'I do realize it. And I'd have to say that I can't imagine the man I knew being involved in murder of any kind,' said Madeleine slowly.

'Oh, I'm so pleased to hear you say that. What was he like?' Clearly Hilary had been wanting to ask this. She leaned forward eagerly.

Madeleine smiled. 'He was good-looking and he could be quite mischievous. Witty and charming. His wife—'

'*Wife?*'

'Yes, he was married to a lady called …' She frowned. 'Hold on, dears, I'll get it in a minute … Something rather foreign-sounding, it was … Sonja, yes, that's it. Sonja. I only met her two or three times, but I know that in her youth she was one of those remarkable ladies who campaigned for women's votes. She was well over fifty when I knew her and I found her a bit alarming, but then I was very young in those days, so I'd likely be alarmed fairly easily.'

'What else? I mean, what else can you remember about Toby?'

'I'm not sure what his involvement was in the first world war,' said Madeleine, 'although I think he was in France for most of it.

He was certainly with my father on the ENSA tours in the second world war – North Africa and India and the Middle East. The headquarters for ENSA was Drury Lane, you know; by the end of the war it was a very big and very respected organization. My mother usually went with them, and I think Sonja went as well. I'm remembering my father used to joke about Rinaldi starting off as a stage manager and ending up as a leading performer.'

'Then Rinaldi – the real Rinaldi – could have been a stage manager?'

'I think so. It's how people thought of him – of the man I knew,' said Madeleine. 'Certainly by the time I was in my teens, he was performing on stage. Not in this country though, I don't think.'

'That would fit if Toby really did use Rinaldi's identity,' said Robert. 'He couldn't risk being recognized.'

'But he gradually regained his old life of entertaining audiences,' said Hilary. 'When did he die?'

'At the same time as my father. They were both in Italy – Sonja was with them. She usually was – she and Rinaldi were always very close, very in tune with each other. People said it was because they never had children, but I used to think it was more than that. My mother had been dead for some years by then, of course, so it was just the three of them. The car they were in crashed somewhere outside Trieste and they were all killed outright.' She saw Hilary's expression, and reached out a hand to her. 'It's long enough ago not to matter now,' she said.

'It is, isn't it?' said Hilary firmly. 'You know, I've been trying to find Toby – properly find him, I mean. For research and for a possible radio biography and for – well, just because I think he sounds interesting. But I've been looking in the wrong places: I've been looking for Toby Chance, but I should have been looking for Rinaldi. D'you know what his first name was?'

'I don't think I ever heard it. Everyone just called him Rinaldi. Even Sonja did.'

'Well, if he was involved in the first world war, we could look up

456

the Debt of Honour Registers and war memorials,' said Hilary. 'They're all available these days. Rinaldi isn't a common name, not in this country at any rate. I believe I'll talk to Caley Merrick in a bit more detail – he seems to have made it almost a life's work to research the Tarleton's history, he might know all kinds of snippets of useful stuff. I'd like to go through the attic again as well if you don't mind, Madeleine?'

'You can demolish the entire house as far as I'm concerned. But,' said Madeleine, smiling at Hilary's enthusiasm, 'don't let's forget the Tarleton and the night to reclaim the past.'

'Oh, I'm not forgetting it,' said Hilary at once.

CHAPTER FORTY

August 1914

'If Rinaldi had to be buried anywhere in the world, he'd want to be here,' said Flora very firmly, 'in the Tarleton. And I know what we're considering offends every shibboleth, but—'

'But it would be the solution for Toby,' said Hal.

'For him to become Rinaldi.' Flora said it cautiously, as if trying it out.

'Yes.' Hal thrust his hand through his hair distractedly and for a moment there was a startling resemblance to his son. 'Let's look at the facts before we make the decision. If we let Rinaldi's death be known, arrange a proper burial and so on, we'd end up facing a coroner's jury. I think that's inescapable; bullet wounds can't be concealed.'

'And,' put in Flora, 'it would remind people that once upon a time you and I and the Tarleton were part of another coroner's inquest. I wouldn't care about that for myself, but it might mean unwelcome attention.'

'Rubbish, people are too caught up in the war news,' said Toby. 'And it was nearly thirty years ago.'

'No, it's not rubbish,' said Alicia, unexpectedly. 'Lady Chance is right. Even with wars going on, people still like local scandals. Perhaps they like them even more in times of war, because it's homely. They'd fasten on – on whatever happened between you all those years ago, and they'd pick over the bones like vultures. And thirty years would be a mere fleabite in this situation.'

'Well spoken,' said Flora, looking at Alicia with approval. 'Go on, Hal.'

'Well,' said Hal, 'thirty-year-old scandals aside, if we let Rinaldi's death be known, there's no guarantee the truth would be believed. I'd put money on Anton Reznik being out of the country by lunchtime tomorrow, anyway. And whether we were believed or not wouldn't matter, because by then the whole Sarajevo business would have blown up in our faces. Everything we've striven to keep secret – everything the government wants us to keep secret – would be public knowledge. There'd have to be an inquiry – even perhaps a trial.'

'I'd face a trial,' said Toby. 'I'd fight to prove my innocence. And if we could prove it was Anton who killed Rinaldi that would discredit the statement he made in Bosnia, wouldn't it?'

'It might,' said Hal a bit dubiously.

'And it might not,' said Alicia. 'Toby, earlier on, you told me something that Anton said while you were in the cellar. He said if you hadn't escaped him in Sarajevo, he was going to make very sure you were found guilty and executed.'

'He said there would have been other statements as well as his,' remembered Toby.

'We always knew that,' said Hal. 'If Anton Reznik and that grisly old baroness could have been discredited, we might have taken the chance and let the whole thing come out, but Reznik has too many followers. Even if Tranz's people had all gone underground, he'd have found half a dozen eye-witnesses – all probably perfectly reputable people – prepared to describe how Toby helped activate the bomb or even fired one of the shots.'

Flora said, 'And there's Sonja to consider. A trial would drag her in.'

'There's also this,' said Alicia, 'Rinaldi was trying to save you from Anton tonight, Toby. He was, you know. How – how *ungrateful* it would be if you let that go to waste.'

They looked at one another. 'Then,' said Toby, 'we leave Rinaldi where he is. And I become Rinaldi.'

'Also, we build a wall to hide his body and hope it's not discovered until it's so far in the future it will have ceased to matter,' said Hal. 'Dear God, I don't believe this conversation is real. I don't believe the situation is real, either. We're discussing the concealment of a body, denying it Christian burial – D'you realize that in the past few days I've gone from being a respectable and respected member of His Majesty's Foreign Office to a man committing half the crimes in the Newgate calendar. Toby, you're the most infuriating liability—' He broke off.

'Sir Hal,' said Alicia, 'can it really make any difference to Rinaldi's immortal soul if he's dropped in the ground at Highgate Cemetery with a few prayers chanted over him, or left quietly at rest in the theatre that represented his life.'

'You appear to have the soul of a pagan, Mrs Darke,' said Hal.

'Paganism is a very interesting religion, Sir Hal. You should try some of its traditions for yourself.' The look she gave him was nearly, but not quite, an invitation.

'Let's examine the practicalities,' said Flora. 'Would building such a wall be a problem?'

'If Rinaldi was here,' began Toby, and then broke off. 'Sorry,' he said. 'I suspect we'll keep talking about him as if he's still alive. But I don't think a wall would be too difficult to build. It might take three or four days. The difficult part will be to get the materials into the theatre without being noticed, but the ghost legend ought to cover that. The ghost can carry in hods of bricks – that will have to be Frank's task; I don't think he'll mind, though. And he and I will build the wall together. Neither of us is the best in the world at practical things, but we'll manage it.' He paused again, and said, 'We'll treat that dear old boy with respect, of course.'

'We know that.'

'You do realize,' said Toby suddenly, 'that it will mean sealing off almost half the entire under-stage area?'

'Yes,' said Flora. 'I'd seen that ten minutes ago.'

'We'll need to make sure no one can get down there any other way. It won't matter about the cellar door because once the wall's in place, anyone going down those steps will just see a blank wall. But the grave trap itself will have to be sealed.'

There was a sudden silence.

'Sealed on stage, d'you mean?' said Flora.

'Yes. We've got to make very sure no one can get down to the cellar and find Rinaldi's body. So the floor of the trap will have to stay up – to be permanently flush with the stage,' he said, by way of explanation for Alicia. 'We'll have to disable the pulleys and nail the floor itself into position – with steel brackets or something like that, so no one can lower it and get under the stage that way. I think I can manage that,' said Toby. 'There are plenty of odds and ends of timber and bits of steel brackets in the carpenter's room.'

'You're right,' said Hal. 'We can't risk that body being found for a very long time. Not until there's no longer the possibility of identification. If you do take Rinaldi's identity, it's vital the real person is never found.'

'Can we do it, though? There are dozens of people in London who'd know you both,' said Flora.

'But I'm not going to be in London,' said Toby. 'I'm going to be somewhere in Europe – France probably, helping the war effort. I don't know yet what form that help will be, but I'll certainly do something. There's no reason why strangers wouldn't accept that I'm called Rinaldi, is there? Or is there? If you see any flaws, for goodness sake say so now.'

'I can't see any flaws,' said Hal, frowning. 'No, I think that will hold water.'

'Is the grave trap ever used?' asked Alicia.

'Only occasionally,' said Toby. 'It's sometimes useful for Christmas shows and pantomimes. Or for moving heavy scenery – it saves dragging things down the stairs.'

'People will ask why it's nailed up,' said Flora a bit doubtfully. 'Which is the one thing we can't risk.'

'You're right,' said Toby. 'What do we do? Is there an answer to this?'

'I think there is,' said Flora. 'It's an answer that would solve just about everything, but it's not an answer I like.' She looked at him. 'You already know, don't you?'

'We've got to close the theatre,' said Toby. 'Indefinitely.'

'Yes.'

All the time he and Frank worked on the wall, Sonja and Flora both looked in to provide food or simply encouragement and companionship, but Toby's mind was in turmoil. This may be the last thing I'll ever do here, he thought. How much do I mind? He was surprised to find he minded less than he would have expected.

'Your father and I have discussed the Tarleton's future,' said Flora, after the wall was finished.

'Has it got a future any longer?' The words came out flippantly, but Toby knew his mother would understand that the flippancy hid his real feelings.

'No,' said Flora, 'not for a very long time. Perhaps not for as long as twenty years.'

'Everything has got to completely die down, hasn't it?' said Toby. 'Sarajevo and this war – however long that lasts.'

'It might last a very long time. Your father doesn't believe all this over by Christmas talk.'

'Nor do I,' said Toby. 'So all that's got to settle. All the echoes, all the memories of Tranz have got to fade into nothing. And I've got to become accepted as Rinaldi – but by people who didn't know him. After all that's over, I might have to create a life away from the Tarleton. Perhaps even away from England.'

'I don't think anyone will see it as peculiar if the theatre closes for the duration of the war,' said Flora. 'I know there's the famous tradition of theatres staying open to boost morale, but your father thinks a great many people in this part of London will become involved in the fighting. The younger men will join the army or the navy and they'll go off to France or Belgium or wherever the battles are. The older ones and the women will help with voluntary work – nursing and food parcels for the troops. I'm already hoping to set up a travelling company for entertaining the soldiers in their barracks, as you know. We'll try to let it be thought that you're part of that if we can. So I don't think closing this place would cause much comment.'

'But the Tarleton will still need someone to keep an eye on it,' said Toby. 'To make sure it isn't burned down or blown up or washed away. I'll be out of England more or less permanently and it sounds as if you'll be whizzing round the camps. And father will be buried under bureaucracy at the Foreign Office—'

'We've thought of that.' Flora hesitated, and then said, 'How would you feel about ceding the place to Frank Douglas?'

'I don't know.' Toby considered this. 'It's a hell of a responsibility to place on his shoulders.'

'I think he'd do it, though.'

'I wonder if he would. It would sever the link for you and for me, wouldn't it?' said Toby after a moment. 'The Chance link to the Tarleton?'

'Yes. Would that hurt?'

'Not as much as it would have done a couple of months ago,' said Toby. 'People have their own links to one another, don't they? They don't need bricks and mortar for it. And there seems to be so much ahead that's far more important. This war – finding out how to help fight it,' said Toby.

463

'That's how I feel.'

'It would have to be done very discreetly.'

'Your father thinks a Deed of Gift would meet the case.'

'He usually knows about that kind of thing,' said Toby. 'But could we specify some kind of a restriction on reopening it? Write in – I don't know the legal terms – but something to ensure it stays closed for a number of years?'

'I don't know,' said Flora. 'But we could try. Toby – when we came up with this bizarre plan, you said if Rinaldi had to be anywhere in the world, he'd want to be here. Probably a part of him always will be. But I think a part of you will always be here, as well, no matter where you go after all this.'

Toby looked round. 'Yes,' he said, softly. 'Yes, I think part of me will always be here.'

The Present

'The ghosts will still be there,' Hilary said to Caley Merrick as the preparations for the Tarleton's opening gathered momentum. 'Ghosts are one of the great traditions of English theatre – of all theatres in the world, I should think. So you won't lose them. And if you like, I could get permission for you to attend a few rehearsals, so you'd see the place sort of emerge from the darkness.'

He was hesitant at first, but in the end he accepted Hilary's suggestion, sitting quietly in the back of the auditorium, unnoticed by most people. She thought that after the first time he rather liked it; he had thanked her very carefully, although Hilary had no idea if he had accepted the opening of the theatre he had haunted so strangely and so faithfully for so many years, and into which he had poured his lonely music. Nor did she know if his ghosts were still there for him.

But there was one ghost he gave her and it was a ghost she had not expected.

'It was in the box of my family's things,' he said. 'You remember about that? Madeleine said she snatched up papers and photo-graphs more or less at random that day? I was given them eighteen years later.'

'Of course I remember.' Hilary noticed he did not yet speak of Madeleine as his mother.

'This was among them,' he said. 'It didn't mean much to me – it was just some scribbled lyrics for a song. But I kept it with everything else, because it was another of the links for me.'

He handed her the sheet of paper, and Hilary took it, not thinking too much about what it might be.

But when she looked down at it, she saw it was the lyrics of Toby's lost song about the Sarajevo assassination.

They had not managed to track down everything from the Tarleton's last, long-ago closing night, but Hilary thought they had a lot of it. There was a really good comedy sketch about a man trying to travel between two places and becoming hopelessly lost. There were also dances from the era – Judy Randall had unearthed an old playbill in a St Martin's Lane print shop, with the name of Elise Le Brun and the Rose Romain dancers. They had no idea if the playbill was for the relevant night, but it was dated as being from 1914, so they had used it.

There were other songs and comedy acts, and also a Shake-spearean monologue which Prospero Garrick had referred to in his book. 'Because we can't possibly miss the old ham out,' Hilary said, and one of the agencies had found a semi-retired actor with a marvellously rich voice who mostly did voice-overs for commer-cials and bit parts in costume dramas. He said his grandfather had met Prospero after the first world war, and expressed himself as being delighted to be part of the Tarleton's reopening. He would give them the old boy's rendering of Henry V's St Crispin Day speech if that would suit, he said, and added something about the tradition of Irving and Tree, leaving Hilary with the feeling that she might almost have encountered the ghost of Prospero himself.

'We don't want any celebrities or TV soap stars,' she had said firmly to the theatrical agency. 'Just good ordinary working actors and actresses and musicians, doing their job. That's what the Tarleton always was, and that's what its owner would like it to remain.'

'Even so,' said the agent, 'you'll be making a few names with this one, Miss Bryant. We've very much enjoyed this association with the Harlequin, by the way – can we hope for more of the same things in the future?'

'That would be very nice indeed,' said Hilary, and went away, trying not to grin like the Cheshire Cat at this prospect of new ventures for the Harlequin.

It was looking as if there might be another reason to grin as well. Two days ago, the senior member of the Harlequin's trust had phoned to say how pleased they were with what she was doing. 'Especially since you were more or less thrown into Shona Seymour's place with no warning,' he said. 'A dreadful business, that. They say she's unlikely ever to be released from Thornacre Asylum.'

'I know.' Hilary had resolved to visit Shona again after the Tarleton's opening, to describe the evening for her. She knew Shona would probably only stare at her with that distressing sly hostility, but there was still the chance that something might get through. She was going to take the programme for Shona to see, and if possible a few photographs.

The senior trust member said, 'When this Tarleton opening is over, perhaps we should talk about making things a bit more official for you, if you'd be interested.'

'Yes, I would,' said Hilary. 'I'd be very interested indeed.'

As she and Robert walked along Burbage Street, Hilary thought: this is it. This is the night I hoped would happen: the night when an old legend is laid to rest and a new one born. I wish I could take hold of this moment and keep it cupped in my hands for ever. She glanced at Robert, and the delight increased, because Robert was another thing in her life for Cheshire-cat smiling, and it was absolutely right that he should be with her tonight.

As they stepped inside the foyer, she knew at once the ghosts were still here. They were not obtrusive, they would not force their presence on this twenty-first-century audience, but they were here all the same and they were interested in what was happening. It's your night as much as anyone else's, said Hilary silently to these gentle, inquisitive ghosts. Whoever you were and whatever you were, you're all part of this. All the memories and the echoes and the happinesses and sadnesses. I was right when I told Caley you wouldn't vanish.

They were quite early, but the theatre was already filling up with people and TV cameras – there were two small outside broadcast crews, who would edit a brief story for the end of the main news programmes, probably calling tonight another layer of theatre history for Bankside and another fragment of the past reclaimed to put alongside the Rose and the Globe. There were also local TV and radio stations who would give a bit more coverage. Journalists from several dailies and Sundays had accepted invitations, and there would be features in at least three of them. This was all deeply satisfying.

The theatre sparkled and spun, and when Hilary and Robert went into the auditorium Hilary thought the atmosphere was so electric that if you could somehow reach out to touch it, you would receive a full-volt shock. She had reserved seats in the third row – 'Near enough to the front to see everything, but not to have to crane our necks to the stage,' she said. Several of the Harlequin Society's governing board were present; they nodded and smiled to Hilary and the one who had made the suggestion of promotion put up his hand in a half salute.

Judy Randall was at the other end of the row with several of the Harlequin's freelancers. They waved to Hilary and gestured that this was all absolutely terrific and Hilary gestured back that yes, it was. Madeleine was near them; Hilary had worried that it might all be too much for her, but Madeleine had said, 'If you think I'm missing tonight, you can think again. I might have to be tanked up with pills and potions, but I'll be there if I'm carried.'

She had not had to be carried, of course; she had walked slowly and rather carefully, but she was in her seat, looking about her with bright-eyed delight. Caley Merrick was with her; he was not saying much, but he was listening to what people were saying, and when Judy Randall leaned forward to make some remark to Madeleine, Hilary saw him laugh.

The lights went down and the stage lights came up, and with a sigh of pure delight, Hilary plunged completely and marvellously into the Tarleton's past.

In the first interval Robert said, very quietly, 'Hilary. Before the scrum in the bar I want you to see this. I found it on the internet about a week ago and I've saved it for tonight, because I wanted to give it to you here, inside the Tarleton.' He passed her a single sheet of paper, a printout of a website. The heading was 'Debt of Honour Register: 1914–1918'. Hilary did not read the rest of the heading, because directly beneath it were the words:

Awarded to Leo Rinaldi (b.1890) Distinguished Conduct Medal for distinguished conduct and bravery in the field of battle and secret intelligence during the years, 1916–1917.

Distinguished conduct. Secret intelligence in the field of battle. Emotion swept over Hilary in a huge engulfing wave, so she was quite unable to speak. I think I've found you, Toby, she thought, staring at the printed words. I can't be absolutely sure, but I think this is you. Bravery and secret intelligence . . .

As the audience reassembled and the music began for the closing item, she looked up at the stage, and saw it through a blur of tears.

*

The audience listened with interest to the brief introduction explaining that the finale for tonight's performance was an almost lost fragment of a Chance and Douglas song, which it was not thought had ever been performed in public before. 'An intriguing set of lyrics,' the compere said. And then, as Hilary had asked, he said, 'We are performing it tonight in memory of Frank Douglas and Toby Chance.'

The music rolled in; there had been no melody to work from, but Hilary had asked that it be tried to the tune of the old song, 'The Man Who Broke the Bank at Monte Carlo', as Toby's letter had suggested, and although she had not yet heard it played or sung, the pianist had told her it worked very well.

It was instantly plain that the audience liked this song, and liked the hint that there might be something more to it than just a music-hall song. The cameras whirred and the journalists leaned forward to write the words in their notebooks.

This is it, then, Toby, thought Hilary. This is what you wrote all those years ago and what you wanted people to hear one day. Only they never did because it somehow got put into a box of papers and photographs and no one realized what it was.

> When they threw the bomb and fired the shot,
> The Kaiser shouted out, 'Mein Gott –
> That's another Habsburg who's got shot,
> We're losing really quite a lot.
> And it isn't even the dead of night
> Not a floosie or hunting lodge in sight,
> So I think I'll find new arms and go a-warring.'

Hilary looked round. Did they all recognize the subtle references – the tragedy of the Mayerling hunting lodge death affair in the 1880s, that offhand reference to the Kaiser's crippled arm? Some would.

When the cards are dealt, the Hand is Black,
The joker's invisible in the pack,
But he's hiding there, be sure of that
And he's got his own plan of attack;
There were people who were counter-plotted,
Outwitted and almost garrotted:
They're not wolves inside the lambskins, they're assassins.

Jokers and counter-plots, thought Hilary. And 'the Hand is Black'. That's the secret Serbian organization formed in 1911 – I didn't know about that when Caley gave me the lyrics, but I know it now because I read about it. It had other names, but was known as the Black Hand. That one's too far back for the audience, I suppose, but it doesn't matter.

As the car went down the long Appel Quay
The Archduke said, 'My goodness me,
They're assassins I believe I see
And of several nationalities.
But although I look with all my might
There is never an Englishman in my sight.
There is never a Chance of the English trying to kill me.'

Never a Chance. Toby had written that with an unmistakable upper-case C which wasn't, of course, apparent in the singing. You were counter-plotted, Toby, thought Hilary. Because there were jokers in the pack, and they nearly outwitted you. That's what you wanted to say to anyone who eventually heard this. We don't know who they were, those plotters, and we'll probably never know. But we know you survived. And your theatre's survived as well.

As people were filing out, heading for the Oyster Bar or Linkman's, Robert said very softly, 'Hilary. Look up there.'

'Where?'

'The stage box,' he said.

'We didn't open any of the boxes,' said Hilary. 'There're only six anyway, and apparently no one ever used the stage box except the owners, so we thought we'd stay with the tradition and not use it either.'

'There's someone there, though,' said Robert. 'I don't know how long he's been there – I noticed him when they started the Archduke song. He liked it. I saw him nod and I think I saw him smile.'

'But there's no one—' began Hilary, and then stopped, aware of an extraordinary sensation.

Standing in the stage box, not quite in the light of the auditorium but not quite in the shadows, was the figure of a man wearing what looked like a long, rather old-fashioned evening cloak. He was just visible against the folds of the box's curtain and as Hilary stared she thought he half turned his head, and for a mind-splintering second she had the impression of dark, slightly too-long hair and of mischievous eyes smiling straight at her. Then the lights came fully up, and after all there was nothing there.

Only the fall of the curtain.